PRAISE FOR SUS

"Susan Stoker knows what women want. A hot hero who needs to save a damsel in distress . . . even if she can save herself!"

—CD Reiss, *New York Times* bestselling author

"Irresistible characters and seat-of-the-pants action will keep you glued to the pages."

—Elle James, *New York Times* bestselling author

"Susan does romantic suspense right! Edge of my seat + smokin' hot = read ALL of her books! Now."

—Carly Phillips, *New York Times* bestselling author

"Susan Stoker writes the perfect book boyfriends!"

—Laurann Dohner, *New York Times* bestselling author

"These books should come with a warning label. Once you start, you can't stop until you've read them all."

—Sharon Hamilton, *New York Times* bestselling author

"Susan Stoker never disappoints. She delivers alpha males with heart and heroines with moxie."

—Jana Aston, *New York Times* bestselling author

"Susan Stoker gives me everything I need in romance: heat, humor, intensity, and the perfect HEA."

—Carrie Ann Ryan, *New York Times* bestselling author

"Susan Stoker packs one heck of a punch!"

—Lainey Reese, *USA Today* bestselling author

TRUSTING SKYLAR

DISCOVER OTHER TITLES BY SUSAN STOKER

Silverstone Series

Trusting Skylar

Trusting Taylor (March 2021)

Trusting Molly (July 2021)

Trusting Cassidy (December 2021)

Mountain Mercenaries Series

Defending Allye

Defending Chloe

Defending Morgan

Defending Harlow

Defending Everly

Defending Zara

Defending Raven

Ace Security Series

Claiming Grace

Claiming Alexis

Claiming Bailey

Claiming Felicity

Claiming Sarah

Delta Force Heroes

Rescuing Rayne

Rescuing Aimee (novella)

Rescuing Emily

Rescuing Harley

Marrying Emily

Rescuing Kassie

Rescuing Bryn

Rescuing Casey

Rescuing Sadie (novella)

Rescuing Wendy

Rescuing Mary

Rescuing Macie

Delta Team Two Series

Shielding Gillian

Shielding Kinley

Shielding Aspen

Shielding Riley (January 2021)

Shielding Devyn (May 2021)

Shielding Ember (September 2021)

Shielding Sierra (TBA)

Badge of Honor: Texas Heroes Series

Justice for Mackenzie

Justice for Mickie

Justice for Corrie

Justice for Laine (novella)

Shelter for Elizabeth

Justice for Boone

Shelter for Adeline

Shelter for Sophie

Justice for Erin

Justice for Milena

Shelter for Blythe

Justice for Hope

Shelter for Quinn

Shelter for Koren

Shelter for Penelope

SEAL of Protection Series

Protecting Caroline

Protecting Alabama

Protecting Alabama's Kids (novella)

Protecting Fiona

Marrying Caroline (novella)

Protecting Summer

Protecting Cheyenne

Protecting Jessyka

Protecting Julie (novella)

Protecting Melody

Protecting the Future

Protecting Kiera

Protecting Dakota

SEAL of Protection: Legacy Series

Securing Caite

Securing Sidney

Securing Piper

Securing Zoey

Securing Avery

Securing Kalee

Securing Jane (novella; February 2021)

SEAL Team Hawaii Series

Finding Elodie (April 2021)

Finding Lexie (August 2021)

Finding Kenna (October 2021)

Finding Monica (TBA)

Finding Carly (TBA)

Finding Ashlyn (TBA)

Beyond Reality Series

Outback Hearts

Flaming Hearts

Frozen Hearts

Stand-Alone Novels

The Guardian Mist

A Princess for Cale

A Moment in Time (a short story collection)

Lambert's Lady

Writing as Annie George

Stepbrother Virgin (erotic novella)

TRUSTING SKYLAR

Silverstone, Book 1

Susan Stoker

Montlake

Published by Montlake, Seattle

www.apub.com

ISBN-13: 9781542021340
ISBN-10: 1542021340

Cover design by Eileen Carey

Printed in the United States of America

TRUSTING SKYLAR

Chapter One

Carson "Bull" Rhodes walked slowly and silently toward the target building. He knew his fellow Delta Force teammates were close behind him. They had his back, just as he had theirs.

They'd snuck into Pakistan to find a high-value target (HVT) the Army had assigned them to eliminate. Fazlur Barzan Khatun, the leader of the Harkat-ul-Mujahideen terrorist group, had claimed responsibility for the ambush and killing of forty-seven American and British soldiers in Afghanistan the year before. The State Department had also learned the group was actively planning large-scale massacres in both the United States and France as well.

Khatun was at the top of the FBI's *Most Wanted* list.

Bull's heart was beating double time in his chest, and he felt energized. He and the others were good at their jobs. They were the best of the best, which was why the Army hadn't hesitated to send them undercover into hostile territory. The team had been dropped near the Pakistan border twenty-four hours ago and had reached the last place Khatun had been seen.

Bull motioned for Smoke and Eagle to take positions on the left and right of him. They'd cleared buildings like this more times than they could count. With Gramps taking up the rear, the four of them were a well-oiled machine, moving silently into the two-story building.

They could hear voices from above, and without a sound, the men entered the stairwell and started climbing. Holding up his fist to stop his team, Bull peered around the corner once they'd reached the second floor. Upon seeing no one in the hallway, he gestured for everyone to follow.

He paused outside a door, where they could all clearly hear a lively discussion taking place. They couldn't understand the words, but that didn't matter. Their job was to find Khatun, kill him, and retreat. Their body cameras would record the conversation, and linguists would later translate everything that was said.

After looking back at the best friends he'd ever had, Bull nodded at Eagle. He was the most important member of the team at times like this. He had the uncanny ability to recognize anyone after meeting them or seeing their picture only once. He had a near-photographic memory. If Khatun was inside the room, Eagle would know it. It wouldn't matter if he'd cut his hair or otherwise tried to change his appearance, no one tricked Eagle. There'd been more than one op when Eagle had prevented them from killing the wrong person or had been instrumental in making sure the target didn't get away with saying he was someone else.

Bull pointed two fingers at his own eyes, then pointed into the room. Eagle nodded and raised his rifle.

Looking back at Smoke and Gramps, Bull saw they'd crept up behind Eagle. The team was ready to breach the room. Taking a deep breath, Bull cleared his mind. The second they stepped into the room, all hell was going to break loose. Since he was leading the team, if the occupants were armed, it was likely he'd be shot first. But he couldn't think about that. He was wearing his body armor and had a job to do. Namely, to kill Khatun.

Lifting a hand, Bull held up three fingers. Then he counted down. *Three. Two. One.*

Bull kicked in the door, and he and his teammates burst into the room.

Chaos erupted immediately.

There were around ten men in the room and a handful of women. The men immediately stood up and reached for weapons that had been leaning against the walls around them.

"Don't move!" Bull yelled in a tone that was meant to be obeyed. Of course, no one listened, so Bull did what he did best.

He aimed and fired.

Bull had received his nickname in basic training because of his ability at the shooting range. In his weapons qualification course, he'd had a perfect score. It didn't matter what weapon he was using, he was perfect every time. Pistol, rifle, even the grenade. Wearing a gas mask on the night range? Perfect. Everyone had started calling him Bullseye, but over the years, it had been shortened to Bull.

And that was the reason he was leading the assault into the room filled with terrorists. He always hit his target. *Always.*

Taking his time, Bull shot the hand off one man who was reaching for a gun and immediately turned his attention to the man next to him and did the same. The shots were loud in the room, and the screams and yells only added to the chaos.

After what seemed like ten minutes, but in actuality was under sixty seconds, Bull held up his fist to alert the team to stop firing. The second the scene was secure, Gramps strode over to the nearest man and shoved him toward the others. Smoke assisted, and before long, all ten men were on their knees, all bleeding in some shape or form but not mortally wounded, glaring up at Bull and his team.

"Fazlur Barzan Khatun?" Bull barked, knowing the coward wouldn't admit who he was but wanting to give him a chance to save the others anyway.

As he thought, none of the men indicated they were who the team was looking for.

"Third from the right," Eagle said in what some people might've thought was a bored tone. But Bull knew better. His friend was deadly serious. There was no discussion or questioning Eagle. If he said the man was Khatun, the man was Khatun. Bull and the others had no doubt whatsoever.

Without hesitation, and without giving the man time to deny he was the FBI's most wanted terrorist, Gramps lifted his rifle and shot the man between the eyes.

The man swayed on his knees for just a moment before falling backward, his eyes staring sightlessly at the ceiling.

The other men immediately began wailing. Bull wanted to roll his eyes at the commotion, especially considering they were probably Khatun's most trusted advisors and neck deep in blood they'd shed themselves.

They'd successfully completed their mission, but Bull wasn't about to exit without making sure they didn't leave behind someone who was just as deadly and ruthless as Khatun. "Eagle?" he asked, knowing the other man would understand what he wanted.

As the remaining men glared at him, Eagle stepped forward and studied each of their faces carefully. He pointed to the last man in the line. "Nabeel Ozair Mullah."

If Bull hadn't been looking directly at the man, he would've missed the look of surprise that crossed his face. But he *didn't* miss it. It was as clear as day that Eagle had correctly identified the man.

Mullah was also on the FBI's *Most Wanted* terrorist list. He was currently ranked at number six, but with Khatun now dead, the entire team knew he was next in line to take his place in the terrorist organization.

"No! I not him. I Muhammad Amir. Servant," the man said in surprisingly good English.

Eagle snorted. "And I'm the king of England."

The man moved surprisingly fast, getting the drop on all four Deltas.

He leaned over and grabbed the arm of a young woman who'd most likely been serving the men before the meeting had been interrupted. She shrieked and struggled against Mullah but was no match for the man.

Gramps, Smoke, and Eagle turned their rifles on the other men, yelling at them to stay where they were, while Bull's attention stayed focused on Mullah and the now-crying woman. She was desperately tugging on the arm around her throat, trying to get free and probably to get air into her lungs.

"I kill!" Mullah threatened, and Bull knew he could easily kill the young woman with his bare hands.

"Let her go," Bull ordered, dropping his rifle to hang around his torso and pulling out his pistol. He had no fear that one of the other terrorists would shoot him. His teammates had his back. His only job right now was to take out number six—now five—on the FBI's list, preferably before he broke the young woman's neck.

Mullah shook his head. "You not allowed in Pakistan," he said.

"And yet, here we are," Bull said calmly.

"US pay for sticking face where it not belong!" Mullah protested.

"You and your cronies shouldn't have killed our countrymen," Bull told him.

"They deserve. Should not have come," Mullah sneered. "They die like coward. Crying like baby!"

The teenager in Mullah's arms had closed her eyes, and Bull could see that she was on the cusp of passing out. He had no more time to listen to this asshole's disparagement of the brave men and women he'd had a hand in killing. Mullah was using the woman as a shield, but there were plenty of places on his body that weren't hidden behind her.

Bull fired his weapon, taking off Mullah's ear.

The man shrieked, and as Bull had thought he'd do, one hand flew up to immediately cover the bleeding mess on the side of his head.

As Mullah moved, Bull shot again, taking off several of Mullah's fingers. His grasp on the woman loosened, and she did the sensible thing by dropping to her knees and crawling away from her captor.

And that left Mullah without protection from Bull's lethal bullets.

Taking three shots in a row, Bull hit the ruthless terrorist twice in the heart and once in the forehead. Mullah dropped like a stone, face-first to the floor.

The other men didn't make a sound. It was almost eerie how quiet the room was. It was as if everyone recognized they were one word, one movement away from having the barrel of Bull's gun zeroed in on them.

"Incoming," Smoke said quietly.

Nodding, Bull holstered his pistol and reached for his rifle once more. In tandem, all four men took a step backward toward the door to the room.

No one spoke. No one moved.

Bull knew Gramps would've taken the necessary pictures to prove they'd eliminated two of the most evil terrorists the world had ever known. They hadn't been tasked with killing Mullah; they'd just been lucky to find him there. Two ruthless terrorists had been eliminated rather than just one.

The four quickly headed back down the stairs and out of the building. They could hear sirens in the distance, but because of the time of night and the upper-class neighborhood they were in, no one was lurking about.

As the team disappeared into the Pakistani night, Bull felt proud of what he and his team had accomplished. When he'd joined the Army, he hadn't thought he'd ever look forward to killing another human being, but after seeing firsthand what men like Khatun and Mullah were capable of, the destruction they left in their wakes, he had no problem killing to protect his country and all the innocent lives at stake.

He had no illusions—innocent lives *were* at stake. Killing the two men tonight wouldn't be looked at very favorably, but it probably set back any terrorist plan to attack US citizens on American soil at least a decade. The Harkat-ul-Mujahideen would have to regroup, put new leadership in place, and that could take years. The infighting and power struggle within the organization would be immense and would cause chaos for the group.

Bull grinned. Yes, he and his team had dealt the terrorist organization a blow they wouldn't easily recover from tonight. And even though few back home would ever know about it, even though their actions would never be praised on the nightly news, they'd done their patriotic duty.

~

Bull stood at attention next to Smoke, Eagle, and Gramps, trying to comprehend what the fuck was happening.

How had they gone from being high on their success a month ago to standing in what amounted to an Article 15 hearing now?

Instead of being thrilled with the outcome of their mission, their commander had been livid that they'd killed Mullah. It made little sense, and the more Bull and the others had tried to explain the importance of the man's death, the more upset the Army brass had become.

Apparently, one terrorist ending up dead was acceptable, but two at the same time? In a country the US wasn't supposed to be in? That was suspicious. Accusations from the Pakistani government that the

United States had deployed spies into their country had flown, and the president wasn't happy that he'd had no idea what was happening.

Personally, Bull thought the man was simply pissed he couldn't take credit for both Khatun and Mullah being dead, but that was purely speculation on his part.

As a result of their actions, Bull, Smoke, Eagle, and Gramps had been brought up on charges of disobeying a superior officer and had to defend their actions from the mission in Pakistan.

It was utterly ridiculous, and Bull was *beyond* pissed.

"After reviewing the body cam footage of your actions, it's been decided that while you successfully completed the original mission honorably, you subsequently made decisions that were detrimental to the overall safety of this country. You killed a man you were not one hundred percent sure was a terrorist and jeopardized international relations between the United States and the Middle Eastern nations. It will take years before any of the governments in that area of the world will trust the US Army again."

Bull ground his teeth together and forced himself to stay quiet. Everything the general was saying was bullshit. Everyone in the room knew it. They needed a scapegoat, and he and his team were the logical targets. Everyone was fucking thrilled Mullah was dead, but they couldn't admit it publicly. He forced himself to pay attention as the general continued speaking.

"Because the man you eliminated *was* Mullah, it's been decided that you will not be punished by a reduction in rank or being chaptered out of the Army."

Bull inwardly breathed a sigh of relief but stiffened when the general continued.

"But as a result of your actions, it's been decided to break up your team. You will all be given a permanent change of station to different bases. You won't be allowed on any Delta Force teams in the future and will be integrated into various infantry units. You will report to the captains in charge of your new teams, and while we aren't stripping you of your ranks, you will be under a suspension of favorable actions and will not be allowed to reenlist once the end of your current term in the US Army is over. Any questions?"

Bull could barely believe what he'd just heard. They were splitting up him and his team? Was this a joke? He didn't care that they'd be forced out of the Army; after everything that had happened, he wasn't inclined to stay in anyway. But separating them from each other was a huge blow.

"If there are no questions, you are dismissed."

Bull turned without saluting the man—fuck that, he didn't deserve his respect—and filed out of the room. He looked at his friends and saw the same disbelief and shock he was feeling reflected back in their eyes.

"Fuck," Smoke said under his breath.

"I won't do it," Eagle swore.

"We don't have a choice," Gramps replied with a sigh. "None of us is up for reenlistment. We're at their mercy until we can get out."

Bull wanted to say something positive, to lead his team as he'd done for as long as they'd been together, but the words wouldn't come. He couldn't imagine not seeing these guys every day. He trusted them with his life and knew he'd never have that kind of bond with any other team. As far as punishments went, what the general had done was worse than stripping their ranks and making them work extra duty . . . and the bastard knew it.

Doing his best to pull himself together, Bull took a deep breath. "Tonight. Meet at Hank's. We need some time to process, then we'll discuss our next steps."

The other three nodded, and with chin lifts goodbye, all headed for their own cars in the parking lot.

Four hours later, Bull, Eagle, Smoke, and Gramps sat in a dark corner of Hank's Bar and Grill near Fort Hood. It was a crappy bar in a crappy part of town, but it was private, and they wouldn't run into anyone they knew from the base. The bar was actually off limits to Army personnel because of the number of fights and drug busts that had happened there, but Bull and his team didn't give a shit. They needed to discuss their future, and this was as good a place as any.

"This is such bullshit," Eagle said in disgust.

"They can't do this to us," Smoke agreed.

"Unfortunately, they can. And did," Gramps said, then took a long swig of his beer.

Bull wished he could tell them he'd come up with a plan in the hours between when they'd learned their fate and now, but he was still at a loss. They all knew within a day or two they'd get their PCS orders and be sent to opposite corners of the country. And being put in ordinary infantry units was a step down. Since they were under a "suspension of favorable actions" reprimand, they weren't permitted to take leadership positions and would end up serving in minor staff slots.

While the infantry were badass in their own way, they weren't Deltas. It was like sending a professional flutist to play in a high school orchestra.

Bull opened his mouth to say something, he wasn't sure what, when a voice interrupted. "May I sit here?"

All four men looked up to see a man standing next to their table. He was wearing a pair of black slacks and a white shirt buttoned almost all the way up. Only the top button was undone. He had on a shiny pair of black shoes and actual cuff links. The man looked as out of place in the seedy bar as a homeless man might've looked in a fancy country club.

"Who the fuck are you?" Gramps asked.

The man didn't seem upset at his tone and merely raised an eyebrow and nodded to the empty seat at the table.

Bull smirked. He had no idea who this guy was, but he had to give him credit. He had some balls. Bull kicked the chair out and nodded.

"Thank you," the man said and sat, as if he didn't have a care in the world. He placed his drink on the table in front of him—whiskey, if Bull had to guess—and leaned forward.

"So," the man said. "Heard you didn't have the best day today."

Bull frowned. Their hearing wasn't a matter of public record. Because they were Delta Force soldiers, anything shared in that room today was supposed to be for those who had the highest security clearance only. And the fact that this man seemed to know what had transpired was intriguing . . . and alarming as hell.

Knowing better than to offer up information, Bull merely shrugged.

The man nodded, as if pleased by his reticence, and pinned him in place with a gaze. "What if I were to offer the four of you a way to stay together? To be able to do what you do best without the government hovering over your shoulders and watching and judging your every move?"

"I'd say you were full of shit," Bull answered without missing a beat.

The man chuckled and took a sip of his drink. "A cynic. I'm not surprised."

"Look, you either need to get to the point or get the fuck out of our faces," Eagle said.

The man turned to him. "Ah, the Eagle Eye doesn't know who I am. I suppose I should be pleased about that."

With every word out of the man's mouth, Bull was more and more intrigued. He obviously knew who they were, including their nicknames and individual skills.

"You've been quiet, Smoke," the man said with a head tilt. "Nothing to say?"

Smoke merely shrugged.

"And you, Gramps? Although, for the record, the fact you got that name merely because you're the oldest of your crew is ridiculous."

"I still want to know who the fuck you are," Gramps said.

The man nodded, and Bull could swear he saw respect in his eyes. "My name is Gregory Willis. I work for the FBI. Intelligence. And before we go any further, I have to say, on behalf of all of us in the FBI and Homeland Security, job well done with Khatun and Mullah. We all worked our asses off to get information on Khatun's whereabouts to you, and we were fucking thrilled that Mullah was dumb enough to be there at the same time. Good shooting, Bull."

FBI . . .

Bull didn't even want to know how the man had found them in a seedy bar in Texas. They hadn't decided to go to Hank's until *after* their hearing.

"You're going to sit there and tell us you've not only seen our body cam footage, but you're responsible for getting the intel we needed for that op?" Eagle asked skeptically.

"Well, not solely responsible, no. That would be pretty damn conceited of me, wouldn't it? But yes, I've seen the footage, and yes, I assisted in getting the info. I will admit, however, that it *was* my idea to include the dossier on Mullah with the intel about Khatun that you received before you left. Pretty damn lucky, huh, Eagle? You wouldn't have known that asshole was there if you hadn't seen his picture and name."

Bull sat back and observed the FBI agent. He was average height and had an ordinary countenance. If he hadn't stuck out like a sore thumb because of the clothes he was wearing in the dive bar, he probably would've blended in, and no one would've taken a second glance at him. He had a feeling this Willis guy had dressed that way on purpose. The intelligence in his eyes was hard to miss.

"You have our attention," Bull told him.

"Good," Willis said, and the humor faded from his expression. He took the time to look each of them in the eye before he continued. "I'm here to offer you a chance to keep doing what you're doing, but not for the Army. It's obvious you have a connection that can't be faked. The way you worked together on the Khatun mission was nothing short of beautiful. You barely spoke ten words to each other, and yet each of you knew what the others were going to do before they did it. Bull, your expertise with a weapon is impressive as hell. Eagle, your skill with facial recognition is something I've never seen before and should *not* go to waste. I know Smoke's the ghost of the group, who can appear and disappear. And Gramps, every team needs a peacekeeper. Bull might be the leader, but you're the glue that holds you all together."

"Yeah, it's obvious you've done your homework," Smoke growled. "Get on with it."

"Right. The Army is going to deliver your PCS paperwork tomorrow. Bull, you're going to Fort Bragg, North Carolina. Eagle, you're assigned to Fort Lewis, Washington. Smoke, you're headed to Fort Carson, Colorado, and Gramps, you're slated for Fort Benning, Georgia . . . as an assistant instructor for Ranger School."

"Fuck that," Gramps muttered.

Willis went on, as if he hadn't just shocked the shit out of the four men sitting in front of him. "I've been authorized to get you out of the rest of your Army commitment. If you agree, you'll be free to go where you want, when you want."

"What's the catch?" Eagle asked.

"Patience," Willis said with a smile. "As I said, if you agree, tomorrow you'll be free to go where you want and do what you want with your life. Smoke, I believe your uncle recently passed away—my condolences—and he left you his garage in Indianapolis. Called Silverstone, is that right?"

"You know it is," Smoke answered suspiciously.

"And not only that, he also left you more money than you'd ever be able to spend in this lifetime. Around a hundred million dollars."

Bull knew his eyes were huge, but he couldn't help it. "He did? Jesus, Smoke, why didn't you ever say anything?"

"Because it doesn't matter," Smoke replied. "I wasn't going to quit the Army and leave my team."

"Damn, dude," Gramps said.

Smoke glared at Willis. "What's your point?"

It was obvious their teammate was uncomfortable with his secret being brought to light, but Willis merely grinned. "My point is that you can all move to Indianapolis, make a go of Silverstone, and work for yourselves . . . with the FBI's assistance, of course."

"Doing what?" Bull asked for what seemed like the hundredth time. He was getting tired of Willis beating around the bush. He couldn't deny what he was suggesting sounded good. Damn good. Much better than going to fucking Fort Bragg without his team.

"Exactly what you do now. Finding and eliminating HVTs."

His words seemed to float in the air around the table. They were both shocking and expected at the same time. That *is* what they did now. They tracked down and killed terrorists that were hell bent on killing anyone they could to get their warped agendas across to the world.

"Who would we work for?" Gramps asked.

"Well, that's somewhat tricky. Technically, you're on your own . . . which is where Smoke's money would come in handy. However, the FBI would like to be informed about which missions you take on. We're willing to assist in intel gathering and of course getting you in and out of the country if your target is outside the US."

"So we'd go from working for the government to working for the government, but we'd have to pay for everything," Gramps summed up skeptically.

"Yes and no," Willis said. "You wouldn't be working for us but rather working *with* us. There's a difference. We hope you'll help us track down the men and women on our *Top Ten Most Wanted* list, but it's not a requirement for us to help *you*. Obviously, you can't go around killing anyone who looks at you cross-eyed."

"So, you want us to be assassins," Eagle said.

Willis merely shrugged. "I don't care what you call yourselves. All I care about is finding and eliminating the sex traffickers, terrorists, and serial killers of the world."

"What's in it for us?" Gramps asked.

"You get to stay together," Willis answered swiftly. "You do what you were obviously born to do—use your skills to make the world a little safer. If not legally, at least with the support of the federal government. We can use our clout to get you in and out of the country with whatever firepower you need. We can give you intel. And most importantly, you're not susceptible to the whims of the political climate and the Army."

"We'd want complete immunity for anything that might happen while we're on a job," Bull said, his mind going a million miles an hour.

"You'll have it . . . to a point," Willis said. "I was authorized to make this offer because of the Department of Justice's special 'black' budget. The money spent from this fund is untraceable and unreported. As far as immunity goes, there are a few rules you'll have to follow. There has to be a positive ID through fingerprint and/or DNA collection of any target you wish to eliminate, and we'll practice plausible deniability if you're captured outside of the country."

"So if we find ourselves up shit's creek without a paddle, you'll deny our existence and leave us to our fate," Gramps said dryly.

Willis nodded once.

"That's not too different than being Delta," Eagle replied with a shrug. "We all knew we were pretty much on our own."

Everyone nodded. They'd known the score going into each mission.

The four men stared at Willis for a long moment, each lost in thought.

Then Bull said, "This sounds too good to be true. Why should we trust you?"

Willis had relaxed back in his chair at some point in the conversation, as if he hadn't a care in the world. But at Bull's question, he leaned forward, and his expression turned dark. "My wife and daughter were killed in France a few years ago. They went out shopping while I stayed at the hotel to do some work. They were kidnapped and held hostage for two weeks, their bodies ultimately found dumped in a back alley. They'd both been tortured and repeatedly raped. And for what? Because some asshole thought it was fun and wanted to hurt Americans. He didn't care that Molly was only thirteen years old. And he didn't give a fuck that my wife was diabetic and didn't have her meds and was suffering.

"It took two years for us to track him down, and when we did, we had to treat him with decency and turn him over to the French government so they could put him on trial. It was a fucking joke. He was sentenced to forty years in prison—they don't have the death penalty—and for the last year, he's been living a happy and healthy life behind bars. It's like Club Med for him. He deserves to die for the blood that's on his hands, and I'll do whatever it takes to make sure the man pays for what he's done. And not only to my family, but for *every* life he's ruined."

Bull nodded. *This* was something he could understand. The man had been wronged and wanted revenge. That kind of motivation seemed more genuine than anything else he could've told them. "We'll need to discuss it," he told Willis.

And just like that, it was as if a switch had been flicked off inside the other man. His shoulders relaxed, and he sat back in his chair once again. He picked up his drink and took another sip. "Of course. I understand."

"This better not be a trap," Eagle said. "As you know, I never forget a face. Gregory Willis might not be your real name, but if you fuck us over, I'll find you . . . and you'll pay."

To his credit, Willis didn't even flinch. "I know you will, and this isn't a trap, and I have no intention of fucking you over. We all know there are people in this world who are pure evil. Who need to be stopped. If there was a group like yours in the past, maybe Hitler wouldn't have been able to kill as many Jews as he did. Maybe Stalin wouldn't have risen to power. Maybe Pol Pot wouldn't have destroyed Cambodian civilization. Osama bin Laden wouldn't have killed over three thousand people on September eleventh."

And with that, he pulled out a business card and put it faceup in the middle of the table. He brought his drink to his lips and drained the glass. Then he nodded at the card. "Call me when you've made a decision. I can have the paperwork to get you out of your Army commitment on the general's desk tomorrow . . . instead of your PCS paperwork. You can be in Indianapolis and working at Silverstone next week. It's up to you. Gentlemen, it's been a pleasure meeting you. Again . . . good job on the Khatun and Mullah deal."

And with that, Gregory Willis stood up and strode toward the door. But Bull saw him far differently now, after hearing his story. He'd lost his family, and that loss was weighing him down significantly.

Strangely, not one person harassed the out-of-place man as he made his way toward the exit. No one called out to him, made fun of him, or otherwise made a move to fling the nerdy-looking man across the bar.

And Bull knew for a fact it wasn't because the men in the bar right now weren't capable of doing so. They were. He'd seen it happen. It was something about Willis himself. Some sort of palpable aura of danger that surrounded the man. Even in slacks, his white shirt, and fucking cuff links, the man oozed a "hands off" vibe. And everyone respected that.

The second the door closed behind Willis, Bull turned his attention back to his team. "Well?"

"Did that just happen?" Eagle asked with a shake of his head.

"I want to talk about Smoke's hundred million dollars," Gramps said, staring hard at his friend.

Smoke held up his hands in capitulation. "I know, I know, I should've told you. But honestly, it means nothing. I wasn't going to leave the Army or the team. What did it matter?"

"It mattered because we're friends. Teammates. We don't keep secrets from each other."

Smoke nodded in agreement and apology.

"Tell us about Silverstone," Bull said. "If we're even going to consider this insane idea, we need to know what we're getting into."

"Honestly, I don't know a lot about it. You know that my uncle raised me after my parents were killed. I knew he wasn't hurting money-wise, but we never talked about it. We lived in a large house with a ton of acreage, and I knew he worked in a garage, but I was too interested in my own shit to pay much attention."

"So anyone know anything about automotive stuff?" Bull asked.

No one said a word.

"Kind of hard to operate a garage without knowing anything about fixing cars," Bull said dryly.

"As far as I know, the garage has been closed since my uncle died," Smoke admitted. "I didn't see the point in keeping it going after he passed away. I helped the employees find other jobs, and I sold off most of the equipment."

"So . . . you own a garage that isn't a garage," Eagle said with a snort.

They were silent for a while, then Smoke said, "What if we reopened? Not as a garage, but something similar."

"Like what?" Gramps asked.

"A towing company?" Smoke suggested.

"How's that different from a garage?" Eagle asked.

"Because we wouldn't actually be working on cars. We'd just tow them from accident scenes to the junkyard or a service station of the client's choice. If people have a flat tire, we could help with that, but not with any mechanical issues. We'd just tow them where they wanted to go. We could buy a couple tow trucks and start from there."

Smoke's idea had merit, and Bull couldn't help but feel a spark of interest. "You'd probably be fronting the bill for a while until we could make it work," he warned.

Smoke merely shrugged. "I don't need that money. I'd never be able to spend that much dough. If it can help us not get shipped off to the four corners of the country and have to answer to some newbie captain, I'm all for it. Besides, can you see Gramps spending the rest of his career training wannabe Rangers? What a disaster."

Everyone chuckled. Gramps's childhood had been tough, and he wasn't one to keep his mouth shut when he had something to say.

"Are we really going to trust the FBI to have our backs? I mean, not if we're caught going in or out of a country that isn't thrilled we're there; he already said we were on our own," Eagle said. "But to give us accurate info and to help grease the wheels when we need to bring weapons or other supplies into a foreign country?"

"Honestly? I don't know. But as long as Willis is involved, I'd say there's a pretty good chance," Bull said.

"Are we okay with being assassins?" Smoke asked quietly.

Bull shook his head. "We aren't assassins," he said emphatically. "We're the owners of Silverstone Towing."

"Who just happen to take extended trips overseas now and then," Eagle said with a laugh.

"What happens if any of us find women we want to spend the rest of our lives with? What do we tell a woman who wants to know where we're going and what we're doing?" Smoke asked.

"Let's not get ahead of ourselves," Bull said with a snort. "We haven't exactly had women knocking down our doors as it is."

"It's a valid question," Eagle countered. "I can't imagine a girlfriend being okay with us acting all secretive about where we're going or what we're doing. She'll assume we're cheating. We can't exactly tell anyone that we're killers."

"No, we can't. At some point, we'll have to be honest," Bull said. "I, for one, am not ashamed of what I've done as a Delta. We just eliminated one of the worst terrorists the world's seen in ages. I refuse to be ashamed of that. When and if any of us find someone we want to spend the rest of our lives with, we'll just have to be honest. If she can't deal with it, then it's not meant to be."

"So you're saying if you love someone, and she can't deal with the fact that you go around killing people, you'll just let her go?" Gramps asked skeptically.

"Yes," Bull returned without hesitation.

The four men eyed each other for a long moment, then Smoke said, "I'm in. I'll use the money my uncle left me to get Silverstone Towing up and going. If I'm honest . . . I'm kind of excited. We won't have to look over our shoulders and second-guess what we're being told to do. We can choose our own marks. I have faith that we can make this work."

"I'm in too," Eagle said. "But before we let Willis know, I want to scour the internet and see if I can't find him, make sure he is who he said he is. And I'll check out the story about his wife and daughter too. That should be easy enough."

"I'm in," Bull said simply.

All three looked at Gramps.

He sighed and nodded. "I can't let you three yahoos go at this alone. Someone's got to keep watch over you."

Everyone chuckled.

Bull held up his beer in a toast. "To Silverstone Towing. And a hell of a new adventure."

"To Silverstone Towing," the other three said in unison as they clinked bottles.

Chapter Two

Five Years Later

Bull sat back in the seat on the private plane and sighed. They'd just finished a job in Lima, Peru, for a good friend they'd made since starting Silverstone Towing . . . and their side job as a team who eliminated the worst humanity had to offer.

They still didn't like to call themselves assassins. They avoided the term at all costs.

Over the years, Willis had been instrumental in helping them figure out logistics for their new venture. At first, they'd gone after and eliminated only people on the FBI's *Top Ten* list, but as the years went by, the team had gotten more comfortable at identifying targets on their own. They'd killed the richest of the rich and the poorest of the poor. They'd eliminated serial killers, sex traffickers, mafia bosses, terrorists . . . anyone who proved themselves to be evil inside and out.

Del Rio was exactly the kind of person their team was made for. He was the lowest of the low, the leader of a sex-trafficking operation that had no problem enslaving women and children, girls *and* boys.

Ten years ago, he'd gotten his hands on a woman whose husband had done everything he could to find her, even forming his own team to rescue repressed women and children from all over the globe. He'd miraculously found his wife alive, and Bull and the others had been happy to head down to Peru to finish the job their friend Rex couldn't do because he was busy getting his wife out of the country.

Del Rio hadn't died an easy death. Silverstone had made sure of that.

And now they were almost home. Back to Indiana and the company that had been more successful than they ever could've imagined. They'd made Silverstone Towing one of the most reliable and affordable towing services in Indianapolis. They showed up quickly when called and didn't charge exorbitant rates. Everyone from law enforcement to automobile associations had them on speed dial.

They now had a dozen tow trucks and over two dozen drivers. It looked like they might need to hire half a dozen more drivers in the next six months or so as well. The garage that Smoke's uncle had left to him had been expanded to house the expensive vehicles they now owned. The garage itself wasn't in the best part of the city, and from the outside, no one driving by would think there was anything special about the building. But Smoke and the others had worked hard to make it comfortable and luxurious on the inside.

The men and women who worked for them deserved a place where they could be safe and relaxed when they weren't on a job. It had a state-of-the-art kitchen, sleeping rooms, a couple of small media rooms where people could play video games or watch movies, and even a finished basement.

All in all, Silverstone Towing had been just what the friends had needed when they'd been forced out of the Army.

They'd been bitter and disillusioned, and their new venture had given them the sense of normalcy they needed between jobs.

While Bull had no problem making sure a man like del Rio knew who was behind his death—and why he had been tortured before he'd been killed—he knew if he went straight to his sterile apartment, he'd never get to sleep. "I'm gonna head to the garage when we land," he told his friends.

"You sure?" Gramps asked.

Bull nodded. "Yeah." He didn't need to explain. Didn't need to tell his best friends that he'd been getting more and more restless after their missions. They'd seen it. Smoke had tried to talk to him about it, but Bull hadn't been ready. It wasn't that he wanted to quit or that he was morally disturbed by what they were doing. It was just that, five years in, he wanted more from his life. What that "more" was, he had no clue—which made his restlessness seem ridiculous even as it increased the feeling.

Smoke pulled out his phone and clicked on a few buttons before saying, "Looks like it's been pretty busy tonight so far. Bart's on dispatch, and most of the others are out on jobs."

"Right. I'll let Bart know I'm coming, and he can put me on rotation. Anyone driving Old Betty tonight?"

Old Betty was the first tow truck the team had purchased when they'd started Silverstone. She was old, as the name implied, and didn't have all the bells and whistles the newer trucks had. Most of their drivers preferred to take the newer trucks, which was fine with Bull. He preferred Old Betty. She'd never let him down, and there was just something about the faint smell of cigarette smoke from the previous owner that they'd never been able to get rid of and the way the leather seats crackled when he moved that soothed him.

Eagle chuckled. "As if anyone would choose Old Betty over the other trucks."

Smoke nodded in agreement. "Eagle's right. She's all yours."

The employees all took turns doing dispatch. When they'd started the business five years ago, the four men had discussed what they thought it would take to make Silverstone a success. Good pay and benefits were at the top of the list. As was having the employees know how to do all the jobs at the garage. Dispatch wasn't anyone's favorite, but knowing how to get all the pertinent details from a caller and how to navigate the software and maps made them all better drivers in the long run.

Because of the way their employees were treated—along with the luxurious interior of the garage, above-average salaries, and generous sick and vacation policies—the men and women who worked there were very loyal. The last time a person quit had been a year ago, and that had only been because the young man's fiancée lived in Chicago. He'd been upset to leave, but Silverstone had given him a glowing recommendation, and the last they'd heard, he was doing okay for himself in his new city.

Five years ago, Smoke had taken on the entire cost of the operation himself. But Bull, Eagle, and Gramps had used the money they'd earned from the business to buy into it, and now they were equal partners. They all did their share of driving and dispatching, losing themselves in the day-to-day operations of the company when not on a mission.

Tonight, Bull needed a distraction. Needed to feel . . . *normal.* Connect to normal people doing normal things. Sometimes answering a call for help wasn't safe—there had been several instances of people trying to either steal the truck or rob the driver—but Bull hadn't ever felt as if his life was in danger when he went out on the road. In fact, he felt as if helping stranded motorists somehow balanced out the other part of his life. The dark and dirty side of murderers, terrorists, and those who preyed on the weak and helpless.

An hour after they'd landed and Bull had said his goodbyes to his teammates, he was standing in the great room of Silverstone Towing. He looked around and smiled. He felt at home here. There were dirty dishes in the sink, and he could hear the hum of the dishwasher. He knew the refrigerators would be full of food and snacks for the drivers to enjoy when they were between jobs. There was a blanket lying discarded on one of the leather couches, and a pillow that still had the indentation of a person's head had tumbled to the floor. It was obvious someone had been taking a nap when they'd been dispatched and had left in a hurry.

Bull walked over and folded the blanket and picked up the pillow. There were two recliners, which never failed to put him right to sleep when he sat in them, along with the two large couches in the room. The fluffy rug under his feet was red and yellow, bringing a bright, happy vibe to the room. The scent of coffee was ever present, and Bull shut his eyes and took a deep breath. Just being here was good for his soul. Making him feel more connected to the decent men and women of the world. He and his friends dealt with the dregs of society on a regular basis, and he needed this . . . goodness.

Lately, in addition to his restlessness, Bull had begun feeling a bit cynical. No one outside the team knew what they were doing, and they wouldn't understand even if they did. They'd call them killers, probably want them tossed into prison and the key thrown away.

They also wouldn't care about the endless research he and the others put in before deciding on a mark.

They only chose the worst of the worst for their personal brand of justice. And in order to decide if they really *were* the worst, they had to study pictures, news stories, firsthand accounts of their possible marks' crimes.

Seeing men, women, and children tortured in the most horrific ways possible, and reading about the terror their marks left in their wake, was leaving its own mark on *Bull*.

His life was full of evil, and five years in, he was having a hard time witnessing enough decency to balance that out. He didn't know where to find more innocence, more good in the world, but he knew he needed it.

Taking a deep breath, he walked through the quiet space and down a long hallway toward the dispatch room. Bull opened the door, making enough noise to let Bart know he was there before walking up next to the other man. There were three large computer screens in front of him: one had *Die Hard* playing on it; another had a map of Indianapolis with blinking dots illustrating where the Silverstone employees were currently located; the last screen displayed the software system into which the dispatcher and drivers typed their notes to keep track of where they were and what they'd done.

Bart wore a headset and turned to look at Bull when he approached. A huge grin crossed his face. "Hey, boss," he greeted enthusiastically. "I wasn't expecting you in tonight."

"You know me, got bored," Bull told him.

Silverstone employees had no idea that when their bosses disappeared for days at a time, they were off ridding the world of evildoers. The team had decided from the beginning to keep their second life a secret from everyone. Their families, friends, and employees. The only people who might one day be told were the women they'd eventually . . . hopefully . . . spend the rest of their lives with.

"Well, I'm glad to see you," Bart said. "We've been unusually slammed tonight. We started off nice and slow, but I sent Alice out twenty minutes ago, and we've got two pickups waiting."

"What are they?" Bull asked, happy that he could get right to work and maybe stop thinking about how the shadows in his soul were beginning to overtake everything else.

"The police are on the scene of a hit and run. Car was totaled, vic is on his way to the hospital. And the second is a lady whose car started making weird noises on the 465 out by the airport. She pulled over, not wanting to make shit worse, and is waiting on a tow to a shop."

"I'll take the woman," Bull said without hesitation. Just the thought of a woman alone, sitting in her car on the side of the highway at night, made his protective instincts kick into gear. It was likely she was fine and could take care of herself, but he'd seen too many instances of people in broken-down cars being taken advantage of by the unscrupulous and desperate.

Bart smiled. "Figured you'd pick that one. Old Betty is in the bay waiting on ya. I'll send her location to your cell."

"Sounds good. Thanks."

"Sure thing."

"What's her name?"

"The chick? Skylar something-or-other."

Bull wanted to roll his eyes at his employee. He figured Bart knew exactly what the woman's name was, but typically he only doled out what he deemed the most pertinent details. And someone's last name was never high on his list of important information.

Bull nodded at the other man and left the dispatch room. He jogged toward the door that led into one of the huge bays housing the tow trucks. There were two other buildings on the property, but Old Betty was always kept in the one attached to the main building.

He grabbed the keys off a hook next to the door and smiled as he approached the old tow truck. Pausing just long enough to pull on a pair of overalls with the Silverstone Towing patch on the upper-left chest, Bull climbed up into the cab. He turned the key in the ignition, relieved when it started right up. He took the time to look around and make sure everything was in order. Nodding in contentment when it was, he clicked open the garage door and pulled out into the dark Indiana night.

It took about twenty minutes to get to Skylar's location. And when he did, he frowned, not happy at all about what he was seeing.

The ten-year-old brown Toyota Corolla had its hazard lights on but was barely pulled off to the side of the road. Not only that, but the woman had stopped right next to a large, dense grove of trees. The security-conscious side of Bull knew it would be easy to pull someone into those trees and do unspeakable things.

Because of his work with Silverstone, and dealing with the scum of society, Bull always saw the bad that could happen in any given situation, his mind immediately jumping to the depraved images he'd seen in reports way too often. Which was part of his problem.

Taking a deep breath, Bull forced himself to concentrate on the job at hand. He'd parked so his truck would prevent anyone who might not be paying attention from plowing into the disabled car on the side of the road. He turned on the bright spotlights on the front of the tow truck, lighting up the car and the area around it as if it were daytime.

He approached the Corolla from the passenger side, staying a respectable distance away from the vehicle.

Before he could knock on the door, the woman—Skylar, he assumed—climbed out of the driver's side and held up her hand to shield her face from the bright lights of his truck.

"Hi! I'm so relieved to see you! It feels as if I've been sitting here forever, even though I know it hasn't really been that long—"

"Stop," Bull ordered gruffly as she began to walk around the front of her car toward him.

She froze and stared at him uncertainly.

"You should make sure I'm who you think I am. That I'm actually the tow truck you called."

She frowned in confusion and looked at him, back toward Old Betty, then back to Bull. "You're in a tow truck," she stated in confusion.

"I am," Bull agreed. "But I could be a random driver who saw your car and decided to stop. I could be trying to steal business from the company who's actually coming to help you, or more importantly, I could be here to do you harm."

She inhaled sharply. "People *do* that?"

The depth of this woman's naivete slammed into Bull with the force of a sledgehammer. He knew he was gawking at her, but he couldn't help it. Was she really *that* clueless? "Yeah, unfortunately, they do."

"Okay. I hadn't thought about that. Though, I'm perfectly aware that sitting on the side of the road isn't exactly safe. I've been nervous since I pulled over. I was relieved to see you . . . but now I'm thinking you're kind of a jerk. I'd call another tow company, but I've already waited what feels like forever."

Bull couldn't help but smile. He liked that she was standing up for herself. He took a deep breath. "I'm sorry for coming off so harshly. It's just that . . . I don't like to see people, especially women, being taken advantage of and hurt."

They stared at each other for a long moment before she said, "I'm assuming you are who you say you are, since you're warning me against people who would do unscrupulous things."

"I am. But you should still call to verify. You can call Silverstone Towing and ask the dispatcher for a description of the driver who was sent to help you. Ask him if the driver has arrived. There are GPS trackers in all of the trucks, so they'll know."

The woman studied him for a beat before nodding and pulling her cell phone out of her pocket, looking down at it to hit a button.

He waited as she made the call. He appreciated the fact that she'd walked back to the driver's side and put some space between them while she talked to the dispatcher. He could still probably bum-rush her and drag her into the woods alongside the road, but at least she was attempting to keep herself safe.

Bull took the time to examine her as she was talking to Bart back at Silverstone. She was a tiny little thing, especially compared to his six-foot frame. He'd estimate her at no more than five-six, max. She wore black dress pants and a cream blouse with flowy sleeves and a V-neck that hinted at some generous cleavage. He'd also noted her heels before she'd retreated, making his guess on her height off by at least two inches.

Her hair was pulled back into an austere bun at the base of her neck . . . and Bull had the strangest urge to release the clip holding it to see exactly how long it was. He unconsciously took a step closer, the sudden desire to know more about her overriding his common sense.

She looked up then and smiled sheepishly. "He said you were here," she informed him.

"So I am," Bull replied. He held out his hand and walked toward her. "Maybe we can start over. I didn't exactly make the best first impression. I'm Bull."

She wrinkled her nose. "Bull?"

He smiled slightly. "My real name's Carson, Carson Rhodes, but no one calls me that."

"Not even your mom?" she asked as she put her hand in his own.

Bull flinched slightly with the jolt that seemed to go through him when their palms touched. Her hand was smooth and felt incredibly soft against his own calloused and roughened skin. "Never knew my mom," he said, barely paying attention to his words. "She left when I was a baby. It was just my dad and me growing up. He died when I was seventeen."

"Oh my God," she said, eyes widening in horror at her faux pas. "I'm sorry."

"It's okay. Long time ago," Bull said.

"Still. That was extremely rude of me. I should know better."

Bull was keenly aware that she hadn't pulled her hand away yet, and he'd be damned if he'd be the first to break what seemed to be an unexpected connection between them. "And your name?" he asked. He knew it, of course, but protocol must be followed.

"Oh, it's Skylar. Skylar Reid."

"Hi, Skylar," Bull said, wanting to hear her name on his lips.

"Hi, Carson."

They smiled at each other for a heartbeat before she gently tugged on her hand. Bull reluctantly let go.

"So . . . ," she said, looking back at her car.

"What happened?" Bull asked, trying to get things back on a professional level. He couldn't help thinking of how nice his given name had sounded coming from her, though.

"I don't know," she said, the distress easy to hear in her tone. "I was on my way home from work and—"

"Work? This late?" Bull couldn't stop himself from asking.

She nodded. "Yeah, I teach at Eastlake Elementary School, and we had teacher-parent meetings tonight. I stayed later than usual because a few of my parents didn't get off work until after six."

"You're a teacher," Bull stated. "What grade?"

He knew he was being nosy but couldn't seem to stop himself.

Skylar shrugged. "Kindergarten."

Bull inhaled deeply. Of *course* she was a kindergarten teacher. For just a second, he'd entertained the idea of asking her out, maybe going on a few dates with her. But how ridiculous was the idea of *him* with a kindergarten teacher? He knew the stereotype of all women teaching little kids being pure and innocent was ridiculous, but he couldn't help feeling that he was way too jaded for her.

"Is there something wrong with my job?" she asked, sounding a little defensive.

Realizing she hadn't missed his reaction, Bull did his best to backpedal. "Of course not. Not at all."

"Yeah, right," she said, turning away from him.

That made Bull even more anxious. She shouldn't turn her back on a strange man. Especially not when it was dark and she was stranded on the side of the road and had no way of escape. "Don't turn your back to me," he ordered.

She glanced over her shoulder to look at him. "Are you seriously ordering me around again?"

Bull did his best to gentle his tone, not sure he'd succeeded when he said, "You shouldn't turn your back on someone you don't know. Especially when you're on the side of the road in the dark and there's a copse of trees not even a hundred yards away that you could be dragged into."

Her eyes got huge once more, and he saw her dart a glance over his shoulders to the trees behind him. She licked her lips, and Bull suppressed the groan that threatened to escape. He'd never been attracted to someone the minute he'd met them . . . but he was to Skylar. He had no idea what it was about her. Her vulnerability? The fact that she so obviously needed his help? The fact that he'd always been drawn to petite women?

He had no clue, but it was extremely uncomfortable.

Instead of ripping his head off for being rude or for scaring her, Skylar Reid tilted her head to the side and stared into his eyes for a long moment. When she spoke, she nearly knocked him off his feet.

"You've seen a lot of bad things in your life, haven't you?"

Bull nodded once, not sure his voice would work.

"I know I'm not that worldly," she told him. "I've lived around here my entire life. I've never been outside the US and have only been to a few other states. But I've seen my share of bad things as well. Kids who've been beaten at home and come to school with bruises and insist nothing's wrong. Children who are so hungry they resort to stealing snacks from their classmates any chance they get. Some of my students wear the same clothes every single day. And believe it or not, bullying starts in kindergarten."

Bull nodded again, not surprised in the least by anything she was saying.

"But I've also seen the good in people. Those kids who get their lunches stolen? The next day, some bring extra food to help feed their friends. And when the students come in wearing the same thing they had on the day before, their classmates are happy to help them pick an outfit from the 'extra clothes' cabinet I keep so their clothes can be washed during the school day."

"And the bullying?" Bull asked.

Skylar shrugged. "I do my best to nip it in the bud, but unfortunately, there's only so much I can do about that."

"I don't think I've ever heard that phrase, 'nip it in the bud,' come from anyone's mouth in real life," Bull told her.

"Whatever," Skylar muttered. "My point is, I know that I'm naive in a lot of ways, and I haven't seen or experienced the kinds of things you probably have. But I know a good man when I see one."

Bull snorted and shook his head. "You have no clue, sweetheart."

Deep inside, he was aware the last thing he was thinking about was del Rio and Peru and the job he'd just finished. He was one hundred percent focused on Skylar. She'd somehow, just by her presence, made the evil things he'd seen and done in the last two days retreat into the background.

"Maybe not," she retorted. "But from the first moment you spoke, even though you were kind of a jerk about it, you've had nothing but my best interests at heart. You would no more attack me and drag me into the woods over there to rape me than I'd hurt a child."

The fact that rape was the worst thing she thought he could do to her was as telling as anything else. Skylar Reid was innocent to the core.

And Bull found himself wanting to do whatever it took to keep her that way.

"So you were driving home from work as a kindergarten teacher, and your car broke down?" Bull asked, needing to move this along to get her off the side of the road. He was well aware of the cars whizzing by at eighty miles an hour or more.

She nodded, allowing the change of subject. "Yeah. It started making a clacking noise, and I was scared a wheel might fall off or the engine would blow up or something. So I pulled over. I've had my car for years, and it's always been dependable. I figured it was smarter to call for help than try to limp it somewhere and do more damage." She grimaced. "I can't exactly afford a new car right now."

Bull had heard that sentiment more times than he could recall. "Do you have a shop you want me to take her to?"

Skylar smiled again. "Why do men do that?"

"Do what?"

"Make all cars female?"

Bull chuckled. "It's just a thing."

"I guess. Anyway, there's a shop not too far from my apartment that I suppose would work. It's called Jim's Autobody."

"Nope," Bull told her firmly.

"What? Why not?" Skylar asked. "It's convenient."

"And Jim is a crook. There's no way I'm taking you or your car there."

Skylar sighed. "I don't know anywhere else. My dad usually takes my car to his mechanic, but that's all the way up in Carmel. I can't afford to be that far away from work."

"You live near Jim's?" Bull asked, telling himself he was only interested in a professional way, but knowing he was lying.

"Yes. I live in Southpoint Apartments."

Bull eyed her incredulously.

She held up a hand. "Don't start. I've heard it all from my dad already. I know it's not the best area of town, and the apartments are kinda shitty, but it's not far from work, and it's affordable."

"They're not kinda shitty," Bull said. "They *are* shitty."

Skylar stared at him without another word.

"Fine. How about Stanley Automotive? It's halfway between Eastlake and your apartment. They've got a few loaner cars. If one's available, you can use it while yours is in the shop."

"That sounds expensive," Skylar noted.

Bull kept his face impassive. She was right, they weren't cheap, but Stan was fair. He went out of his way to help his clients, even going to the junkyard to find parts for older-model cars when possible, just to keep their costs as low as he could make them.

He'd have a word with Stan to let him know that he'd be helping Skylar pay for repairs . . . on the down-low, of course. He had a feeling the feisty woman would never accept his help. "Stan's a good guy," he told her. "He'll be honest with you and won't make repairs you don't need."

Skylar hesitated and bit her lip as she contemplated what to do. Bull didn't rush her. As much as he wanted to tell her to hurry so he could get her off the side of the road, he let her come to her own decision in her own time.

"You probably know a lot about cars," she told him.

Bull shook his head. "Nope. I can change a tire and check the oil, and that's about it. But I *do* know a lot about which garage owners are honest and which are pieces of shit."

"Why are you helping me?" she asked. "I mean, I'm grateful, don't get me wrong, but I can't imagine you do this for every person you help on the side of the road."

"Why not? Maybe I do," Bull insisted.

Skylar shook her head. "No, I think you do exactly what they tell you to, even if you know they're making a mistake. I'm guessing you don't suffer fools gladly, and if someone acts superior, I bet you completely dismiss them."

She was so right, it was almost scary.

"Maybe I just feel sorry for you," he told her, lying through his teeth. The last thing he felt was pity for Skylar.

"Maybe," she agreed. "But I'll gladly take your advice. Car shops are your area of expertise, not mine."

Bull sighed in relief. He would've taken her car to Jim's if she'd insisted, but he wouldn't have been happy about it. He gestured toward Old Betty. "I'd feel better if you waited in the truck while I get you all hooked up," he told her.

Skylar nodded. "Can I grab my stuff first?"

"Of course," Bull said.

She headed around her car and opened the passenger-side door. She leaned over to gather her things—and Bull just about swallowed his tongue at the sight of her ass. She was nice and curvy, and it was all he could do not to reach out and palm her fleshy globes.

As far as he could tell, Skylar was built perfectly. She carried extra weight on her, but it was all in those curves and made her look soft, which he loved, as he was anything but.

Skylar stood up, and Bull sighed in relief. He should *not* be lusting over her. First, because she was a customer. Second, because it was rude.

And third, because he'd just met her. But that didn't seem to matter to his libido. She intrigued him and turned him on, and it had been a long time since a woman had caught his attention . . . and he knew Skylar wasn't even trying. Which was even *more* of a turn-on.

She had a giant messenger bag over her shoulder that looked heavier than she was. Bull could see papers sticking out from the top, and it made him smile. She'd also put the strap of her purse around her head and shoulder and held a bedraggled bouquet of wildflowers in her hand.

At his raised eyebrow, she said, "One of my students gave them to me. If I leave them in my car, they'll die."

Bull wanted to tell her the flowers looked half-dead already, but he kept his mouth shut. He walked next to her over to Old Betty and grinned when it was clear she'd only now realized how tall the cab of the truck was. She turned to him and wrinkled her nose. "Men and their trucks," she said with a laugh.

Bull couldn't help but chuckle. "It's a tow truck. She has to be big to be able to do her job."

"I'm guessing you have a huge pickup truck parked in your own driveway, though."

"You'd be wrong," Bull told her, not worried in the least about sharing personal information. He never told women about his personal life when he'd just met them, but around Skylar, he couldn't seem to keep his mouth shut. "I live in an apartment, like you, although it's in a safer part of town, and I drive a 2015 Nissan Altima."

She blinked up at him. "But that's so . . . normal."

Bull couldn't help it, he barked out a laugh. When he got himself under control, he asked, "Would it make you feel better if I told you it was red?"

Skylar smiled. "Yes, actually."

"Come on, I'll help you up," Bull told her, holding out a hand.

Without hesitation, she put her palm in his once more and let him give her a boost.

He could see her better in the light from inside the truck when he'd opened the door, and he finally noted her hair was a beautiful auburn color. Green eyes seemed to sparkle as she looked down at him.

Bull stared up at Skylar and made a decision. He was going to ask her out. He had no idea if she'd say yes or not—if she was smart, she'd decline, and they'd go their separate ways—but he was desperate to spend more time with her. To see if she continued to make him feel as lighthearted later as she had in the last twenty minutes.

He had no idea if the pull he felt toward her was because of the job he'd just finished and he was desperate for her kind of goodness, or if it was more. But he wanted to find out.

"Everything all right?" she asked uncertainly when he continued to stand at the door and stare up at her without saying a word.

He mentally shook his head and berated himself. "We're good," he said, then shut her door and jogged around to the driver's side. He hauled himself into the truck and pulled it in front of her Corolla. "Stay here," he told her. "I'll have your car hooked up in no time, and we'll be off."

Without waiting for her agreement, he jumped out of Old Betty and slammed the door. He had a job to do, and he needed to get on it.

The entire time he was hooking her car up, though, all Bull thought about was how he should ask her out . . . and if she'd be brave enough, or stupid enough, to say yes.

Chapter Three

Skylar put a hand on her chest and willed her heartbeat to slow. Ever since she'd seen the huge man next to her car, it seemed as if she couldn't take a full breath. She'd tried to tell herself it was because he was so intimidating, but she knew that wasn't it.

From the second she'd put her hand in his, she'd felt in tune with him. She didn't know why; he'd been kinda harsh with her, and she knew he thought she was way too naive. But there was something in his gaze that drew her in. She'd seen it in some of her students' eyes over the years. A desperation for a connection.

But Carson was no child. He was a man through and through.

He towered over her, which wasn't exactly anything new. At only five feet four, she was shorter than most people. But standing next to Carson made her feel as if she could let all of her worries go. Maybe it was because he was so muscular, or maybe it was the protective vibe he'd exuded from the very first words out of his mouth. Whatever it was, Skylar felt comfortable with him.

His black hair was short, but still long enough to be a bit mussed, as if it hadn't seen a comb for quite a while, and the beard on his face made him seem even more unkempt. But he had such gentle eyes.

And Skylar knew if anyone could hear her thoughts, they'd think she was certifiably insane. Gentle eyes?

But she knew she wasn't crazy. Living where she did and working at the school both had their downsides. She came into contact with plenty of tenants and parents who were drunk, high, or simply pissed off at the world. And she'd learned when they had a crazy look in their eyes to stay away from them.

When she looked into Carson's eyes, she saw a yearning so acute she was drawn *toward* him rather than warned away. She wanted to find out exactly what his demons were and slay every one. Which was crazy. Carson wasn't a man who looked like he'd allow anyone to fight *anything* for him. He could take care of himself.

Shaking her head, Skylar mumbled, "Get yourself together, Sky. You just met the man, he's towing your car. He's doing his job."

She turned around in her seat to watch through the back window as Carson hooked up her little car to tow it to Stanley Automotive. She wasn't sure how she was going to get home from the shop, but she'd cross that bridge when she got there.

Studying her surroundings to try to turn her thoughts away from the all-too-intriguing man who'd shown up to help her, Skylar noticed the children's car seat in the back of the tow truck. It looked out of place, and she couldn't help but wonder why it was there. She noticed other things as well. The interior of the truck was spotless. Not a piece of garbage anywhere to be seen, and when she inhaled deeply, she smelled a bit of old smoke, but the scent of fresh linen was much more prominent. She was somewhat surprised, as she'd thought a work truck like this would smell like grease, dirt, maybe a lot more strongly of smoke.

Holding on to the bedraggled flowers tighter, she startled badly when the driver's side door abruptly opened, interrupting her thoughts, and Carson climbed into the seat next to her.

"You okay?" he asked, obviously seeing her jerk.

"Yeah. That was fast."

His lips moved up into a half smile. "Been doing this for a while now, sweetheart. Not hard to hook up a car. You ready?"

She should've told him that calling her *sweetheart* was presumptuous since they'd just met, but instead she simply nodded.

Carson nodded to her seat belt. "Buckle up."

Mentally shaking her head, Skylar reached for the seat belt. She couldn't believe she'd forgotten it. She always wore her seat belt. Always. Even when she was on a school bus, she buckled the lap belt. She was cautious by nature, and it was a little surprising that she'd had to be reminded to buckle up by the large man next to her.

"Here, let me hold those," Carson said, reaching for the small bouquet she was still clutching. His fingers brushed hers as he took them, and Skylar barely repressed the reactionary shudder at feeling his touch again. When he'd introduced himself and she'd taken his hand earlier, it had felt as if she'd grabbed hold of a live wire. A jolt had gone through her and left her feeling a bit off balance.

She buckled the seat belt and took the flowers back from Carson, being careful not to touch him this time. "For the record," she blurted, "I'm not usually so careless with my safety."

He blinked in surprise at her words, then shrugged.

"I was just flustered by the situation," she further explained.

Carson put on his hazard lights and started driving down the shoulder of the highway. Once he'd gained enough speed, he pulled out onto the main road. "When you're flustered and unsure is when you should be even more careful."

Skylar wanted to be irritated, but she knew he was right. "I know. I appreciate you encouraging me to call Silverstone to verify you were sent by them."

She wasn't sure how she'd expected Carson to respond. Maybe something about how she should be more careful the next time. Or that he was glad everything had worked out all right. But whatever she'd expected, it wasn't what he actually said.

"There are too many people in the world who are looking to take advantage of those they think are weaker than them. They'll exploit, steal, and intimidate whoever they can to get what they want, and damn the consequences."

His words lay heavy in the cab of the truck, and Skylar wasn't sure what to say.

But she didn't have to say anything.

"Sorry," Carson muttered. "It's been a long twenty-four hours."

And that struck her as odd as well. He didn't say it had been a long day. But a long twenty-four hours. It was subtle, but there was a difference between the two phrases.

"When have you last slept?" she asked gently. Now that she was nearer to him, and more or less at eye level, she could see the dark circles under his eyes.

"I'm okay to drive," he said instead of answering her question. "I'd never put you or anyone else in danger."

Skylar nodded. "Okay." His response didn't answer her question, but then again, it kinda did.

"Tell me about your students," he asked after a moment.

Blinking in surprise, Skylar asked, "My students?"

"Yeah. You said you were a kindergarten teacher. I bet you've got some cute kids in your class."

She usually didn't talk about her kids. She was protective of them, and as he'd pointed out earlier, not everyone's interests were innocent. But she couldn't help but trust Carson. She didn't know what it was about him, maybe that he'd gone out of his way to make her more safety conscious, but she didn't even hesitate to answer his question.

"There are fourteen kids in my class. They're all from lower-income families, because of where Eastlake is located. But I've never had such supportive parents as I've gotten this year. They might not have a lot of extras at home, but they all want the same thing for their children . . . for them to be happy and loved. And for them to get an education so they can get a good job and hopefully break out of the box their parents seem to be stuck in."

"That's good," Carson murmured.

Seeing that he genuinely seemed interested, Skylar went on. "I've got a good mix of ethnicities in my class this year. It's pretty evenly split between Hispanic, African American, and white kids. Which I love because I can hopefully teach them that it's not the color of one's skin that makes someone good or bad, it's what's inside that matters."

Carson nodded. "Got any favorites?" he asked.

"Of course not," Skylar said immediately. "I care about them all the same."

She couldn't help but smile when Carson glanced over at her skeptically.

"That's the official party line, I get it. But come on, there have to be some that tug at your heartstrings harder than others," Carson cajoled.

"If you tell anyone, I'll deny it," she warned sternly, but inside she wanted to grin.

"Who would I tell? Stan? I don't think he's gonna care who the little teacher likes better."

"Fine. Let's see . . . there's Chad and Brodie, who are super adorable. Chad is black, and Brodie is white, and they honestly think they're twins. They're inseparable and do everything together. One day they were both wearing similar navy-blue shirts, and they came up to me with their arms around each other and said, 'Look, Ms. Reid, we're twins! Bet you can't tell us apart.' So for the rest of the day, I played along and called them by each other's names, smacking myself in the forehead when they informed me I had it wrong. It was hilarious and adorable . . . especially because Brodie has bright-red hair, and Chad has some of the darkest skin I've seen in a very long time."

She eyed Carson to see if she was boring him, and he nodded at her with a small smile, so she went on. "Ignacio's parents are from Mexico and, from what I can tell, are probably in the country illegally, but he was born here. They work extremely hard, and he's one of the smartest kids in the class. He's got a lot stacked against him, but I have a feeling he's going to go far in life. Gwen's mom is a stripper at night, and during the day she's a waitress. She's a single parent who spends every second of her free time with her daughter, if what Gwen tells me can be believed. She's having a hard time learning to read, but I think it's because they don't have a lot of money for books. Every penny goes toward keeping a roof over their heads and food in their stomachs."

"Let me guess, you've managed to find books to give her," Carson said.

Skylar shrugged. "The public library is always having sales on old inventory, and they practically give the books away. It's not a big deal for me to grab some and give them to my kids." She liked the warm look he aimed her way at that.

"Anyway, Karlee and Marisol are thick as thieves . . . and if there's trouble, those two are usually involved. They're super smart, and I can't help but laugh at their attempts to look innocent when they're caught in the act. Zahir is from Afghanistan, and although he doesn't speak a lot of English yet, I can see every day that he understands more and more. During their first week in class, Cedric took him by the hand and towed him around the playground, showing him every piece of equipment and how it worked. They now play together every day.

"Keilani's parents are Hawaiian and moved to the mainland last year when her dad got a job here in Indy. I think they all miss the beach. Keilani is always cold, so I'm happy to snuggle with her during nap time. Then there's Sandra . . ."

"Sandra?" Carson asked when she didn't continue.

Skylar sighed. "Her mom died last year, and her dad is raising her, except he works all the time. His parents aren't in the picture, and I guess his in-laws—who are wealthy—didn't approve of their daughter marrying a white man, and they refuse to help him in any way. They've never even met Sandra. He's working three jobs, and while I admire how hard he's trying to provide for his daughter, I worry that she's spending too much time on her own. She participates in the after-school program for kids whose parents work, but she's always the last one to be picked up, and most of the time I stay after the program is over so she's not alone until her dad can get there to pick her up. She seems happy enough, but I can see the worry in her eyes. She's too young to worry as much as she does."

"What does her dad do?"

"I've only met him once. He hasn't been able to come to the teacher-parent meetings because he's always working, but he explained their situation at the beginning of the school year. He works as a short-order cook for a diner in the mornings, then goes back to their housing complex and starts his job as a landscaper . . . mowing the grass, shoveling snow, and doing whatever else needs doing. At night, after Sandra is home, he feeds her, then goes to his third job as a janitor."

Carson whistled. "That's a lot. Does he leave his daughter home alone?"

"Yeah, I think so. But it happens with a lot of students," she told him with a small shake of her head. "I know he loves that girl more than anything. She told me he took her to the beauty parlor so the ladies there could teach him how to braid her hair. She's biracial and I guess looks a lot like her mom, who was African American . . . and she definitely got her hair. She always speaks of her dad with love. She's not neglected, although I do think she's starved for attention."

"Hmmm," Carson said. "What's his name?"

"Her dad's name?"

"Yeah."

"Um . . . Shawn Archer. Why?"

Carson shrugged. "Just wondering."

"Anyway, there are a few other kids in my class, but I love them all. It's a privilege to teach them, and it's exciting to see them grow up and become amazing boys and girls. I always go to the fifth-grade graduations and cry when I see the little kids I knew moving on."

She looked over at Carson and saw he had a small smile on his face as he drove. "What?"

His gaze flicked over to her before returning to the road. "Nothing."

"No, seriously, what?"

"I hope those kids know how lucky they are to have you in their corner."

Skylar knew she was blushing, but she hoped the darkness hid it. "They're good kids. They may not have been born to families with money, but that doesn't mean their parents are uninvolved. Or that the kids don't deserve to have the best education they can get. They have enough strikes against them, I just don't want their education, or lack of it, to be another."

"As I said, they're lucky. What about you? Where'd you grow up? You said you've been in the Indy area your entire life."

"Yeah, I have. I grew up in Carmel and went to college at IUPUI, downtown. I've never lived anywhere else. I love it here. And yes, I grew up with every privilege a kid could have . . . and I'm very appreciative of that."

"Your parents still live here?"

"Yeah. They're still in Carmel."

"How do they feel about their little girl working and living in a not-so-nice part of Indianapolis?"

Skylar wrinkled her nose. "My dad wants to pay my rent and move me to another apartment complex, but while the neighborhood might not be the best, I love most of the people who live in the apartments around me. We're all just trying to make a buck and to get through life as well as we can. At first they were wary of me because of the color of my skin, just as I was with them, but when the apartments the next building over caught fire . . . we all kinda bonded. That could've been us. Ever since then, we look out for each other."

"Any siblings?"

"Nope. I'm the only one. My dad teases me and says that they couldn't handle another baby after me. I guess I was a holy terror."

Carson chuckled. "We have that in common."

"You were a terror too?" Skylar teased.

"I meant that we're only kids. My mom wasn't thrilled about having me, and she made it clear that she wanted nothing to do with my dad, or me, by leaving."

Skylar couldn't help but gasp. She reached over and put a hand on Carson's arm. "I swear I don't make a habit of sticking my foot in my mouth. I'm so sorry."

Carson looked at her, then down at her hand still resting on his arm. Then he covered her hand with his and squeezed gently.

Visibly, Skylar stilled. But the feel of his warm, calloused hand on hers made her thighs clench and her belly roll. His hand dwarfed hers, and she had the urge to turn hers around and clasp their fingers together.

Which was crazy.

Insane.

Ridiculous.

Wasn't it?

But when he began to speak again, it was almost as if he didn't realize his hand was still lying on hers. He didn't say anything suggestive. He just continued speaking, as if he wasn't practically holding hands with a woman he'd picked up on the side of the road.

"Don't feel sorry for me," he told her. "My dad was awesome. I miss him every day. Even though my mom treated him like shit and left him with a screaming kid, he was never bitter about it. He took to being a dad like it was the easiest thing on earth. We didn't have much money growing up, but he spent as much time with me as he could. We went camping all the time, mostly because it was free, but I'll never forget those trips. It was just me and him and the huge sky above us.

"He told me that life was hard, and if I expected it to be easy, I was bound to be disappointed and disillusioned. He taught me that having true friends was more important than having money, and treating others with respect was the measure of a good man. Most of all, he taught me that when the time came, and I found a woman I wanted to spend the rest of my life with, that my job was to protect her . . . not because she's weak, but because she's important enough to *be* protected."

Skylar simply stared at the man next to her. She'd just met him, but somehow she felt as if they'd been friends forever. She had no idea if he was blowing smoke up her ass with that last line about treating his woman as if she was important, but she didn't think he was.

He continued, as if he hadn't just rendered her speechless.

"When he died when I was seventeen, I floundered for a bit but eventually got my ass in gear, graduated from high school, and went into the Army. While there, I met the best friends I could ever hope to have and learned, not for the first time, that my dad was right. Having true friends is more important than anything."

"You still keep in touch with them?" Skylar asked.

He looked at her and smiled. And it was an honest, genuine smile that seemed to light him up from the inside out. "Oh yeah. They co-own Silverstone Towing with me."

Skylar blinked in surprise. "You *own* Silverstone? I thought you just worked for them. What in the world are you doing rescuing stranded motorists?"

He squeezed her hand, answering her question about whether he realized he was still touching her. Though she had a feeling that if she pulled on her hand the least little bit, he'd release her immediately. "The best way to make sure things are running smoothly is to get in the trenches, so to speak," he explained. "Besides . . . I needed the distraction tonight."

Skylar wanted to ask why, but Carson began to slow down as he exited the interstate. He released her hand and put both of his on the wheel. "Stan's place isn't too far from here. I called him when I was hooking up your car, and he's going to meet us there to get the paperwork done and to give you the keys to your loaner."

"Wow, really?"

"Yup."

"I was just going to take an Uber or something."

"No way," Carson said with a shake of his head. "If you thought for a second I was going to simply leave you there, you were wrong."

"Well . . . thanks. I appreciate it."

"You're welcome."

"Can I ask a question?" Skylar asked.

"Of course. You can ask me anything," Carson told her.

"What's up with the baby seat in the back?"

She watched him carefully to see if he looked guilty about something or tried to lie to her, but his facial expression didn't change in the least. "We've got seats in about half our trucks, and dispatchers are trained to ask if the pickup includes children. We just want to be prepared to transport little kids if necessary."

It was a good answer. A very good answer.

"And under your seat is a bag with stuffed animals," he continued. "We get called to a lot of wrecks, and sometimes the kids are scared and upset. If the firefighters or cops haven't already given them a toy, we'll do the honors."

"That's . . . amazing."

Carson shrugged. "It's all part of being a decent human being. Caring about others. My friends and I want Silverstone to be a good place to work and able to offer a safe service for people in need. Most of the time when our services are needed, it's because someone isn't having a good day at all. Making their life easier by having a car seat or making their kid smile by giving them a stuffed animal makes the experience just a little bit better. Or at least we hope it does."

Then he smiled. "And if they have a good experience with Silverstone, maybe they'll tell their friends, and our business will continue to grow and prosper."

Skylar chuckled. "I'd say that business model is working for you. Silverstone was the first towing company I thought of when I pulled onto the side of the road."

"Good. That's what we want." Carson flipped on his blinker, and the next thing Skylar knew, they were pulling into a service station. He maneuvered the tow truck with her car behind it as easily as if he were driving a small sedan. He pulled up at the front door of the business and said, "Hang on while I come around," before jumping out of the truck.

Skylar shook her head and undid her seat belt. She could manage to get out of the truck just fine on her own. She opened her door . . .

Okay, maybe she couldn't. She knew the truck sat high but hadn't realized exactly *how* high until she was looking down at the ground from inside.

Then Carson was there in front of her, grinning knowingly. "Let me help," he said, not commenting on the fact she obviously hadn't planned to wait for him.

Not sure how this was going to work, Skylar squeaked in surprise when large hands gripped her around the waist and physically lifted her off the seat. She managed to keep hold of the flowers even as she grabbed his biceps for balance when he put her on her feet.

"Thanks," she said a little breathlessly.

"You're welcome," he returned.

Neither moved for a long moment. Carson's hands stayed at her waist, and she stood there holding his arms, staring up at him, her mind a complete blank.

"Hey!" a loud, cheery voice called, startling them both.

But instead of dropping his hands, as if he'd been caught doing something he shouldn't, Carson merely shifted his hold. He turned to stand next to her, and one of his hands rested lightly on the small of her back.

It should've felt creepy. Having a man she didn't really know put his hands on her. But it didn't.

"Hey, Stan," Carson said, reaching out to shake the other man's hand. "Thanks for coming out so late."

The large black man merely shrugged as he shook Carson's hand. "You said it was important, and I know you don't say that shit just to say it. So here I am."

"It wasn't *that* important," Skylar protested.

Both men ignored her. "Skylar's a kindergarten teacher over at Eastlake, and her car started acting up on the 465. Made weird noises. She pulled over, and here we are. She needs something to get her to Eastlake and back to Southpoint Apartments safely until her car is fixed."

"I've got a nephew who goes to Eastlake," Stan said.

"Yeah? What grade?" Skylar asked.

"Fourth. Name's Terrell Johnson."

"I know Terrell!" Skylar smiled. "I didn't have him in my class, but I hear he's really smart."

Stan chuckled. "A little too smart for his own good sometimes. But I love him. You live in Southpoint?" he asked.

Skylar nodded. "Yes. And before you say anything negative, I love it there. I've got great neighbors, and we all look out for each other."

"I wasn't gonna say nothin'," Stan said with a smile.

Skylar rolled her eyes.

"Come on, while Bull unhooks your car, you can fill out some paperwork, and then I'll let you pick which car you want to use while I'm workin' on yours."

"Oh, anything will do. I'm not picky."

Skylar looked back when they got to the door to the building and saw Carson hadn't moved to start unhooking her car. He was staring at her instead. Goose bumps broke out on her arms, but she raised her eyebrows at him in question.

He smiled then, and she loved seeing it. She sensed he didn't smile a lot, and it made her feel good to know she could do that for him. He gave her a chin lift and turned away to head for the back of the tow truck.

After ten minutes of paperwork and teasing from Stan, Skylar followed him back outside to see her car sitting in a parking spot in front of the garage. She'd left her keys in the ignition and assumed Carson had moved it.

"I said I was gonna give you a choice as to the loaner you wanted, but I changed my mind," Stan said, holding out a key ring to her. "You're takin' the Volvo."

Skylar didn't much care which car she drove as long as it got her to school and home in one piece. But when she saw the car in question, she couldn't help but wince. The white older-model car looked like it had seen better days. The paint was peeling, and there was rust around the edges. It looked like a hunk of junk, but she'd never tell Stan that.

"Don't judge a book by its cover," Carson told her, obviously seeing her dismay. "It looks like a piece of shit, but I can guarantee she purrs like a kitten. If any of his loaners broke down, Stan would take it personally."

"I'm sure it's fine," Skylar said politely.

Both Stan and Carson chuckled.

"She just got a new engine a few months ago," Stan reassured her. "She was a complete overhaul. You'll never drive anything as smooth as her, I promise. But considering you live at Southpoint, you couldn't exactly pull in there with a Mercedes. It would draw too much attention. Nobody'll take a second look at this piece of crap. They won't try to steal it, because they'll assume it won't run well. Go on, get in and start 'er up. You'll see."

Skylar conceded his point, though she wasn't exactly convinced the car wouldn't fall apart around her. But when Carson held out his hand for the bouquet of flowers, she didn't have much of a choice. Smiling at Stan, she climbed behind the wheel and put the key in the ignition. When the engine turned over, she looked up in surprise.

Once again, both men chuckled.

"Told ya," Stan said.

"It's so quiet!" Skylar exclaimed.

"Yup. She'll get you where you need to go safely. She's got no flash, but you don't need any more attention on you than you've got already."

Frowning, Skylar asked, "What does that mean?"

Instead of answering her, Stan turned to Carson. "She serious?"

Carson nodded. "Yup."

"Damn. All right, I've got your digits. I'll give you a call after I get under the hood of your car tomorrow," Stan told her.

Skylar saw a look pass between the men that she couldn't interpret. She had a feeling there were a lot of things going over her head, but she wasn't about to ask. She'd always been kind of clueless when it came to innuendos, so she let it go.

"Sounds good," she told Stan. "And I really appreciate you coming out tonight to meet us."

"Of course. Bull's a good man. One of the best. If you see Terrell, tell him you saw me and I said to be good," Stan said. Then he turned and headed back for his shop. He locked the front door and went around the corner, probably to where he'd parked his own vehicle.

"You good?" Carson asked as he handed her the flowers he'd been carrying around. He'd also grabbed her messenger bag and gave that to her too.

Skylar looked up at him after putting the bouquet and bag on the seat next to her, feeling at a disadvantage since he was so tall and she was sitting in the car.

As if he could read her mind, Carson squatted beside her door so they were more or less eye to eye.

"I'm good," she told him. "Thank you for coming."

"Of course." He paused, then said, "I'm going to follow you home. Not because I'm being creepy, but because I want to make sure you get there all right."

"Stan's loaner car isn't as good as he claimed?" she asked.

"No, it's not that. That car would get you all the way to California and back without any issues whatsoever. I just want to make sure you get home all right. It's getting late and . . ."

"And you don't like where I live," Skylar finished for him.

He merely shrugged.

"It's not that late," she protested. "It's only like nine."

"Even so," Carson said.

"Nothing I say is going to change your mind, is it?" she asked.

Carson didn't even break a smile. "If you told me it honestly made you uncomfortable and you didn't want me to follow you, I'd respect that. But I swear that I only have your best interests in mind."

"It's okay if you follow me," Skylar told him.

His lips twitched.

"But I've made it a rule not to let strays stay if they follow me home," she joked.

The twitch turned into a real smile, and her heart swelled.

"What would you say if I asked if you'd like to go out for coffee or lunch sometime?" he asked.

Skylar stilled. She couldn't believe this beautiful man was asking her out. Some people might assume he asked out every woman he picked up for a tow, but she had a feeling he was acting out of character. And when she paused a bit too long before answering, she knew for sure that he didn't do this kind of thing all the time. A mask seemed to fall over his face, as if he wasn't feeling anything at all. As if her answer wouldn't faze him one way or another.

Hating that blank mask more than she wanted to admit, especially after making him smile and laugh several times that night, her hand landed on his forearm. He'd braced it on his knee, and it tightened at her touch.

"I'd like that. But I'm not free until the weekend . . . because, you know . . . teacher."

"You don't get time off for lunch at school?"

"I do, but I usually eat with the kids. It gives me time to catch up with former students, or if any of my kids needs some extra affection, that's a great time to give it without being distracted by lessons or other classroom stuff that takes my attention during regular class time."

He didn't say anything for a long moment.

"Carson?" she asked tentatively. "Is that okay? I'm not blowing you off."

"I know you aren't," he told her. "I bet you're an amazing teacher. Your students are extremely lucky to have you."

Skylar knew she was blushing once more. "I don't know about that."

"I do," he said firmly. "And if you're free this Saturday, I'd love to take you to lunch."

Saturday. That was three days from now. Skylar wasn't sure she could wait that long. But she forced herself to smile sedately. "Sounds good."

The blank look had fallen off his face, and he looked relaxed and happy once more. She liked that.

Before she could ask for his number or give him hers, he picked up her hand from his arm, kissed the back, then stood. "Drive safe," he said, then shut her door.

Skylar stared at him in bemusement as he strode confidently toward his tow truck. She wasn't sure how they were going to make arrangements for their date. She didn't know where they were going, what time they were meeting, or anything.

But even though she hadn't known Carson that long, she had a feeling he'd take care of it. He knew where she worked, he was about to find out exactly where she lived, and he knew the man who had her car. It wasn't as if Carson couldn't find her.

She supposed she should be a little more concerned about how much the man knew about her and how much she *didn't* know about him, but he exuded a certain vibe that made her feel safe regardless.

Deciding to let things happen as they would and that she'd worry on Saturday morning if she hadn't heard from him, Skylar pulled out of her parking spot and waited until the huge tow truck was behind her before pulling out and heading toward home.

And Stan had been right. She'd never driven a car that ran as well as the loaner.

Smiling to herself, she decided for a night that hadn't started out very well, she was pretty darn content with how things had ended.

Chapter Four

Bull sat in the safe room underneath Silverstone Towing with his three friends. It was Friday, two days after they'd returned from Peru, and time to get back to work. Every morning, they met to scour the news from around the world and to review the FBI and Homeland Security reports Gregory Willis sent securely via computer files.

Five years ago, when they'd all sat down to discuss remodeling the garage, all four of them had decided they'd feel more comfortable having a space they could be one hundred percent certain was secure. It had been one of the best decisions they'd made. The employees knew about the room, since it was part of the basement, but not what went on inside.

There was a circular table to the left after entering, where Silverstone had most of their meetings. It was big enough to spread out maps and to share the briefings Willis sent over. There were no windows in the room, but on the right side was a sink, a microwave, and a small refrigerator. The cabinets above the small kitchen were filled with MREs and other food goods that wouldn't go bad.

A closet on the back wall contained blankets and cots in case they had to spend the night in the room or if one of their meetings went long and they didn't want to go home and the rooms upstairs were occupied. There was also a small bathroom behind another door.

There were several computers in the room, their screens all turned away from the door, just in case someone unauthorized entered. They didn't want to risk anyone seeing what they were researching.

All in all, the room was pretty utilitarian. The comforts of the rooms upstairs and just outside the door in the finished basement were nowhere to be seen in here. This was an office where extremely serious shit went down.

As Bull got as comfortable as he could at the table, he looked over the newest files they'd received.

There were a few men and one woman Silverstone was keeping an eye on. The man currently on top of their list of people they wanted to take down was Abubakar Shekau. He was the leader of Boko Haram, a jihadist terrorist organization in northeastern Nigeria. They also had ties to Al-Qaeda. The group became more well known after they kidnapped over two hundred schoolgirls in Nigeria because they believed girls shouldn't be educated and instead should be wives or slaves.

All of that was unacceptable, but what pushed the man onto Silverstone's radar was news that he was planning another raid. This time on a primary school, with the intent to enslave and marry off girls as young as seven. The entire situation made Bull's stomach turn, and he knew his friends felt the same way.

"So . . . ," Eagle began. "Bart told me that you went out on a job when we returned from Peru and were gone an extraordinarily long time . . . then when you got back, you told him you were done for the night and disappeared. Want to tell us what's up?"

Bull knew his friend was fucking with him. He loved Eagle and the rest as if they were brothers, and they'd discussed women they'd dated in the past, but somehow this seemed different. Skylar wasn't like any other woman he'd been interested in, and it made him uncomfortable to admit it. So he shrugged and said, "I just needed to decompress. I towed a lady to Stan's garage, made sure she got home all right, and everything caught up to me. I went home and crashed."

The explanation left out a lot, but Bull wasn't sure he was ready to talk about Skylar to his friends yet.

But of course they weren't going to let the topic go.

"You made sure she got home all right?" Smoke asked with a raised eyebrow. "That's not like you. In fact, I remember us telling our employees that there wasn't time to do that sort of thing when they're on the job."

"Yeah, well, as part owner, I'm not tied to the same rules as our drivers, am I?" Bull said a little more defensively than the situation warranted.

"It's fine," Gramps said. "You can do whatever the hell you want, and you know it. I'm sure you had a good reason to want to make certain she got home safely." The last was said with a questioning tilt of Gramps's head.

Bull sighed. He still wasn't sure he was ready to put into words how Skylar made him feel, but these were his friends. His family. If he couldn't talk to them, who *could* he talk to?

"She lives at Southpoint," he said.

All three men around the table nodded, as if that explained everything. But Bull knew it was only the tip of the iceberg where his feelings were concerned. "She claims that she feels safe there, that her neighbors watch out for each other, but we all know the reputation of that apartment complex."

Eagle nodded. "Police blotter said there were shots fired there last night. The cops investigated but didn't find anything."

His friend's words made Bull's stomach clench, but he went on with his explanation. "Skylar teaches kindergarten at Eastlake Elementary School. Her engine started making weird noises Wednesday night when she was on the way home from parent-teacher meetings. It was pitch dark, and she was stranded on the side of the road. I know that's nothing new for us, we see people in the same situation every day. But something about her made me want to make sure she got home all right."

"She petite?" Smoke asked, knowing Bull had a soft spot for small women.

"Yeah. About five-three or four. But that's not what really hooked me." Knowing admitting his interest in Skylar was opening himself up for a lot of shit from his friends, Bull went on quickly. "It was the aura of innocence that surrounded her like a shroud. There she was, standing by her disabled car on the side of the road, a copse of trees right behind us, cars whizzing by at eighty miles an hour, and she acted as if we were meeting at a fucking tea party. She would've gotten into my truck without calling to verify I was from the towing company she'd hired. After del Rio, and knowing what he did and how easily he seemed to get his hands on women—including here in the States—it bothered me. A lot."

"And?" Gramps asked.

"And what?" Bull retorted.

"Don't get me wrong. Del Rio was a piece of shit who deserved everything that happened to him. But most of the people we roll up on are just as clueless as this woman. They don't think to call and verify who we are. What made her so different?"

Bull didn't take offense, as he could tell Gramps was honestly trying to understand. The problem was, Bull didn't know if he could put into words what it was about Skylar that had struck him so hard. "I can't explain it," he said somewhat lamely. "When you meet her, you'll understand. There's just something about her that makes me want to protect her from the mean ol' world. She's . . . special. She's a damn kindergarten teacher, for God's sake."

"Which doesn't mean jack," Eagle pointed out. "I dated a preschool teacher once, and she was the kinkiest woman I've ever been with. Insatiable in bed. I actually found myself making up excuses for why I couldn't see her, because she exhausted me. Teaching kids doesn't automatically equate to innocence, Bull."

"I know," Bull agreed. And he did. Intellectually, he knew that what someone did for a living didn't mean they were good or bad, innocent or jaded. "But Skylar's different. She *is* innocent. And it's part of her charm. She didn't ogle me like a lot of women do when they get into the cab of the tow truck. In fact, she went out of her way to *not* catch my eye. And you should've heard her talking about the kids in her class. She loves each and every one of them for who they are, not because of the color of their skin or how smart they are. She wants to help their parents, simply because it's the right thing to do. She lives in a shithole apartment complex, but she made sure I knew she'd personally met each of the people who live around her and that they've formed their own little community. How many of you know *your* neighbors?"

All three of his friends shrugged. Bull had no clue who lived in the apartments around his. When he went home, he didn't want to socialize with strangers. As long as they were quiet and didn't burn the place down, he didn't give a shit who they were.

"You ask her out?" Smoke asked.

Bull nodded. "Lunch tomorrow."

"You sound serious about her," Gramps noted. "You thought about the long-term ramifications of being with her? That what you do might be too much for her delicate sensibilities?"

Bull wanted to be pissed that Gramps had brought it up, but he couldn't deny he'd thought about it a lot in the days since he'd driven away from Skylar's apartment complex. None of them had dated anyone seriously since they'd gotten out of the Army and started Silverstone Towing . . . or their secondary job. And frankly, it was ridiculous to even be thinking about how to break the news to Skylar that he and his friends did shady mercenary work for the government.

But he hadn't stopped thinking about her in two days. He'd never, not once, been so enamored of a woman that he thought about her day and night. Wondered what she was doing and if she was having a good day.

Love hadn't worked out for his dad, but that didn't mean he hadn't wanted it. Hadn't taught his son the right way to treat a woman.

"There's a possibility she won't be able to deal," Bull admitted.

"And you're going to take the risk anyway, aren't you?" Smoke asked.

Bull nodded. "Yeah. Something tells me she's worth making the effort to get to know her. She might reject me when she learns about what I do, but I have to take that chance."

"You're going to bring her by so we can meet her, right?" Eagle asked.

"Yes. Though . . . she was extremely skeptical when Stan showed her the loaner car she was going to use. I could read her face easily. She couldn't believe she was going to have to drive such a piece of shit."

The others all chuckled. "Stan loves doing that," Gramps said. "Making a car that looks like it's on its last legs run better than a brand-new one off the lot."

"Yup. She started it up and was floored. It was hilarious. So I can't wait to show her Silverstone," Bull said with a quirk of his lips.

"Because it looks like a building on the verge of collapse from the outside, but inside it's quite palatial?" Eagle asked with a smile.

"Palatial?" Smoke echoed. "What are you, a fucking thesaurus now?"

"Fuck off," Eagle told his friend.

"Oh, there's something else I wanted to run by you guys," Bull said before the two men got too enthusiastic about jerking each other's chains. "Skylar mentioned that one of the kids in her class is being raised by a single father . . . and he's struggling. Has three jobs and not a lot of time to spend with his daughter."

"What's he do?" Gramps asked.

"Short-order cook in the mornings, works for a landscaper in the afternoons, and he's a janitor at night."

Smoke, Eagle, and Gramps all looked at each other, and Bull saw the second they came to the same conclusion he had.

"Seems to me a man like that would be pretty handy around here," Smoke said.

"Yeah, no one can really cook worth a shit, and I'm sick of walking in and smelling burnt-ass food," Eagle agreed.

"And while everyone does their best to clean up, sometimes this place smells like a fucking middle-school boys' locker room," Gramps chimed in.

"I'm okay with the bushes and shit being a bit overgrown, but the other day, I dropped my keys and just about lost them in the weeds," Bull threw in.

"When do you think he can start?" Smoke asked.

Bull smiled. He loved these men. On the outside, they were hard-asses. They'd all killed without a moment of remorse, but they never hesitated to do the right thing for someone in need. Smoke had bank-rolled the business for the first couple of years, but now Silverstone Towing was making good money. Very good money. And what they spent that income on—401(k) investments for their employees, insurance deductibles, and higher-than-average wages—was worth every penny. The men and women employed by Silverstone were loyal and hardworking. It was a win-win combination.

"I don't know. I'll need to talk to Skylar and see what I can find out about her student's father. We'll also need to do a background check and of course interview him . . . and that's if he's even interested," Bull said.

"He'll be interested," Eagle said.

Bull knew he was right. The job would mean he'd be able to spend more time with his daughter, save for retirement, and make just as much money, or more, as he was making now with three separate jobs. He'd be crazy to turn down the opportunity to work for Silverstone.

"I'm happy for you," Gramps said quietly.

Bull snorted. "Don't be. We haven't even had one date yet."

"Yeah, but I know you. And if you're this interested after meeting her once, she *is* something special. And take it from me, you'll regret it if you let her get away without at least making an effort to see what the two of you might have together."

Bull eyed his friend. He and his Silverstone team were *very* close . . . but he couldn't remember Gramps ever talking about a relationship in his past that hadn't worked out. And when Gramps looked away quickly, Bull knew now wasn't the time to press for more details. "I'll see if I can't come up with an excuse to come by here Saturday after lunch."

"We'll be here," Eagle assured him.

"Now . . . can we talk more about Abubakar Shekau and his plan to abduct more girls?" Smoke asked.

Everyone nodded and turned back to the intelligence Willis had sent them.

But Bull gave himself one more moment to think about Skylar . . . and about the surprise he had for her later that afternoon.

Skylar stood behind Sandra and pushed her as she swung on the swing set in the school's back playground. The area was smaller than the main play area and was mostly used by the lower grades. It was five forty-five, and the little girl's dad was late picking her up . . . again. But since she truly didn't mind playing with Sandra, Skylar couldn't make herself get upset.

As she absently pushed Sandra higher and higher, Skylar's mind drifted to Carson, as it often did lately. When she'd arrived home Wednesday night, she'd unlocked her door and turned to wave at him. He'd lifted two fingers from the steering wheel of the big tow truck and driven off.

And she hadn't been able to stop thinking of him since. She hadn't been this excited about a date in a long time.

Okay, part of that was because it had been ages since she'd even been *asked* on a date. But for the first time in forever, she really wanted things to work out. She didn't want to say anything dorky on their date or give him a reason not to ask her out again. Skylar knew she could ask *him* out, but she was old fashioned in a lot of ways, and more than that, she never wanted to push herself on someone if they weren't interested.

"Ms. Reid, stop pushing!" Sandra yelled, bringing Skylar out of her musings. "I want to play over there!"

Skylar caught the chains of the swing and stopped it, laughing as Sandra hopped out of the seat and ran full tilt over to the edge of the small yard to hang from the monkey bars. Knowing the little girl would find something else to entertain herself with in a minute or two, Skylar didn't follow. She watched from afar as one of the last cars pulled out of the faculty-and-staff parking lot behind the play area. Almost everyone had left for the weekend, but Skylar was used to being one of the last to leave the building.

She supposed she should be impatient to get home herself, but she literally had nothing to look forward to in her little apartment. No one waiting for her. No big plans for a Friday night. She'd hoped to hear from Carson before their date, but so far she hadn't received one email, text, Facebook message, or phone call. Of course, they hadn't exactly exchanged information . . .

Sighing, she watched as Sandra fell to her knees, then, a millisecond later, stood and aimed a thumbs-up in her teacher's direction. Skylar returned the gesture with a smile.

Out of the corner of her eye, she thought she saw someone standing at the back of the teacher's parking lot.

Sandra chose that moment to yell something. By the time Skylar had turned to look at her student, then back at the parking lot, the person was gone.

Shrugging and assuming she'd either been mistaken or was simply seeing things, Skylar motioned for Sandra to head back toward the doors to the building. According to the note she'd gotten from the principal's secretary, Sandra's dad would be arriving in about twenty minutes. She needed to get Sandra ready to go, including putting a bunch of books in her backpack to help keep her entertained over the weekend. Shawn was probably going to be working, and as much as Skylar wanted to protest that Sandra was too young to be left alone, she knew the man didn't have money for a babysitter.

She didn't like a lot of things that happened with her students, but that didn't mean she could change them.

Sandra ran up to her and threw her little arms around Skylar's waist. She looked up at her teacher and said, "I'm gonna miss you this weekend. I wish I could go to school every day!"

Skylar simply smiled. A seven-day workweek sounded like hell to her, but she understood why Sandra wished for it. She had to be lonely locked up in their apartment while her dad was working. Lonely and probably worried too.

"I know, I'll miss you too," Skylar told her as she walked them both toward the school doors. She kept one arm around the little girl's shoulders as she said, "I've got some special books for you to take home. But you need to take very good care of them. Can you do that for me?"

Sandra nodded solemnly.

The little girl was exceedingly smart. And, except when she was running around the playground, she typically acted much older than her five years. She'd had a lot of responsibility put on her young shoulders because of their financial situation.

"And you know what else?"

"What?" Sandra asked.

"I've got a date tomorrow."

Sandra stopped and looked up at her teacher in awe. "With a *boy*?"

Skylar chuckled. "Yeah. His name is Carson, but his friends call him Bull."

Sandra wrinkled her nose. "That's a weird name."

"I know. I don't know what it means."

"Does he have a ring in his nose like Ferdinand?"

Skylar smiled again. She'd just read *The Story of Ferdinand* to her class, and Sandra was obviously thinking about the ring in the bull's nose. "No," she told her.

"Does he have horns?"

This time, Skylar laughed out loud. "No. How about this . . . I'll ask him why his friends call him that, and I'll let you know on Monday."

Sandra beamed. "Okay!"

In the past, Skylar had said things like that to her students, thinking they'd forget all about it over the weekend, but to her surprise, come Monday morning, the children always remembered. Always asked about whatever it was she'd promised to tell them as soon as they saw her. She knew Sandra would be no different. She'd just committed herself to asking Carson about his nickname . . . and if for some reason he called off their date, she'd have to make up something to appease the girl.

She went inside with Sandra and helped her pack her little secondhand backpack with as many books as would fit. Skylar also slipped in some of the snacks she had in her classroom for children who hadn't had any breakfast or who couldn't make it through the day without something to eat. She wanted to do more. Wanted to offer to babysit for free but knew she needed the two-day break the weekend would give her. Sandra would be all right. She was a smart little girl who never disobeyed her dad.

At quarter to six, Skylar walked Sandra out of the classroom toward the front office at the school. Her dad always met them there after checking out his daughter with the secretary. This time, however, when she approached the office, she saw another man was standing in the office with Mr. Archer.

The second the other guy turned around, Skylar gasped in surprise. It was Carson.

She had no idea what he was doing there, but as she watched, he shook Mr. Archer's hand. Shawn was grinning from ear to ear, and when he saw Sandra, the smile only grew.

"How's my girl doin'?" he asked as he opened his arms.

Sandra ran straight to her dad and leapt into his arms and squealed in happiness when he stood and twirled in a circle. Sandra might have gotten a lot of her physical characteristics from her mother, but there was no doubt she and her father had a special bond.

Skylar followed a little more sedately and smiled at Mr. Archer.

"Sorry I'm late again today," the man said.

"It's okay. We played outside for a bit. Sandra's all set with extra books and things," she told him.

"I 'preciate all you do, Ms. Reid," Shawn said.

"It's my pleasure," she told him, doing her best not to fidget under Carson's gaze, which she could literally feel on her.

"I'm hoping my luck'll change soon, and then I won't be such a pain," Shawn told her cryptically as he glanced over at Carson, then down at Sandra.

"You aren't a pain," Skylar told him honestly. Yes, staying late to watch over kids wasn't in her contract, but it wasn't exactly a hardship. She genuinely liked Sandra.

"Ready to go home, pumpkin?" Shawn asked his daughter.

Sandra nodded enthusiastically. "I felled down and scraped my knees," she told her dad.

"You did? I guess you're gonna want a Band-Aid, huh?"

Sandra shook her head. "Ms. Reid already gave me one. It even has Elsa on it!"

"Cool," her dad said, looking back at Skylar as they walked out and mouthing, "Thank you."

Skylar waved at them and finally turned to look at Carson. "Hi," she said somewhat uncertainly.

"Hi," he responded, his deep voice doing weird things to her insides.

"Do you know Mr. Archer?" she asked, remembering how the two men were shaking hands when she'd approached.

"Just met him," Carson said easily.

Skylar mentally shrugged. "What are you doing here?" she asked when he didn't say anything else.

He looked at the secretary, who was watching the two of them from across the room with both impatience and a little too much interest. "You about ready to go home?" he asked instead of answering her question.

"Yeah. I just need to go back to my room and grab my stuff." She hesitated, then asked, "You want to come see where I spend most of my days?"

"Thought you'd never ask," he said, his lips twitching.

It wasn't a full-fledged smile, but Skylar would take it.

"Sandra was the last student to be picked up," the secretary said. "I'm gonna head out . . . if that's all right."

"Sorry you had to wait," Skylar told her. "I'll see you Monday."

"Bye!"

Carson watched the other woman reach for her coat as they left the office. He turned to her. "You're often the last one out, aren't you?" he asked.

Skylar shrugged as they walked down the hall toward her room. "Yeah. Most of the other teachers are married and have kids, so they want to get out of here as soon as possible. Get home to their families."

"It's not safe to walk to your car when it's dark."

Skylar nodded. "I know, but I don't have a choice."

"No security?"

"For an elementary school? No. The middle and high schools have resource officers, but they aren't usually assigned to primary schools. But the back lot is well lit, and I try not to park in the last spaces by the trees, where it's darker." She looked at him as they walked. "I know

I'm short, and a woman, but the world isn't as scary as you seem to think it is."

"Wrong," he said in as serious a tone as she'd ever heard from him. "It's scarier. But I can't help but love that you don't know anything about that side of life. I'd like to keep it that way. You have a flashlight? Mace? Your cell out and 911 already punched in as you go to your car?"

"Uh . . . I keep my keys in my hand with one of them poking through my fingers," she told him.

Carson shook his head. "Not good enough. If you have to punch someone, you'll hurt yourself more than them if you hold your key like that. You're better off carrying Mace."

"I don't feel comfortable having that stuff in my purse. I keep imagining it going off accidentally and me having to evacuate my classroom so my kids don't get sick."

"They have safety switches on them," Carson told her.

"Right, safety switches that are probably childproof and would do me no good if I had to figure out how to work it if someone ran at me in a parking lot. I'd drop the stupid thing and be attacked anyway," she retorted. Skylar didn't know why she was fighting this so hard. She just couldn't imagine herself ever carrying around Mace. "I can't even open those stupid aspirin bottles that are childproof. And don't get me started on the pod detergent lids. Once I get the thing off the first time, it stays off."

She saw his lips twitch again and loved that she'd gotten another almost smile.

"Right. What about wasp spray?"

Skylar blinked up at him in surprise as they reached her room. "What?"

"Wasp spray. You can get it anywhere, and I'm assuming you don't think it's as scary as Mace."

She frowned. "It's not scary. It's the wasps that are scary."

"Wrong," he said again. "I mean, not about wasps, hate those little shits. But wasp spray is just as effective as Mace, maybe more so. It's made to be accurate at great distances, so you can nail an attacker in the face, or at least in the chest, from quite a ways off. It's caustic and will sting like hell. It would give you a chance to make noise, use your phone to call for help, or simply run. And now that I'm thinking about it, you should keep that stuff in your room in case of an active-shooter situation."

Skylar couldn't help but shake her head. "You want me to carry wasp spray from here to my car in the parking lot?"

This time, he didn't even crack a smile. "No. I want you to be safe. To do what you need to do to protect yourself. I'm guessing you spend all your time worrying about your kids and their families and not enough about yourself."

"I'm okay, Carson," Skylar said softly, realizing for the first time he was one hundred percent serious about all of this. He wasn't kidding around even a little. Wasn't making suggestions offhand.

"I just want you to stay that way," he told her.

"I'd be stupid not to think about my kids' safety. I'd like to say that no one would ever come to Eastlake and start shooting up the place, but unfortunately, I can't. And I have to admit that I'm way more comfortable with having a bottle of wasp spray in the classroom than anything else."

"Good," he said with a nod. "We'll figure something out about your walk to your car in the dark. We'll find something you're comfortable with that's still effective if someone tries to jump you."

Skylar didn't want to think about someone jumping her, so she changed the subject. "I wasn't sure if you were serious about tomorrow. I haven't heard from you," she blurted.

"Oh, I'm serious," he told her, *looking* serious. "I didn't want to freak you out by blowing up your phone with 'I can't wait to see you' and 'I'm looking forward to Saturday' texts."

"But you don't have my number," she said stupidly as they reached her classroom.

Carson grinned, and it lit up his face. Skylar knew she'd do whatever she could to put that smile on his face in the future.

He pulled his cell from his back pocket and fiddled with it for a long moment, his fingers flying over the keys.

From across the room, inside her purse, Skylar's phone dinged with the special tone she'd assigned for text messages.

"I have your number," Carson told her.

Skylar couldn't take her eyes off his. "Oh. Right." Of course. She'd confirmed her number with the Silverstone dispatcher when she'd called for a tow.

"Fuck, you're cute," Carson said, brushing a lock of hair that had come loose behind her ear. "How old are you?"

"You mean you didn't research that info already?" Skylar asked cheekily.

His grin widened. "Nope. Wanted to find out about you from *you*."

"I'm thirty-two," she told him immediately, liking that he seemed sincere. That he wanted to *talk* to her to know more about her. "And before you say anything, I know I look younger. I think it's because I don't wear a lot of makeup and I'm short. How old are you?"

"You're perfect the way you are," he reassured her. "And I'm thirty-six. Six feet tall and have been part owner of Silverstone Towing for five years."

"You were in the Army before that, right?" Skylar knew she should be getting her stuff so they could leave, but she literally couldn't keep herself from asking questions. She wanted to know as much about the man standing in front of her as possible. Besides, when they left, she'd have to go back to her boring apartment. Talking with Carson was much more interesting and exciting.

"Yeah. My friends and I served together."

Skylar nodded. "Are they as big as you?"

This time, she got a chuckle. "I'm the short one."

"Oh Lord," Skylar said under her breath.

Carson looked around her classroom, and she held her breath. It was crazy to want him to be impressed with her room. But she'd put a lot of work into it. Making it seem comfortable and inviting to her students, and yet still giving them an atmosphere where they could get some quality learning in.

"There's a lot of trucks," he observed.

Skylar grinned. "Yeah, my class this year loves trucks of all kinds. They're kind of obsessed. I read them *Little Blue Truck* at the beginning of the year, and now that's all they want to read about. Fire trucks, dump trucks, eighteen-wheelers, even big ol' pickup trucks . . . they love them all."

"Would they . . . or you . . . be interested in Silverstone bringing some of our tow trucks over here so they could check them out firsthand?" Carson asked. "I don't know how that kind of thing works, what kinds of permissions we'd need. But we could park them in the lot out back, and they could sit inside the cabs, and we could even hook up someone's car to show them that too . . . if you think they'd enjoy it."

Skylar stared at Carson with big eyes. "Seriously?"

"Well, yeah," he said with a shrug. "I wouldn't have offered if I wasn't serious."

"They would *love* that!" Skylar exclaimed happily. "I could teach a whole lesson on car safety and why seat belts are important . . . you know, in case there's an accident. And I could explain that tow trucks are necessary to come and get the crashed cars. Maybe I could talk to the fire station guys around the block and even the police. Oh, I bet the other grades would be interested too! You could talk to the older kids about careers and stuff."

Skylar realized she'd been babbling on and became embarrassed, but when she looked up at Carson, he didn't seem irritated in the least.

"I'll talk to Eagle, Smoke, and Gramps. I'm sure they'd be happy to come too."

"Are those your friends?" Skylar asked.

"Yeah. And co-owners of Silverstone. I'll introduce you to them soon."

"I'd like that," she said honestly.

"Come on," he said, putting a hand under her elbow. "Let's get your stuff so we can get you home."

She noticed his use of the plural pronoun but didn't call him on it. She walked over to her desk and grabbed her purse. Her room was a mess, and she usually straightened it before leaving, just so she didn't have to do it when she came to work the next time, but she'd just have to deal with it on Monday. Right now, she wanted to hang out with Carson.

He'd waited by the door as she'd gone to get her bag, and she couldn't help but notice he'd kept his eyes on her the whole time. If her hips swayed a bit more than usual as she walked back toward him, she'd never admit it.

He didn't touch her as she came up beside him, but he did stay close as they walked back down the hall toward the door that led to the teachers' parking lot in the back of the building. Skylar could feel the heat coming off his body as he walked beside her.

Carson pushed open the door and held it for her, and she ducked under his upraised arm to get past him. The second she raised her head to glance toward the parking lot, she let out a surprised gasp.

"My car!" she exclaimed. Turning to look up at Carson, she said, "How'd my car get here? Stan said it wouldn't be ready until next week!"

"He lied," Carson told her. "I talked to him yesterday, and there wasn't much to do. So he got it done, and I asked Eagle to help me get it here. I'll get the loaner back to Stan if you give me the keys."

"But . . . I haven't paid for it," Skylar told him anxiously. "What was wrong with it? Will it be okay now? Do I need to worry about it breaking down again?"

"Do you think I'd bring your car back if it wasn't one hundred percent safe for you to drive?" Carson asked in an almost disappointed tone.

Skylar looked up at him. "Well . . . I don't really know you. And you don't know me. Why would you care?"

"I care," he answered immediately. "Hell if I understand why, when I haven't known you that long, but I do. And it doesn't matter what was wrong with it. It's fixed now."

Skylar narrowed her eyes. "You didn't do one of those over-the-top alpha things like tell Stan to overhaul the entire engine and then decide to tell me it was just a bit of spilled oil or something that caused the weird noise, did you?"

"You need a reliable car," he told her, not answering her question. Not one muscle in his face twitched, but Skylar somehow knew that was exactly what he'd done.

She sighed. She could choose to be pissed and stomp her foot and demand to know what was done and how much it cost, but she had a feeling Carson wouldn't tell her.

She couldn't exactly afford a huge bill. Her dad would most certainly help pay for whatever had been done, but she hated leaning on him. She was an adult, and her parents had done more than enough for her in her lifetime. "I'll call Stan tomorrow and pay him," she said instead.

Surprisingly, Carson merely nodded.

She raised an eyebrow. "You mean you haven't already paid for it?"

This time his lips twitched, and Skylar knew she was in trouble. One smile from him, and she'd forgive him anything.

"Nope. I knew you'd be pissed if I did."

"I appreciate you bringing it to me," she told him.

"Figured if I got it to you tonight, we wouldn't have to waste our time tomorrow dealing with it."

"Speaking of which . . . where are we going? What time? What should I wear? Should I meet you somewhere? Do I need to bring anything?"

Carson chuckled. "You've been worrying about this, haven't you?"

"No," Skylar said immediately, then wrinkled her nose. "Maybe. I'm a planner. It's what I do."

"I'd like to surprise you with where we're going, if that's all right. I thought I could pick you up around eleven thirty, if that works. As far as what to wear, be comfortable. And all you need to bring is yourself," he said.

"Are jeans okay?" she asked. "Since I don't get to wear them at work, I tend to like to dress down on the weekends. But I can wear a dress or a skirt if I need to."

She loved the way Carson was looking at her. As if he couldn't believe she was actually standing in front of him. As if she was the most important thing in the world at that moment. He wasn't looking around, although she had a feeling he was more than aware of every car that drove by and every piece of trash that was blowing around the parking lot.

"Jeans are perfect," he reassured her.

"Okay. Eleven thirty. I can do that," she said a bit nervously. Hell, if he'd said he was coming over at six in the morning, she would've agreed.

"Come on," he said, putting his hand on the small of her back, encouraging her to head toward her car.

His hand seemed to burn through her blouse, but in a good way. Walking next to him, Skylar felt safe. She didn't have to look around, didn't have to wonder if someone was hiding behind her car or had somehow broken in and was waiting in the back seat. She knew he thought of her as naive, and she was in a lot of ways, but she went overboard when getting in her car after shopping or working.

He opened the driver's side door of her now-spotless Corolla, and she got inside with a smile. Gasping, she realized that it had been detailed *inside* as well as out. It smelled fresh and clean, and she could hardly believe it was her old battered Toyota.

"Wow, it looks amazing," she said.

"Start 'er up," Carson ordered.

So she stuck the key in the ignition and grinned at how easily and quietly the engine turned over. "Wow." Skylar turned to Carson. "*Did* Stan overhaul the entire engine?"

He chuckled. "Not that I know of. He just cleaned some things up and replaced spark plugs and whatnot."

Skylar knew that wasn't all that was done to her old car, but she was more than grateful. "Thank you," she breathed.

"I didn't do it," Carson deflected.

"But you brought me to Stan. And I'm sure that you had at least one conversation with him about my car, and that's why it's running as smoothly as it is right now. And you brought it to me so I didn't have to deal with retrieving it. *And* you're going to return the loaner. So . . . thank you."

"You're welcome," Carson told her. "Is it okay if I follow you home to make certain everything's all right with your car?"

Skylar had no doubt he'd already made sure her car was fine, but she also had no problem with him following her . . . again. "Yes," she told him.

"Great. Drive safe. I'll see you tomorrow at eleven thirty," he said before closing her door and heading for his red Altima parked two spots over.

Fifteen minutes later, Skylar was once again waving to Carson from just inside her apartment door. He lifted two fingers, as he'd done the last time, and pulled out of the lot. When Skylar closed the door, she remembered the text that Carson had sent her when they were inside her classroom. She'd forgotten about it until now.

Standing just inside her closed and locked door, she pulled out her cell.

I can't wait to see you. I'm looking forward to Saturday.

She smiled. He'd told her he hadn't wanted to freak her out by sending a bunch of texts that said that exact thing. She typed in a short reply and saved his contact information.

Skylar: Me too.

Not caring that it was Friday night and she was once more spending it alone in her apartment, Skylar put her phone back in her purse and went to change into her pajamas. She was going on a date tomorrow. With a man who just seemed to get better and better the more she got to know him.

Skylar knew no one was perfect. *She* certainly wasn't. But for the first time in a long time, she had high hopes that maybe, just maybe, things might work out with Carson.

Chapter Five

Bull pulled into Skylar's apartment complex at eleven fifteen. He was early, but he'd done everything he could think of to procrastinate so as not to arrive hours before their agreed-upon meeting time. When he'd woken up that morning, his very first thought was that he'd get to spend a few hours with Skylar.

He'd gotten her text the night before, and even though it was only two words long, seeing her response on his phone had made him feel really good. It was ridiculous. She could turn out to be a psycho, but he didn't think so.

After meeting Shawn Archer the day before and hearing him talk about how amazing Ms. Reid was and that he wouldn't be able to work the jobs he did without her helping out with Sandra in the afternoons after school, Bull knew his feeling about her was spot on.

He hadn't had time to talk to Archer in depth about his situation, but he'd briefly mentioned that Silverstone might be looking to hire someone to be a jack-of-all-trades. The other man's eyes had lit up, and he'd said he would definitely be interested. Bull had gotten his phone number and said he'd be in touch. They had some research to do on the man, to make sure he had a clean record, but from what Skylar had told Bull and given how hard the man was working to give his daughter a safe roof over her head and food to eat, Bull had a feeling he'd be perfect for Silverstone.

But at the moment, thoughts of hiring Archer were a distant second. All Bull could think about was Skylar. He was nervous for this date. Him, *nervous*. It was insane. He was a former Delta Force operative who had fought in the gnarliest fights and been all over the world, face to face with some full-on evil types.

How he could be nervous to spend a few hours with a woman, Bull had no idea. But that didn't change the situation. He'd second-guessed himself over and over about their plans for today. He didn't want it to look like he was trying too hard, but then again, he didn't want her to think he wasn't trying at all to impress her.

Internally rolling his eyes at how ridiculous he was being, Bull shut off his car and took a deep breath. He was early. He could sit in the parking lot for ten minutes before going upstairs to knock on Skylar's door, but that seemed silly. He was there, and he didn't want to wait another second to see her again.

Climbing out of his Altima, Bull took a deep breath and walked up the outer stairs to the second floor. Southpoint Apartments had all exterior doors. It almost looked like a motel, with all the doors facing toward the parking lot.

As he walked by one of the doors on the way to Skylar's apartment, it opened, and a middle-aged Hispanic woman stuck her head out.

"You must be Carson," she said with a smile. She was missing one of her front teeth, but it didn't diminish the friendly vibe she exuded.

"That's me," he told her with a polite nod.

Then the door on the other side of Skylar's apartment opened, and an African American woman stepped out onto the walkway. She was easily six feet tall and very slender. "You Carson?" she asked, a little less friendly than the first woman.

Bull wasn't sure why or how these women seemed to know who he was, but since they were Skylar's neighbors, he wasn't about to do or say anything rude. He remembered how Skylar had said the people who lived in her building stuck together. "Yup," he answered the second woman.

She crossed her arms across her rather large bosom and pinned him with a glare when he stopped in front of Skylar's door.

"Sky's a good woman," she said, telling Bull something he was already aware of. "A little clueless sometimes about shit that's goin' on around her, but good. You treat her just as good, or you'll have to answer to *us*."

Before Bull could respond, Skylar's door opened, and she stepped outside. "Tiana, leave Carson alone. The last thing I need is you scaring him away before we even have our first date." Then she turned to the woman on the other side. "Maria, did you behave yourself?"

She held up her hands. "Hey, all I did was ask if he was your date. It's probably a good thing Susan isn't home," Maria said, gesturing to the door next to her own. "She's even more protective than we are. Besides, Tiana's the one with the bad temper."

"You know your temper is just as bad," Tiana scoffed, and Bull was beginning to feel as if they were in the middle of two dogs circling a juicy bone. His head whipped back and forth between the two women as they teased each other.

"Maybe, maybe not, but at least I didn't jump down Sky's date's throat the second he showed up!"

"I'm just trying to make sure he treats her right. She ain't been out with anyone in forever, and the last thing she needs is some asshole trying to get down her pants on the first date."

"Kill me now," Skylar whispered, and Bull ignored the other two women to look at the one he couldn't stop thinking about. She had on a pair of jeans that hugged every curve of her legs. A pair of strappy sandals gave her an extra three inches of height. She wore a forest-green blouse with the shoulders cut out, and the sight of her creamy skin—complete with freckles—made him want to brush his lips against her shoulders to see if she was as soft as she looked.

And her auburn hair was down around her shoulders. It was the first time he'd seen it loose from the bun she'd worn the previous two times he'd been with her. The strands framed her lovely face . . . and Bull wanted to thrust his hand into the luscious locks and kiss the hell out of her.

He vaguely heard Tiana and Maria still arguing, but he only had eyes for Skylar. "You look beautiful," he told her.

She looked up and met his gaze. "Thanks. You look good too."

Bull had on a pair of jeans, his customary black work boots, and a navy-blue short-sleeve polo. For him, this was dressed up.

He was anxious to get this date started, but first he wanted to take away the discomfort in Skylar's eyes. He turned his head and interrupted Tiana mid-sentence. "I'm assuming you're close to Skylar and want the best for her," he said to both women.

They stared at him for a beat, then nodded.

"Right, so you have to know you're embarrassing her—and that's not cool. We're going to lunch, not for a midday tryst at a pay-by-the-hour motel. We're going to talk and get to know each other better. I'm hoping she'll enjoy our time so she'll say yes when I ask her out again. But if you make her feel self-conscious about going on a date with me in the first place, she might decide seeing me isn't worth the hassle. I'm sure she'll tell you all about me and our time together when she gets home."

"Damn straight she will," Tiana retorted.

"We just wanted to make sure you knew Sky's got people lookin' out for her," Maria added.

"That's obvious. And while I'm glad she's got you two at her back, us talking about Sky while she's right here is making her uncomfortable. I know she cares about the two of you and that you all look out for each other, which I appreciate. But you need to stop now so I don't say something that'll irritate Skylar and put us off on the wrong foot."

He was relieved when both Tiana and Maria grinned.

"He'll do," Tiana said. "Have fun, Sky. We'll talk when you get back."

"Don't do anything I wouldn't do," Maria chimed in.

They both waved and disappeared behind their respective doors.

"Wow, sorry," Skylar told him when they were alone once again.

Bull knew both women were probably peeking out at them through their curtains. "I'm not," he told her. "I'm glad you've got such good friends to watch over you."

She chuckled. "Is that what they were doing? I thought they were going to try to steal you for themselves."

Bull was glad she could shrug off the embarrassment she'd felt earlier. He didn't mind reassuring her that her friends didn't bother him, but if she'd continued to apologize for them or let their behavior put her in a bad mood, it wouldn't have boded well for their relationship.

And yes, he'd already thought of the two of them as having a relationship.

"You ready to go?" he asked.

Skylar nodded. "Yeah. Are you going to tell me where we're going?"

"Not yet," he said as she stepped out onto the landing and turned to lock her door.

Bull opened his mouth to remind her it wasn't smart to turn her back on a man she'd just met, that he could easily push her into her apartment and overpower her, but the words stuck in his throat. If he thought her jeans looked good from the front, that was nothing compared to how they looked from this angle. Her ass was full and perfect, and it took everything Bull had not to reach forward and put his hands on her.

She turned around, and he knew she'd caught him staring at her ass. But he didn't apologize, and other than a slight pinkening of her cheeks, she didn't call him on it.

He motioned for her to walk ahead of him, and he couldn't resist resting his hand on the small of her back as they headed for the stairs.

When they got to his car, he opened her door and waited until she was settled inside before shutting it and walking around to the driver's side.

When he was sitting, instead of immediately turning on the car, he turned to look at Skylar. "Sorry I was early," he said. "I couldn't wait anymore."

She smiled at him. "It's okay. I was ready about an hour and a half ago and was pacing my apartment waiting for you to show up."

Sighing in relief, Bull nodded. "For what it's worth, I like your friends."

Skylar shook her head. "They're a bit brash, but their hearts are in the right place."

"You're lucky to be close to your neighbors."

"I mean, we don't hang out or anything. It's more just talking when we see each other in passing and letting each other know when stuff has gone down in the complex."

"I don't even *know* my neighbors," Bull told her. "I think one is an older gentleman, and the other is a woman who works way too much, because I literally never see her."

"Carson?"

"Yeah?"

"Tiana was right about one thing . . . it's been a long time since I've been on a date. I spend most of my time with five-year-olds. If I do or say anything inappropriate, could you please overlook it and not think I'm a weirdo?"

Bull couldn't help but chuckle. "It's been a long time for me too. I figured I'd just go low key today. No over-the-top, trying-to-impress-you antics. There's a diner not too far from work that serves some of the best food I've ever eaten. I thought we could go there, then if you were interested, I'd give you a tour of Silverstone. But if you need to come straight home, that's okay too."

He watched as she visibly relaxed in the seat next to him. "That sounds great."

Wanting to do nothing but sit there and stare at her, Bull forced himself to start the engine and pull out of the parking spot. He was well aware that he and Skylar were probably being watched by her neighbors. It felt a little like when he was in high school and wanted to make out in the car with his date, but knew her dad or brothers were watching from inside the house.

They made small talk as he drove to the diner. He pulled into the parking lot and winced at the sight of the place. The roof needed repairing, and the sign above the door had seen better days. Things he didn't care about or notice on a regular basis. And he hadn't lied, Rosie's Diner had some of the best food around. He'd spent more than his fair share of time in the restaurant.

He parked and jogged around the car in time to take Skylar's elbow as she stood up. He shut her door and, after looking around to make sure there weren't any vagrants lingering in the parking lot, walked slightly behind her to the door. Pulling it open, Bull braced himself for the greeting he knew was coming.

"Bull!" a loud and boisterous voice called out after he'd entered behind Skylar. A tall slender woman came bustling out from behind the counter. She grabbed him by the arms and air-kissed both of his cheeks. "I haven't seen you in forever . . . it's been, what, a week or so?"

"Cheeky." Bull grinned. Then he gestured to Skylar. "Rosie, I want you to meet someone. This is Skylar. She's a kindergarten teacher over at Eastlake. Skylar, this is Rosie Spencer . . . she owns this place and manages it with an iron fist."

"Oh, you," Rosie said, smacking Bull on the arm. Then she turned to Skylar. Bull tensed slightly; like Skylar's neighbors, Rosie wasn't one to mince words. If she liked someone, she was quick to let everyone know. But if you rubbed her the wrong way, that was it. You weren't ever going to get a second chance, and she had no problem letting you know that you weren't on her list of favorite people.

But he needn't have worried.

"It's so good to meet you," Skylar started before Rosie could say anything. "Carson's told me wonderful things about this place. And I have no doubt he was one hundred percent honest, because if the smells are anything to go by, I'm going to want to bring a mattress and live here for the rest of my life."

Rosie chuckled, and Bull could see that with just a few sentences, Skylar had another fan. "Carson, huh?" Rosie asked. She gave Bull a side-eye before turning back to Skylar. "So you're a teacher?"

Skylar nodded. "Yeah, over at Eastlake."

"That's in a rough part of town," Rosie noted.

"Honestly, why does everyone say that?" Skylar complained good-naturedly. "I mean, yeah, the neighborhood has had its share of issues, but the kids aren't to blame. They're smart as all get-out and soak up every scrap of information they can get. If people could look past their skin color, how much money their parents have, or where they live, I don't think they'd see any difference between them and the kids where I grew up in Carmel."

Rosie nodded and looked back over at Bull. "I like her. Go on, Bull, pick a seat, and I'll send someone over as soon as possible. It's good to see you again."

"Thanks, Rosie," Bull told her and didn't hesitate to put his hand on the small of Skylar's back once more. He loved having any excuse to touch her. It was too early to hold her hand or put his arm around her shoulders or waist, so for now, he had to make do with guiding her to a booth on the side of the restaurant.

He waited until she'd settled on one side of the booth before scooting into the other side. He leaned his elbows on the table and couldn't help but run his gaze over her.

"I guess you know Rosie pretty well," she said.

"I've been coming here for the last five years, ever since we started Silverstone. As you could see from the outside, it doesn't look like anything special. But I was driving by and smelled the most amazing smell and just had to turn around and come in to check it out. I was hooked by that first meal."

"He's like a stray we can't get rid of," a woman said from next to their booth.

Bull looked up and smiled. He stood and gave her a hug before sitting back down. "Skylar, this is Julie. She's one of several waitresses who work here."

"Hi," Skylar said. "It's good to meet you."

"Back atcha," Julie said. "Do you know what you want yet?"

"Oh!" Skylar said in surprise. "I hadn't had a chance to look at the menu."

"You should let Bull order for you. He's literally eaten every dish on the menu. He won't steer you wrong."

"Julie, this is our first date," Bull told her. "I'm sure Skylar would prefer to choose her own meal. I don't even know what she likes and what she doesn't yet."

"You allergic to anything?" Julie asked Skylar.

"No."

"Vegetarian?"

"No."

"Need gluten-free, low carbohydrate, on a diet?"

"No, no, and no," Skylar said with a smile.

"You're good," Julie told Bull.

Knowing that the older woman wasn't going to budge from the side of their table until they'd ordered, Bull gave in. "I'd like a water, and I'll have the number four. I think a number ten for the lady."

"Good choice," Julie said. "And to drink?" she asked, looking at Skylar.

"Iced tea, please."

"Coming right up," Julie told them. She wasn't carrying a pad of paper or anything and spun around to go and tell the cook their orders and to get their drinks ready.

"So, what'd you order for me?" Skylar asked.

"Sorry about that," Bull said. "Maybe this wasn't such a good idea. I should've brought you to Chili's or TGI Fridays or something."

She reached across the table and put her hand over his. "It's fine. This is great. I'm not that picky of an eater, and I know I'll like whatever you ordered for me."

"I got myself a gyro with tzatziki, and I went safe for you with the philly cheesesteak."

"Yum," Skylar said. "Have you really had everything on the menu?"

"Yup," Bull told her. "It's all amazing too."

They gazed at each other for a moment, then Julie was there with their drinks.

After she left, Bull leaned forward once again. He could look at Skylar forever. He didn't think he'd ever get tired of studying her face.

"Ask me anything," he said.

"What?"

"Ask me anything," he repeated. "I don't want this to be weird. I want you to feel as if you can talk to me about whatever strikes your fancy."

She chuckled. "Strikes my fancy? Who says that?"

"I think I just did," Bull told her.

"Okay then. Why do people call you Bull? Sandra asked me why you had such a weird name, and I had to tell her I didn't know. I promised I'd ask and report back."

Bull knew he was smiling like a crazy person at that question, but couldn't help it. He'd never smiled so much as he did when he was around her. She had an uncanny ability to catch him off guard. He hoped that would never change. "I got the nickname when I was in the military. I'm a good shot. Hit the bull's-eye every time." He shrugged. "Bullseye eventually became Bull, and it stuck."

"I suppose that's better than the things Sandra guessed."

After she told him some of the things the little girl had suggested, Bull had to agree with her.

"Now you," Skylar said.

"Now me what?"

"Ask me something. Isn't that how these things are supposed to go?"

"These things? You mean dates?" Bull asked.

"Yeah."

"Well, as it's been a very long time since I've been on a date, I wouldn't know. I don't want this to feel like twenty questions," he admitted.

"You asking *me* stuff would make me feel better about asking *you* questions," Skylar said.

"Did you always want to be a teacher?" he asked immediately, not wanting her to feel uneasy for even one second.

And with that, the ice was broken. Julie brought over their meals, and as they ate, they both asked and answered questions back and forth, getting to know each other . . . and the more Bull learned about Skylar, the more uneasy he became.

She was funny, pretty, down to earth, and she didn't seem to have any dangerous vices. He couldn't find anything that didn't intrigue him.

For his part, Bull was keeping a huge secret from her. It didn't sit well with him, but he couldn't exactly just blurt out that he and his friends were hired killers. He had a bad feeling that it might be the one thing that could end their relationship. And he definitely didn't want to mess things up right when they seemed to be going so well.

In the end, he decided he'd keep that side of himself from her until he was more sure things would work out between them. Who knew—in a week or two, or a few months, they might find out they weren't as compatible as they seemed right at this moment. Just because he couldn't find anything that made him want to run the opposite direction didn't mean a long-term relationship was in the cards.

There was no need to tell her about what he felt was his true purpose in life . . . yet.

"I can't wait to meet your friends. They sound hilarious. Can you tell me more about them?" Skylar asked.

Bull took a long drink of water, washing down the last of his gyro before leaning back in his seat. "Kellan, otherwise known as Eagle, is the same age as me, and we're complete opposites in looks. He's light to my dark . . . with his blond hair and blue eyes, he looks more like a surfer, and I look like I could be one of Darth Vader's minions."

"You do kinda look like a bad boy," Skylar said with a grin. "But don't women go for that sort of thing?"

"I don't know, do they?" Bull asked.

"This one seems to," Skylar said a little shyly.

They sat there gazing into each other's eyes for a heated moment before Bull continued describing his friends. "Eagle has the unique ability to recognize anyone after only meeting or seeing their picture once. It's uncanny, really."

"Wow, that's amazing. I bet he'd be great with a police lineup or as a witness to a crime."

She didn't know how right she was. Bull pressed on. "Smoke—whose real name is Mark—is thirty-eight, and when you meet him, you'll understand his nickname. He's completely average. At six-one, with nondescript brown hair and brown eyes, he blends in with most men. He just seems to disappear in a crowd."

"Like a puff of smoke, right?" Skylar asked.

Bull nodded. "Yup. One second he's standing there next to you, and the next he's gone. Don't ever play a game of hide-and-seek with Smoke . . . you'll lose," Bull said with a smile.

"Gotcha. No hide-and-seek. Check," Skylar teased. "What about Gramps? I'm guessing he's the oldest of the bunch?"

"You'd guess right," Bull said. "He's ancient at forty-five. He joined the Army late, but since he's really hard to rattle, and he stays calm ninety-nine percent of the time, he excelled. Before you ask, his real name is Leonardo. His grandparents came to the US from Mexico, and he grew up in El Paso. He's proud of his heritage, even if his parents aren't full-blooded Mexican. And you can't miss him when you meet everyone, as he's the tallest at six-four."

"Oh jeez. I feel short most of the time, but around you guys, I'm gonna feel like a shrimp," Skylar moaned.

"You're the perfect size," Bull told her, being completely honest.

"Thanks. My mom's short too, around my height, but my dad's almost six feet. It took me a long time to admit I wasn't going to grow any taller than what I am now. That I'd be short and dumpy my entire life."

Bull took her hand in his and stared into her eyes intently. "You aren't dumpy," he said a bit too fiercely. "You're curvy. And believe me, curvy is good. It's *very* good."

Skylar licked her lips, and Bull couldn't help but follow the movement with his eyes. It took everything in him not to haul her across the table and find out for himself how soft and wet those lips were.

"Thanks," she said after a heated moment.

"You guys done?" Rosie asked from beside them.

Bull felt Skylar jerk in surprise, though he'd known the woman was approaching them long before she'd arrived at their table. It was one of the only reasons he hadn't kissed Skylar there and then. He held on to her hand until he knew she'd calmed, then Bull leaned back and reached for his wallet.

"We're done," he told her. "You have our bill?"

As he'd figured she'd do, Rosie rolled her eyes. "You aren't paying, Bull," she scolded.

"Rosie," he warned.

"Nope. Not happening. You and Silverstone have done more for this place than you'll admit. You helped us get back up and running after we had that kitchen fire. You've donated a ton of money to help feed the homeless. And we all know you and your friends talk us up to anyone who'll listen, and most of the business we have today is because of you. No, you're not paying for your meal today, or *any* day."

Bull growled under his breath.

"And you don't scare me with that shit. Just say 'Thank you, Rosie,' and take your girl and show her a better time than this dump," the woman ordered.

"This isn't a dump," Skylar protested. "It's awesome. The vibe in here is homey and comforting, and the service was perfect. Julie was attentive but not obnoxious about it. You should be proud of this place."

Rosie beamed, and Bull knew Skylar had a friend for life without even trying. Praising Rosie's Diner was akin to telling her that her baby was the prettiest little girl she'd ever seen.

"Right. Get on with you," Rosie said. "And tell the others to get their asses in here. It's been too long since they've come in to get their Rosie fix."

"Yes, ma'am," Bull said.

Rosie winked at him, then turned and headed back for the counter. The diner was fairly busy by now, and Bull knew many of the men and women who were having lunch. Most were business owners from the area. They all knew a good thing when they tasted it, and Rosie's Diner was definitely a good thing.

"Do you want to go to Silverstone, or have you had enough of me?" Bull asked.

"Oh, I definitely want to go to Silverstone," Skylar said. "Will your friends be there?"

"Probably." Bull knew they'd absolutely be there. He'd told them he was taking Skylar to lunch and had planned to give her a tour of Silverstone, and all three had said they wanted to meet her. They were curious as to what kind of woman had caught Bull's attention so strongly. They'd each had their share of women, but no one had come close to getting serious with any of them. So Bull's interest in Skylar had them all intrigued.

He stood and held out his hand for Skylar. Just like when they'd first met, sparks seemed to fly when she put her hand in his. When she was standing, Bull reached into his wallet and took out fifty bucks and placed it on the table as a tip for Julie. This was his and Rosie's game. She refused to charge him for any meal he ate, and he tipped as generously as possible. Julie and the other waitresses could all definitely use the extra money. Everyone involved was satisfied with the arrangement. Bull because he got to eat an exceptional meal, the waitresses because they knew they'd get a generous tip, and Rosie because a satisfied employee meant a happy employee. It was a win-win-win situation.

Skylar smiled at him when she saw what he'd done, but she didn't comment on it.

When they were once again seated in his car and on their way to Silverstone, she said, "Thank you for lunch."

"You're welcome."

"Did you really do all those things Rosie said?" she asked.

Bull shrugged. "Yeah. But so did Eagle, Smoke, and Gramps. I'm not flying around the city being a do-gooder all by myself."

Skylar giggled, and Bull loved hearing the sound.

"And now I'm gonna have that image in my head the rest of the day. You in a cape and tights, sprinkling hundred-dollar bills around."

Bull couldn't help but laugh along with her. "I'm not sure about the tights," he quipped, which made Skylar laugh harder. She was so busy joking around, she obviously hadn't realized how close they were to Silverstone.

"Here it is," Bull told her as they approached the garage.

Skylar looked up, and her eyes widened as she gasped.

"What?" Bull asked, concerned about her reaction.

"You're secretly in a motorcycle gang, aren't you?" she blurted.

"What? No. Why would you say that?" he asked.

Skylar gestured to the garage without a word.

Bull looked at Silverstone and tried to see it through her eyes. Then he chuckled. It did kind of look like a compound . . . one a motorcycle club might use for their nefarious activities. "Wait until you see the inside," he said, then pulled up to the fence around the property, which was topped with razor wire, to input a code into the security system. He waited for the gate to open before pulling inside.

Chapter Six

Skylar couldn't take her eyes off the disaster in front of her. She'd gotten the impression that Bull and his friends were doing pretty well for themselves. With everything he'd said about the multiple tow trucks Silverstone owned, the reputation Silverstone had, how Rosie had talked about his volunteering, and then that generous tip, she'd thought his business would look prosperous.

But what she was seeing looked anything but.

It wasn't just the formidable fence that surrounded the large lot; it was the thigh-high weeds and grass growing around the various buildings. It was the peeling paint on the garages. The austere cinder block buildings that probably housed the tow trucks when they weren't in use didn't help either.

There was a large sign proclaiming the business to be **SILVERSTONE TOWING**, above what she assumed was the main building. The second *S* in Silverstone was crooked and looked as if it was about to fall off the sign altogether. There was a motorcycle parked haphazardly at the front door, but she saw no other cars. She assumed the employees' vehicles were parked around the back of the buildings.

"It's . . . big," she said diplomatically.

She knew Carson was laughing at her, but she couldn't do anything to keep the surprise off her face. She wanted to seem impressed with his business, but it was hard to reconcile what seemed to be a run-down, sketchy establishment with everything she'd heard about Silverstone Towing until now.

Carson parked his car next to the motorcycle and cut the engine. He turned to her. "You trusted me to order lunch for you. Can't you trust me now too?"

Skylar did her best to give him a reassuring smile. "Of course."

But Carson obviously saw right through her bravado. "I know it seems bad. But look around. You see the neighborhood we're in?"

Skylar turned her head to look past the fence and buildings and saw what he meant. Her school wasn't in the best part of town, but it looked like paradise compared to where they were now. There was an abandoned gas station across the street, its pumps long since removed. The glass was broken, and the walls were covered with graffiti.

"We didn't put it out of business, if that's what you're wondering," Carson said. "It was already abandoned when we moved in five years ago. As were the two businesses on either side of this main building. We bought the lots, put up the fence, built the new garages to house our tow trucks, and here we are today."

Skylar nodded and did her best to put aside her first impression and looked around once more. Now that she knew the large garages were only a few years old, she could see that they did look pretty sturdy. They were made out of cinder blocks and not painted, but she could see large silver locks on the sliding doors as well as the door on the side of the nearest building. There was no graffiti on the Silverstone side of the fence . . . and there was that security panel where Bull had to punch in numbers before they could enter. And he'd put in a *lot* of numbers. At least ten. That would be almost impossible to crack for anyone who was wandering by and tried to get past the gate surrounding the property.

Skylar realized that she'd been extremely rude and had jumped to conclusions. She'd done the one thing she hated most of all—judged Silverstone based on what she saw on the outside rather than what was on the inside.

"I'm sorry," she said softly.

"You have nothing to be sorry about," Carson said firmly. "You saw exactly what we wanted you to see. A run-down, piece-of-shit business . . . that no one in their right mind would want to break into."

Suddenly, everything she saw made sense. "Damn," Skylar said under her breath. "It's like the car Stan loaned me. That's ingenious."

"It was all Smoke's idea. This place belonged to his grandfather once upon a time before his uncle inherited it. It was an actual garage, like Stan's. But it sat empty for a while, and when we got out of the Army, we decided to make a go of it. Since none of us know anything about fixing cars, we had to shift the business plan a bit. And . . . voilà. Silverstone Towing was born. The location is actually perfect, as we're close to 465 and I-65 and can get into the city easily as well. It's a good home base, and customers don't care where we're located . . . they just care if we can get to them as fast as possible."

"Very true," Skylar said.

"Come on," Carson urged. "I can't wait to show you the inside."

"I'm guessing it doesn't match the outside?" she asked.

"Come see for yourself," Carson told her.

He was right there at her door by the time she stepped out of the car, and she leaned into him slightly as his palm landed on the small of her back. Skylar loved the feel of his hand there. His fingers felt as if they spanned her entire lower back. The heat from his hand seeped through her shirt, making her wish he was touching her skin on skin.

Shaking her head, she did her best to get herself together as Carson reached around her and punched in another code in the box next to the door, and after a click, he opened it and held the door for her.

"After you."

Taking a deep breath, Skylar stepped inside.

The room she entered was nondescript and plain. There was a battered couch along one wall and a few hard-looking chairs. Glancing at the magazines on the one table in the room, Skylar saw that they were a few years old. She turned to Carson and raised an eyebrow.

He smiled but didn't say anything. Walking over to a door at the back of the room, he punched in another set of numbers on yet another keypad. The door opened, and once more he gestured for her to enter.

"Why do I feel like the fly being invited into the spider's parlor?" Skylar quipped.

She started when Carson burst out laughing.

She could only stare at him in disbelief. He'd laughed. Actually *laughed*. Out loud. And it was glorious.

"I think you'll be pleasantly surprised by what's on the other side of this door," he told her.

Knowing she'd do whatever he asked as long as he kept smiling at her, Skylar walked past Carson and into a small foyer. But it was what lay beyond that foyer that had her mouth opening in shock. "Holy crap!"

"Told you," Carson said smugly. "Come on, let me show you around."

Skylar didn't know where to look first. It was as if she'd entered a multimillion-dollar home. The floors were hardwood, and the leather couches in the room looked extremely comfortable. There was a huge TV on the wall and a giant picture of a garage with a **SILVERSTONE** sign alongside the road. She imagined it was the old garage before Carson's friend Smoke had revived it.

But it was the chef's kitchen along one side of the room that really had her gawking. Stainless steel appliances, granite countertops . . . everything was top of the line. Once she'd understood that the outside of the business was unkempt on purpose, she'd expected to see something nice on the inside, but this was beyond her imagination.

"This is the main room," Carson was telling her. He walked over and straightened a pillow on the couch and picked up an empty glass sitting on the coffee table. "When our employees aren't on a job, they sometimes hang out here. Their shifts are eight hours, and they're welcome to watch whatever they want, to help themselves to the food in the kitchen. I'd like to say the stove gets a good workout, but unfortunately, it doesn't." He snorted. "Who am I kidding? None of us can really cook worth a damn, so we eat a lot of sandwiches and frozen meals. Come on, there's more to see," he said, gesturing toward a hallway with his head.

Skylar followed him in a daze. More?

"Down here are the smaller rooms we added on. Some have beds in them, and others have PlayStations and Xboxes set up. It gives everyone a chance to sleep if they need it or to entertain themselves by playing a game. When we first opened, these rooms were used a lot more than they are now. We weren't as busy back then." Carson shrugged. "At the end of the hall is the dispatch room. I'm not sure who's working in there today, but I want to introduce you."

Skylar's head was spinning. She glanced inside one of the small rooms and saw that it wasn't a secondhand setup. There was another large TV, although not as big as the one in the main room, and a leather easy chair in the room, as well as a small love seat. It was a bit messier than the large room. She could see a cup and some food wrappers, but it wasn't a pigsty by any means.

Carson opened the door at the end of the hall and stood back, letting her enter. A desk was set up to the right, facing a large window, and sunlight streamed inside. A woman was sitting in front of three large computer screens, and when she heard them enter, she turned to greet them.

"Bull! Hey! Didn't expect you in today. Everything all right?" she asked.

"It's fine. Skylar, this is Leigh Coleman. Leigh, this is my friend Skylar."

"Hi!" Leigh said cheerily and stood, holding out her hand.

Skylar shook it, a little surprised at the friendliness of the other woman. It wasn't that she thought she'd be mean or especially grumpy, but it *was* a beautiful Saturday, and she was stuck sitting behind a computer.

"How're things going?" Carson asked.

"Busy as usual," Leigh said as she sat back down. "I've got eight trucks out, but so far we aren't backed up, which is good. Bart and Thomas are on break and will go back in service in thirty minutes or so. Christine is finishing up at an MVA; Rob just left the police impound yard and is on his way to a flat tire on I-65; Jose radioed in to say he's dropping off a lady and her daughter at home—who he picked up on the east side—after he drops off their car at the Ford dealership; and Shane just arrived on the scene of a suspended driver."

Skylar's head spun with all the info Leigh rattled off. She didn't know what an MVA was and had no idea how the woman kept everything straight.

Just then, the radio came to life, and Leigh gave them a little smile and turned back to the computer.

"Wow," Skylar said as she looked up at Carson.

"A good dispatcher knows where her or his people are at all times. We've got trackers in each of the trucks, for safety, but things can go sideways in seconds, and if she needs to call for help, she needs to know exactly where she's sending the cops."

"Do things go bad a lot?" Skylar asked nervously.

"Not really," Carson said with a nonchalant shrug, but that didn't exactly reassure her.

"She looks content enough in what she does," she observed quietly after a moment.

"The drivers all rotate in and out of dispatch," Carson told her. "No one gets out of it. It's part of being a Silverstone driver. There was pushback at first, but after a while, they got it. Being behind the radio makes them a better driver. And having to work in here makes everyone more patient when they're behind the wheel. It's an ideal situation."

"Eight-hour shifts, breaks, this amazing building . . . it seems as if it's a good place to work," Skylar said more to herself than Carson.

But it was Leigh who responded. "It's the best place I've *ever* worked," she said. She'd turned in her seat and was facing them once more. "Bull, Eagle, Smoke, and Gramps actually care about their employees. We're not just another name on a piece of paper to them. They know everything about us. Don't you, Bull?"

He smiled. "How was Larry's math test this week?"

Leigh raised both eyebrows at Skylar, as if to say, "See?" Then she said, "Passed with flying colors, thanks to you tutoring him the other day." Then she turned back to Skylar. "Because of my job here, I was able to move into a safer apartment. The pay is way higher than anything else I could find without a high school diploma. I have a 401(k), holiday pay—which is time and a half—free food on my shift, and bosses who give a shit. Some people might look down at me for being a tow truck driver, but I'll be thankful every day of my life that I was hired on here."

Skylar could tell Leigh meant every word that came out of her mouth. Carson hadn't set this up. Hadn't planted her to say all the nice things about his company. She was genuinely thankful to be working there . . . and it showed.

"That's great," Skylar said.

"Sorry," Leigh apologized with a grimace. "I tend to go overboard when talking about Silverstone. I just feel sorry for everyone who's working their asses off out there for shit pay and who get no respect. Like my son's teacher, for example. She gets to the school at six in the morning and doesn't leave until around six at night. She has to deal with ungrateful kids and uncooperative parents all damn day. I make at least ten grand more than she does a year, *and* I only work eight hours a day and get a ton of extra perks."

Skylar shifted uncomfortably.

"Leigh," Carson warned.

"I'm just saying," Leigh went on, oblivious to Skylar's discomfort. "Teachers are just one example. One of Larry's friends' parents is an admin assistant over at IUPUI, and I even make more than *her*. She's got a college degree! I can't help but gloat a little that someone like me, who was working as a waitress in a piece-of-shit bar and barely getting by and never seeing my son, now has a freaking 401(k) and stability. The turnover here at Silverstone is zero. No one who gets hired on would leave if they could help it."

"Skylar's a teacher," Carson said bluntly.

Leigh's face drained of color. "Oh shit. I'm sorry. I didn't mean anything by all that. I was just saying that you guys work your asses off and should be paid more . . ."

"It's okay," Skylar told her, feeling bad that the *other* woman felt bad. "I knew what you meant."

"I just wanted to let you know that Bull is a good guy. The best. And his friends are too. They've changed my life for the better. I obviously went about it the wrong way, but I get shit all the time from my family and friends who don't understand why I'm working here, instead of trying to get a 'real job'—their words, not mine."

Just then, the radio crackled to life again, and Leigh turned around to do her job.

"Come on," Carson said.

Skylar allowed him to steer her out of the room. "It was nice to meet you," she called out softly before the door shut behind her. Leigh raised a hand in acknowledgment, but since she was still dealing with the driver she was talking to, she didn't verbally respond.

Carson stopped her when they were outside the door. "You good?" he asked.

Skylar looked up at him in surprise. "Yeah, why?"

"Well, my employee just insulted the hell out of you."

"No, she didn't," Skylar protested. "She was just being honest. She loves working here, and it's obvious you care about your employees. I can't get insulted by that. Maybe *I* should apply to work at Silverstone," she teased.

"No," Carson said seriously, and for a second, Skylar *was* kind of insulted at his quick response. But then he continued.

"You're right where you're supposed to be. You're a good teacher. You *care* about your kids. And most of them need that kind of caring. You spend more time with them than their parents do . . . not dissing their moms and dads; it can be brutal to make enough money to raise a kid. I just hate that society doesn't see the value in teachers. You should be making twice as much as you do. Maybe if states started paying their educators what they should, test scores would go up, we could keep the good teachers in the classrooms, and our young people would be more respectful and grateful to go to school in the first place."

Skylar wanted to cry at his words. She'd long ago come to terms with the fact that her job wasn't well respected. She'd been yelled at by parents for daring to request they read to their kids. She'd been told she wasn't doing her job when a child failed a test, when she'd bent over backward to try to help them learn. And she'd even been spit on a time or two by pissed-off dads.

But deep down, she loved what she did. Loved seeing little faces happy to see her each morning. Loved that moment when a child "got" what she was teaching. Loved to hear the laughter and joy when her students were playing. Yes, her pay was crap. Yes, there were a lot of headaches with her job, and she worked long hours. But Carson was right, she felt as if she was right where she was meant to be.

"Thanks," she said sincerely.

"Want to see the rest of the place and meet my friends? Or I can take you home . . ."

"There's more?" Skylar asked in surprise.

Once again, she was rewarded by his lips quirking up in a smile. "We've got a finished basement downstairs. It's also a place where the employees can go if shit goes down outside."

Skylar's eyes got huge. "Have they ever needed to use it?"

"Once," Carson told her. "There was a shooting down the way in some apartments. Cops showed up. Things got ugly. The three employees who were here went down there just in case. Turns out nothing happened, but I feel better knowing they have a safe place if things go sideways."

"I'm sure they do too," Skylar said simply. Carson hadn't moved away, and she could smell the soap he'd used in the shower that morning. He towered over her, and Skylar wanted nothing more than to rest her forehead against his chest and lean into him. But since he hadn't even held her hand yet, snuggling up to him seemed a bit forward.

As if he could read her mind, Carson's hand skimmed up her arm and came to rest on the back of her neck. He gently massaged her there, which made Skylar want to melt into a puddle of goo at his feet. She closed her eyes and leaned into his touch.

"Feel good?"

She nodded.

"You're tense," he muttered.

"It's been a long week," she responded.

"What would you be doing today if you weren't hanging out with me?" he asked. "What's a typical Saturday like for you?"

"Sleeping in, then doing errands before all the crazies are out and about. Then I'd probably lounge around my apartment for a while, watching TV or reading a book. I usually talk to my parents at least once on the weekend, and sometimes I head up to Carmel to visit them. If I do go up there, I have dinner with them. And if not, I make myself something and snuggle under a blanket and veg. Sunday nights, I work on my lesson plans for the week."

"I'm sorry I've disturbed your routine," he told her.

Skylar opened her eyes and looked up, aware that he hadn't dropped his hand from her nape. "I'm not. I'm thirty-two, and my life is boring. I'd much rather be here with you, seeing where you work and meeting your friends, than schlepping around the grocery store buying too much junk food and thinking about watching *Live PD* later."

They stared at each other for a long moment. Then Carson's head dropped a fraction of an inch.

Skylar's heart stopped beating in her chest. Was he going to kiss her? *Please let him be about to kiss me.*

"Sky?" he whispered.

"Yes," she said eagerly, giving him consent to do whatever the hell he wanted. She went up on her tiptoes to further demonstrate that she was one hundred percent all right with him kissing her.

His lips brushed across hers once in a gentle caress. For such a large man, he was being extremely careful with her. Skylar wanted more. It had been a very long time since she'd desired someone like she did Carson. She might be little, but she wasn't going to break.

Moving her own hand up, she palmed the back of his head, loving the way his short hair felt against her skin, and urged him closer.

He took the hint, tilting his head and nipping her lower lip. Skylar gasped, and he took that opportunity to thrust his tongue inside her mouth.

Groaning now, she deepened the kiss.

How long they stood outside the dispatch room in the hall making out, Skylar had no idea, but when Carson finally lifted his head from hers, her chest was heaving, and she felt almost light headed.

Carson Rhodes could kiss. *Damn* could he kiss.

Licking her lips, Skylar loved how his eyes followed the motion. His thumb brushed back and forth over the sensitive skin of her neck, and Skylar realized that while they had been kissing, she'd plastered herself to his chest. Or maybe he'd pulled her there. She didn't know, and she didn't care.

One of her hands was behind his head, the other was flattened against his pec. He still palmed her nape, and his other hand was on her lower back, his fingers just resting at the top of her ass.

Taking a deep breath, Skylar could only smell *him*. She was so turned on, and all she could do was stare up at Carson.

"We have to stop," he told her after a moment.

"Why?" she blurted without thought, then blushed at how eager she sounded.

Carson brushed his fingertips against her cheek. "Because Silverstone has cameras. Eagle, Smoke, and Gramps are probably watching and judging my performance. The last thing I'd ever want to do is embarrass you."

"Oh," Skylar said, not really caring that his friends had probably just watched Carson kiss the hell out of her.

"Yeah, oh," Carson said seriously. "In case I forget to say it later, I've had a really good time on our date. And I want to take you out again."

"Okay," she told him without hesitation.

"Fuck," Carson swore.

Skylar had no idea what he was swearing about, but since he didn't seem upset with her, she didn't give it another thought.

Neither moved. They just stayed wrapped up in each other there in the hallway.

Chapter Seven

Fuck, Bull thought to himself as he held Skylar in his arms. She fit against him perfectly. He could feel her tits against his chest, and she'd opened to him so trustingly, it made him want to throw her down on the floor and take her right there in the hall.

Her innocent reaction to his kiss just brought home their differences all the more. How in the hell was this going to work? She was a kindergarten teacher, for fuck's sake. And he was . . .

What was he? Co-owner of a successful business, yes, but ultimately, he was a hired killer. He had more blood on his hands than he could ever wash off. He was the grim reaper, and she was a beautiful, innocent angel.

And all he could think about was making her his.

They'd never work out. He should end this, whatever this was, right now.

But then Skylar laid her cheek on his chest and sighed in contentment, and he was a goner. Her fingers curled into his shirt, as if she was trying to hold on to him, and he knew he wasn't going to back away from this. He was going to take everything she offered, and when it came time to tell her what it was he and his friends did—and he *would* tell her—hopefully she'd be so in love with him that it wouldn't matter. She'd accept who he was, and they'd live happily ever after.

Fuck, Bull swore again. Jesus, he was practically planning their wedding in his head on their first fucking date. He was an idiot. He'd probably do something boneheaded way before they got too deep into a relationship, and that would be that.

"Carson?" she asked tentatively.

He knew he'd been quiet for too long, and they should head downstairs, where his friends were most certainly waiting impatiently. "Yeah?"

"You're a good man."

Her words hit a nerve. He wasn't really. But he tried to make up for what he did by helping others as much as possible. He didn't think he'd ever wipe his slate clean enough to be called *good*, but he was doing what he could. "If we don't get downstairs, Eagle will probably come stomping up to get us," he said, deflecting her words easily.

Bull pulled back, and his stomach clenched at the rush of cold air that wafted over his body where she'd been curled into him. He dropped his arms but snagged her hand. He smiled, squeezing her hand, and turned toward the door nearby that led downstairs.

They walked down the plain stairwell, through a heavy steel security door, and into the lower level of Silverstone. There were Ping-Pong and foosball tables, a pinball machine, a vintage *Pac-Man* video game, and some comfortable chairs around the space.

Eagle, Smoke, and Gramps were sitting at a table playing gin rummy. Bull encouraged her to walk over to his friends, and they all stood, waiting patiently for him to introduce them.

"Skylar, I'd like you to meet my very best friends. This is Eagle, Smoke, and Gramps."

She shook each of their hands in turn. "It's very nice to meet you all." She looked at Gramps. "I think you got the short end of the stick when it comes to nicknames. The *last* thing I think when I look at you is *old man*."

The ice was broken, and everyone burst out laughing.

Gramps reached for her and bent her backward over his arm. “Run away with me, Miss Skylar. I can take much better care of you than this young whippersnapper can.”

Bull was afraid for a second that Skylar would panic, or otherwise feel uncomfortable at being basically manhandled by his friend, but he relaxed when she rolled her eyes and smacked him on the arm.

“I would, but I’m afraid you’re simply too tall for me.”

Gramps chuckled and brought Skylar upright. He was at least a foot taller than her, in fact, and she indeed looked absolutely tiny next to Bull’s friend.

“Damn,” Gramps said theatrically.

Bull didn’t hesitate to reclaim Skylar. He put his arm around her waist and pulled her into his side. To his relief, she immediately wrapped her arm around him and gave him some of her weight in return.

“What’s behind that door?” she asked, pointing down the short hallway.

Bull tensed, but did his best to keep his tone casual. “Another bathroom, a storage room, closet, things like that.” What he didn’t say was that the space at the very end was a safe room protected with a biometric lock. It was where he and his team researched and discussed the missions they went on. He trusted Skylar, but a first date wasn’t the time or place to spring that on her.

“Cool,” she said with a nod.

“You play rummy?” Eagle asked, bringing her attention back to them.

“I don’t just play rummy,” Skylar told him. “I’m practically a gin rummy pro.”

“A pro, huh?” Eagle said as he pulled a chair out from the table. “This I gotta see.”

The others all chuckled, and Bull smirked. “You want something to drink?” he asked before sitting down.

"I'm good," she told him. "I'm ready to kick some gin rummy butt."

An hour later, Bull knew he had a stupid smile on his face, but he couldn't help it. He'd hoped his friends would get along with Skylar, but they were not only getting along—it was as if they'd known each other their whole lives. She *was* kicking their butts in the card game and gloating about it more with each hand they played.

"How the hell are you this good?" Eagle complained.

Skylar smiled and laid down four eights. Bull inwardly grimaced. He'd been hoping to get an eight to complement the six, seven, and nine he was holding in his own hand. Damn.

"My dad taught me to play when I was nine," she told Eagle with a smile. "We play every time we get together. No one else in the family likes to play with us anymore."

"I can see why," Smoke grumbled. He put down three twos and scowled at them.

"Bull said you grew up in Carmel," Gramps commented as the game continued.

"I did."

"What do your parents do?" he asked.

Bull knew the question wasn't as innocent as it might sound. He threw Gramps a warning glance, but his friend ignored it.

"My dad's the CFO of ADESA, and my mom retired this year from Assembly Biosciences."

Smoke whistled. "Wow. Impressive."

Skylar shrugged. "It is. But to me, they've always just been Mom and Dad."

"We bought one of our trucks from ADESA," Smoke said. "Their vehicle auctions are well run, and they sell at fair prices. We haven't had any issues with that truck either, which we appreciate because it means they aren't selling lemons."

"My dad's not involved with the auctions, per se," Skylar said. "He's just the money guy."

"What did your mom do at Assembly Biosciences?"

"She wasn't a scientist, so don't get too excited. She worked in their fundraising sector. She helped get sponsors and to plan their galas and parties and things. She's happy to get to stay home, although Dad complains that she spends all of her time trying to plan his life now. They have more get-togethers with their friends than ever before, simply because Mom needs something to do."

When it was Skylar's turn again, she picked a card off the top of the stack, then smiled broadly.

She laid down her cards and said with a grin, "Gin."

"Fuck," Smoke groused.

"Shit," Eagle said.

"Damn!" Gramps swore.

Bull merely grinned and threw his cards to the center of the table. He loved seeing the happy glint in Skylar's eyes. She'd beaten them for the third time, fair and square.

She leaned her elbows on the table and asked no one in particular, "So, you guys met in the Army?"

"Yup," Eagle said. "We were stationed together at Fort Bragg, North Carolina. We were put in the same unit, and when the time came for us to reenlist, we all asked to stay together, and they moved us to Fort Hood, Texas."

"Did you like it?"

"We loved the Army," Smoke told her.

"Why?"

"It's hard to explain," Bull said. "There's just something about the danger that really brings you closer to your teammates. Knowing that they have your back and you have theirs is pretty amazing. Not to mention the shared goal of keeping our country safe."

She nodded. "I'm guessing you were deployed?" she asked.

Bull exchanged a look with his friends before saying, "Yeah, we were deployed. More than once."

"Oh, that's so hard. Thank you all for your service. I know that's something lots of people say nowadays, but I really mean it."

"You're welcome," all four men said at the same time.

"If you liked it so much, why'd you get out?" she asked.

This question was a bit tougher, and Bull never wanted to lie to her. He might skirt the truth, but an outright lie seemed to be a bad way to start out a relationship. And the longer he was around her, the more he wanted that relationship.

Before he could answer, Gramps said, "Smoke's uncle died. He left him Silverstone, and the four of us decided to try to make a go of it. The Army's a tough mistress. She'll chew you up and spit you out without a second glance. And the bureaucracy was getting the better of us. We wanted to make our own decisions, not be tied to what our superior officers said we had to do."

"Well, I'd say you're doing all right for yourselves," Skylar said with a smile, accepting his explanation without a second thought. "I think it's great that you're still friends and that you get to work together."

"Some people think it's weird," Eagle said.

"Not me," Skylar said emphatically. "If I had friends who I was as close to as you guys seem to be, I'd want to go into business and spend all my time with them too. Family isn't necessarily a matter of blood relation. It's the people who would bend over backward to help you, no matter what time it is or if they have to drive a thousand miles to get to you."

"You have friends like that?" Smoke asked. "You sound as if you know what you're talking about."

For the first time, Bull saw her natural sunny disposition slip a bit. "Unfortunately, no. I mean, I'm close to the teachers at my school, but they're busy with their own families, and during the school day we're all busy with our classrooms. I would've called a friend to come help me with my car if I had anyone I was that close to. Instead, I had to call Silverstone."

She sounded so sad, Bull couldn't help but reach out and put a hand on her arm. He waited until she looked over at him before saying, "You called Silverstone and got *me*."

He could see his words struck home, because she paused for a moment before nodding. "I got you," she agreed.

"And us," Gramps threw in. "See, the thing is, we're kind of a package deal. Not in the sense that we want to swap spit with you or see each other naked or anything, but if you can't get ahold of Bull, you can call one of us. No matter what time it is, we're here for you."

Skylar looked at each of the men at the table with an odd expression on her face.

"What's wrong?" Bull asked her.

She met his gaze. "This is our first date," she answered.

"And?" he asked.

"I'm just . . . confused. This isn't how things usually go."

"Don't care how they usually happen," Bull said firmly. "We're different."

She swallowed hard and nodded.

"Life's too fuckin' short to ignore what's happening between us, Sky. I'm not asking you to marry me. But we've already agreed to a second date. We're gonna set up a time when Silverstone can come to Eastlake and entertain the kids and hopefully teach them some car-safety stuff. You've met my family," Bull nodded to the men silently watching them, "and I want to meet yours. We'll take things one day at a time.

"But I know a good thing when I see it, and I'd be a complete fucking idiot if I didn't give this relationship one hundred percent of my time and effort. And believe me, Sky, I'm not an idiot. And neither are my friends. They know this is different, *you're* different. How many people do you think we let into our inner sanctum here at Silverstone?"

Skylar bit her lip and looked around the room once more, then back at him. She shrugged.

"Other than family members of our employees, who are welcome here at any time, no one else visits the garage. We want this to be a safe place where our employees can hang out without feeling awkward about it," Bull told her. "I'm not telling you this to freak you out, but to explain why Eagle, Smoke, and Gramps are offering you their friendship and support so easily and quickly. I know I'm kinda pushy, and things between us seem to be moving quickly, but . . . well, I'm hoping you're feeling even a tenth of what I am when I'm around you."

Gramps pushed back in his chair and stood. "We'll just leave you guys alone for a bit," he said.

Eagle and Smoke also stood, but Skylar whipped her head toward them and asked, "How many times have you guys saved Carson's life?"

Bull's friends stared at her in surprise and confusion at her abrupt question. "Uh . . . we haven't kept count," Gramps said.

"But you *have* saved his life," she pressed.

"Yes. And he's saved ours," Smoke said.

"Then as far as I'm concerned, you have a right to be here," she finished.

Eagle crossed to where Skylar was sitting and held out a hand. She took it, and he pulled her up so she was standing. Then he gave her a short hug. Smoke came over and did the same thing. Then Gramps.

"We like you, Skylar," Eagle told her. "You're good for Bull, and frankly, you're good for us too. It's been a long time since we've all just sat around and played like we did today. So thank you for being who you are."

And with that, he turned and headed for the stairs, followed by Smoke and Gramps.

When it was just the two of them, Bull reached out and ran his fingers down Skylar's cheek gently. "You're freaked out," he said quietly.

She shook her head, then shrugged. "A little. I mean, I do like you, Carson. A lot. But this is the first time we've hung out. I'm just a little confused."

Bull wanted to pull her onto his lap and hold her tight, to try to make her feel better, but he knew that would only confuse her more. And the last thing he wanted to do was make her pull away from him. He might know how special she was, and that he'd be an idiot to let her slip away, but she hadn't seen what he had. Hadn't seen the evil that seemed to be so prevalent in the world. He liked her innocence and would do whatever it took to keep the evil at bay for her. And if that meant pulling back, giving her space, that was what he'd do.

"I'm sorry," he told her, dropping his hand. "I'm coming on too strong, I know. I'll do my best to check that."

"It's not that I don't want to date you," she told him. "I do, but—"

"But you're not ready to bring me home to Mom and Dad . . . or for such intensity," he finished for her.

She bit her lip and nodded.

"Noted," he told her. "Are you still willing to let me and the guys come to your school and entertain the kids?"

"Yes," she said without any hesitation. "They'll love it. I'll talk to my principal and some of the other teachers and see if we can't coordinate a 'truck week' or something."

"Good. And that second date? I didn't move too fast and make you have second thoughts about that, did I?"

She shook her head. "No. I want to see you again."

Bull let out a sigh of relief and returned her small smile. "It's getting pretty late in the afternoon. I know you've got things to do, and I've monopolized enough of your Saturday," he said.

"I've had a wonderful time," she told him. "I can't remember when I've had such a nice first date."

Bull held back his wince. *Nice* wasn't exactly the adjective he was looking for, but he nodded anyway.

"Carson?"

"Yeah?"

"I've been burned in the past by a man who seemed too good to be true. I fell really hard. And fast. My dad tried to tell me to slow down, but I didn't listen. I wanted to be married. Wanted a family. Wanted the closeness that came with having a loving husband. But in the end, he wasn't what he seemed."

"Did he hurt you?" Bull growled, the thought of anyone putting their hands on Skylar more than he could stand to even think about.

"No. Not physically. But everything about him was a lie. He said he was an orphan, but his parents were alive and well and living in Chicago . . . he just didn't want to introduce me to them. He said that he'd never been married, which was another lie. He had *two* ex-wives. He told me he worked at the Subaru factory up in the Lafayette area, which was why he couldn't see me on weekdays, because he was working, but that ended up being a lie too. It was . . . a bitter pill to swallow."

Bull came back toward her and put his hands on her shoulders. "I've never been married. I don't know where my mom is and wouldn't want to find her now anyway, not after she abandoned me and my dad. My dad really did pass away, and the last thing I want to do is mooch off you. Honestly, I don't need to. No offense, but I have a feeling I have a lot more money in the bank than you do."

"You're unlike any guy who's ever been interested in me, and while I don't think I'm a bad person or anything like that, you kinda feel out of my league. I'm not even sure why you're interested in me," she said.

"I'd really like to hug you," he told her, unable to resist holding her in his arms any longer. But he also didn't want to do anything that would make her uncomfortable.

She nodded and stepped into him and laid her head on his chest. He felt her arms tighten around his back, and her warmth seemed to seep into his very bones. "I'm not sure I can explain it," he told her.

"Try," she said dryly.

Bull chuckled. "Fine. You've made me smile and laugh more in the short time I've known you than I have in the last entire year. You remind me that the world is full of good people, not just those who want to take advantage of and hurt others. It sure doesn't hurt that I'm physically attracted to you as well. You're curvy, and I fucking *love* curves, and your hair makes me want to wrap my hands in it and never let go. You exude an innocence that I want to bottle up and hoard from the world. But mostly . . . you make me feel like a better person when I'm around you."

"Wow," she whispered. "I'd say you explained it just fine."

Bull pulled back a bit, but didn't let go of her. "All I'm asking is for a chance to get to know you. I want to know what makes you laugh, what makes you cry . . . and to have a chance to make it better. I want to see you interact with your kids at school and watch you beat the pants off my friends in gin rummy again."

He couldn't read what she was thinking as she stared up at him, and Bull hoped he hadn't just ruined things.

"You're different from anyone I've ever dated," she said after a moment.

"Is that good or bad?" he asked.

"I haven't decided," she said honestly. "I feel comfortable with you. Which is kind of scary. I mean, here I am, in the basement of your business. No one knows I'm here, and you can overpower me and do whatever you want with me, and I'd have absolutely no way of escaping. But instead of being scared or unsure, I'm completely confident you won't hurt me."

"I won't," he said emphatically.

"Maybe it's because of how we met, how the first thing you told me was to double-check your identity. Even though you were kinda rude about it, you've been open and honest with me from the start. I trust you, Carson."

"You can trust me to do what I think is in your best interest," he told her, not comfortable with her assessment that he was open and honest, especially when he knew he was keeping a huge secret.

"And for the record, I'm attracted to you too. I'd have to be dead not to be," she said with a small chuckle. "You've got muscles upon muscles, and something about knowing you could bench-press me, but wouldn't hurt me, is a huge turn-on. But I'm asking you to have patience with me. It's not in my nature to jump into bed with a man, which has been an issue in the past."

"I'll never pressure you," Bull told her.

"See, guys say that, then two weeks later they claim they have blue balls and I'm a tease," she said a little sarcastically.

"Sweetheart, I have a hand, and I know how to use it. I've gone a year without having sex, I'm not going to shrivel up and die if we don't make love anytime soon."

"A year?" she asked, her eyes widening.

He nodded. "Yeah. I've been busy. How about you?" Bull couldn't believe he'd asked, but he couldn't have stopped the question if his life had depended on it.

"Um . . ." She looked away from him.

Bull put a finger under her chin and tilted her head up so she had no choice but to look at him. "No judgment here, Sky."

"About nine months. But it was only once, and the guy turned out to be a jerk. He didn't even get me off. Just did his thing and rolled over when he was done."

Bull winced, then promised, "If you ever let me in your bed, or let me take you to mine, I *guarantee* you'll be satisfied."

"For some reason, I believe you," she told him quietly.

"As you should. I give you my word that I won't pressure you to have sex with me. We'll go at your speed. If and when we ever get to that point in our relationship, it means that I'm all in. That this isn't just a casual thing for me. I'm too old to be interested in having sex just for the sake of getting off."

She licked her lips, and he swallowed a groan. There was nothing Bull wanted to do more than lean down and cover her lips with his own. But he'd just promised to move at her speed. He wouldn't make her doubt him this early in their relationship.

"So we'll take things one day at a time?" she asked.

"Absolutely. I know you work every day, but I'd like to see you on the weekends as much as possible. I also know you need to get your lessons planned, but maybe I can hang out with you when you do them? And I can schlep your bags when you run errands, if you'll let me tag along."

"I think I'd like that," she said.

"Me too," he told her. "Now, it's probably time I got you home so you can reflect on everything we talked about. I'm an intense guy," he said honestly, "but you have to know that I'll always treat you with care. I want to see where things between us can go."

"Okay, Carson. I want that too."

Nodding, he reluctantly dropped his hands. He gestured toward the stairs. "After you, my lady."

She rolled her eyes but preceded him up the stairs and into the main room. This time, there were two of the drivers sitting on the couch, watching TV. Eagle and Smoke were in the kitchen, arguing with each other about whatever it was they were making. Gramps was nowhere to be seen.

"Bull!" Jose and Shane yelled at the same time.

"Who's the babe?" Shane asked.

"My girlfriend, Skylar, and I'll ask you to be polite, or I might have to beat you," Bull told the other man.

Shane laughed but nodded at Skylar respectfully. "Sorry, ma'am."

"Oh Lord," she told him. "That makes me feel as if I'm ancient. Skylar will do."

"You leaving already? Before we have a chance to get to know your woman?" Jose asked.

"Yup. She's got shit to do," Bull told his employees.

"Maybe I can come back, and you'll play a round of gin rummy with me," Skylar said with a wicked smile.

"Ooooh, I can teach you all the tricks and how to win," Jose said.

Eagle and Smoke burst out laughing from the kitchen at that.

"What? What'd I say?" Jose protested.

"I'd like that," Skylar said, doing her best to hide her smile and failing.

Bull walked her to the door. "Be back in a bit," he told his friends. "Tell Leigh she can put me in the rotation when I get back."

"Will do," Eagle told him.

Bull walked Skylar out to his car, and soon they were on their way back to her apartment.

"You really do get along with your employees, don't you?" she asked.

"I do," he agreed. "I like them. They work hard, and they're all good men and women."

She didn't say anything the rest of the way to her apartment complex, but the silence was comfortable rather than awkward. Bull pulled into a parking spot and got out to walk her up the stairs to her door.

This time, her neighbors didn't poke their heads out of their apartments, but he wondered if they were still watching.

"I had a good time," Skylar told him as she paused outside her door.

"Me too."

She stared up at him and bit her lip nervously.

"I'll call you later, if that's okay," Bull told her.

She nodded. "I'd like that."

"Have a good rest of the day. Relax, enjoy your Saturday," he said.

"I will."

Wanting to take her in his arms and kiss the hell out of her, Bull forced himself to lean down and kiss her briefly on the lips instead. It was a chaste kiss, and he almost moaned when she licked her lips after he pulled back, as if to savor his taste.

"Be safe," he told her, the words popping out of nowhere. Then Bull stepped away and walked backward, staring at her as he left. When she didn't move, he nodded toward her door. "Go in, sweetheart, so I know you're inside safely."

She nodded and unlocked her door. She opened it and turned back to him once more. "Bye," she said.

"Bye," he told her with a lift of his chin. Then he forced himself to turn and head toward the stairs. He wanted to go inside her place and talk with her some more. Hear more about her childhood, if she liked high school, her relationship with her parents, and more stories about the kids in her class . . . but he kept walking. He'd have time to learn all those things later. He hoped.

He got into his car and looked up at her apartment. The door was shut, and he couldn't see any sign of Skylar. Then his cell vibrated with a text. Before he headed out of the parking lot, he looked down at his phone.

Skylar: Thanks for a great time. Can't wait to talk to you later.

He loved that she hadn't hesitated to contact him. That she didn't seem to be playing games. And that he'd been upgraded from *nice* to *great*. He immediately texted her back.

Bull: Best first date ever.

Bull: I'll call later.

Bull: Have a good rest of the day.

Then he put his phone on the seat next to him and smiled. Skylar Reid was the best thing that had ever happened to him . . . and he'd do whatever it took to convince her of that fact.

Chapter Eight

Sunday evening, Skylar sat on her couch, staring into space. Carson had called the night before, just like he'd said he would. They'd talked for about an hour about nothing in particular. Then he'd called this afternoon, and they'd actually FaceTimed. Again, they hadn't discussed anything specific, but at no time had the conversation lagged or felt awkward.

In fact, she was more comfortable with Carson after only a few days than with some of the men she'd dated for weeks. He seemed interested in her job and asked about her students and what she had planned for them this week. They talked about when he and the others from Silverstone might be able to come and show off their trucks. The more Skylar talked to him, the more she liked him.

This morning when she'd come back from the grocery store, Tiana and Maria had cornered her and wanted all the details about her date with Carson. They'd also let her know they approved of him. They hadn't seen much of him, but after hearing about their date and what had happened at the diner with the tip, they'd been impressed.

When her phone rang, Skylar jumped, wrenched from her thoughts. Laughing at herself, she saw it was her parents' number on the display.

"Hey, Mom," she said as a greeting.

"I might've been your dad, you know," Dayana said with a chuckle.

"Mom, you've been calling me every Sunday night since I moved out. I knew it would be you."

"True. How are you? Did you have a good weekend?"

"I'm good. I had a great weekend," Skylar told her mom, not able to keep the pleasure from her tone.

"Yeah? What happened?"

"I met someone."

"Like, a boy someone?" her mom asked.

Skylar chuckled. "Well, yeah. I actually met him last week when my car died on the 465."

"Are you all right?" Dayana asked in concern, momentarily forgetting the meeting-a-guy thing. "What was wrong with your car? Why didn't you call your dad?"

"Mom, I'm fine. It would've taken Dad forever to get there, and he wouldn't have been able to do anything anyway. I called for a tow."

"I hope it wasn't one of those disreputable places," her mom cautioned. "Where's your car now? Do you need to borrow one of ours until yours is fixed?"

"It wasn't, and my car's already fixed."

"Really? What was wrong?"

Skylar didn't want to admit that she wasn't sure. When Carson had brought it back to her at the school, he hadn't offered specifics about what had been done, and when she'd called Stan to take care of the bill, he'd quoted her some paltry amount that she'd known couldn't be right. When she'd challenged him on it, he'd gone on and on about clogged air filters and other car stuff she had no idea about. In the end, it was easier to just thank him, pay what he asked for, and move on.

"Nothing serious," she told her mom. "But the man I met is part owner of the towing company that I called. He was the one who showed up."

"Really? Tell me more," Dayana said.

Skylar chuckled. "His name is Carson, and his company is Silverstone Towing. He's tall, has black hair, is an Army veteran, and he tips really well."

"Hmmmm, all that sounds good, but does he treat you well?"

"He does," Skylar told her mom. "I kinda worry that he's *too* nice."

"In what way?"

"I don't know. I mean, we've only been on one date so far, a lunch date yesterday. But everyone at Silverstone seems to really like and respect him. I met his friends, the guys he owns the business with, and they were all very polite too. Thanks to Daddy, I kicked their butts at gin rummy, and they didn't even get upset. They seemed to think it was hilarious that I was so good at it. Anyway, I've only been out to lunch with Carson, but . . . Mom . . . we really clicked."

"Have you talked to him since your date?"

"Yeah. He called last night, and today we FaceTimed." Her mom was quiet for so long, Skylar was afraid the connection had cut off. "Mom?"

"I'm here," Dayana said.

"What are you thinking?"

"I'm thinking *you're* thinking too hard about this guy. You don't have to decide if you're going to marry him right this second. Go out, have fun, see where things can go."

"But what if he hurts me?"

"What if he does? Skylar, you're an adult. Just because one boyfriend hurt you doesn't mean they all will. You're old enough to use your words to tell him when he's overstepped and when he does something you don't like. You know as well as I do that even in the best relationships, being hurt is inevitable. The main point is how you deal with that. And I'm not talking about physical hurt. If this Carson guy so much as gives you a bruise, you drop him like a hot potato. But if the hurt is because of miscommunication or a misunderstanding between you, then you need to talk about it like adults."

"You're being awfully encouraging about this," Skylar observed. "In the past when I've told you that I'm dating someone, you've cautioned me to go slow, to make sure I'm not with him just because I'm lonely or because everyone else around me is married."

"You're right," Dayana told her daughter. "But this guy's different."

Shocked, Skylar asked, "How do you know that?"

"I can hear it in your voice," her mom said confidently. "You've had other men call you right after a date, and you were annoyed by it. You thought they were moving too fast. That you'd only been on one date, and you weren't sure you wanted to see them again. This Carson guy has called you twice since yesterday, and instead of being annoyed, you sound as if you're thrilled."

"True," Skylar admitted.

"What makes him different?"

Skylar thought about her mom's question for a moment, then sighed. "It's hard to say. He just seems . . . unsure. And that sounds weird, because he's definitely not unsure about wanting to go out with me. I think if he had his way, I'd be wearing his letter jacket and have his class ring on my finger."

Her mom chuckled, and Skylar continued. "It's just something I sense, that he wants to be with me, but something is telling him to back off, that he's not worthy or something. I don't know."

"What *do* you know about him?" her mom asked.

"His mom left when he was little, and his dad died when he was seventeen. He joined the Army right after high school, and he met his friends there. They all got out at the same time and started Silverstone Towing. I guess one of his friends inherited a lot of money, and that's how they got it going. But, Mom, you should see this place. From the outside it looks awful. Like a run-down, piece-of-crap business. But inside, it's so nice. I mean, *really* nice. Full kitchen, video games for the employees, sleeping rooms. And all of the employees I met seemed so happy to be there. I can't help but think that's because of Carson and his friends and the way they run the company. It's impressive."

"Has he ever been married? Does he have any kids?"

"He said he hasn't been married, and I don't think so on the kid thing, but we're still getting to know each other," Skylar said a little defensively.

"I wasn't criticizing," her mom rebuked gently. "You know your dad and I want you to be happy. And this Carson sounds lovely. You also know I wouldn't be your mom if I didn't caution you to make sure you know who he is inside before you blindly accept what you see from the outside. He might be muscular and good looking, but if that hides a black heart, it won't matter *how* cute he is."

"I know," Skylar said, and she did. She valued her mom's opinion more than anyone else's in the world.

"Are we going to get to meet him?" she asked, surprising the hell out of Skylar.

"Wow, really?"

"Yes. I've never heard you so excited about someone before. If Carson has impressed you this much after one date, then your dad and I want to meet him sooner rather than later."

"I'd like to bring him by for dinner sometime, but I'm not sure when."

"Does he work a lot?"

Skylar thought about that. She wasn't sure about *that* either. Yes, he'd come to help her when she'd called Silverstone, but she'd gotten the impression that he and his friends worked when they wanted, that they didn't have a set schedule. "I'm not sure. I mean, I would think so, since he co-owns the business."

"Okay, well, if he's free one weekend, you just let us know, and we'll welcome him up here for lunch or dinner."

"Thanks, Mom."

"Of course. We love you and just want the best for you. And if this Carson is it, then we'll be thrilled. Now . . . how's work? How are those adorable kids of yours?"

For the next twenty minutes or so, Skylar caught her mom up with what was going on with her students. She told her that Sandra's situation hadn't changed. Her dad was still working an incredible amount of hours to try to keep a roof over their heads, which meant she was staying late practically every day until she could be picked up. The after-school program only went until five o'clock, and Skylar was hanging out with Sandra on the playground until Shawn could come get her, which was usually five thirty at the earliest.

She told her about finding matching T-shirts at Goodwill and giving them to Chad and Brodie and how they had been so proud to wear them and prove that they really were twins. Keilani was teaching everyone some basic hula steps that she'd learned back in dance class in Hawaii, and Zahir was learning English so quickly that Skylar thought he'd be the best reader in the class by the end of the school year.

"I'm so glad you've found your calling," her mom told her when Skylar finally ran out of things to say about her students. "It's obvious you're not only good at what you do, but that you love it too."

"I do," Skylar said. "They're all so innocent at this age. I'm not an idiot, I know bullying has been starting earlier and earlier, but in my class, at least, none of that is happening this year. I love seeing Gwen help Zahir with his colors and was so proud when Cedric comforted Marisol when she tripped on the playground last week. I wish they could stay innocent forever."

"I used to think that about you too," Skylar's mom said.

"I'm pretty sure Carson thinks I'm still completely naive," Skylar said. "I guess he's seen a lot from his time in the military and because he was orphaned so young."

"Back to Carson, huh?" Dayana said with a chuckle.

"Oh . . . sorry," Skylar said sheepishly.

"Don't be. I love how excited you are about him. Growing up where you did and how you did—with plenty of money, food on the table, and no worries about having a roof over your head—definitely spoiled you. But I won't apologize for it. If Carson's any kind of man, he'll do whatever he can to preserve the rosy outlook you have on the world."

"I know the world can be a bad place," Skylar protested. "I see it every day with my students."

"You see it, but you don't live it," Dayana said. "There's a difference."

"I know, Mom," Skylar said, feeling irritated.

"All I'm saying is that I'm glad your Carson sees who you are. I love how you see the good in people. That you have compassion for your fellow man. You've got a tender heart. You always have."

Skylar knew her mom was right. She was always moved to tears when she saw homeless families panhandling. She sometimes volunteered at a homeless shelter downtown, but it made her so depressed that she couldn't do more to help the people there. She tried to overtip when she could, and she never hesitated to give her time to help others . . . like the Archers. She was a true believer in karma, that those who worked hard would be rewarded, and those who did harm to others would get what they deserved someday. "I love you, Mom."

"Love you too, Sky. Keep me updated on your young man, okay?"

"I will. Tell Dad that I love him."

"I will. I know you've got lesson plans you need to do since it's Sunday, so I'll let you go. Have a good week."

"You too."

"Bye."

"Bye." Skylar clicked off the phone and stared into space for a few minutes. Talking to her mom always made her feel better about whatever was going on in her life.

Taking a deep breath, she reached over and pulled her computer onto her lap. She needed to get to work and plan the week's lessons. She'd never be able to stick to her plan exactly—how could she with fourteen kindergartners—but if she didn't have a plan, things usually ended up in chaos. So she'd learned to do what she could to schedule each day and then do her best to stick with it.

Looking ahead, Skylar thought she might be able to get the other teachers in her unit to agree to concentrate on trucks the week after next. That gave them enough time to gather books to read, prepare bulletin boards, and generally turn their rooms into truck central. She'd talk to everyone tomorrow to see what they thought. Then she'd check with Carson about his schedule.

The more she thought about the large tow trucks coming to Eastlake, the more excited she got. The kids, young and old, would love it. And so would she. She'd get to see Carson outside the weekends.

Loving the feeling of anticipation and hoping what seemed like a promising relationship worked out, Skylar turned her mind to her computer and planning for the week.

~

The next morning, Bull sat in the safe room with his friends.

"We like her," Eagle said without beating around the bush.

Bull didn't need his friends' approval, but he couldn't deny he was relieved to get it anyway.

"She's spunky," Smoke observed.

"I see what you mean about the naive thing," Gramps added. "And I don't mean that in a bad way."

"I know you don't," Bull reassured him.

"It's just that she's such a breath of fresh air. Her emotions are right there on her face to read. She wasn't sure about meeting us, but she was still friendly and open. And she didn't seem to look down her nose at Silverstone because it's a blue-collar operation," Gramps went on.

"Well, you didn't see her reaction to the outside," Bull said with a small chuckle. "The camo job we've done seems to be working."

"Speaking of which, the weeds are out of control," Smoke complained.

"Not to mention the place was a fucking mess this morning when we came in," Eagle added. "No one did the dishes last night, and the trash stunk to high heaven. Someone brought in Chinese and didn't finish it. The shrimp smelled like shit in the trash can this morning."

"Why'd someone bring takeout when we've got a whole refrigerator full of shit for them to eat?" Smoke asked.

"Well . . . we did last week, but apparently just about everything's been eaten, and this morning, the pickin's are pretty slim," Gramps said.

Bull didn't mind that the topic of conversation had shifted away from Skylar. She was on his mind pretty much all the time, but that didn't mean he really wanted his friends dissecting their relationship.

"Fuck, I hate food shopping," Eagle said.

"I might have a solution to the lack of food, the out-of-control weeds, *and* the sloppiness of the rooms around here," Bull said.

He suddenly had three pairs of eyes focused on him.

"Yeah?" Smoke asked, definitely interested.

Bull went on to explain what he wanted to do, and not even ten minutes later, they had a plan. Bull was in charge of setting the wheels in motion, which he'd do as soon as possible, and Eagle would get on the computer and do some research.

They decided to come back that afternoon and check up on the news from the weekend, but in the meantime, Gramps and Smoke would clean up the public areas and start washing the sheets from the bedrooms. Eagle reluctantly volunteered to do a food run to refill the cupboards and fridge, and Bull was in charge of making sure all the trucks were stocked with toys for kids and the car seats were still secure and checking that they all had plenty of windshield-washer fluid.

As Bull headed outside, he couldn't stop his mind from wandering to Skylar once more . . . and he didn't want to. He'd called her twice that weekend, and for a man who never talked on the phone, he'd been pleased to sit on his ass and chat with her.

Skylar was funny. Smart. And she made him feel as if he was normal.

Bull knew he'd *never* be normal. He could fake it well—he'd learned to do that during his time on the Delta Force team, and he'd certainly perfected it over the last five years living in the civilian world. But he and his friends were always one step away from leaving normal in their dust.

Bull knew Skylar couldn't do lunch during the week or even really talk to him, but that didn't mean he couldn't let her know he was thinking about her. The more he considered it, the more the thought appealed to him.

Before beginning his chores with the trucks, he made a quick call.

He'd have enough time around lunch to run to Eastlake and leave a small gift for her before coming back to Silverstone and getting down to business. He should have enough time to get everything done. Besides, if he was a bit late, Eagle and the others wouldn't care. His flexible schedule was one of the many things he loved about owning his own business.

~

Skylar had just dropped her class off at the music room and had thirty minutes to herself. She was about to head back to her room, to enjoy the peace and quiet, when the school secretary caught her in the hall. "You've got a delivery in the main office."

Skylar scrunched her nose. "Are you sure?"

"I'm sure. It's on my desk. I'm heading to grab a quick lunch."

Skylar thanked the woman and turned to go the opposite direction, toward the office at the entrance of the school.

"Oh, and Skylar?"

She turned back around. "Yeah?"

"He seems like a keeper."

With those parting words, the secretary hurried in the direction of the teachers' lounge.

Feeling butterflies in her belly, Skylar headed for the main office. She saw the delivery the second she opened the door. A brown paper bag with her name written on it in large block letters sat on the desk. She walked over, and instead of looking inside the bag, she dislodged the small envelope that had been stapled to the bag and opened it.

> I thought maybe I'd help get your students excited about truck week.
>
> ~Bull

She'd figured the gift was from Carson, after the secretary's hint, and she was right. But her guess that he'd brought her lunch or some other small gift had been completely wrong. When she opened the bag, tears sprang to her eyes.

She pulled out one of the cellophane-wrapped sugar cookies inside. It was brightly decorated and in the shape of a tow truck. Whoever had decorated the confections had done an amazing job, making them as lifelike as possible.

Carson had brought her *students* a present. Not her.

Nothing could've endeared him to her more.

She put the cookie back in the bag and picked it up, carrying the sack to her room as if it contained precious jewels.

He didn't know that Ignacio had celiac disease and couldn't eat gluten. Or that Karlee was a diabetic. He'd just been trying to do something nice for her . . . and her students. She'd had boyfriends give her flowers before. One man had even bought her a necklace. But no gift meant as much as the two dozen sugar cookies in the plain brown paper bag that she held in her hands at the moment.

She'd talked to the other teachers that morning, and they were all one hundred percent in for truck week. Skylar just had to coordinate with the local fire and police departments to see if they'd also come with some of their vehicles one day the week after next, and things would be perfect.

She'd let her students know what was coming up, and they'd have cookies in the shape of tow trucks. It would mean they'd be hyper that afternoon, but Skylar didn't care.

She set out the cookies, and grabbed one of the gluten-free snacks she had on hand for Ignacio, as well as some low-sugar fruit snacks for Karlee. Waiting impatiently, Skylar looked at the clock. The kids would be back shortly, and she couldn't stop smiling.

~

Bull was studying the Department of Justice's information sheet on Jehad Serwan Mostafa, when his cell phone rang. Eagle, Smoke, and Gramps were also looking for more information on Mostafa, a US citizen fighting with a Somalia-based terrorist organization. He'd grown up in San Diego but had left the States and joined Al-Shabaab after his Muslim beliefs had gotten more and more radical.

They'd gotten reports that he'd recently been identified and was reportedly living in a small town in Kenya. He was on the FBI's *Most Wanted* list because of his involvement with the terrorist organization. He played an active role in terrorist acts and would continue to do so if he wasn't stopped. And if the latest information they'd received panned out, it was likely Silverstone would be sent in to eliminate him sooner rather than later.

But when Bull saw Skylar's name on the display of his phone, all thoughts of their next target were wiped from his mind.

"Are you all right?" he asked in lieu of a greeting.

"Thank you," Skylar said immediately. "Your gift was perfect."

Bull did his best to get his heart to stop beating so fast. He shouldn't have been so alarmed when he'd seen her name on his phone, but for some reason, he was. "You're welcome."

"Seriously. I hadn't planned on telling the kids about truck week yet, but the cookies were a perfect way to introduce the topic and to get them excited. And believe me, they're excited."

"Good. We helped a lady who owns a cookie shop not too long ago, and I thought she might be able to make some cookies in the shape of our tow trucks. She gave me a huge discount since it was the first time she'd tried it, but if you ask me, they looked pretty darn good."

"They were perfect," she told him softly.

"Where are you now?" he asked, looking at his watch. It was six fifteen. He hadn't realized he and the others had been in the safe room, poring over the intel they'd received on Mostafa, for so long.

"I'm still at school. Specifically, I'm watching Sandra play on the playground. Her dad called to say he'd be even later than usual today. He had some meeting that went long, and then they were trying to finish up a landscaping job."

A pang of guilt struck Bull, and he almost admitted what he'd been up to that day but decided to keep it to himself until it was a done deal. "I'm sorry you're still at work."

"All part of the job," she said, not seeming put out at all. And Bull realized she probably wasn't. She honestly didn't mind staying late to make sure one of her students was safe.

"I got all my planning done when Sandra was at the after-school program. Hanging out with her for a while after five o'clock isn't a big deal. I just wanted to call and thank you. You didn't have to do that."

"I know. I wanted to," Bull told her.

"And you made quite the impression on the secretary," Skylar said.

"I didn't say much to her," Bull admitted. "She had to look inside the bag to make sure I wasn't bringing in an explosive or something, but otherwise, I told her it was for you, and she said she'd make sure you got it. That's it."

"Well, it's not every day that someone brings something to the school for an entire class like that. Not someone who isn't related to one of the students, I mean."

"Your students are important to you," Bull said. "Therefore, they're important to me."

She didn't say anything for a long moment.

"Sky?"

"I'm here. I just . . . you scare the hell out of me, Bull."

Bull looked up and saw his friends watching him, not even pretending to give him space. One of them dating seriously *was* a new thing . . . for all of them.

"You have nothing to fear from me," he told her honestly.

"Right." She huffed out a laugh. "Only having my heart broken when you get tired of me working so much and being second fiddle to a bunch of five-year-olds."

"I work too," he reminded her. "And I can't put into words how impressed I am with your determination to give those kids a good start in life. Most of the time how a person turns out as an adult is shaped when they're a kid. And with you in their corner, they've got a hell of a good example."

"Thanks, Carson."

"You're welcome. I know you're busy watching Sandra, and Archer will probably be there soon to get her. Drive safe, and let me know when you get home?"

"I will."

"You up to talking a bit tonight?" he couldn't help but ask. "I won't keep you up late. I'd just love to talk more later."

"I'd like that," she told him. "I usually go to bed around nine thirty, so . . . maybe we can talk around nine?"

Bull did his best to not think about Skylar in bed. "Sounds perfect. I'll talk to you later."

"Okay. Bye, Carson."

"Bye, sweetheart."

"That was slick," Smoke commented after he'd hung up.

"Cookies for her class. Damn, you've got moves, bro," Eagle said with a smirk.

"Fuck off," Bull told his friends.

"What else do you have planned?" Gramps asked.

Bull wasn't surprised his friend had asked. Gramps always seemed to be thinking ahead, and he knew Bull better than he probably knew himself. He smiled. "Oh, a little of this and a little of that."

"Fuck, I should be taking notes," Eagle said. "I probably would've just sent her flowers or something."

"I wanted to do something different," Bull noted.

"She know about Archer?" Smoke asked.

Bull shook his head. "No. I don't want to get her hopes up until it's a done deal."

"But he seemed interested when you talked to him today, right?" Gramps asked.

"Oh yeah. Especially when I told him he'd be working eight-hour days, forty-hour weeks, getting double what he's getting at the three jobs he's doing now, *and* benefits. He's definitely interested. He signed the background-check papers today and told me he's clean. I believe him. No one can work as hard as he does and be on drugs or drinking himself into oblivion all the time."

"Time will tell with the background check and the inquiries we've put in to his current bosses," Smoke said.

"True. He did ask if he could stay on with his current jobs for the time being. He wanted to give an appropriate amount of notice. He didn't want to leave anyone in the lurch, especially at the diner. He seemed very worried about leaving his boss without a breakfast cook."

"Hard worker and loyal. A good combination," Gramps noted.

"That's what I thought too. I told him it wouldn't be an issue. That he could continue to work until they hired his replacements, no matter how long it took, and he was welcome here anytime. Even if he's not officially on the clock, he was still part of the Silverstone Towing family," Bull said. "We can figure out what hours will work best for him after he's cleared to be hired."

"Skylar's gonna probably want to give you a *very* personal thank-you gift for hiring her student's father," Eagle said, wagging his eyebrows suggestively.

"I didn't do this to try to get in her good graces," Bull argued. "I did it because it's the right thing to do . . . for Silverstone Towing, Archer, *and* his daughter. She shouldn't be by herself as much as she is. This past weekend, Skylar told me that he wakes Sandra up at three thirty in the morning to bring her next door to his neighbor's house when he leaves to go to the diner. She gets the little girl up and ready and to the bus stop so she can get to school. She never sees her dad, and that's just not right."

"I agree," Smoke said. "I also think it's the right thing to not tell Skylar until it's a done deal."

Bull nodded. He knew it was. He'd also not lied when he'd said he wasn't trying to get Archer hired at Silverstone Towing to try to get in Skylar's good graces . . . or her pants.

"I don't know about you guys," Gramps said, "but my eyes are crossing looking at this shit. The tip about Mostafa seems to be legit."

"It pisses me off that he was raised in the US, went to college out in San Diego, and *now* he's instructing terrorists on how to kill Americans," Eagle said in disgust.

"The fact that he's knee deep in things over there, conspiring with other terrorist groups, and was caught on that leaked video, gleefully using explosives in one of their camps to blow up his own countrymen, is fucked up," Smoke added.

"So we're in agreement that he needs to be stopped?" Bull asked.

All three of his friends nodded.

"I'll talk to Willis," Gramps said. "See what else he can get us. If we're going to go to Africa to find this asshole, we need a lot more intel. We don't want to be wandering around there aimlessly. Get in, get out. That's the goal for this op."

"Isn't that the goal for every op?" Eagle asked with a grin.

"Yeah, but you know what I mean," Gramps said with a smirk.

"I do. And there's nothing else we can do tonight. Let's go home, and we'll start this up tomorrow afternoon, after Gramps has time to get in touch with Willis," Smoke suggested.

Standing, Bull put his hands on the small of his back and leaned backward, groaning. He'd been sitting for a long time, and his body was letting him know it.

He said his goodbyes to his friends and headed through the basement and up the stairs. He couldn't wait to talk to Skylar later tonight. He hoped it would be the beginning of a routine for them. He couldn't imagine anything better than hearing her voice right before he went to bed.

~

Jay Ricketts lay still in the dense foliage of the woods bordering the parking lot at Eastlake Elementary School. He wasn't afraid of being spotted. He had on his camouflage pants and shirt. And besides, he'd been staking out the playground for two weeks now, and not one person had noticed him.

He knew he shouldn't be there, but he couldn't help himself. He stared at the red-haired teacher who was typically at the playground every day with the little black girl. The woman had just hung up her cell phone and put it in her pocket and was now pushing the girl on the swings. Both were laughing, and Jay's heart literally ached at the sight.

She was beautiful. He couldn't keep his eyes off her.

It had been a long time since he'd fallen for someone, and she'd caught his eye one day when he'd been walking by the school. He'd been mesmerized by how pretty she was. Then he'd heard her laughing . . . and that was that.

He wanted her.

And what Jay wanted, he got. It was just a matter of watching and waiting for the right time.

The woman looked at her watch and stopped pushing the girl. They both walked back toward the doors to the school together, and Jay looked at his own watch. He slowly pulled out the little notebook he always had on him and recorded the time.

Most days, the duo left the playground earlier than they had tonight. He frowned. He didn't like when schedules changed.

There were only a few cars in the parking lot, and Jay could see the gate at the back of the playground without a problem. It was broken. He'd come to the school at two in the morning one night and made sure it would swing open easily without looking as if it was malfunctioning. He'd bent the locking mechanism, so the gate would close but wouldn't latch.

His plan had to be perfect, with no miscalculations, if she was going to be his.

But the later hour that they were at the playground bothered him. He needed to be *sure* about his timing. If he was going to steal her away, he had to be able to account for every variable. He wasn't going to prison again. He wouldn't survive a second stint locked up. He had to be smarter than the cops, smarter than everyone.

Jay stayed exactly where he was until the petite teacher walked out of the school and entered the small parking lot. He watched as she looked around for anything that might be a danger to her. Little did she know, he was lying nearby—and if he wanted to, he could have her incapacitated in seconds.

But it wasn't time. Not yet.

She clicked the locks on her shitty Corolla and got in.

Jay waited until she was long gone before slowly easing out of his hiding spot. He cut through the small patch of woods toward the abandoned row house he'd made his own for the time being. His plan was to bring his prize back there, lie low for a few days, then get the hell out of Dodge with his new bride.

His cock twitched in his pants, and Jay couldn't help but smile.

Making sure no one saw him, he ducked under the board that was nailed horizontally over the back door of his temporary dwelling. He didn't disturb the cobwebs that hung throughout the rooms on the first floor as he made his way to the basement.

He'd found a mattress in the trash that didn't look to be too dirty and had brought it inside. He checked the chain he'd fastened to the floor and was satisfied when it didn't budge. The handcuff at the end would go around her ankle, and she'd be well and truly captured. His to do whatever he wanted.

Lying on the mattress he'd brought here for her comfort, Jay's hand went to his groin. As the waning sunlight crept across the room from the small window high up in the wall, he closed his eyes and fantasized about the one who would be his.

"Soon," Jay moaned as he pleasured himself.

Chapter Nine

Two weeks. That's how long it had been since their first date. Skylar couldn't believe it had only been fourteen days. It seemed like she'd known Carson forever. That was probably because they'd talked every day since he'd taken her to the diner and given her a tour of Silverstone Towing.

Sometimes they only talked for ten minutes, but most of the time they were on the phone for at least an hour. He'd often call when she was on her way home from work, and they'd talk through her making dinner and eating, as she decided what to wear the next day, and after she got settled on her couch. Sometimes he even called back after she'd checked her lessons to make sure she was still on track for the week and after she'd climbed into bed.

Those were the times she liked best. It seemed very intimate to be talking to him when she was cuddled up under her covers. He'd asked to FaceTime one night, and while she'd been reluctant, she'd let him talk her into it. She'd propped the phone up on the pillow next to her, and she'd actually fallen asleep while he'd been talking. She'd woken up an hour later to see that he hadn't disconnected the call. He'd been watching her sleep.

Skylar knew if she told anyone about that, they'd say it was creepy, but she hadn't felt weirded out in the least. When she'd woken up, he'd said, "If possible, you look even more innocent when you sleep. I didn't want to disconnect and have you wake up and be embarrassed that you fell asleep on me. I'll talk to you tomorrow, okay?"

Carson knew her so well, even after only two weeks. She *would've* been embarrassed for falling asleep on him.

Talking every day had possibly forged a deeper bond between them than if they'd gone on dates each of the last fourteen days. They often talked about nothing important, but she'd also learned more about how close he and his friends were.

Carson had told her that he and his team had been disciplined, which had prompted them to get out of the Army. She didn't know the details because he'd said they were classified but that getting out had been the best decision they'd made. She also knew he and his friends had once been captured by an enemy and tortured. She'd cried when she'd heard that story, and he'd quickly assured her they'd been rescued within a few days and pointed out that they were all okay.

Skylar had told him about her first year teaching, how awful she was. She hadn't been prepared at all, and she feared she'd hurt her young charges more than helped them. He, of course, had disagreed and tried to make her feel better by telling her that Silverstone's first year of business had been a disaster. Every single employee had quit at some point during the year. They'd learned from their mistakes and realized that the power of Silverstone was the employees themselves. Not how fancy the trucks were or that the owners were veterans.

They'd gone out last weekend. Carson had picked her up around ten in the morning on Saturday, and they'd spent the entire day together. They'd had lunch, played some cards at Silverstone, watched a movie in one of the small sleeping rooms. She'd lain against him and simply enjoyed being held as the movie had played. He'd taken her home and kissed the hell out of her in his car before walking her up to her apartment.

Then he'd brought her Chinese takeout on Sunday. He hadn't stayed, saying he knew the weekends were the only time she had to catch up on her errands and to plan her week, but he'd wanted to make sure she ate all right.

And almost every day, he'd delivered something to the school. Sometimes it had been a treat for her entire class, other times it had been just for her.

It had only been two weeks, but Skylar knew she was head over heels for Carson. Yes, she'd fallen fast, but how could she not? Everything he did seemed sincere.

Though, every now and then, she caught a glimpse of . . . something . . . in his tone. As if he was just waiting for the other shoe to drop, and she'd tell him she wasn't interested.

She had no idea why someone like Carson had such low self-esteem, but she hated it. He was considerate, patient, funny, protective, and very smart. He had great friends, and everyone at Silverstone Towing seemed to respect and like him.

Today was Friday, and Carson was picking her up at school. She'd left her keys with the secretary earlier so Carson could pick up her car and drive it to her apartment. One of his friends was going to pick him up there and take him back to Silverstone Towing until it was time for their date. They were going out for dinner, and she couldn't wait. Normally, she'd want to go home and get changed and doll herself up, but Carson had promised dressing up wouldn't be necessary.

Sandra's dad was picking up his daughter around five thirty, and then Skylar was free for the rest of the weekend.

They were outside on the playground, as usual, when Skylar thought she saw something moving in the trees behind the teachers' parking area. There was only one car in the lot, the secretary's, as Carson had already picked hers up.

Tilting her head and squinting to try to see better, Skylar didn't notice anything out of the ordinary. The wind blew the leaves on the trees, and she decided that had to be what she'd glimpsed. And she knew talking to Carson was making her just a little paranoid. He was constantly warning her to be safe, to be on the lookout for someone who might want to do her harm as she went about her daily activities. She even had a bottle of wasp spray on one of the tall shelves in her room—out of reach of little hands, but still available—just in case.

Spotting movement out of the corner of her eye, she turned to watch Shawn's beat-up vehicle pull into the guest parking area.

"Sandra! Your dad's here!"

The little girl scrambled off the monkey bars and came running toward her teacher as fast as her little legs could carry her. They went inside and grabbed her backpack, loaded down with more books and snacks that Skylar had packed earlier, and went down to the office to meet her dad.

Skylar smiled at the enthusiastic greeting Sandra gave her father. She was always happy to see him, which made Skylar's heart feel good.

"I wanted to thank you again," Shawn said.

"For what?" Skylar asked.

"Well, for not minding when I'm late to pick up Sandra."

"It's fine, Shawn. We've been over this. I truly *don't* mind. It lets me get caught up on schoolwork so I don't have to do it when I go home."

"Well, I also wanted to tell you that in the near future, it won't be an issue anymore."

"What do you mean?" Skylar asked.

"I got a new job. A *good* one," Shawn said. "I'll be working eight to four, so I can be here to get Sandra on time."

"That's great news!" Skylar said, genuinely pleased for the man, and for Sandra.

"And I have *you* to thank for it."

"Me?" she asked in confusion.

"Yeah. I know you had to have said something to Bull. When I met him a few weeks ago, he said he'd heard good things about me, and he had a proposition for me. When he told me about the job, I about fell over! Sounded too good to be true, if I'm being honest. I don't know nothin' about cars, but he didn't care."

Skylar was stunned. Carson had offered Shawn a job? "What kind of work?" she asked.

Shawn chuckled. "Well, doin' what I'm doin' now. Cleanin', landscapin', and cookin'." He leaned toward her and said softly, "With *benefits*. He's paying me more than I was makin' doin' three jobs! It's a miracle, and I have *you* to thank. So on behalf of me and Sandy, thank you."

Skylar swallowed hard and put her hand on the man's biceps and squeezed. She was thrilled for both Sandra and her dad. This *was* a miracle for them, and her heart felt as if it was going to burst. "I'm so happy for you."

"I didn't want to quit without givin' notice, so I'm still gonna be late picking Sandra up for two weeks or so, if that's all right."

"It's no problem," Skylar assured him. "Sandra and I get along just fine, and it's my pleasure to look after her until you can get here to pick her up. I'm happy for you, Shawn. I know how hard you've been working."

"Thanks." Shawn looked down at his little girl. "Want to stop and get some chicken nuggets for dinner? We're celebratin'!"

"Yay!" Sandra said happily.

Shawn nodded at her, then turned and headed out of the little office.

"Knew that man of yours was a keeper from that first bag of cookies he dropped off," the secretary said.

Skylar turned to her and smiled. "He's pretty amazing."

"And speak of the devil," the other woman said, nodding to the large window in the office.

Skylar looked into the hallway and saw Carson speaking with Shawn. They shook hands before Carson turned to head to the office. He caught sight of her through the window and smiled.

She had a feeling that smile would always make her knees go weak. Skylar grinned back, said goodbye to the secretary, and exited the office to meet him.

"Hey," he said, but she didn't give him a chance to say anything else. She went up on her tiptoes, put a hand on the back of his head, and tugged him down to her. He didn't resist, and her lips met his in a fierce kiss. Not caring that they were standing in the middle of the hall in an elementary school, Skylar showed him without words how amazing she thought he was.

She was panting when she drew back from him. He'd wrapped both arms around her and was holding her against the length of his body. "What was that for?" he asked. "Not that I'm complaining, mind you."

Chuckling, Skylar said, "Because you're amazing. I just heard what you did for Shawn."

Carson merely shrugged. "You said he was a hard worker, and the jobs he had were all exactly what we needed at Silverstone."

Cupping his cheek, she couldn't find the words to tell him how happy she was. Skylar knew she was a goner. Whatever this man asked of her, she'd gladly give. No questions asked.

"You ready to go?" he asked.

"I need to grab my purse and bag."

Without another word, Carson wrapped his arm around her waist and turned her in the direction of her room. They walked down the hallway arm in arm, and Skylar knew she'd never been so happy.

When they got to her room, she made a beeline for her desk to grab her things. She couldn't wait to hang out with Carson. She enjoyed talking to him on the phone, but she loved being with him in person a lot more. She hoped she never lost that giddy feeling that filled her whenever she saw him.

"Are you sure I look okay for where we're going? If you swing by my place, I can change really fast. It won't take more than five minutes."

"You're perfect," Carson told her. "I thought, if it's okay with you, we might go back to my place. And I promise this isn't a chance for me to pressure you for anything. I just thought after a long week of work, you might like to kick back a bit and not worry about what you're wearing or other people. I've ordered from Mama Carolla's. Eagle said he didn't mind picking it up for us and bringing it by my apartment. I know Italian is kind of out of favor, what with all the carbs and stuff, but I guarantee you haven't eaten better Italian than Mama Carolla's."

Skylar's mouth began to water just thinking about it. "I love that place," she said. "I haven't eaten there in forever."

"So you're okay with coming back to my place? I swear I'm not trying to angle for sex. We can go out if you prefer."

"I can't think of anything better than relaxing with you in comfort," she told him honestly.

His smile returned. "Good."

"Carson?" Skylar asked.

"Yeah?"

"I'm falling for you," she blurted. She noticed the surprised look on his face, but kept going before she lost her nerve. "I know it's only been a few weeks, and we haven't really hung out much, but I feel as if I know you really well from all our phone conversations. But . . . I'm kinda freaking out."

"About what?"

"I just . . . please don't be playing me. If you make me fall in love with you and then turn out to be a closet abuser, or you're putting on a huge show, it'll destroy me."

He put his hands on either side of her neck and tilted her head up so she had no choice but to look him in the eyes. "I'm not an abuser," he told her seriously. "I'd rather pull my own fingernails out by the roots than do anything that would hurt you. And I'm in the same boat as you. I've become a clock watcher . . . waiting impatiently for five thirty to roll around so I can hear your voice again. I'm not perfect, but being around you makes me want to be a better man. Makes me wish sometimes that I was more worthy of being *your* man. But if you're falling . . . Sky, I'm already there. I can't believe no one has snatched you up already, but that's their loss and my gain."

"Carson," she whispered, his words making goose bumps break out on her arms.

"I've got secrets," he admitted. "Some people would say that you should stay far, far away from me. But I swear to you that nothing I've done, and nothing I'll do in the future, will ever touch you. You're safe with me."

Skylar wasn't sure what he meant, and she felt a little uneasy with both his words and the intensity behind them. But any discomfort over what he'd meant was lost with his *next* words.

"For a long time, it was only me and my dad against the world. He meant everything, and I lost him. I thought I'd never feel that type of connection again. Then I met Eagle, Smoke, and Gramps. I'd found a new family. I'd do anything for those guys. But having you in my life these past couple weeks has made me realize that while they're important to me . . . you're even more so. I want to be the kind of man you look up to and respect. I want to be *everything* to you, just as you're beginning to feel like everything to me."

Skylar swallowed, not sure what to say.

"Shit, I know. Too soon. Sorry. Just know that I don't take you for granted. You can trust me. I'll be there when you need me, always."

In a lot of ways, he was correct. It *was* too soon. But deep down, it felt right.

After taking a deep breath, she said, "How about we eat some Italian tonight and see where things go from there?"

For a second, Carson's grip on her tightened, then he nodded and brushed her cheek with the back of his fingers. "Deal," he said. He reached for her bag and swung it over his shoulder, and they walked hand in hand out of her classroom and toward the visitors' parking lot.

Skylar ogled him as he rounded the front of the car to the driver's side after making sure she was comfortably seated, marveling that he was hers. Everything about their relationship had been in fast-forward, but as promised, he hadn't pressured her. Not once. In fact, he'd reminded her more than once they'd move at whatever speed she was comfortable with.

But sitting next to him as he drove them to his apartment, Skylar was more certain than ever that Carson was the man she'd been waiting for her entire life. She'd begun to think she'd never find him, but then one clanking car later . . . there he was.

Resting her head on the seat behind her, Skylar took a deep breath. She was excited to see Carson's apartment. She didn't know what kind of secrets he might have, but how bad could they be? He co-owned a towing business with his friends. His employees respected him, and she had firsthand knowledge that he was a good guy.

He was probably worried about what he'd done while in the military and thought she might judge him for it. Well, she wouldn't. Being in the Army was honorable, and if he thought she was going to run because of what he'd done in his past, he would find out she was made of sterner stuff than that.

Until he was ready to share his secrets, she was going to enjoy spending time with him and getting to know him better.

~

Four hours later, Bull sat on his couch with a drowsy Skylar snuggled up against his side. She'd told him how much she loved his roomy apartment. It had three bedrooms and a huge living room that opened to the kitchen. It was modern, and she'd commented on how many safety measures were in place simply to get inside the building. There was a code to get into the parking garage, then another to get into the lobby. There was a security guard stationed there who checked everyone's ID before they were allowed onto the elevator. Finally, Bull used a keycard to give the elevator access to his top-floor apartment.

Of course, he then had several locks on the actual door to his place.

Considering what he did for Silverstone, Bull wasn't taking any chances with his safety. Or hers. He knew she thought it was overkill, but he didn't care. No one would hurt her when she was with him. No one.

Eagle had shown up not too long after they'd gotten home and delivered the food from Mama Carolla's. Bull hadn't been sure what Skylar might want, so he'd ordered way too much food, but Italian was always better the next day anyway. They'd gorged themselves on fried ravioli, veal marsala, chicken involtini, and tiramisu for dessert. He loved that Skylar hadn't picked at her food. She'd dug in, as if she hadn't eaten in weeks.

And conversation had never lagged. Not once. They talked about her students, what she had planned for truck week starting on Monday, the jobs that he'd been on, and how Archer had come to be the newest employee at Silverstone Towing.

He'd suggested they watch a movie, and she'd agreed eagerly. They'd argued good-naturedly about what to watch, but Bull honestly didn't give a shit. He was happy to sit next to Skylar and marvel at the fact that she was there at all.

In the end, she'd decided on *Central Intelligence* with Kevin Hart and Dwayne "The Rock" Johnson. He'd seen it several times and enjoyed it. But he liked it even more watching it with Skylar. She freely giggled and gasped . . . and by the end, she was practically sitting on his lap.

It was ten o'clock, and as much as she was attempting to pretend otherwise, it was obvious Skylar was exhausted. Bull wanted to be selfish and keep talking to her, maybe even put in another movie and have her fall asleep on him. He hated the thought of returning her to her crappy apartment complex, but knew he didn't have a choice.

"You tired?" he asked.

"Mmmmm."

After chuckling, Bull kissed the top of her head. "I should get you home."

"Carson?"

"Right here, sweetheart."

"Do you want to come to my parents' with me next weekend?"

"Do *you* want me to come to your parents' with you next weekend?" he asked.

She looked up at him, and even in the dim light he could see how beautiful her green eyes were. Right now they seemed as if they were a dark-forest hue. But in the sunlight, they lightened to more of a jade. "I'd like that," she told him.

"Then nothing could keep me away," he said.

She smiled up at him, and Bull made a vow to do whatever he could to always put that look on her face.

"It's nothing special. Just lunch on Saturday. I try to get up there to Carmel at least once a month."

"You've got Silverstone scheduled to come to the school next Friday, right?" he asked.

She nodded. "Yeah. The fire department is coming on Wednesday, the police on Thursday, and you guys are closing out the week."

"How about you come with me after school again next Friday?" he suggested. "I'll return the truck to Silverstone, then we could do what we did this week . . . have dinner here, relax, then I'll come by Saturday, pick you up, and we can head up to Carmel."

"Sounds perfect," she said, then licked her lips.

And just like that, Bull was a goner. He moved before he'd even thought about what he was doing. His head dropped, and he was devouring her.

She opened to him immediately, and he felt her fingernails dig lightly into the sensitive skin at his nape. She moaned, and he pulled her up and over his lap until she was straddling him.

Bull put a hand on the small of her back and hauled her closer until her core was pressed against his hard cock. Then he tilted his head and kissed her as if his life depended on it. For just a second, he wasn't concentrating on what Sky might want. He was taking what he needed. Her.

When she squirmed against him, Bull came to his senses and tore his mouth away. He dropped his arms, ashamed at how aggressive he'd just been. Afraid he'd scared her.

Bull took a deep breath and forced himself to look at her.

What he saw made his erection throb in his jeans.

Skylar's lips were pink and swollen, and as he watched, she licked them sensually. She leaned into him, running her hands up his chest and into his hair. Her nipples were visible under the light-blue blouse she wore, and he swore he could feel the heat from between her legs burning him alive.

He slowly smoothed his hands up her legs and rested them at her hips. He'd scared himself for a second by just taking what he wanted rather than making sure she was on the same page. He was a big guy and could easily overpower someone as small as Skylar.

"That was so much better than my dreams," she whispered shyly.

Bull groaned, his fingers tightening. "You've dreamed about me?" he asked.

She blushed but nodded.

"Tell me," he ordered.

She hesitated, and he mentally smacked himself on the head.

"I mean . . . if you want," he backpedaled.

"You know you're hot when you get all growly and demanding, right?" she asked instead of answering him.

"I don't want to scare you," Bull said honestly. "I don't want you to think that I'd ever do anything you don't want."

"I know," she told him. "And believe me, you hauling me on top of you and kissing the hell out of me definitely didn't scare me."

Bull sighed in relief and let himself move one hand up the side of her body, brushing her breast as he went. He smiled in satisfaction when her nipple beaded once more. "Tell me what you've dreamed about," he ordered again. He hoped she wasn't kidding when she said she liked his bossy side.

Her cheeks were still rosy, and he could see splotches of pink on her upper chest, but he didn't back down. He wanted to hear what she had to say. *Needed* to hear it.

The room was semidark, with only a glow from the kitchen and illumination from the TV lighting the area. With her on his lap and his arms around her, the atmosphere was intimate—and he'd never wanted someone as much as he wanted Skylar. Hearing her sexual fantasies might kill him, but he wasn't going to take her tonight. He wanted her desperately, but this didn't feel like the right time.

"We were at my apartment, which I know you haven't seen the inside of yet, but since I hadn't seen *your* place, that's where I pictured you. Anyway, you backed me into my room—we were both already naked for some reason—and when I fell onto my bed, you crawled between my legs, shoved them wide, and immediately starting making love to me."

"Fuck," Bull swore, her words painting a visual that made him want to do exactly what she was describing.

Skylar looked away from him, focusing on a point behind his head. "I was already soaking wet, so you didn't hurt me at all. You were really passionate, almost bossy, and you moved me however you wanted as you pumped in and out of me. No one's ever really cared if what they were doing felt good to me, but you kept checking, making sure you weren't hurting me and that I was enjoying it. I orgasmed once and thought that was that, but you kept going. Not letting me come down. It was amazing."

Bull's cock was so hard it felt as if he was going to bust out of his pants. He put a hand at the back of her head and wound her hair around his fist. Her head tilted back, and he waited until she was looking at him before speaking. "I'm gonna *love* fucking you," he said in a low rumbly tone. "I'm gonna make you come over and over until you're begging me to stop."

"Carson," she said breathily.

"When we get together, you come first. Every time. Always. Understand? Any man who doesn't make sure their woman is pleased in bed is an idiot. And Skylar . . . I'm no idiot."

She swallowed and nodded.

Keeping his hand wrapped in her hair, Bull used the other to brush his knuckles over her chest. Skylar's breathing sped, but she didn't pull away. "You're very responsive, and I'm gonna love unwrapping you," Bull murmured, forcing his eyes away from her hard little nipples. "Don't be afraid of me," he ordered. "When we get together, it's gonna be powerful. I might do things you haven't done before, but I'll always make sure it's good for you. Okay?"

"Okay," she answered immediately.

Reluctantly, Bull untangled his fingers and caressed the back of her neck before moving his palm to her back. "Thank you for sharing that with me."

Skylar shrugged. "You make me feel as if I can tell you anything."

"Good," he said in satisfaction. "Because you can."

"Thank you for not making this weird . . . or weirder than it already is."

"Come here," Bull said and gently pulled her forward until she was lying against him. Her weight on his chest felt good. Right. Her hair tickled his jaw, and she was warm and relaxed, and nothing had ever made him more content. Bull had no idea what he'd done to deserve this. Deserve *her*.

He wanted to tell her about Silverstone right that second, about what he and his friends did. But even more, he didn't want the closeness he felt with her to end. He was too selfish.

And he knew it *would* end. Telling someone you killed other people for a living wasn't exactly a warm and fuzzy thing. She'd be shocked and confused . . . and he might lose her.

He wasn't ready to lose her.

How long he sat there on his couch cuddling with Skylar, Bull didn't know, but eventually he knew he had to get her home. He shifted and stood with her in his arms. She didn't even flinch, making him feel ten feet tall. She trusted him not to drop her, and that trust meant the world.

Maybe, just maybe, she'd be able to deal with what he did. Maybe she'd see it as he did . . . that he was protecting his country, the world, from the evil that resided within it.

"Am I going to see you tomorrow?" Skylar asked sleepily as he carried her toward his door.

He carefully put her on her feet and held her close to him so she wouldn't fall. "Do you *want* to see me tomorrow?" he asked.

"Yes."

"Then yes, you'll see me tomorrow," he told her.

"And Sunday?"

Bull's lips twitched. "Yeah."

"Good. I miss you during the week. Maybe you can come over for dinner sometime? I mean, we talk on the phone, so you might as well be there in person, right?"

Bull's heart swelled. "Right."

She smiled up at him. "Carson?"

He loved how she frequently did that. Said his name as a way of requesting permission to ask him something. As if he'd deny her anything. "Yeah, Sky?"

"I'm happy."

Those two words almost did Bull in. "Me too," he told her honestly. He hadn't realized how much he'd just been going through the motions of living until he'd met her. He hadn't been *unhappy* before, but he hadn't really found much to smile about. Until Sky.

It took only a minute or two for her to put on her shoes and get her stuff, then they were going back down to the lobby and into the garage.

Bull walked her up to her apartment, noting that at least there were several lights in the parking lot, and everyone around her place had their outside lights on. She opened her apartment door and asked shyly, "Do you want to come in?"

His cock twitched, but Bull ignored it. "No. Not tonight. You need to get some sleep. You're exhausted. I can see the circles under your eyes." He traced one with his finger.

She wrinkled her nose. "Thanks for pointing it out," she griped.

"You're beautiful with or without those circles," Bull said honestly. Then he leaned in and said softly, "When we go to bed the first time, we're both going to be wide awake and not tired from working all day. I want to see your apartment, but we've got time. I'm not going anywhere."

She nodded. "I had a good time tonight. Thanks for everything."

"You're welcome." He moved even closer and took his time kissing her goodbye. Bull wanted to shove her against the wall and take her the way he'd dreamed about, but he forced himself to pull back. "Sleep well."

"You too," she said breathily.

"I'll call in the morning, and we can decide what we want to do. Okay?"

"Sounds good."

Bull kissed her once more on the forehead, then made himself step away from her. "Go inside and shut and lock your door," he ordered.

Skylar rolled her eyes, but did as he asked.

Only then did Bull head down the walkway toward the stairs to go back to the parking lot.

On the way home, he thought a lot about why he was so drawn to Skylar. Part of it was her innocence, which made him want to wrap her up and protect her from the world, but the other part was her enthusiasm for life. She also didn't hesitate to say what she was thinking—he couldn't believe she'd actually told him about her dreams of the two of them. Just thinking about it made his cock hard once more.

He'd had an erection more often in the last two weeks than he'd had in the last two years. And it was just from listening to her *talk*. He couldn't imagine what it would feel like to be skin to skin with her. To be inside her.

Forcing himself to pay attention to the road, Bull thought instead about the upcoming week. He and the others were very close to getting the intel they needed to head to Africa and find Mostafa. If the man thought he could get away with training terrorists to kill his own countrymen, he was mistaken.

But Bull had to think about what he was going to tell Skylar regarding where he was going. They'd both gotten used to talking to each other every day. He couldn't very well tell her he was going out of the country without an explanation of why. He hadn't wanted to break the news about what he did so soon into their relationship, but he was beginning to suspect he'd have no choice.

Maybe it was better this way. If she couldn't accept who he was and what he did, they didn't have a shot in hell at making things between them work long term.

That thought made him want to punch something, but he took a deep breath after he parked his car instead. The thing that sucked the most was that he knew he was already one hundred percent committed to the relationship. He was going to meet her parents, and he couldn't imagine even going one day without talking to her. If she couldn't handle Silverstone, he had a feeling he'd never recover.

Deciding he had little choice but to take things one day at a time, Bull got out of his car and made his way back into his apartment. He was going to get to see her tomorrow and Sunday. Then, at her invitation, he'd make it a point to get over to her place at least twice next week for dinner. Friday, he'd get to spend most of the day with her . . . and her class . . . but he'd have her all to himself that night. He'd meet her parents, hopefully make a good impression . . . and then he'd worry about telling her about Silverstone.

He had time.

He hoped.

Chapter Ten

Skylar looked down at her fourteen kindergarten students with affection. They were extremely worked up and hyper today. After a few days' worth of lessons about different kinds of trucks, they'd been in heaven to get to climb on the fire truck Wednesday afternoon. They'd gotten to sit inside an ambulance and go up in the bucket on the fire truck as well. On Thursday, they'd gotten the opportunity to set off the siren of a police car and explore a SWAT truck.

Today it was Silverstone Towing day. Carson and his friends were bringing by two of their newer trucks to show off to the kids. Skylar had been over the agenda with Carson, and he hadn't seemed worried at all about entertaining a class full of kids. She wasn't sure if he was simply clueless as to how rambunctious kids could be or if he really was *that* sure of his ability to handle them.

"Remember, boys and girls," Skylar told her kids, "you can't touch anything without permission, and you need to put on your listening ears, okay?"

Everyone nodded their agreement, and all Skylar could do was hope for the best.

The last week had been amazing. Saturday, Carson had picked her up, and they'd gone for a bike ride along the Monon Trail. It was a former railroad that had been made into a biking-and-walking trail. Of course, somehow Carson had known she wasn't much of a biker and had rented her an electric bike. She never would've guessed that she could enjoy biking so much . . . but it was because she'd been with Carson. Afterward, she'd brought him back to her apartment, and they'd spent the rest of the afternoon talking, eating dinner, and watching another movie.

Skylar had been disappointed when he'd left without doing more than kissing her, even though it had been a thirty-minute make-out session.

Sunday, he'd picked her up and taken her to Rosie's Diner for breakfast. Then he'd reluctantly dropped her back at home so she could get her weekend errands done.

But what had made her week even better was when he'd asked if he could stop by and have dinner with her on Tuesday. Then he'd done it again on Wednesday.

Skylar freely admitted to herself that she was addicted to the man. She wanted to be with him all the time and lived for talking on the phone when she couldn't see him in person.

He'd reeled her in, hook, line, and sinker—and she couldn't be happier.

A knock at the door distracted her, and after whirling around, she saw Carson standing there with Eagle, Smoke, and Gramps.

"Girls and boys," she called out, "our guests are here. How about you show them how polite and welcoming we can be?"

"Welcome to our class!" all fourteen little voices shouted at once.

Skylar hurried over to the men. "Come in," she told them. Then she lowered her voice and teased, "They don't bite . . . at least not very hard."

All four men chuckled, and Skylar relaxed. This was going to be fine.

She'd talked to the guys before they'd arrived, and they'd all agreed to sit with little groups of students and read stories to them and discuss them before heading outside to the trucks. She'd found a few books appropriate for the occasion. Carson was reading *Tow Truck Joe*, Eagle was reading *Sunny's Tow Truck Saves the Day*, Smoke had *Little Green Tow Truck*, and Gramps had *How Many Trucks Can a Tow Truck Tow?*

Skylar knew she had a goofy smile on her face watching the big, muscular, *very* masculine men read the silly books to her students. She even snuck a few pictures because she knew she never wanted to forget this day.

Sandra, Brodie, and Chad were with Carson, and he had their complete attention. He was a natural with kids, and Skylar felt as if her ovaries were going to explode at any minute—which was a shock. She supposed her biological clock *should* be ticking by now, but even at thirty-two, she'd never felt a huge need to procreate. She spent almost every day with little kids, and she enjoyed her kid-free time when she went home.

However, seeing Sandra put her little hand on Carson's knee and lean into him, looking up at him with adoring eyes that clearly showed she was hanging on his every word, Skylar could picture Carson with kids of his own.

Shaking her head at her ridiculousness, she walked around the room, listening to the small groups and encouraging the children to ask questions. When it was obvious the kids were more than ready to go outside and see the trucks for themselves, she gathered them around her on the special rug in her classroom.

"Okay, everyone. We're going to go outside and see a tow truck up close in a minute. But before we go . . . who can tell us when you might need to call for a tow truck?"

Almost every hand went in the air, which Skylar loved. She wanted each and every one of her students to feel confident in their answers and to get used to speaking in front of not only their classmates, but the strangers in the room too.

"Ignacio?"

"Mama's car gets a flat!"

"Good," Skylar praised. "When else? Gwen?"

"When Dad forgets to put gas in the car and it stops."

"Right. Running out of gas isn't good. When else?"

She got a few more answers out of her students before they couldn't think of any other reasons. "We talked to the nice police officers yesterday. Do you think our guests today work with the police?"

"Yes!" her students all cried out.

Smiling, Skylar nodded. "You're right. When there's been an accident, the police officers sometimes call for a tow truck. Should you be scared of the men and women who show up with their *big* trucks to tow your car away?"

All fourteen students shook their heads.

"Exactly. They're here to help." Skylar lowered her voice and leaned forward, as if telling her students a secret. They ate it up and leaned toward her in response. "But sometimes," she said softly, "adults don't like it when a tow truck has to come. Know why?"

"Because money," Zahir said.

"Because it means our car is smashed," Karlee responded.

"Because the driver is big and scary," Marisol said timidly.

Skylar nodded. "Yes to all of those. But you know what?"

"What?" everyone asked.

"The person driving the tow truck didn't cause the accident, and your car might be smashed, but *you* aren't, and we've talked a lot about how someone's looks don't tell you anything about what kind of person they are on the inside, haven't we?"

Everyone nodded.

"Our guests—they're big, right?"

All the kids' heads turned to stare at Carson, Eagle, Smoke, and Gramps. They all agreed that the four men were indeed big.

"I have it on good authority that they're all very nice. Not only that, but they keep little presents to give to scared children when they get called out to an accident." She could tell that got their attention. She probably shouldn't have said anything, because now they'd all expect a toy if and when their parents had to call for a tow, but it was too late to take it back now.

"Who's ready to see a big tow truck?"

All fourteen children threw their hands up in the air, and Skylar chuckled. She stood and got them into two lines at the door. She glanced over at Carson—and almost stumbled at the look he was giving her. She saw respect and admiration . . . but also what she thought was lust.

Which was crazy. She knew her hair was coming out of the bun she'd put it in that morning, she wasn't wearing makeup, and she was in her "teacher mode."

But there was no denying the heat she saw in his gaze.

Ignoring Carson was impossible—she was well aware of where he was every second—but she did her best.

Gramps and Smoke walked at the back of the lines, and Eagle and Carson walked up front with her. They headed down the hall and out the door toward the teachers' parking lot, where the staff had blocked off some spots for the trucks.

They cut through the playground, since it was faster, and headed for the gate in the back of the large grassy lot. It swung open easily when Skylar pushed on it; the latch had broken a while ago, and it still hadn't been fixed.

Her students were hyped up, and Skylar couldn't blame them. They'd had so much fun with the fire trucks and the police vehicles they were expecting another amazing time with the tow trucks. There were two parked in the lot, and they looked huge compared to the other cars.

Skylar broke the children up into two groups. Gramps and Eagle took seven kids, and Carson and Smoke took the other seven.

Skylar hovered for a while, making sure the men had things under control, and when it was more than obvious they did, she stood back and simply watched the men of Silverstone Towing charm her students.

The kids wanted to flip every switch, of course, and see the tow trucks in action. Carson talked her into letting him hook up her car so everyone could see how it was done. Skylar wouldn't have guessed it at the start of the week, but the tow trucks were definitely the highlight . . . more so than the police cars or fire trucks.

By the time the demonstration was over, it was the end of the school day. Skylar brought her amped-up kids back into the school and got them sorted. Those who were being picked up by their parents, those who were riding the school bus, and those who were going to the after-school program.

Eagle, Smoke, and Gramps left with the trucks, and Carson stayed behind with her. Sandra would be at the after-school program for a while longer. She'd come back to the classroom to wait for her dad after it was over.

Sighing in relief at the blessed silence of the classroom, Skylar glanced over at Carson. He was standing at the side of the room, leaning against the wall. He had his arms crossed over his chest . . . and was staring at her with that same look she'd seen earlier.

The moment he saw he had her attention, he pushed off the wall and stalked toward her.

For a second, Skylar wanted to back away, his intensity so potent, but she held her ground and tilted her head to look at him as he approached.

He didn't say anything, simply took her face in his hands and leaned down to kiss her. The kiss wasn't long, a hard press of his lips against hers, but he didn't pull away when he was done. He stared down at her for a long moment before saying, "You're amazing."

Skylar knew she was probably blushing, but she reached up and grabbed hold of his wrists—not to pull him away but to feel a deeper connection with him. "Why?"

"Why are you amazing?" he asked. Then, not giving her a chance to respond, he went on. "Because you're giving these kids an amazing jump start to their school experience. You're patient with them, answering all of their questions without irritation; you give them affection without strings; and it's clear that you love what you're doing."

"I'm just doing my job," she protested.

"No. You aren't. I had plenty of teachers growing up who were obviously just going through the motions. The bureaucracy of teaching had beaten them down, and they were merely existing, getting through each day so they could earn their paycheck. I'm sure you're underpaid, maybe you even struggle with paying your own bills, but don't think I haven't noticed the stash of snacks behind your desk for those who can't afford enough to eat, or the pile of stickers and little toys that I'm sure you dole out for a job well done. Not to mention the markers, books, construction paper, and the countless other things you've paid for yourself in order to make your classroom a welcoming and happy place to be."

"Carson, there are thousands of teachers just like me out there," Skylar argued. "We all spend our own money because there simply isn't enough in the school budgets."

He shook his head. "But you *care*," he said. "You know what Sandra told me today?"

Skylar swallowed and shook her head. She'd seen the two talking earlier, and they'd looked mighty cozy together, but she'd been busy and hadn't had a chance to go over and see what they had been discussing so intently.

She knew Sandra had asked him about his nickname. Even though Skylar had told the little girl all about it, she hadn't been surprised Sandra wanted to hear it from him. She also knew Carson had downplayed the Bullseye thing—he couldn't exactly tell a little girl that he was an excellent shot—but she had no worries that he'd said something inappropriate. It was a wonderful surprise, but he seemed to be really good with kids.

"She told me that sometimes she got sad she didn't have a mommy, but when she came to school, she could pretend *you* were her mom," Carson said, bringing her out of her musings.

Skylar's eyes teared up at his words.

But he wasn't done.

"She told me she knew it was you who'd somehow gotten her daddy a new job. Because he was sad he couldn't be with her as much as he wanted. She said she got scared at night when she was by herself but that she knew if she said anything to anyone, they'd take her away from her daddy. She was so excited that he'd be working at Silverstone Towing, that now he'd get to stay home with her at night. And she knew it was because of *you*. She said you're her angel."

Skylar was outright crying now. The tears slipped down her face.

Carson used his thumbs and brushed them away.

"I didn't get her dad that job. I didn't even know Silverstone was hiring," she protested.

"But you were worried about Sandra. *And* her dad. You might not have known he would be perfect for us, but you cared enough about them both to express your concern. Having that empathy is what makes you not only a good teacher, but someone I wasn't able to stay away from. I want to bottle up your caring nature and carry it with me to pull out when I encounter the worst the world has to offer."

The way he said that last part had Skylar frowning in concern. "Are the customers you come into contact with really all that bad?" she asked.

Her question seemed to bring him out of whatever intense moment he'd been in, because Carson closed his eyes and took a deep breath. "Sandra's special. All your kids are special. And you've made a huge difference in their lives, whether they know it or not. You're an amazing teacher, Skylar. I hope you realize that."

Feeling a little embarrassed by his over-the-top praise, Skylar simply shrugged.

"What can I do to help you while we're waiting for five o'clock to come around and for Sandra to come back until Archer can pick her up?"

Skylar figured saying "Make out with me until I can't breathe" wasn't exactly appropriate for the time or place, so she sighed and said, "If you really want to help, you can put all the chairs back under the tables and clean them off for me while I type up a short review of the week for the principal. She wants to share it in her monthly report to the school board."

"Done," he said—then didn't move away from her.

"Carson?"

"Yeah?"

"You have to let go of me if I'm going to get anything written."

"I know," he said, but still didn't drop his hands.

If she was honest with herself, Skylar loved that he didn't want to stop touching her. She felt the same about him.

And suddenly she wanted more. More of his touches. More of his kisses.

She wanted it all.

He'd been nothing but a gentleman since they'd met, which she'd appreciated, but she was officially over it. Tonight, she'd make sure he knew she was ready for the next step. For him to stop holding back.

"What's that look for?" he asked with a tilt of his head, obviously seeing some of what she was thinking on her face.

Skylar grinned. "Nothing."

"Lord help a man when his woman says 'Nothing' but then smiles like that," he said.

She loved being called *his woman*.

Carson leaned down and kissed her once more. This time it was gentler, more reverent. Then he dropped his hands and took a step back. He held eye contact with her for a moment before turning to grab a chair.

Skylar went to her desk and sat, pulling her laptop over and opening it. There was nothing she wanted to do less right now than write up a synopsis of how the week had gone, but she knew if she got it done, she wouldn't have to worry about it later . . . and she could concentrate all of her attention on Carson.

So while he cleaned her room and put it back to rights, she quickly and efficiently wrote a glowing review of truck week.

~

A little after five o'clock, Bull stood with Skylar outside on the playground and watched Sandra run around. She was an extremely happy little girl. You'd never know how little she and her dad had by looking at her. Some people might feel sorry for her, being a minority living in a not-so-prosperous part of Indianapolis, but Bull had a feeling she'd grow up to be an incredible woman. She was already smart and empathetic toward others. She had a father who would do anything for her, and she had the perfect start to her educational journey with Skylar as her first teacher.

"She's happy," Skylar said from next to him. "I love that."

"She is," Bull agreed. Then asked, "What about you?"

She turned to look at him. "What about me what?"

"Are you happy?"

Instead of immediately answering, she thought about his question for a moment.

"I am. I've got a job I love that pays enough for me to eat and have a roof over my head. I have amazing parents who raised me to see the best in people and who love me unconditionally. I've got some great neighbors who watch out for me, and while we might not be best friends, I know if I needed them, I could definitely call them, and they'd be there." Then she blushed and said, "And I have an incredible boyfriend. Yes, Carson, I'm happy. Are you?"

He should've seen that coming, but for some reason, he hadn't.

Bull frowned. Was he happy? If he'd been asked that question a month or so ago, he would've shrugged and said he was content with his life. It wasn't that he'd been *un*happy, but he hadn't exactly been brimming over with joy either.

But now? He woke up excited to start each day because he knew he'd get to talk to and hopefully see Skylar. She was like a ray of sunshine in his otherwise dull life. Even looking over reports on the dregs of society and reading about the horrible things one person could do to another didn't affect him as it used to. And it was all because of the woman standing in front of him.

"Yeah, Sky. I am," he said simply.

She beamed up at him and slipped her hand into his. They stood there watching Sandra for a moment before the little girl called out, "Come push me, Ms. Reid!"

"Looks like duty calls," she told him with a smile.

Bull reluctantly let go of her hand. "I'll wait here."

"Okay." Skylar gave him a smile and headed toward Sandra and the swings.

Bull shoved his hands in his pockets and watched her walk away. The more time he spent around Sky, the deeper he fell for her. She was honestly just so damn *good*, it made his heart hurt.

He knew he should break things off. He was going to contaminate her. There was no doubt about that. It wasn't as if he could keep what he did a secret forever. He never wanted to be in a relationship where he had to lie to his woman.

Unfortunately, the time was fast approaching when he'd have to sit down and have a serious talk with Skylar. He wasn't ready. It didn't feel as if they'd been together long enough. There was every possibility she'd learn about what he and his team did, and she'd leave his ass right then and there.

It was looking as if next week, Silverstone would be headed to Africa. The previous reports had been confirmed. Mostafa *was* there, allegedly preparing to train a new group of terrorists to attack Americans on US soil. If Bull and the others could prevent another 9/11, they would. That they'd take the job wasn't even in question.

As he watched Skylar push Sandra on the swing and heard them both laughing, his belly tightened with anxiety. He consciously did his best to relax, tried to think about the upcoming weekend instead. Sky was coming home with him, and they were going to have dinner and hang out. Then he'd pick her up in the morning, and they'd drive north of Indy to Carmel to have lunch with her parents.

He was going to get to spend almost the whole weekend with her. He needed to concentrate on that in the upcoming week, not on the death and destruction he would bring upon a man who more than deserved it.

~

Jay Ricketts watched the playground from his vantage point in the trees and frowned. He didn't know who the man standing by the building was, but he didn't like him on sight. He watched his girl with way too much interest. He was a complication Jay didn't need or want.

Jay had been watching him all afternoon. Watched *all* the men from that towing company flirting. They'd gotten up close and personal with *his* girl, and jealousy was eating Jay up inside.

He wanted to be the one she smiled at. The one she looked up to.

And now one of the men had stayed behind. He and the teacher were definitely into one another. The man could throw a huge monkey wrench into his plans.

He knew he needed to get his shit together and move his timetable up. He couldn't hide here and watch her forever. He needed to act. And act fast. He still had to get some of the details nailed down on how he was going to get to Chicago with her, but once that was ironed out, he'd make his move.

He hadn't thought anyone would miss her, but watching now, he knew that might not be the case. They'd have to lie low for a short while. There would likely be a search party, but he could hide right here under their noses, and then when the coast was clear, they'd get the hell out of Indianapolis and start over in Chicago.

She'd be reluctant at first. She'd probably cry and beg him to let her go, but he wouldn't. He was *never* letting her go. That was what had gotten him in trouble the first time. He'd believed the last one when she'd promised she wouldn't tell anyone what he'd done. He wasn't going back to prison. No way.

He was keeping this one. She'd be his forever. Eventually, she'd learn that she belonged to him, and she'd obey him and do whatever he asked.

He should leave before the man spotted him. He had the same air as the guards in prison, constantly scanning the area, looking for danger. But if Jay stood up now, he'd definitely be caught. His best bet was to stay where he was until they all left the playground.

"She's mine," Jay growled when the man's gaze returned to the pair at the swing set. "You can't have her. I saw her first."

Chapter Eleven

Skylar was nervous. She was cuddled against Carson on his couch. Her knees were drawn up, and one of his arms was resting on them. His thumb gently caressed her skin as he held her close.

They'd eaten dinner and were both pretending to watch TV, but all Skylar could think about was how much she wanted him. Deciding the best way to move things along between them was to just tell him what she wanted, she took a deep breath. "Carson?"

His lips twitched. She knew he found it funny when she said his name like a question when she wanted to ask something.

"Yeah, Sky?"

"I'm ready," she blurted.

His eyebrows came down in confusion. "For what?"

Shit, this was embarrassing. Skylar knew she was probably beet red, but she forged ahead. She was thirty-two years old. Not fifteen. They were both adults, they were having an adult conversation about sex. She could do this.

"To have sex."

The three words seemed to echo in the air around them, and she winced.

But she definitely had his attention now.

"I mean, we've been talking every day. I know you better than I've known any of the men I've slept with. Not that it's been that many, and it's been quite a while, as you know. But you told me that we'd move at my pace, and, well, I'm ready. That is, if you're still interested."

One second she was against his side, and the next she was on her back under him on the couch. He loomed over her, his weight heavy against her body. She stared up at him in surprise.

"Are you sure?" he asked.

Skylar nodded. "Yeah. I wouldn't have said it if I wasn't."

"If you change your mind, let me know," Carson told her seriously.

"I won't," she said confidently.

"Birth control?" he asked.

"I'm on the pill . . . to help control my periods, but I was thinking you'd wear a condom too. I trust you, but—"

"Was already planning on it," he said.

"Do you . . . I don't have any on me," Skylar said. Talking about safe sex was harder than she thought it would be.

"Been carrying one around since a few days after I met you," Carson told her with a small smile.

Skylar gawked up at him. "You have?"

"Yeah. Knew I wanted you from the time I dropped you off at your shitty apartment and you turned around to wave at me before you went inside. I mean, who does that? Waves at a stranger they've just met as if they'd hung out for hours and hours?"

Skylar shrugged. "I guess I do."

"Yeah, sweetheart, you do. And it's fucking adorable. I wanted you then, and I want you now. But if at any time you change your mind, all you have to do is say the word, and everything stops."

Skylar tilted her head and teased, "Are you trying to tell me you've got an alien penis with barbs and ridges and shit, and it might scare me into calling this off when I see it?"

In response, Carson burst out laughing, and Skylar simply stared up at him. He was good looking on a regular day, but laughing so hard he couldn't stop? He was absolutely beautiful.

When he got himself under control, Carson looked down at her once more. His black hair was tousled, and his brown eyes twinkled with mirth. "Hate to disappoint you, but I've just got a regular cock, Sky. It's not monster huge, but it's not small either. You aren't gonna leave my bed unsatisfied."

"We aren't in your bed," she blurted.

Without a word, Carson lifted himself off her, then leaned down and picked her up off the couch.

Giving a little squeak of surprise, Skylar wrapped her arms around his neck, holding on for dear life. Within seconds, they were heading down the hallway toward the master bedroom. She'd seen it the first time she'd been to his apartment when he'd given her a tour.

Carson nudged open the door with his hip and strode toward his king-size bed. The sheet and comforter were thrown back, as if he'd just crawled out from under the covers. Skylar had time to notice that there was a stack of books on the table next to the bed and that the hamper in the corner was overflowing with clothes before she was unceremoniously dropped onto the mattress.

Giggling, Skylar looked up to see Carson already pulling off the Silverstone Towing polo shirt he'd been wearing all day. His gaze met hers, and without looking away, he undid his belt and jeans and shoved them down his legs.

Skylar's eyes roamed down his body, and she felt her heart begin to pump faster.

Carson "Bull" Rhodes was the epitome of masculine perfection.

He had a smattering of chest hair that made her want to run her fingers through it. His biceps bulged, and he didn't seem to have an ounce of fat on him. He wasn't as muscular as the bodybuilders she'd seen on television, but he'd obviously kept in shape after getting out of the military.

Her eyes strayed to his groin, and she swallowed hard. Skylar knew he'd said his nickname had come from his shooting ability, but she couldn't help noticing he was hung like a bull as well.

He wore a pair of tight black cotton briefs that outlined his cock perfectly. His thigh muscles tensed, and then he was on the mattress with her. He crawled up to hover above her. Even though she was still fully dressed, Skylar felt at a definite disadvantage.

Carson straddled her thighs and put his hands on the mattress, next to her shoulders. He leaned down until she could feel his chest brush against her own. Skylar couldn't deny that she loved the feeling of being under him. She grabbed hold of his arms and waited for him to take the lead. She seemed to have run out of steam after initiating the sleeping-together and birth control / safe-sex conversations.

"You good?" he asked gently.

Skylar nodded.

"You nervous?"

She nodded again. "A little."

"Why?"

"Why?" she echoed, a little confused.

"Yeah. Why?" he repeated. "I'm not going to hurt you. In fact, everything that happens in this bed is gonna make you feel really good. What, specifically, are you nervous about?"

Now she felt kind of stupid. She dropped her eyes and stared at the pulse she could see beating in the side of his neck. "I don't know."

"Look at me," Carson demanded.

Licking her lips, Skylar met his gaze.

"I think you're beautiful," he told her gently. "And it's more than physical. I've been attracted to you since I first saw you. Your red hair is fucking gorgeous, and the way your green eyes sparkle when you're excited is something I wish I could capture in a picture to keep with me always. I haven't been able to stop thinking about seeing and touching your luscious body. But I'm even more attracted to who you are as a person. You're good down to the marrow of your bones. You're compassionate, giving, caring, and I have no doubt you'd give your last dollar to someone else if they needed it. You make *me* feel like a good person simply by being around you."

"Carson," Skylar whispered, overwhelmed by his words.

"If you're nervous about being naked with me, don't be. If you're nervous about whether you'll please me, don't be. If you're nervous about my size, *don't be*. And if you're nervous about making love because it's been a long time since you've been with someone . . . I'm right there with you."

Carson's words made any anxiousness she'd felt disappear. His admission that he wasn't quite as sure as he seemed about what they were about to do made her feel not quite so alone.

She smiled up at him. "Kinda hard to make love when I'm completely dressed," she teased softly. "Seems to me I remember both of us needing to be naked for this to work."

Without a word, Carson moved. He sat up and, keeping his weight off her but still straddling her hips, brought his hands to the hem of her blouse. Arching her back and raising her arms to help him, Skylar barely breathed as he eased her shirt up and over her head. He threw the material to the side without taking his eyes from her body.

Skylar had worn the lacy black bra today on a whim. Usually she preferred her comfortable cotton and sports bras. But this morning when she'd been getting ready for work, knowing she'd be going home with Carson and wanting to do everything possible to give herself confidence, she'd put on the pretty underwear.

She was very glad she had.

Carson's eyes were glued to her chest. Her cleavage was more impressive when she wasn't on her back, but she wasn't disappointed with his reaction.

He placed his hands on her stomach before slowly drawing them upward. They went up and over her breasts and caressed her shoulders. Then he leaned forward, and his hands went to her back. Arching once more, Skylar gave him access to the clasp. Within seconds, she was bare from the waist up.

For some reason, considering how slowly Carson had been moving with her, she thought he'd proceed with caution once they got to this point. But she'd been wrong. Very wrong. One second she was staring into his eyes, the pupils dilated with lust, and the next she gasped as he leaned down and took one of her nipples into his mouth.

"Carson!" she exclaimed breathlessly.

He didn't respond, but suckled hard on her nipple. Skylar arched her back, and one of her hands flew into his hair and grabbed hold. His hand went to the other breast that he wasn't suckling and squeezed the fleshy globe. His fingers began playing with that nipple, pinching and rolling as he did his best to drive her out of her mind with his lips and tongue.

"Holy crap," Skylar said, panting as her brain tried to process what she was feeling. His mouth on her almost hurt, but not exactly. Her legs opened as far as possible with him straddling her, and she thrust her pelvis upward, needing more.

Carson let go of her nipple with a loud pop, and he raised his head so he could see her face. "Tell me if I hurt you," he demanded, his voice rougher and lower than she'd ever heard it.

She shook her head. "You aren't."

"I want you so fucking bad, Sky," he admitted, then squeezed the breast he still had in his hand.

Skylar could only nod. Her skin felt as if it was on fire, and she wanted him inside her. Now.

At her acquiescence, he let go of her and sat up once more. His hands went to the button of her jeans and ripped the zipper open. He didn't move from his position, merely pulled both her pants and underwear over her hips.

Skylar helped as much as she could, doing her best to get the jeans off while not kicking him in the process. Carson straightened on his knees, shoved his own underwear down, then, quick as a flash, rolled onto a hip next to her and peeled them off before moving over her once again.

She only caught a glimpse of his hard cock before he lay down between her legs this time. He pressed on her inner thighs with his hands until she was spread open right in front of his face.

"Carson, please, I need you."

"And you'll get me," he told her. "Once I know you can take me without pain."

"I don't . . . I'm not comfortable with that."

At her words, Carson went stock still, but he didn't move up from between her legs. "With what?" he asked in confusion, studying her face.

Embarrassed now, Skylar motioned between her legs with her hand. "You know, *that*."

"Me looking at you? Me eating you out? Coming while I watch? What?"

"Yes!" she said in exasperation. "All of it."

"Why?"

"Jeez, not this again," she complained.

"I'm serious. Why?" Carson asked. "Did you have a bad experience? Did someone hurt you?"

"No, nothing like that," she said, lying back and staring at his ceiling. "I just . . . I've never done it. None of the other guys have bothered. And it's just embarrassing to have you looking at me so closely like that."

"First of all . . . can we please not talk about other men when you're in my bed?" Carson growled. "Second of all, I have to admit I kinda love that you're embarrassed. Your innocence is a huge fucking turn-on."

"I'm not innocent," she protested.

"You sure as fuck are—and I'm gonna corrupt the shit out of you."

For a second, Skylar wasn't sure she'd heard him correctly, but when his words sank in, she couldn't help but chuckle. "Seriously? If you corrupt me, I won't be innocent anymore," she said.

"Yes, you will," he countered. "But you'll crave me and *only* me. No one else will be able to do to you what I can."

He sounded awfully sure of himself, and a lot conceited, but Skylar found she didn't care. Also, he was probably right. She *already* craved him, and they hadn't done more than make out. After he made love to her, she knew everything between them would be different. More intense.

Skylar wasn't sure what to say, and she didn't know what he was waiting for. He lay patiently between her legs, his thumbs caressing her inner thighs, watching her expectantly.

After licking her lips, she asked, "Why are you looking at me like that?"

"I'm waiting for you to give me permission to eat you out. To give you an orgasm that will make you forget everything but how good you feel. If you truly are uncomfortable, I'll stop. But I've dreamed of this for weeks. Of having you under me and hearing your whimpers as I taste you."

How could she say no to that? She couldn't.

"Okay," she whispered.

"Okay what?" he insisted.

Damn, he took this consent thing seriously. "You can lick me there, if I can return the favor."

At her words, his hips jerked once as he humped the mattress under him. His eyes closed for a fraction of a second before they opened again, and he pinned her in place with his gaze. "You wanna suck my cock?" he asked.

His words made her stomach tighten. She nodded.

"*Fuck.* I've fantasized about *that* too," Carson told her. "Your lips stretched over me, licking and sucking."

Blow jobs weren't her favorite thing, but Skylar had a feeling it would be a completely new experience with Carson. Just as him giving her oral was about to be.

Then, without another word, Carson's head lowered—and just like when he'd sucked on her nipple, he didn't ease into things. His lips closed around her clit, and he used his tongue to tease the small bundle of nerves.

Skylar squirmed in his grasp, and she wasn't surprised when he inched up the mattress a bit, put one arm over her lower belly to hold her still, and continued to drive her crazy.

His tongue felt like a vibrator against her, and when he alternated licking with sucking and nipping at her clit, Skylar felt herself dripping with arousal. She was so wet, she could smell herself. For a second, she worried about how she smelled and tasted to him, but then when he used his free hand to probe her folds, she forgot about anything except how he was making her feel.

His finger was gentle compared to what his tongue was doing to her clit. He pressed inside her body, then retreated to caress every inch of her folds. Then he added a second finger.

Groaning at the feel of him filling her, Skylar thrust toward both his hand and his face as he continued to push her toward an orgasm.

How long he kept her on the edge, Skylar wasn't sure. At one point, she looked down because he'd stopped sucking on her. His fingers were still pushing in and out of her body, and she was still thrusting up to meet them, while Carson watched her writhe under him, as if he'd never seen something so amazing in all his life.

His chin and lips were glistening with her juices, and he made no move to wipe his face. He seemed enthralled with her body and what he was doing to it. He caught her gaze, and Skylar couldn't even see the brown irises in his eyes, his pupils were so dilated.

Then he looked back down between her legs and lowered the hand that was on her belly until his thumb was pressing against her clit.

"God!" she exclaimed.

He didn't say a word, and the last thing she saw before his head descended was Carson licking his lips.

Then he once more began sucking on her clit. But this time it was obvious he wasn't just trying to work her up. There was no teasing. His fingers pushed inside her, and he turned his hand so it was palm up. Then he began pressing on her inner walls, as if he was looking for—

Skylar gasped as he hit her G-spot with his fingertips, and her body jerked, hard.

She felt him smile against her, but he didn't lift his head. The sucking against her clit turned almost painful as he caressed her deep within her body.

The orgasm swept over Skylar without warning. She was about to push his head and hands away from her because she didn't think she could take one more second of this erotic torture, but then every muscle in her body tensed, and her back bowed as she came.

Carson still didn't back off. His fingers began to push in and out of her faster, hitting her G-spot with every thrust, and Skylar knew she was humping his hand, as if she couldn't get enough.

He lifted his head finally, but his thumb went back into motion, pressing hard on her clit, prolonging her orgasm until she thought her heart was going to burst out of her chest.

Her thighs were still twitching, and she was gasping for air when she felt Carson lift up and off her. She barely registered him reaching for his pants, which were still on the edge of the bed. He rolled a condom over his impressive cock and then was back between her legs. Scooting forward on his knees, he spread her legs even wider than they'd been before.

Skylar knew she'd be sore in the morning, as she hadn't stretched her muscles like this in a very long time, if ever. But at the moment, she couldn't think about anything other than Carson getting inside her. She felt empty without him.

The air of the room was brisk against her soaking-wet folds, but she didn't care about that either. Skylar couldn't take her eyes off Carson's cock. From this angle, with him hovering over her, his dick in his hand, he looked huge.

"You okay?" he asked once more.

"Fuck me," Skylar whispered, needing him inside her more than she'd needed anything.

"I've never heard you swear," Carson said as he ran the tip of his cock between her folds, lubricating himself. "It's fucking sexy."

Skylar dug her nails into Carson's thighs and begged, "Please, Carson!"

Then, as he'd done everything else that evening, he leaned forward and didn't hesitate to take her. He sank inside her body without pausing to let her adjust.

Even though she was soaking wet, there was still a pinch of pain as he bottomed out inside her. But once he was all the way in, he didn't move at all, giving her the time she needed to acclimate to his size.

Panting and holding on to him for dear life, Skylar looked up into Carson's face.

His head was thrown back, and a muscle in his jaw was ticcing furiously. It was more than obvious being inside her was absolute ecstasy for him.

And just like that, Skylar didn't feel any more pain. Having this man at her mercy was as heady as anything she'd ever experienced in her life.

"I'm yours," she said softly. "Take me."

~

Bull had never felt anything as good as being inside Skylar.

He'd been on the edge ever since he'd first seen her perfect tits. His cock had pulsed against the mattress as he'd eaten her out. When Skylar had begun to fuck his hand, he'd thought he was going to lose it.

He hadn't lied; corrupting her was exciting as hell. He knew without asking that she'd never been as turned on as she'd been right then. She'd soaked his hand, and when he'd found her G-spot, it'd been obvious she'd never been touched there.

After her orgasm, he'd fumbled putting on the condom.

When she'd said "Fuck me," he'd realized he'd never heard her swear. He'd been doing everything he could to distract himself from how much he wanted to push inside her, but then she'd begged . . .

That had been it. He'd given her every opportunity to tell him no, that she'd changed her mind. That she didn't want to make love. But she hadn't. She'd *begged* him to fuck her.

So he had.

He'd meant to go slow, but as soon as her heat had closed around the tip of his cock, he'd been a goner. He'd shoved himself to the hilt, hating himself every second, but he hadn't been able to stop.

He'd seen Skylar wince, and Bull had held on to his lust with every bit of inner strength he'd had. He'd stayed stock still, giving her time to adjust, even if it had been a bit too late. He'd thrown his head back, grinding his teeth together to try to get the control he knew he needed so as not to hurt the precious woman under him.

"I'm yours," he heard her say. "Take me."

His hips moved without conscious thought. Bull pulled back and thrust into her. When she didn't yelp in pain or try to push him away, he did it again. And again.

Then they were fucking. They weren't making love. He was fucking his woman so hard her tits bounced up and down with their movement. But one look at Skylar's face, and Bull knew she loved it. She gripped his arms so tightly he'd have marks from her fingernails.

With every thrust, she moaned and pushed her hips up toward him, egging him on. Encouraging him.

At that moment, Bull knew he loved her.

He'd never felt this way about a woman before. Ever. Skylar Reid was made for him.

Reaching down, he grabbed one of her butt cheeks, opening her up a little more. She moaned in ecstasy.

"You're *mine*," Bull growled as he fucked her even harder.

"Yourssssss!" she groaned.

Bull wanted to feel her come on his cock. Stopping his thrusts by sheer force of will, he sat back on his heels and hauled Skylar's ass onto his thighs. The position forced her pelvis up, and he couldn't really thrust inside her at all, but at the moment, he needed to see and feel her come again more than he wanted to fuck her.

His thumb eased between them, gathering up some of her juices, and he pressed hard on her clit. She about jumped out of his grip at the touch.

"Carson!" she exclaimed. "Too sensitive."

"Come for me again, Sky," he told her. "You can do it. Let me feel you squeeze my cock."

Her nipples were standing straight up, and Bull wished he had four hands so he could touch her all over.

"I can't!" she wailed.

"Yes, you can," he told her. He wasn't one hundred percent sure she *could* orgasm again, but he was going to push her hard. She was *his*. His to corrupt.

Bull groaned when her inner muscles tightened around him almost to the point of pain. He reached up with his free hand and pinched one of her nipples ruthlessly.

That did it. Skylar exploded so hard in orgasm she almost bounced off his lap. Bull grabbed her and held her to him as she shook and did her best to strangle his dick. He'd never felt anything so amazing in all his life. He swore he could feel her pleasure as if it were his own.

Then the overwhelming need to thrust took him. Bull eased her off his lap, picked up her legs, hooked her knees over his arms, and leaned over her spent body. She was bent almost in half, but he didn't stop to ask if she was okay. He took what he wanted.

And what he wanted was Skylar.

The noises their bodies made as he fucked her were loud, almost overshadowing everything he was feeling. The slap of their skin as his thighs smacked against her butt was heightening the experience.

Bull felt his balls draw up toward his body and knew he was going to blow.

He thrust inside Skylar twice more, then pushed himself as deep inside her as he could and exploded. He felt almost light headed as he came. It seemed as if he wouldn't ever *stop* coming. He had the fleeting concern about whether the condom could actually hold all the fucking sperm he was ejaculating but decided he didn't care.

When he could breathe again, Bull realized that he was practically squishing Skylar under him. He quickly leaned back and helped her lower her legs. He didn't pull out of her, though. He knew he should. He needed to take care of the condom, but he couldn't bring himself to leave her yet.

He settled himself over her, careful not to give her all of his weight. His elbows rested next to her head, and he caressed her sweaty face with his fingertips. Her eyes were closed, and she was panting heavily. He could feel her heart beating against his chest.

"Sky?" he asked.

"Hmmm?" she answered without opening her eyes.

"I'm sorry."

At that, her eyes popped open, and she stared at him in confusion.

"I'm sorry that I was so . . . rough. I meant to make love to you nice and slow our first time."

Skylar's lips quirked upward, and she shook her head. "I've had slow. I've had nice. That was . . . I've never had *that*, and I'm not sure I can ever go back. I think I talked to angels, I came so hard."

Bull chuckled and couldn't help but feel ten fucking feet tall. "So . . . I corrupted you?"

"Yeah, Carson. You definitely corrupted me," she agreed. "I wasn't . . . it was good for you too?"

He stared down at her in disbelief. "Are you kidding? I couldn't wait to get inside you, and I know I hurt you in the process. Then I didn't last more than a couple thrusts because the feel of you coming on my dick was so overwhelmingly good, I busted a nut almost immediately. If it was any better for me, I'd be dead."

She smiled then. A wide honest smile that made Bull's heart almost hurt. He couldn't believe she'd been unsure for even a second. He made a mental note to make certain she knew how much she pleased him in the future. It was unacceptable for her to not be confident in her ability to turn him on.

She sighed in contentment, and her eyes closed.

"I need to take care of the condom. I'll be right back," Bull said as he slowly pulled out of her body.

They both groaned at the feel of him leaving her. Skylar turned on her side, and Bull straightened the blanket and sheet to cover her. Then he went to the bathroom and disposed of the condom before hurrying back.

He stopped in the middle of the room and stared at the woman in his bed.

She was still on her side. Her hair had come out of the bun she kept it in and was spread across his pillow. He could see her naked shoulders sticking out from under the sheet, and his heart literally hurt from the sight. Putting a hand to his chest, Bull knew Skylar had the power to hurt him more than anyone ever had in his life.

He'd never wanted this to happen. Not before he told her about Silverstone. He'd wanted to protect his heart so he could walk away without being hurt if she couldn't handle it. But it was too late. He was in too deep. It had happened quickly, so fast she'd snuck in under his shields.

Bull took a deep breath and walked the rest of the way to the bed.

He slipped under the covers, and Skylar snuggled into his side. She laid her head on his shoulder and wrapped an arm around his stomach. One leg hitched up and rested on his thigh. He felt claimed, and it was fucking amazing.

"You want me to take you home tonight?" he asked.

Bull felt Skylar stiffen against him before she asked, "You want me to leave?"

"No!" he said immediately. "But if you want to go, I'd never force you to stay."

"I want to stay," she said as she relaxed against him. "If it's okay with you."

"It's more than okay with me," Bull told her.

"I need to go home tomorrow before we head to my parents' house so I can change and shower."

"You can shower here," Bull told her. "And you know, to conserve water, we should probably shower together."

He felt her smile against his chest. "Of course," she agreed. "Carson?"

Bull couldn't help but smile at that, as always. "Yeah?"

"Thank you for being so amazing. Not only in bed, but in general. You're one of the best men I've ever met, and sometimes I think you're too good to be true."

Bull's heart squeezed. For a split second earlier, he'd considered telling her everything about Silverstone. And he should have. He needed to talk to her before he and the others left for Africa. But for now, in this moment, he was going to enjoy the relaxed and sated woman in his arms . . . maybe for the last time.

"Sleep, sweetheart," he told her, kissing her on the forehead.

It seemed as if she was out in seconds.

Bull lay awake for at least an hour trying to come up with the best way to tell her that he wasn't the man she thought he was. He was a killer. Plain and simple. And he wasn't sorry about it either.

That would be the hardest part to admit. That he would gladly do what he was doing for as long as possible because it made women like her safer.

Bull held Skylar close and did his best to put the conversation he had to have with her out of his mind. Tomorrow, he was going to meet her parents, something he knew she was nervous about. They'd moved their relationship to the next level tonight. Not only had they been as intimate as two people could be, but they were sleeping together. *Sleeping.* He could count on one hand the number of women he'd spent an entire night with.

He was going to enjoy this moment and this weekend as much as possible, because he knew the happiness and rightness of being with Skylar could be ripped from him as early as next week.

Chapter Twelve

Skylar could hardly believe this was her life. She'd expected the morning to be awkward with Carson. But when she'd woken up, he'd already been awake and had been quietly watching her.

"What's your morning routine like?" he'd asked.

"What do you mean?"

"Do you like to shower immediately, or do you need to relax and chill a bit first? Do you drink coffee? Watch the news? I know what you like to eat for breakfast since I've taken you out a few times, but I don't know about your routine."

It was true. She knew a lot about Carson too, but not some of the same things he'd just asked about her. "I usually shower first thing. It helps me wake up. I sleep in as late as I can, no snooze button for me, then just get up and get ready for work. After I'm showered and dressed, I have my coffee and check my messages and stuff. I don't like reading or watching the news—it's too depressing."

She hadn't been able to read the look on his face, but she'd relaxed when he'd nodded. "I like to shower right away too, and I don't use the snooze either. Most of the time, courtesy of the Army, I don't need an alarm. I seem to wake up when I have to. So . . . ready to get up and shower?"

Skylar had nodded, and five minutes later, she'd been in the shower with Carson.

He'd kissed her as if it was the first time, then he'd used his hand to get her off. It was a good thing he was there, as her knees had gone completely weak when she'd orgasmed, and she would've fallen to the floor if he hadn't been holding her up.

Wanting to return the favor, she'd gone to her knees and taken him into her mouth. He'd tried to tell her she didn't have to, but Sky had *wanted* to. Wanted to see him lose his incredible control. In the end, she'd had to use her hand to finish him off, but when he'd shot off all over her breasts, the look in his eyes had been completely worth her sore knees and the uncertainty about what she had been doing.

They'd cleaned each other off and gotten dressed, and he'd made them breakfast. Then he'd driven her to her apartment so she could change. Tiana had stuck her head out of her apartment and embarrassed the hell out of her, making comments about Sky not making it home the night before and insisting she was proud of her.

Carson had simply smiled throughout their entire conversation. He hadn't seemed uneasy in the least, and it had only made Skylar fall for him more. Most of the men she'd been out with would've been uncomfortable with her neighbor's teasing . . . and ogling. But Carson had just smirked and let Tiana have her fun.

Now they were on their way to Carmel, north of Indy.

"Carson?"

He grinned. "Yeah?"

She'd tried to stop doing that. Stop starting out every question with his name, as if she were asking permission to speak. But since she knew he was amused by it, by *her*, now she did it on purpose.

"My dad's kinda protective. I know I'm over thirty, but he simply can't stop himself from finding a moment to take the guys I date aside and let them know if they hurt me, they'll have him to deal with."

Carson didn't look put out in the least. "How many guys has he met?"

"Um . . . I think three before you."

He looked over at her then. "Only three?"

Skylar blushed. "Yeah, well, one was in high school, so I'm not sure he completely counts, but Dad scared him so badly he barely touched me all night. He didn't ask me out for a second date. The other was a guy I'd thought was the one. I met him in college and brought him home over Thanksgiving break. My dad thought he was a jerk, and I was devastated that they didn't get along. He broke up with me after Christmas break, saying he was getting back together with his high school girlfriend, who he'd spent a lot of time with when he was home."

"Asshole," Carson muttered.

"The other guy was someone I met four years ago. I dated him for about six months before I invited him home."

"What happened?"

Skylar shrugged. "My parents both liked him. He was a nice guy, but . . ."

"But you didn't," Carson finished for her.

"Pretty much. He was nice. Really nice. Almost *too* nice. I mean, I don't want to date an asshole, but I don't want to have to make all the decisions in our relationship either. I was constantly asking him when we could get together again and where he wanted to go. Not only that, I just . . . never mind."

"No, what? I'm interested," Carson pressed.

She took a deep breath. "Fine. I didn't feel *safe* with him. I always felt as if I was the one who had to be vigilant when we were in parking lots and stuff. He never walked me up to my apartment—I think because he was afraid. One day, there were cops everywhere on our block because a woman with a felony arrest warrant for murder had ditched her car after a chase and was on the loose. He simply told me to be safe and dropped me in the parking lot. It kinda freaked me out."

"That's bullshit," Carson growled. "I'd *never* do that. Hell, if it was up to me, you'd move out of your apartment complex into a safer one."

It was a bold statement, but strangely, Skylar appreciated the sentiment. He wasn't ordering her to move out, and it wasn't as if she didn't already know her apartment wasn't in the best part of town. "I feel safe with you," she told him. "From the moment we met, you've harped on me about my personal safety. And when we're together, you almost go overboard with security."

"That's because you're important," Carson said with a shrug. "If I can't protect the woman I'm with, then I don't deserve her."

"I don't need protecting all the time," she felt the need to say.

"I know you don't. You're a grown-ass adult who's proven she can take care of herself. But that doesn't mean that I'm going to let anything happen on my watch."

"It's just who you are," Skylar said with confidence.

Carson nodded.

"My dad's gonna love you," she said under her breath.

"Good. Not that I care for *me*. There are a lot of people who don't like me. But it's important to you, so I hope it goes well today."

Skylar did too. There were times she felt as if Carson was too perfect, and she really wanted to talk to her mom about him. See what vibes *she* got from him. At this point, Skylar thought she was too biased to see anything but the amazing man he was. He had to have some flaws, but so far she was having a hard time seeing them.

It had been a while since she'd been home, and when they pulled into her neighborhood, Skylar had a moment to be thankful that she'd grown up where she had. After living in her apartment for a few years, she was more than aware of the white privilege afforded her, living in Carmel. She didn't get any side-eye when she shopped in the grocery store, and no one followed her around, wondering if she was going to steal something. She had a positive relationship with the police.

The differences had stood out even more once she'd started at Eastlake. She could easily find children's books with white characters, but had to search hard to find quality ones with Hispanic, black, Asian, Arab, and other ethnicities as main characters. And most importantly, she had the privilege of being insulated from the daily toll of racism. She could go about her life without worrying about being discriminated against or racially profiled. She couldn't say the same for her students or their parents, which was heartbreaking.

Skylar knew she wasn't perfect. She tried hard to be as blind to people's exteriors as possible, but there were still times she found herself purposely trying to avoid someone she saw on the street because of the way they looked.

Growing up in Carmel had been good. Great, really. She loved her parents, and they'd worked hard to give her a good start to life. But coming home also made her uncomfortable sometimes because she couldn't help comparing her childhood to those of the students in her class.

"It's nice," Carson said as he pulled into the driveway of the house she'd grown up in.

Skylar nodded. "It is," she agreed.

"You okay?" he asked.

She took a deep breath. "Yeah. I just want today to go well."

Carson undid his seat belt and put his hand at her nape and pulled her into him. "It's gonna be great. Wanna know how I know?"

She nodded.

"Because these are your parents. They raised you to be the beautiful person you are today. How could I not get along with them?"

Skylar smiled at him. "Thanks."

Then Carson kissed her lightly. It was a casual kiss, one that demonstrated more intimacy than anything else he could've done. She loved that he touched her so much. That he didn't feel awkward about holding her hand or pulling her into him. Or kissing her in his car in her parents' driveway.

He looked her in the eyes for a long moment, then, obviously seeing whatever it was he was looking for, he nodded. "Come on. Let's do this so you can relax."

Carson came around the car and took hold of her hand when she got out. He walked confidently up to the front door. "Do we knock?" he asked.

The question surprised Skylar. She grinned and reached for the knob. "Nope. Mom would probably wonder who the hell was at the door if we did." They walked into her childhood home hand in hand, and she called out, "Mom? Dad? We're here!"

Within seconds, Dayana and Cory Reid appeared.

Skylar saw her dad's gaze go down to her and Carson's intertwined hands, and then she was in his embrace.

"Hey, baby girl," he said softly into her ear.

"Hi, Daddy," she returned. Being held in his arms never failed to make her feel safe. He'd been protective when she was a little girl, and Skylar had never forgotten a single one of the hugs he'd given her to make her feel better when she'd been upset.

She turned to her mom and gave her a huge hug as well, and when she turned around, she saw that Carson was just dropping his hand after shaking her dad's.

"Mom, Dad, this is Carson Rhodes. Carson, this is my mom and dad. Dayana and Cory Reid."

"It's a pleasure to meet you," Carson told them as he shook her mom's hand. "Skylar has nothing but good things to say about both of you."

"Then she's lying," her dad said with a grin.

"Dad," Skylar warned.

"What? You can't stand there and tell your young man there were never times you were pissed as hell at me. What about that time when you—"

"Can we leave the embarrassing stories until we've at least eaten lunch?" she interrupted, rolling her eyes.

"Come on," her mom said, always the peacekeeper. "I've got some appetizers for now until lunch is ready in a bit."

Skylar wanted to shake her head. Who heard of offering appetizers before lunch? But she simply nodded and went with it. She felt Carson's hand brush against hers, and she gladly took hold. She loved that he wasn't afraid of showing a little bit of affection toward her. It would be different, and too much, if he hauled her against him and threw his arm over her shoulder. But holding his hand felt nice . . . and right.

Two hours later, after a delicious lunch, it happened, just as Skylar had known it would.

Her mom said, "Honey, I haven't heard about your students in way too long. Why don't you let your dad and Carson talk for a bit while we catch up?"

It was her mom's not-so-subtle way of giving her dad time to talk to her boyfriend one on one. It annoyed her a little bit, but since she'd known it was coming, Skylar merely turned to Carson and lifted her eyebrows in question. She wouldn't leave him alone with her dad if he was uncomfortable.

But he simply nodded. "Go on. Catch up. We'll be fine."

"You sure?"

"Of course," Carson said with a smile. "You afraid your dad is gonna break out the photo albums and show me all your teenage pictures?"

Skylar winced. "Uh . . . if he does, promise me you'll be a gentleman and refuse to look."

Carson chuckled. "I promise."

She knew he was lying through his teeth. He'd jump at the chance to see what she looked like when she was a teenager. She turned to her dad. "Behave," she warned.

Her dad widened his eyes innocently, as if to say, "Who, me?"

Skylar sighed and shook her head in exasperation, but she stood to follow her mom out of the room. She looked back right before she left to see Carson looking as relaxed as he had been all day, while her dad leaned forward, as if to start the interrogation.

Hoping that Carson hadn't been lying when he'd said he didn't mind if her dad gave him the third degree, she followed after her mom.

~

Bull was almost eager to have this conversation with Skylar's father. It was a little ridiculous that the man wanted to interrogate his daughter's boyfriend when she was in her thirties, but then again, if *he* ever had a daughter, he knew he'd feel the same way. So he didn't mind Cory having his say. Bull had no intention of hurting Skylar, and he'd let her father know that in no uncertain terms.

Cory didn't make Bull wait. As soon as they heard a door shut upstairs, the other man turned to him. "First, I realize my daughter is a grown woman and that she's been making decisions for herself for a very long time. But she's still my baby. So I'm gonna say what I have to say, and we can move on.

"Skylar's always been the kind of woman who leaps before she looks. She's tenderhearted and sometimes doesn't stop to think about the motives behind other people's actions. She doesn't hesitate to help those who she thinks are in need. She gives money to homeless people who aren't homeless. She's paid for groceries for people who've claimed to have lost their credit card who can probably more than afford their food.

"My daughter might also claim that she's perfectly happy being single and living a carefree life, but that isn't what she wants deep down. She wants someone of her own. Someone she can come home to, who she can make laugh. Sometimes I think she was born in the wrong century. She wants a man she can take care of. Cook for, do his laundry, and generally do whatever she can to make his life easier. That's not to say she doesn't want to work, because she does. She's a damn good teacher, and her compassion makes her invaluable to her students."

"You aren't telling me anything I don't already know," Bull said when the other man paused. "Well, maybe except for wanting a man. From what I've seen, she's perfectly happy being on her own."

Cory shrugged. "I think that's because she's learned her lesson a few too many times with assholes who've taken advantage of her giving nature. All I'm saying is that in the past, Skylar's fallen fast for men she's dated, and some weren't worthy of one second of her time and energy. She's been hurt, and every time, all her mom and I can do is sit back and tell her that somewhere out there is a man who was made just for her. She just has to be patient."

Cory's words made Bull sit up a little straighter. He liked that thought. A hell of a lot.

"We tell her that there's a man out there who needs her brand of goodness. Someone who will let her be who she is . . . a little naive and a lot generous. If you're with my girl to get off or because you think she's an easy mark, you can walk out that door right now. It'll hurt her a lot less if you end things now than after she's fallen head over heels for you. I refuse to sit back and let her be taken advantage of anymore. If you aren't prepared to have Skylar fall in love with you, you need to rethink things. Because as her dad, I can tell for certain, she's almost there."

Bull's heart felt as if it was going to burst. He couldn't help but think back to last night and this morning. How carefree and content he'd felt with Skylar in his arms. He liked that her dad thought she was in love with him, because *he* sure as hell was already there.

He leaned forward, resting his elbows on his knees and looking Cory in the eye. "What's between Skylar and myself is not casual," he said carefully. He wasn't going to tell Skylar's dad he loved her before he'd told *her*. "I agree that your daughter is naive. She grew up sheltered, but that's not a bad thing. She's got more compassion in her little finger than most people have in their entire bodies. You and her mother did an amazing job raising her."

Cory shook his head. "Wasn't us," he protested. "It's just her."

Bull nodded in acknowledgment, then continued. "Your daughter and I haven't been dating all that long, and I don't know what the future has in store for us, but I've never felt so content in a relationship before. Skylar is everything you said she is and more. I don't want to change her. I find that standing back and watching her interact with the world, while keeping her safe from those who might want to take advantage, is one of the most exciting and interesting things I've ever done in my life. I'd rather gouge my own eyes out than do anything that will hurt Skylar. She's safe with me."

Cory eyed him for a long moment, then finally nodded. "She had one boyfriend in college who hit her."

Bull sat up straight upon hearing that.

"She never admitted it to us, told us that she'd run into a door, but my girl isn't clumsy. Not at all. I think she was embarrassed she'd cared as much for that asshole as she did. She might be naive, but Skylar's not dumb. She wasn't going to put up with that, not for a second. She told us things weren't working out between them and that's why they broke up, but she wasn't the same for the longest time after that." The older man sighed. "I just don't want that for my daughter ever again."

"I will never lay a hand on Skylar in anger," Bull told him. "The mere thought makes me physically ill," he said honestly. "I can't promise we'll never have a disagreement or that she won't be upset with me for whatever reason, but I *can* promise that I'll always have her well-being in mind."

The two men stared at each other for a long moment before Cory nodded again. "Thank you."

Bull mentally sighed in relief. He hadn't needed Cory's approval, but he'd wanted it. And it had been a long time since Bull had wanted *anyone's* approval. Knowing Skylar's dad was okay with him seeing his daughter felt good. Very good.

In a lot of ways, he reminded him of his own dad. And he definitely liked that he was fierce in his protection of Skylar. "You have a beautiful home," he told Cory, changing the subject.

"Thank you."

"I couldn't help but notice, however, that there are a few things you could do to make it safer."

Cory's head tilted. "Yeah?"

"Yeah."

"Like what?"

"The bushes around the windows in front are huge. They're very nice, don't get me wrong, but they're big enough to conceal a man my size. He could hide there and overtake someone who stops at the front door to unlock it and enter." Bull hadn't really meant to give the other man security tips, but when he thought about *Skylar* being the one taken by surprise by someone lurking in the bushes, he couldn't help bringing it up.

"Hmmm. I've been meaning to call in a landscaper to prune them," Cory said. "What else?"

"The control pad for your alarm system is located where it can be seen from one of the windows by the garage," Bull told him.

"And?" Cory asked.

"And anyone who wants to know if the alarm is activated only has to look through the window and see if it's on or not. It was off when we toured the house, and the big red button on the device would let anyone looking in the window see that."

"Wow, okay, I hadn't even thought of that," Cory said, his brow furrowing.

"Your backyard is gorgeous, but the gate to the fence is located around the side of the house, instead of at the front, where it would be more obvious to neighbors if someone was trying to get in. I also suggest you put a better lock on that gate as well. And you've got a ladder stored under your deck back there. Thieves will use anything they can to make their lives easier . . . why give them a way to get to the second floor?"

Cory didn't say anything for a moment, and Bull thought he'd overstepped. No man wanted to admit he'd fucked up, that the home he'd thought was secure wasn't.

Then Skylar's father nodded. "I can see my Sky's in good hands," he said. "Thank you for the tips. I'll see what I can do to fix those things and get someone in to find out what else we could do to keep ourselves more secure."

After that, the talk turned to more general topics. Cory wanted to know how long Bull had been working at Silverstone Towing, and they talked a bit about the military before Skylar and Dayana returned.

Bull stood to greet them.

"You're still here," Skylar teased with a grin. "Guess that means Daddy didn't have time to get out my prepubescent pictures."

Bull couldn't help but pull her against his side and kiss her temple in response. She stared up at him, and it was as if they were the only two people in the room. "Have a good talk?" she asked softly.

"Of course," Bull told her. "I heard you were in the theater club in high school."

Skylar chuckled. "I was a terrible actress. I never had a main part and was always a 'townsperson' or other random characters in the plays."

Bull loved learning new things about Skylar. Although he'd been pissed to hear someone she'd dated and trusted had put his hands on her in anger, he was proud that she hadn't made excuses for him and had ended the relationship.

"I bet you were adorable," he told her.

Skylar shook her head and rolled her eyes. "I wasn't, but thank you. What did you and Daddy talk about?" she asked.

"Man stuff," her dad responded.

Bull felt Skylar jerk slightly against him, as if her dad had scared her. If he was being honest, he'd kinda forgotten they had an audience himself. He tightened his hand around her and kept it there as she turned.

"Whatever," she told her father. "At least tell me you didn't get out the shotgun and threaten Carson. I forgot to tell you that his nickname in the Army was Bull, short for Bullseye . . . because he was such a good shot."

Bull wanted to chuckle at the look of respect Cory fired at him. It was more than obvious he was okay with him being a good shot . . . as long as his skill was used to protect his little girl.

"Thank you for your service," Dayana said.

Bull nodded. At one time, that phrase had bugged him. If people knew what it was he and his team had done as Deltas, they might not be so quick to thank him, and it irritated him that he was doing the same thing now, but it would be looked at very differently if word got out. Though he'd learned over the years that when people thanked him for his service, it was more because they wanted to show support for the military in general. Citizens hadn't always treated veterans with respect, so he'd learned to take their thanks graciously.

He nodded at Skylar's mom.

"We need to get going," Skylar said in the conversational lull that followed her mom's words.

"Oh, but you just got here," Dayana protested.

"Mom, we've been here for hours," Skylar said with a laugh.

"Not long enough," her mom pouted.

Skylar pulled away from Bull and went over to hug her mom. "I'll be back soon, and you know I'm always just a phone call away."

She hugged her dad then, and Bull shook both of her parents' hands. "Thanks for letting me encroach on the time with your daughter," he told them.

"You're always welcome here," Dayana said.

"After I make those changes you suggested, I wouldn't mind you coming back and taking a look," Cory told him.

Bull nodded. "Just let me know when it's done, and I'll come up."

"What changes?" Skylar asked.

"Next time I'll make that chocolate cake I talked about," Dayana said with a huge smile.

Bull herded Skylar to the door. He liked her parents, but he was looking forward to having her to himself once more. He liked hanging out with her. Thus far in his life, the only people he'd found himself comfortable around were Eagle, Smoke, and Gramps. And now Sky. It was one of the ways he knew this wasn't just another casual relationship.

He watched as Skylar hugged and kissed her parents once more and said goodbye. Then he followed her to the passenger side of his car and made sure she was settled before going around to the driver's side. As he pulled away, Bull couldn't help but chuckle at the vigorous way Skylar was waving to her parents . . . as if she was going to be thousands of miles away from them for the foreseeable future, instead of only an hour or so.

"What changes?" she asked again when they were down the road a ways.

"Nothing major. I just had some suggestions as to how to make the house more secure."

"Wow. All right, then I have to warn you that Dad's probably gonna go a little crazy asking for more advice about that kind of thing," Skylar told him.

"It's fine. I'm happy to help."

A comfortable silence fell between them.

When they were halfway back to the southwest part of the city, Bull observed, "You're close with them."

"I am," she agreed. "I never went through that awkward teenager phase where parents are the enemy. I always knew they had my best interests at heart."

"Tell me about the asshole in college who hit you?" The question burst out of Bull before he could think better of it.

But Skylar didn't get upset. She simply sighed. "I swear to God, my dad always brings that up when I get a new boyfriend."

"He's worried about you."

"I know, but, Carson, I'm old enough to take care of myself. And, I'll note, that asshole only hit me once before I dumped him."

Bull didn't even crack a smile. "What happened?"

"You aren't going to drop this, are you?" she asked.

"No."

Sky shook her head in exasperation. "He was drunk. We were at a party. I was talking to a guy who I knew from one of my classes. My boyfriend got insanely jealous and grabbed my arm, basically force-marching me from the house. I was embarrassed as hell because everyone saw him do it, and he was also hurting me. I let him steer me out into the yard, but then I refused to go any farther.

"He yelled at me, told me that I was 'his' and I'd humiliated him. I tried to explain I was only friends with the other guy, and we were talking about the assignment that was due the next week, but he wasn't listening. Before I even knew what his intentions were, he'd pulled his arm back, and his fist was coming toward my face.

"I turned at the last second, and luckily he got me in the temple instead of my nose, which was what he was aiming for. I fell to the grass and stared up at him in shock, but he didn't even seem sorry for what he'd done. He was drunk and still pissed. He tried to kick me, but three guys at the party tackled him and beat the stuffing out of him. The next day, when his friends told him what he'd done, he tried to get me to talk to him, to apologize, but I refused to listen. I told him we were over and that I didn't want to talk to him ever again."

Bull's fingers tightened on the steering wheel. He wanted to go back in time and beat the shit out of the little punk himself. But he forced himself to sound calm when he asked, "And did he stay away?"

Skylar sighed. "No. He begged me to hear him out. To let him explain. He claimed he was drunk and didn't know what he was doing. That he'd never hurt me intentionally. That I was the best thing to happen to him."

"You didn't give him a second chance . . . why not?" Bull asked. He was *glad* she hadn't given the asshole another chance to hit her, but he wanted to hear her reasoning.

"Here's the thing. I know he was drunk. But if I was so important to him, if I was the 'best thing' to ever happen to him, then I figure he would've known who I was, even if just unconsciously. That he should've been protecting me from *other* people who might hurt me while *they* were drunk." She shrugged. "It sounds stupid, now that I think about it."

"It's not stupid," Bull told her fiercely. "You're dead-on accurate. He was at a party with you, one where there was alcohol, and he shouldn't have gotten so fucked up that he couldn't keep his head on straight. Getting drunk isn't an excuse to hurt someone you love. Ever. You did the right thing, and I'm proud of you for sticking up for yourself."

"I might be naive and clueless sometimes," Skylar said ruefully, "but it's like you said to me once. I deserve to be with someone who will bend over backward to keep me safe and protect me. Not because I'm weak, but because I'm important enough to them that they can't help but do anything differently."

He remembered telling her that, and Bull could still picture his father sitting him down and explaining how it should be between a man and his wife. Telling him that when he met the woman he wanted to spend the rest of his life with, he'd understand what he meant.

"And you know what? I want to find someone I feel the same about. I know I'm a woman, and men are typically stronger and all that jazz, but when push comes to shove, I'll do whatever it takes to protect my man too. That might not be with my fists or with brute strength, but

I'll find a way. I can be pretty sneaky if I have to. I just know I'll support him in whatever he wants to do with his life."

Goose bumps broke out on Bull's arms. Her words struck home and were everything he'd ever wanted to hear from someone. He knew he was a lucky man. His dad had been amazing. And his Silverstone team would follow him to hell and back if he asked it of them. But he'd never found a woman who'd had that same level of fierce loyalty.

He hadn't realized he'd wanted that.

Until now.

Until *her*.

"And now I feel stupid," she said with a wrinkle of her nose.

"No!" Bull exclaimed. Then he took a breath and tried to not sound so crazy. "That was amazing. I'm proud of you for seeing your own worth, even back when you were in college. Too many women don't. They make excuses for their men and believe they must've done something to be abused. And you're exactly right—you aren't weak. You're probably the strongest woman I've ever met. You live your life the way you want and don't let others tell you what you should think or do. It's beautiful. *You're* beautiful."

Bull wanted to pull over and kiss the hell out of her, but he knew that wouldn't be enough. And stopping now just meant it would take longer to get her back to his apartment and into his bed. "You have anything you want to do on our way home?" he asked, not so nonchalantly.

"You mean, like, errands?" she asked.

"Yeah."

"No. What I want is for you to take me back to your apartment so I can show you how much it meant that you came with me to meet my parents. And that you didn't freak out when my dad gave you his 'I have to protect my little girl' speech," she said with a gleam in her eye.

"My apartment *is* safe," Bull said with a small smile.

"God," Skylar sighed. "I love seeing you smile. It's so sexy, especially because you don't do it that often."

"I hadn't had much to smile about until I met you," Bull said, feeling a little sappy admitting that, but the look of delight on her face made opening up to her worth it. He reached down and twined his fingers with hers.

He drove as fast as he dared to get home. He and his friends had a good relationship with law enforcement. They didn't know the exact nature of what Silverstone did, aside from the towing, but some *did* know they worked with the FBI and Homeland Security in some way. They'd even been called upon to help in local active-shooter situations in the past. But Bull didn't want to push his luck by getting a reckless driving ticket.

He and Skylar didn't say much as he drove back to his apartment, but the silence was anticipatory, not strained. The sexual tension in the car was thick, and Bull found himself enjoying the feeling.

The second he parked, both he and Skylar hopped out. She met him at the front of the car.

"In a hurry?" he teased.

"Yup," she told him, then grabbed hold of his hand and began towing him toward the door to his complex. Bull never took security for granted, but just this once, he wished it was easier to get to his apartment.

The second he shut his door behind him, he turned and picked up Skylar.

She giggled and wrapped her legs around his hips, and Bull had his hands under her ass as he carried her to his bedroom. She began to unbutton his shirt as he walked, and when she lightly pinched his nipples, he staggered and hit his shoulder against the wall.

"Careful," she teased as she leaned forward and nuzzled his neck near his ear.

"Fuck," he said under his breath.

"That's the plan," she agreed.

Bull shoved open the door and headed straight for his bed. He had his own plans for his woman . . . namely, showing her how much she meant to him.

Chapter Thirteen

Skylar woke early Sunday morning feeling more relaxed than she'd been in a very long time. She looked over and was surprised to see Carson still asleep.

After he'd taken her hard and fast when they'd gotten home yesterday, he'd made it his mission to kiss every inch of her skin. He'd been tender and loving, and when he'd finally slipped back inside her body, she'd wanted nothing more than for him to take her roughly again, but instead, he'd made love to her gently and reverently.

By the time she'd orgasmed, she'd known if he ever broke up with her, she would be devastated.

He'd ordered pizza for dinner, and after eating, they'd watched half of the third season of *Stranger Things*. Then she'd decided to make love to *him*, and surprisingly, he'd allowed it. He'd let her suck on him for a while, but not bring him over the edge. She'd straddled him and taken him inside her body, but they'd both known she wasn't the one in control. Carson had held her hips and helped her move up and down on his cock until they'd both exploded.

It had been as natural as breathing to stay the night again. Skylar knew she shouldn't get used to it, but she couldn't help it. She loved sleeping next to him.

Even in sleep, Carson looked fierce. His mouth was drawn down into a frown, and Skylar wanted to see him smile. She slowly shifted, getting up onto an elbow—and huffed out a breath in frustration when he immediately opened his eyes.

But she was rewarded by a slow smile forming on his lips. His eyes glowed with happiness.

"Morning," he said groggily.

"Morning. Do you hear that?" she asked quietly.

His brows furrowed as he listened intently. "Hear what?"

"Silence," she told him. "It's never quiet at my apartment. I've gotten used to it, but there are always horns honking, cars and trucks going down the street, train whistles, people yelling at each other, babies crying. Day and night, it never stops. Sometimes it makes me feel alive. As if I'm in the thick of things. Other times it's somewhat scary, especially when I hear gunshots. But I never really understood *how* noisy it was until this morning, when I lay here and realized that the only thing I could hear was you breathing next to me."

She didn't mean her words to be alarming, but apparently they were. At least to Carson. "I hate where you live," he told her.

"I know." There wasn't much else to say. She knew he didn't like it. Neither did her parents. But it was what she could afford. And she had amazing neighbors, which Carson and her mom and dad knew.

Deciding she probably should've kept her mouth shut—because Carson was now anything but relaxed, and he definitely wasn't smiling—she changed the subject. "What are our plans for today?"

And his smile returned. "Our plans?"

She shrugged and tried to pretend she wasn't blushing. "Yeah, well, we're here together, and while I have some things I need to do later this afternoon, I was wondering what we were going to do this morning."

"I need to run by Silverstone," Carson told her. "I have to meet with Eagle, Smoke, and Gramps and make sure things for the upcoming week are good."

"What things?"

"The schedule, truck maintenance, shopping, those kinds of things."

"Oh, that makes sense."

"I can either drop you off at your place before I head over there, or you could come with me."

"I'd love to come with you. I can keep myself busy while you're doing business stuff. It's not as if hanging out at Silverstone is a hardship," she teased.

"True. We've really tried to make it a home away from home. Somewhere our employees like coming to."

"You've succeeded," Skylar told him.

"Thanks. Anyway, then I thought we could go to lunch before I bring you back to your place. I know you have stuff to do."

"Do you . . ." Skylar's voice trailed off. Would it be too clingy to ask him to stay with her? To stay the night? She was well aware her place wasn't as fancy or safe as his, but she couldn't deny she wanted him in her space. In her bed.

"What?" Carson asked, rolling over until she was under him.

She loved when he did that. She felt surrounded by him, as if nothing and no one could ever hurt her when he hovered over her like he was. "I was just going to ask if you wanted to stay with *me* tonight. It's okay if you don't—my place is kinda small, especially compared to here. But it's close to my work, and I wouldn't have to get up as early if we stayed there. You could watch TV or something while I did my lesson plans for the week, then I could make dinner for us, or we could order in." She knew she was babbling but was almost afraid to stop talking, because then he could possibly say no.

Carson leaned down and kissed her to shut her up. When he pulled back, he had a small smile on his face. "I'd love to stay. Thank you."

"Feel free to bring whatever. You can leave stuff over there too. My shower's not as big as yours, but the water heater is really good. There's lots of hot water."

Carson studied her for a long moment. Then he brushed a hand over her hair—which she knew was probably a mess—and caressed her cheek before running a finger over her lips. "My Sky's so sweet," he said softly.

She swallowed hard. She wasn't sure what to say to that.

"A sweet, innocent lady in public and my wild woman in bed," he continued, still grinning. He lifted a bit, and his hand went between them, his fingers playing with one of her nipples.

"Carson," she whispered, arching her back, offering herself up to whatever he wanted to do to her.

It was hard to believe she'd found such a good man. One she couldn't ever imagine hurting her. One who knew exactly where and how to touch her to drive her crazy.

~

After a late start because of the three orgasms Carson had given her, Skylar walked into Silverstone ahead of her man. She loved thinking about him that way. The weekend had been perfect so far, and she'd truly enjoyed spending time with him.

"Hey!" Carson called out as they entered the great room. It never ceased to amaze Skylar that the outside of the building could look so run down, yet the inside looked absolutely beautiful and elegant.

Today it was even nicer because there wasn't one thing out of place. The pillows were perfectly placed on the couches and chairs, the throw blankets were folded and sitting in a basket next to one of the easy chairs, the DVDs were neatly organized on the rack next to the television, and there wasn't a speck of dust anywhere.

"Hey!" a deep voice returned from the kitchen.

Looking up, Skylar saw exactly why Silverstone Towing was so neat. Shawn Archer was in the kitchen, wearing an apron and standing in front of the stove. Sandra was also with him.

"Hi, Ms. Reid! Mr. Carson!" the little girl shouted, hopping down from the step stool she'd been standing on next to her dad and running over.

Skylar caught her and gave her a big hug. "Hey, Sandra. What'cha doing?"

"Me and Daddy did some shopping!" she exclaimed.

"Daddy and I," Skylar corrected. Then asked, "You did?"

"Yeah. And we paid with *money*," Sandra said earnestly.

Skylar looked up at Carson in confusion.

"We do the bulk of the shopping for the week on Sundays. Even though he's not officially on the payroll yet, Archer volunteered to do it this week because Eagle hates grocery stores with a passion. He asked if he could bring Sandra along, of course. And we gave him cash to use."

Skylar's heart almost hurt that Sandra had been so enchanted with the thought of using paper bills to pay for the food instead of probably a credit card or food stamps.

A tug on her shirt had Skylar looking back down at Sandra. "We bought *so* much food! And now Daddy's cooking some up."

"I figured folks wouldn't mind having a nice meal when they came in from their jobs," Shawn said a little sheepishly.

"Anytime you want to cook, you go right ahead," Carson told him gratefully. "One more week until we have you full time."

Shawn nodded. "Yep, one more week until I'm done with *all* my jobs. I'm looking forward to working here full time." He looked at Skylar then. "Which means this coming week should be the last you'll need to stay late lookin' after Sandra."

"I'll miss looking after her," she told him.

"I know. You've been a blessing from God," Sandra's dad told her. "And, Bull, sir, you have no idea how much it means for me to have this job. I'm not going to mess it up."

"I know you aren't. You really didn't have to come in on the weekend to work, Archer. But you have no idea what it means to us to not have to cook and to have someone to help keep this place clean. Our employees are great tow truck drivers but not so good when it comes to picking up after themselves. And while we don't want Silverstone to look too inviting to nefarious riffraff, we don't want it to look like a junkyard either."

"What's knee-far-e-us mean?" Sandra asked, looking up at Skylar.

"Wicked or evil," Skylar told the little girl.

"Oh. Okay. Daddy! Wait! I wanna do it!" Sandra said, running back into the kitchen and climbing up on her stool. Shawn gave her the spoon he'd been using to stir the meat and vegetables that would go into his shepherd's pie.

"He's started working already?" Skylar asked Carson quietly.

"Not officially, but he's come in the last couple weekends of his own volition. He's great. We've never eaten so well, and seriously, look around this place. I'd eat off the floor if I had to."

Skylar giggled. "I'm not sure you need to go that far."

She loved the way Carson looked at her. With a mixture of tenderness, longing, and lust.

"I'm going to head downstairs to talk to the others. You'll be okay?" he asked.

"I'm fine. Go. I'll just get a head start on my lessons for the week," she told him.

Carson nodded, kissed her on the forehead, and headed for the stairs.

She wandered over to the kitchen and sat on one of the barstools. She didn't know how long Carson would be meeting with his friends, but she figured she had plenty of time to socialize and get her work done.

"He's a good man," Shawn said.

"I know."

"All of them are. No matter what it is they get up to in that mysterious safe room of theirs, no one can ever convince me otherwise."

Her brows furrowed. "A safe room? What do you mean?"

Shawn looked at Sandra, then took a step closer to Skylar. He kept his voice down so his daughter wouldn't overhear. "That room in the basement with the fingerprint lock on the door. Those four are more than just the owners of Silverstone," he said without a trace of doubt. "There's enough security in this place to keep the president of the United States safe. Not to mention the amount of time they spend watchin' the news and talking among themselves behind closed doors. Mind you, I've only worked a couple weekends, but . . . wouldn't surprise me if they were spies or somethin'."

His suspicions didn't sit well with Skylar. She hadn't thought at all about the other room in the basement, the one he hadn't shown her when he'd given her the tour. "There's a lot of busywork they have to do to run a business like this," she defended. "And it's good to keep up with current events. I don't like watching the news myself—it's too depressing—but not everyone's like me."

Shawn eyed her for a moment. "I'm sure you're right," he said.

Skylar frowned. She hated when people humored her. And it was more than obvious Sandra's dad didn't believe a word she said. "They aren't spies," she said firmly.

Shawn opened his mouth to respond, but Sandra interrupted him. "Daddy, what next?"

He nodded at Skylar and returned his attention to his daughter.

Sighing, Skylar grabbed her bag and went to sit on the couch. She didn't like Shawn talking about Carson and his friends behind their backs . . . but what she *really* hated was that he'd gotten her wondering what it was they did in that locked room in the basement.

She really *hadn't* thought anything about it before. Was it really a safe room? Like in the movies? But now that she considered it . . . why would they need something like that here? Yes, tornados sometimes hit Indianapolis, but they were rare. And while crime was possible in this neighborhood, why would someone target a towing company? It wasn't as if they had regular cash coming in that was kept on the premises.

Was Carson hiding something?

Hadn't she thought all along that he was too good to be true?

Realizing where her thoughts had led, Skylar shook her head in exasperation.

Why was she always looking for the bad in the men she dated? Maybe because so far, she'd always been let down by her boyfriends. She didn't want to think Carson could be hiding something from her. Remembering how happy she'd been that morning, Skylar did her best to set aside the doubts Shawn had unknowingly planted.

Carson was a good man. He wasn't hiding anything. He was simply a co-owner of a towing company. That was it.

She forced herself to pull her planner out of her bag and concentrate on what she wanted to teach her students in the upcoming week.

~

"So we're sure the intel is one hundred percent accurate?" Smoke asked the others.

The four men were seated around the circular table in the safe room at Silverstone, reading over the latest information they'd received from the FBI and Homeland Security. They would've waited until tomorrow to meet, but Gramps had insisted they needed to talk immediately.

"Yes," Gramps said with a nod and a grim look on his face. "Mostafa has traveled to Somalia, and a new training session has started. It's likely he'll be there at least all this week."

Bull's stomach rolled. He wasn't nervous about traveling to Africa and taking out Mostafa—he was scared shitless about telling Skylar he was leaving the country and what he'd be doing. He knew he could lie and say they were going to a conference or something, but he didn't want to do that to her. To them. He wanted to be honest. He knew he could trust her.

But he wasn't as certain that she'd be able to accept him as he was.

"What about Shekau?" Smoke asked.

"The asshole leader of Boko Haram?" Eagle questioned.

"Yeah. Last we heard they were planning another raid on a school. What's up with that?" Smoke clarified.

"It's on the back burner," Gramps informed them. "The primary school got word that a raid was being planned, and they took measures to mitigate the risk."

"What measures?" Eagle wanted to know.

"Armed guards, mostly."

"That's not going to keep Boko Haram from going after those girls," Eagle pressed.

"I know, but for now, we've got other things to concentrate on," Gramps told them. "Plans are to head out Tuesday morning. We'll make our way to the camp and be there by Thursday morning, their time. We'll strike in the middle of the night, kill Mostafa, and get the hell out. We'll be home early Friday evening."

It would be a quick job, as long as things went according to plan. Bull knew he'd only be away from Skylar for four days, but he still had a sense of foreboding.

"Anyone have any issues with that time frame?" Gramps asked, looking at Bull.

"Nope," Eagle said.

"Not me," Smoke added.

"I'm good," Bull told his friend.

"You gonna tell her?" Gramps asked.

Bull felt all his friends' eyes on him. He nodded slowly. "I have to."

"What if she can't handle it?" Smoke asked.

"Then I'll let her go," Bull said, the words feeling like acid in his mouth.

"Just like that?" Eagle asked in disbelief.

"What choice would I have?" Bull asked. "I'm not leaving Silverstone. I'm *proud* of what we do. We're making the world a safer place—for everyone."

"I think you should fight for her," Gramps argued. "She's bound to be shocked. You can't just drop a bomb like, 'Hey, I kill people for a living, that cool with you?' and expect her to be okay with it immediately."

Bull ran a hand through his hair. "I just . . . I don't want to hurt her."

"Life is full of hurts," Smoke argued. "And we all know you'd rather die yourself than put her in harm's way."

Yeah, of course they did. These men knew him better than anyone in the world.

Smoke went on. "Skylar makes you happy. And no other woman in all the time we've known you has done that. You're more laid back, relaxed. If you don't fight for her, you're making a big mistake, Bull."

He knew his friend was right.

"If she can accept this, can accept *you*, then I feel like maybe we all have a chance to find women of our own," Eagle said quietly.

Bull nodded.

"Besides, she likes us," Gramps said with a smile. "Who else are you gonna find who'll put up with the three of us?"

Everyone chuckled, Bull included.

"I'll talk to her tomorrow night," Bull said.

"If you need assistance, just let us know," Gramps told him. "You know we have your back."

"I appreciate it," Bull said. And he did. He wouldn't call on any of his friends for this, but he knew without a doubt they'd drop everything if he did.

Talk turned to other issues, including Archer's performance thus far. Everyone was extremely pleased with their new hire and couldn't wait for him to be available full time.

But Bull's mind remained on Sky. For the first time in his life, he was scared about a mission. Not because of what he was going to encounter in Somalia . . . but because of what Skylar would think of him after he told her what he did.

Chapter Fourteen

For the first time in her career, Skylar didn't want to go to work. She usually loved Mondays. She got to see her students after the weekend, make sure they were all okay, hear about what they'd done the last two days, and basically reconnect.

But today, she didn't want to do anything but lie in bed with Carson.

He'd stayed over at her apartment, and it had been everything she'd dreamed about. Her bed wasn't as big as his, but that didn't really matter since they slept wrapped around each other.

They'd gone to bed early, and he'd shown her just how dominant he could be. He'd made her orgasm over and over until she'd begged him to take her. And when he'd entered her, she'd sensed a kind of desperation in him that she hadn't noticed before. It worried her . . . but then he'd flipped her over onto her hands and knees and taken her from behind, and she'd convinced herself she'd just imagined it.

This morning, he'd gotten up before her alarm had gone off and made breakfast. He'd woken her up with a gentle kiss and a steaming-hot cup of coffee.

She hadn't wanted the morning to end, but of course the time had come for her to leave to go to school.

"I'd like to come over for dinner, if that's okay," Carson said.

"Yes! You're always welcome here," Skylar told him. But she got the immediate impression that he wasn't as excited about dinner together as she was. "What's wrong?" she asked quietly.

Instead of telling her that he was good, Carson took a deep breath—which scared the hell out of Skylar. Was he about to break up with her? He'd gotten her in bed, and now he was done?

She tried to control her panic. He wouldn't do that. He wasn't that kind of man. She'd bet everything she had on it.

"We need to have a serious talk tonight," he said, making her heart stop in her chest. "Don't panic," he ordered, obviously seeing her distress.

"Carson, nothing good comes from one person telling another, 'We need to talk.'"

She jerked in surprise when he reached out and snagged her by the nape. He pulled her into him, and Skylar went willingly, putting her arms around him and lacing her fingers together at his lower back. Her cheek rested on his chest, and she could hear his heart thumping. One hand stroked her hair, and the other clasped her to him tightly.

"There are things about me that I need to tell you," he said seriously. "But what you need to remember is that you're safe with me. You're *always* safe with me."

Skylar's mind whirled. She had no idea what he needed to tell her, and that made her uncomfortable. She picked her head up and tilted it back to look him in the eye. He looked as serious as she'd ever seen him.

"I know," she said softly.

"Do you?" he retorted.

Frowning, Skylar nodded.

"I hope to God you aren't just saying that," he muttered. Then he took another deep breath and put his hands on either side of her face and leaned down to kiss her on the forehead. It was a chaste, tender kiss, and it made Skylar want to cry. She had no idea what was going on in Carson's head, but obviously he was nervous about telling her something.

Wanting to ease his worry, she said, "I've never felt about anyone the way I feel about you. I know things have happened fast between us, but I have no doubt that we're meant to be together. I can't feel so comfortable and safe with you and not believe that you came into my life for a reason."

But instead of making him feel better, her words seemed to make him more anxious.

"Carson? You're scaring me."

"There's nothing to be scared about," he told her. "No matter what you hear from me tonight, please remember that I'm the same man you've gotten to know over the last month or so. I'm the same man you FaceTimed with in those first two weeks."

"You aren't going to tell me you're married with another family on the other side of the country, are you?" Skylar asked.

"No. I've never lied to you. Never. That's why I need to talk to you tonight."

Nothing about the vibe he was giving off right now seemed good. "Okay," Skylar said uneasily.

"Fuck," he muttered. "Now I've freaked you out. I shouldn't have said anything."

"It's okay," she repeated, wrapping her fingers around his wrists and holding on. "I just hate seeing you so upset."

He chuckled, but it wasn't a humorous sound. Then he leaned down and kissed her on the lips. "I had a good time this weekend."

It was an abrupt change of topic, but Skylar welcomed it. "Me too."

"And you're right, your apartment is noisy as hell."

She smiled. "I've mostly gotten used to it."

"It's getting late," he told her. "You need to get your butt in gear so you can be ready for everyone when they get to school. You know they'll all want to tell you about their weekends."

Everything he said was true, but Skylar *definitely* didn't want to leave now. She wanted to know what he had to tell her. She knew she'd think about it all day, probably getting little actual work done. Six o'clock couldn't come fast enough.

He leaned down and picked up his overnight bag, and she gathered her bag with her lesson plans, and they both headed for the door. Maria poked her head out of her apartment when they walked by and said good morning.

Carson walked her all the way to her car, his head on a swivel, looking for dangers all around them. Although this early in the morning, Skylar knew most of the local troublemakers were probably passed out in their beds.

"I'll come by around six thirty tonight, if that's okay," Carson said after she'd opened her car door.

"That's fine. This should be the last week I have to stay until six. It's going to be weird to not have to look after Sandra when the after-school program is done for the day. I know both her and her dad are excited about him not having to work so late."

"We're excited to have him at Silverstone," Carson said. "He's a hard worker, and we're lucky."

Skylar loved that he felt that way. He was a great employer, and he obviously valued his employees.

"Drive safe, and I'll see you tonight," Carson said.

Then instead of his usual peck on the lips, he tilted her head slightly and kissed her as if this would be the last kiss they ever shared.

As much as it turned her on, it worried her as well.

Closing her eyes, Skylar let Carson take what he obviously needed. A minute later, he pulled back but didn't let go of her. She opened her eyes and saw him staring at her, as if he was trying to memorize her face. Unease snaked its way through her once more.

"Carson?"

"Hmmm?"

"It'll be all right," she said softly.

Her words seemed to break whatever trance he was in, because he dropped his hands from her and took a step back. "Have a good day, sweetheart."

"You too."

"Later."

"Bye." Skylar sat in her seat, and he closed the car door. She waved, and he gave her a chin lift in return. He stood right where he was until she'd turned her car and was driving toward the exit. She looked into her rearview mirror before she drove out of the lot, and the last thing she saw was Carson running a hand through his hair in obvious distress.

Butterflies rolled in her belly. Something was definitely wrong, and she wasn't happy that he'd dropped such a vague relationship bomb on her before she left for work. Now she was going to worry about what he wanted to tell her all day. He *should've* kept his mouth shut and not said anything.

She shook her head. Men. Couldn't live with them, couldn't live without them.

~

Later that afternoon, when Bull was pulling up to Skylar's apartment, he beat himself up for what seemed like the hundredth time that day. He shouldn't have opened his big mouth that morning. He knew Skylar had probably worried all day over what he wanted to talk to her about. He'd stewed about it himself.

While telling her about Silverstone was the right thing to do, it still left a bitter taste in his mouth. Eagle, Smoke, and Gramps were equally worried about how his talk would go.

But this was Skylar. He'd explain that he and his friends were doing exactly what they did when they were in the Army as Delta Force operatives. She'd understand, and they'd spend their night together in bed, and he'd leave in the morning with a clear conscience. Not only that, but her knowing about his secret life would bring them closer together.

He hoped.

He ran up the stairs two at a time to get to the second floor and knocked on her door. It opened almost immediately—and Bull mentally chastised himself once more. Sky was biting on her lip and looking pretty damn anxious.

He acted without thought, pulling her into him and kissing her, as if he hadn't seen her for months rather than hours.

She melted into him, and the ball in his gut loosened a bit. He loved this tiny woman with everything in him. She had the power to ruin him, and she didn't even know it.

He backed her inside and shut the door behind him.

"Hi," he said when he finally lifted his lips from hers.

"Hi," she returned breathlessly.

"How was school? All your kids all right?"

"It was good. Hectic, as Mondays usually are. It took a while for them to get back into the swing of things, but that's nothing new. They're all good. Karlee fell and skinned her knee, and Ignacio learned to ride a bike over the weekend. I'm not sure Marisol had all that much to eat, and I need to make sure I pack some extra food in her backpack on Friday, but otherwise, everyone seemed to have a good break."

"That's good," Bull told her. It was always so easy to see she loved her students. They weren't merely a way for her to make money. She genuinely cared and worried about them. He knew that their life together would probably revolve around "her kids" for as long as she was a teacher. And he was more than okay with that. "Something smells good," he told her.

"Yeah, I made tacos. It was fast and easy. Do you want to talk first?"

Bull's stomached rolled. No, he didn't want to talk first. He was scared as fuck and wanted to keep things easy between them for as long as possible. "I'm starving," he lied. It would be a miracle if he could choke anything down. "Archer made an amazing-smelling casserole for lunch, but I didn't want to ruin my appetite for dinner with you."

She smiled up at him. "Okay, come on."

Throughout dinner, Bull couldn't take his eyes off Skylar. She'd changed into a loose pair of cotton pants and a T-shirt when she'd gotten home. Her auburn hair fell in waves around her shoulders, and he felt like the luckiest man alive to be sharing her space.

He wanted to prolong the night, forget telling her about Silverstone altogether, but after dinner, they sat on her couch . . . and he knew it was time.

Telling himself that things would be fine, that she'd understand and be proud of him for what he was doing, Bull took hold of her hands when she turned toward him.

"What I'm about to tell you, I haven't told any other woman I've dated. And you can't tell anyone either. Not your parents, your neighbors, or anyone. Understand?"

Skylar's brow furrowed, but she nodded.

"It's important, Sky," he said earnestly. "It's a matter of national security, and the safety of lots of people is at stake."

Her eyes widened. "I won't say anything to anyone."

Bull inhaled deeply and nodded. "You know that I was in the Army. Eagle, Smoke, Gramps, and I were all in Delta Force. Do you know what that is?"

"Yes. It's Special Forces, right?" she asked.

"Exactly. Delta Force is the best of the best. We were sent into situations that were too dangerous for regular units. We were good at what we did, Sky. With Eagle's ability to remember the names and faces of everyone he'd ever met or seen documentation about, Gramps's negotiation skills, Smoke's ability to get in and out of situations without being seen, and my accuracy with weapons, we were nearly unstoppable. None of the missions we accomplished will ever be talked about—they're now buried in mission reports in the Pentagon—but we more than served our country."

"I'm proud of you," Skylar said softly.

Bull nodded, then went on. "Our last mission for the Army was one of our best. We were able to eliminate two of the world's worst terrorists . . . but we hadn't been given permission to take out the second man. We were reprimanded, and our team was disbanded. We were going to be separated and kicked out of the Army when our enlistment was up."

Skylar gasped. "Can they do that?"

"Yeah. They can and did."

"I'm sorry," she told him.

"We weren't happy," Bull admitted. "And then someone offered us an opportunity to stay together. To keep doing what we were trained to do. The money Smoke had inherited allowed us to come to Indianapolis and get Silverstone Towing up and running. After a few years, Gramps, Eagle, and I bought into our share of the business. And we're proud of what we've accomplished."

Skylar frowned. "But . . . that's not what you were trained to do in the Army . . ."

"Right. Silverstone Towing is our passion, but it's only part of what we do. The other part of Silverstone is taking up where we left off with Delta. The guy who helped us end our commitment to the Army works with us when we go on missions. We get intel from him, and he greases the wheel when we need to get in and out of foreign countries undetected. But there are risks. If we're captured in the act, or if something goes wrong, the government won't bail us out. We're on our own. So, we get assistance and some funding, but when push comes to shove, we can only rely on each other. Which is okay, because I know the guys have my ass covered, just as I have theirs."

Judging by the confused look on Skylar's face, Bull realized he wasn't explaining things very well. He was beating around the bush, and he knew it.

"What are you saying?" Skylar asked. "Just spit it out."

He wasn't surprised she called him on his lack of clarity. So he laid it on the line. "Silverstone isn't just a towing company," Bull said bluntly. "Eagle, Smoke, Gramps, and I still go on missions to keep the world safe. We're leaving this week, tomorrow, to find another bad guy. Well, not *find*, as we know where he is . . . but to eliminate him as a threat."

Skylar's hands pulled out of his own, and Bull felt bile crawl up his throat. She wasn't taking this well.

Shit.

"You . . . you *kill* people?" Skylar whispered.

Bull winced, but nodded.

"You get *paid* to kill people?" she clarified.

Bull nodded again.

She sucked in a deep breath, and the look of shock on her face made Bull's chest hurt.

"You don't bring them in and put them on trial so they can pay for what they've done legally?"

"No," Bull said. There was a lot more he could say about that, but he'd obviously screwed up this explanation enough already. He was loath to mess it up even more.

Skylar abruptly stood and began to pace back and forth. It was obvious she was upset about what he'd told her, and Bull couldn't blame her. He searched for something reassuring to say, but couldn't think of a damn thing that would make this easier for her. He hated how she was biting her lip. How her forehead was all scrunched up.

And he *really* hated that when he stood and held out a hand to her, she ignored it.

He loved her. And he couldn't stand that the woman he would die for didn't want him to touch her. Wasn't asking more questions. Had simply withdrawn from him.

Bull felt himself go cold. He tamped down the pain he was feeling and dropped his hand. The only thing he could think about was the confusion and fear on Skylar's face. *He'd* done that. He'd promised not to hurt her, and it felt as if he'd done so in the worst way possible.

He wanted to say he was sorry. That he thought she'd understand. That he wanted to marry her someday, and what he did would never touch her in any way . . . but he couldn't say a word. It was as if he were frozen.

If she couldn't work through this, he would lose her. Fuck.

Skylar couldn't believe what she was hearing.

"You're an *assassin*?" she asked Carson incredulously.

They were standing about five feet apart, but it might as well have been a hundred.

"We don't like that word," he said in what sounded like a robotic tone. His face was blank of all emotion.

But Skylar was too shocked about what he'd told her for it to really register. She was having a hard time reconciling the man she knew with being a killer.

"You guys really go out and kill people? Is that even legal? No wonder you said I couldn't tell anyone! Will I get arrested for knowing what you do? Am I now an accomplice?"

"Breathe, Sky," Carson said. "We're working with the FBI."

She noticed he didn't answer her question of whether what he was doing was legal. Of course it wasn't. She felt faint.

"Sit down before you fall down," Carson ordered. He reached for her once more, but Skylar evaded his touch.

"Fuck," Carson muttered. "Will you let me explain?"

Skylar shook her head. She didn't want to hear any more. If the government was willing to hang them out to dry if they were caught, that *had* to mean what they were doing wasn't really sanctioned. That was a huge red flag for her. *Everything* about what he and his friends were doing was questionable.

And suddenly the secret safe room in their basement made more sense.

She collapsed onto one of the chairs in her small dining area. How she'd even gotten there, she didn't know. She stared at Carson, who'd followed her but was keeping his distance. "You said you'd never hurt me," she said in a small voice. "I trusted you, and you just hurt me more than anyone has in my entire life."

It registered again that Carson had not one ounce of emotion on his face. He appeared as she imagined he would while on one of his secret missions. Cold. Hard. Unfeeling.

She put a hand on her chest, as if that could keep her heart from shattering into a million pieces. "I need to think about this," she managed to get out. She didn't want to cry in front of him, but she knew she was only seconds from doing just that.

For a moment, Carson stood his ground, as if maybe he was going to try to rationalize the fact that he killed people for a living.

"Carson," she whispered. "I need some time."

"I don't think I explained things very well," he said quietly. "Please, let me stay. Let's talk through this."

Skylar shook her head, tears stinging her eyes. "You aren't the man I thought you were. The first time I met you, all you talked about was my safety. And the more you harped on it, the more I accepted it's just who you are. Now . . . hearing you say that you and your friends go around *killing* people is so far from who I thought you were it's not even funny. I need some time to digest this, to decide what to do about it. Please."

He winced, his only show of emotion, and incredibly, Skylar felt a little bad for him. But she pressed her lips together, refusing to give in and tell him it didn't matter what he did outside his time with Silverstone Towing.

It mattered. A lot.

"I'll give you some time . . . but this isn't over, Sky," Carson told her after a moment. "I refuse to let you go without a fight. You're the best damn thing that's ever happened to me, and I'm not willing to give up on us so easily. I'll be in touch as soon as I can."

Then he did as she'd requested. Turned and headed for the door.

The first tear fell as he reached for the knob. Without turning around, he said, "Lock this behind me." Then he was gone.

Skylar stood, as if in a trance, and walked to the door and turned the bolt. Then she collapsed on the floor and cried as she'd never cried before.

Her sweet, protective Carson, the man she loved with all of her heart, was a murderer.

She couldn't wrap her mind around it.

He'd sat next to her and explained it as if it was no big deal. As if what he and his friends were doing was perfectly normal.

It wasn't. It wasn't *close* to being normal.

A part of her wanted to be impressed that he hadn't lied to her, at least. But right now, all she felt was pain. The man she'd thought was absolutely perfect was so far from it that it made her head spin.

Chapter Fifteen

When Skylar turned over and looked at the clock and saw it was four thirty in the morning, and she hadn't slept at all, she knew she needed to call in sick. There was no way she could go to work and be happy and outgoing with her kids. She felt like death warmed over and could barely open her eyes, they were so swollen from crying.

She crawled out of bed and got her laptop, shooting off a message to the principal and sending in her lesson plans for whatever substitute was assigned to her class. Then Skylar got right back in bed and curled into a little ball.

Inhaling deeply, she could still smell Carson on her sheets.

She'd been thinking all night about what Carson had told her. He and his friends had been Delta Force. They'd taken out *terrorists*, never receiving accolades or credit.

She thought back to when Osama bin Laden had been killed. The Navy SEAL team who'd done it had been praised and given all sorts of press. Hell, she thought there was even a book and a movie about that mission.

She racked her brain trying to think of a movie she'd seen about any Delta Force team. She thought there were some with Chuck Norris, but didn't know if they were made up or based on real events. Then she remembered *Black Hawk Down* was about events in Mogadishu, and the men portrayed in that film were Army . . . Delta. She recalled the film and being in awe of the bravery of those men. Thinking about Carson doing the same thing for their country, for people like *her*, terrified Skylar and made her prouder than she could ever remember being of someone.

But he'd admitted the government wouldn't come to their aid if they were busted outside the country. That *had* to mean their continued missions were wrong . . . didn't it?

And Carson had said he was leaving today for a mission. He and his friends were going after another terrorist.

Just like that, fear swamped her body.

And not fear *of* Carson—fear *for* him.

Where exactly was he going? Was it going to be dangerous?

Of *course* it was!

God! How could she be so upset with Carson one second, pissed that he was a hired killer, then scared to death he might get hurt while on one of these undercover missions the next?

She was exhausted from not getting any sleep, her head hurt from crying, and her heart ached for the man she'd thought she knew.

It struck her that she'd never know if he was killed while he was overseas, especially if the government bailed on him and his team. He'd be just another "missing person," and no one would know where to start looking for him. Maybe he'd be taken prisoner and kept for decades in some deep dark pit somewhere.

Skylar knew she was overreacting, but she couldn't help it. Thoughts of Carson hurt or dying wouldn't leave her brain.

She needed to talk to him. Needed more information . . .

But she'd told him to leave. She'd called him a *murderer*—hadn't she? Or was that just on repeat in her head? She wasn't even sure what she'd said last night. She'd been so overwhelmed with his confession that everything afterward was somewhat of a blur.

Something else had gutted her almost as deeply as his confession. She'd gotten so used to seeing him smile at her; he did it all the time now. But last night, she'd seen the same blank look on his face that he'd worn when she'd first met him. His eyes had gone completely empty. *She'd* done that. And that hurt almost more than anything else.

But he *killed* people! How could he be so generous, funny, and caring with her and everyone around him, then go out and murder someone?

None of it made sense, and Skylar was as confused as she'd ever been.

She was so exhausted. Bone-deep tired, but every time she closed her eyes, she saw Carson trapped in some dark prison cell, reaching out for help, but no one was there to give him a hand. She was losing it. Completely losing it.

When her cell phone rang, it scared her so badly she let out a small scream.

Knowing if she didn't get herself together she was going to have a heart attack, Skylar leaned over to pick up her phone. It was still really early. Too early for telemarketer calls.

Maybe it was Carson, calling to say he'd told his friends he quit. That she was more important than his "job" and that he wasn't leaving today, after all.

But the number flashing on her screen said *unknown.*

Thinking it could be the school district, Skylar answered. "Hello?"

"Skylar, this is Gramps."

Her shoulders tensed, and she curled back up in a ball under her covers. She didn't know what to say to the man. She thought she'd known him, too, but apparently, he was also a killer . . . just like her boyfriend. Or ex-boyfriend. At this point, she had no idea what Carson was.

But she didn't have to say anything. Gramps began talking without waiting for her to ask why he was calling.

"Bull doesn't know I'm calling. He'd kick my ass if he did. But I had five minutes before we get on our plane, and I had to talk to you. I'm guessing things didn't go well last night."

Skylar wanted to snort, but she just lay there listening.

"You know, we all told Bull that you would be shocked when he explained about us. None of us thought it would go well. How could it? How could anyone understand what we do? But he had the utmost confidence in you. He said with the connection you two shared, there was no way you wouldn't understand. Or at least listen to what he was saying.

"But when we saw him this morning, we knew things didn't turn out as he'd hoped. Look, Bull is one of the best men I know. I've seen him *literally* give the shirt off his back to someone who needed it more than he did. Not only has he saved my life more than once, he's saved Eagle's and Smoke's too.

"When he first joined the Army, he had no one. His mom left him, and his dad had died not too long before. He had no family, no friends, and was trying to find himself. I didn't think much of him when we first met, but once I got to know him, I realized he lived to serve others. Some people are just wired that way. They want to help everyone they meet. He's also a little rough around the edges and doesn't show emotions very well, but deep down, he wants to be loved like anyone else. He's only spoken about it once, but his greatest wish is to find a woman he can love and who'll love him in return. We know he found that with you."

Gramps's words made tears well in Skylar's eyes once more. But he wasn't done.

"Have you heard of Fazlur Barzan Khatun?"

Swallowing hard, Skylar said, "Yes. Who hasn't? I don't watch the news, but everyone knows he was responsible for killing all those soldiers in Afghanistan."

"That's him. He was killed not too long after that, and it was discovered that he was planning a large-scale attack on US soil."

"I remember," Skylar said.

"It was Bull's bullet that ended his life," Gramps said bluntly.

Skylar's breath left her on a gasp.

"We also killed his second-in-command that day, Nabeel Ozair Mullah. But we weren't supposed to. Damn politicians got their panties in a wad, worried because officially, we weren't even supposed to be in Pakistan. But they sent us in after Khatun, and Eagle recognized Mullah, so we eliminated him. Instead of being praised for getting rid of two of the most dangerous men in the world, we were reprimanded, and our team was disbanded."

Skylar remembered Carson telling her about that last night, but she hadn't known the details. She hadn't asked and hadn't given him a chance to share them. "Why are you telling me this? Isn't it supposed to be top secret?"

"It is," Gramps told her. "But Bull trusted you enough to tell you about Silverstone, so I'm trusting you too. I don't know what was said last night or if Bull did a good job of explaining what we do. And I'm not trying to change your mind or tell you that you're wrong in kicking him to the curb, but . . . you *were* wrong," Gramps said harshly.

The man had been nothing but funny and gentle with her previously, but he wasn't being gentle right now.

"The guy who came to us after we learned the Army was going to kick us out works for the FBI and Homeland Security. We aren't some rogue group of guys flitting around the world killing random people. We go after the worst of the worst. Terrorists, sex traffickers, serial killers, drug lords . . . people who don't deserve to breathe the same air as law-abiding, innocent civilians. We work *with* the government, Skylar."

"But Carson said that they wouldn't help if you were caught."

"That's true. The Department of Justice has something called a 'black budget.' It's a budget allocated for classified and secret operations. We fall under that category. What we do is top secret, and we'll never get credit for any of it, but we don't want that shit anyway.

"The bottom line is that Bull is a fucking hero. What we do keeps the bogeymen away. We ask for no thanks, we don't want any damn medals. We do it to keep the ones we love safe. To keep our countrymen and women safe. To let kids like the ones in your class grow up without having to worry about whether their school will be blown up by a terrorist. We do what we do, knowing that if we die on a mission, no one will ever find out. Will never know what we've tried to do—keep the world safe from some of the evil that lives within it.

"Bull loves you, Skylar. He hasn't had much love in his life, and he'd bend over backward to keep his loved ones safe. He accepted me, a Hispanic young man who had a huge chip on his shoulder, without blinking. I'd do anything for that guy, and I know he'd return the favor. All I'm asking is that you think about how you *really* feel for him. I get that what he does is hard to understand or accept. But if he was still in the Army, would you feel the same way about what he's doing? Because believe me, what we're doing now is no different than what we were ordered to do when we worked for the military. Nothing's changed except the uniform. *And* we make one hundred percent sure the people we go after are guilty. We couldn't say the same when we were Delta."

"Gramps . . . ," Skylar started, not sure what else to say. The man's speech had cut her to the quick.

She'd judged Carson harshly. She hadn't given him a chance to explain, not really. But in her defense, he'd left out the part about being recruited by the FBI. Or maybe he hadn't . . . maybe she hadn't heard it through her anger and anguish.

"I gotta go," Gramps told her. "We should be home by Friday night if all goes well."

Once again it struck home what Gramps, Carson, and the others were going to do. They were headed into danger—and she might never see them again.

"Be safe!" she said almost desperately. Skylar didn't know if she could accept what Carson did, but she knew she couldn't stand the thought of him being hurt or killed.

"We always are. We know what we're doing," Gramps said confidently. "This should be a relatively easy job. In and out. Think about what you want," he told her. "Because I'll tell you this—if you choose Bull, you'll never go a day in your life without knowing you're loved. You'll always be safe and protected. That's a damn guarantee. I can't imagine anyone else who will love you as deeply as he does."

Then the line went silent.

"Gramps?" Skylar asked.

There was no answer. He'd hung up on her.

Turning onto her back, Skylar stared at her ceiling. She was even more confused.

Did she love Carson? Yes. There was no doubt.

Could she live with the knowledge that he was out there somewhere killing another human being? Being judge and jury? A killer was a killer, but if Bull and his team were sanctioned by the FBI and being funded by the government, did that make it okay?

She didn't know the answer to that.

~

After finally getting a few hours of sleep, Skylar crawled out of bed and showered. She didn't really feel any better, and the dark circles under her eyes made it obvious something was wrong, but she couldn't lie in bed any longer. She tried to get some work done but couldn't concentrate. She made something to eat and, after only a few bites, realized she wasn't hungry.

She was pacing her apartment, trying to get her head screwed on straight, when she heard Tiana laughing out on the walkway. She hurried to her door and opened it.

Her neighbor had just clicked off her cell, and she jumped and put a hand on her bosom when Skylar's door flew open so suddenly. "You scared the crap out of me," Tiana said on a laugh.

"Can I talk to you?" Skylar asked.

Obviously noting how disheveled and out of sorts she looked, Tiana immediately nodded. "Of course. You want to come over?"

"Yes." Skylar needed a break from her apartment. Everywhere she looked, she saw Carson. He hadn't been in her life that long, but the memory of him permeated every corner of her small living space.

She followed her neighbor inside. She hadn't been in her friend's apartment many times, but it was an exact replica of her own. Tiana put her purse on a table inside the door, already overflowing with other odds and ends, and gestured to the living room. "Sit. I'll get the shots."

"Oh, but I—"

"Nope. I can see whatever's on your mind calls for alcohol. And since you're here and not at the school on a workday, nothing's keeping you from indulging. Go sit, and I'll be there in a second."

Knowing when Tiana got something in her mind, she could be extremely stubborn, Skylar went and sat on the edge of the sofa. Studying her surroundings, she was reminded of how little she knew about her neighbor. Her place was cluttered but not dirty. Tiana was in her early fifties and had grown children. She lived alone and kept a shotgun by her front door and worked odd hours . . . but that was about all Skylar knew.

"Here," Tiana said, holding out a shot glass.

Skylar took it and wrinkled her nose. "What is it?"

"Don't ask. Just throw it back," Tiana advised her.

After taking a deep breath, Skylar did just that . . . and nearly choked at the burning in her throat as the alcohol went down. "Holy crap," she wheezed.

Tiana simply laughed. She did her own shot, then put her glass on the table in front of them. "Okay, talk. I know something's up, since you're never home in the middle of the day on a Tuesday. Are you sick? I probably should've asked you that before I gave you the shot, huh?"

Skylar smiled at the other woman. "I'm not sick."

"Right, then start talking."

Now that she was there, Skylar wasn't sure where to start. Even though she was confused as hell, she wasn't going to break Carson's confidence. He trusted her, and even though she desperately needed someone to talk to, she had to figure out how to get the answers she needed without blurting out what Silverstone did. "Carson told me something last night that has me reeling," she finally said. "The image I had in my head about who he was as a person was shattered into a million pieces."

"Guess the honeymoon's over, huh?" Tiana said with a small laugh.

Skylar didn't see the humor. "I just . . . he's always been so amazing. Overtipping, being a stellar employer, treating me with nothing but respect . . . but learning this thing . . . I just can't get over it."

Tiana leaned forward, all humor gone from her face. "First of all, no one's perfect."

"I know," Skylar said impatiently.

"Do you?" Tiana fired back. "Look, I like you. A lot. You're a great neighbor, you don't cook smelly food that penetrates the walls and makes me wanna gag. You're clean—there aren't any roaches coming from your apartment over to mine. You're quiet, polite, you always take your trash all the way to the dumpsters . . . but you're completely clueless when it comes to some things."

Skylar frowned. "I'm trying to be better."

Tiana chuckled. "Don't try too hard. Honestly, it's part of your charm. You like to see the good in people, which is fine, but you often completely ignore the bad," Tiana told her. "You're too trusting for your own good. Too naive. It's cute but exasperating as well."

Skylar huffed out a breath. "Why do you think it's so bad to see the good in people?"

"It's not bad, but it can get you into trouble. Remember the guy who lived in 3A a while back?"

Skylar nodded. "Yeah, what happened to him?"

"He was arrested for possession with intent to distribute," Tiana said bluntly.

"What?" Skylar asked in surprise. "But . . . he was always so nice to me!"

"See? That's what I mean. You probably wouldn't know what a drug addict looked like if your life depended on it. The man was a druggie, Skylar. He was arrested with enough meth on him to be charged with distribution, but I have no doubt he planned to keep it all for himself. He was nice because he was trying to butter you up. I'm guessing he would've stolen from you at some point. Your car. Break into your apartment. Come up and ask for a cup of sugar to see if you'd let him in."

Skylar was genuinely shocked. "I didn't know."

Tiana's voice gentled. "I know, Sky. That's why Maria, Susan, and I look after you. Everyone around here knows that if they mess with you, they'll have to deal with us. And believe me—no one wants that."

Skylar swallowed hard. "Why?"

Tiana stood up, grabbed Skylar's shot glass, and went into the kitchen. She came back with a full glass. "Drink it," she ordered sternly.

Surprised at the change in Tiana's tone, Skylar did as she'd commanded. Once again, the alcohol burned going down, but not as bad as the first time.

"I'm not the sweet old lady you think I am," Tiana said.

"You aren't old," Skylar protested.

The other woman snorted in laughter. "Right. Most days I feel as if I'm ancient. Anyway, what do you know about my past?"

"Um . . . nothing?" Skylar said with a shrug.

"I grew up on the east side of the city and joined the Vice Lords when I was twelve," Tiana said with no emotion in her tone. "Didn't really have a choice—it was join them or suffer the consequences. I never went to college, didn't finish high school, never got married. I had my first kid when I was seventeen and killed my first man when I was eighteen."

Skylar stared at the woman she'd come to know and respect, stunned, her mouth hanging open.

"I lived that life for more years than I care to admit. But eventually, it got old. I wanted more outta life than running around dodging the cops. I moved over here to the west side and got a job. It wasn't easy, and you never *really* leave the gang life, but I did my best. I managed to keep my kids away from that shit and alienated them in the process. They don't come visit me, but that's okay because I know they're safe and living nice, boring lives away from here. Everyone knows not to fuck with me because I could bring Vice Lords' vengeance on them with one phone call. I'm no longer a gangbanger, but I've still got connections."

Skylar's mind was spinning. "Are you serious?"

"As a heart attack," Tiana said. "I don't go 'round shooting no one up anymore, but I'm not the Goody Two-shoes you seem to think I am."

"I didn't think you were a Goody Two-shoes," Skylar said somewhat defensively.

Tiana ignored her. "And Susan? She's a kleptomaniac. She can't help it. She sees somethin' pretty in the store, and she has to have it. She's been arrested a time or two, but just about everything in her apartment has been stolen."

"She gave me the prettiest handbag last year for Christmas," Skylar blurted.

"Stolen," Tiana said with a nod.

"But—"

"You're the recipient of stolen goods," Tiana confirmed, not sounding concerned at all. "The guy in 12B likes to wear women's underwear . . . but as far as I know, he buys it all legal-like. The husband and wife in 14A sell the painkillers she gets for her bad back."

"What about Maria?" Skylar asked, almost afraid to know.

Tiana gave her an intense look. "Her mom was a prostitute, and she was killed by a client one night. Maria was bullied throughout school and is barely making enough money for rent, but she refuses to turn tricks like her mom did."

"I had no idea," Skylar said, shaking her head.

"My point, my naive friend, is that *no one* is perfect. You can either live in righteous indignation and refuse to talk to anyone who you think is below you, or you can just *live*. And ask yourself . . . whatever Carson's doing, is it hurting you? Because from what I've seen, that man is completely devoted. He doesn't take his eyes off you when he drops you at home until you're safely locked behind your door. He opens car doors for you, he always has his hands on you, ready to throw himself in front of you if necessary to protect you. He keeps his eye on everyone in this complex, and if they so much as twitch in your direction—which they wouldn't, because they know you're under *my* protection—I have no doubt he'd keep them in line."

Skylar could barely believe what she'd just heard. She'd had no idea about her neighbors' pasts or their habits. She'd always enjoyed talking to everyone, and they'd all seemed so . . . normal.

And Tiana was spot on about Carson. She'd always known he was hyperalert when she was around, but she just figured it was what he did for everyone. When he was at his apartment or at Silverstone Towing, he was much more relaxed. Not quite so alert.

Because he knew she was safe in those places?

Her mind spun.

"All I'm sayin' is that if I had a man like that, a man who treated me as if I was the best thing that ever happened to him, I'd overlook a hell of a lot. Again, Skylar, no one's perfect. And I'm guessing whatever he told you was big, since you never call off work—you love your kids too much—but is it too big for you to live with? That's the question."

That *was* the question.

"Do you know who Fazlur Barzan Khatun is?" Skylar asked.

"Of course. He's that motherfuckin' terrorist who killed all those people over in the Middle East somewhere. Good riddance. Fucker wanted to come over here and attack several cities at once. The news said if he would've succeeded, ten times the number of people who were killed in the attacks on the World Trade Center would've died. Whoever killed him did the world a favor, that's for sure. Sorry, I'm babbling. Why do you ask?"

"I just . . . no reason," Skylar said lamely. Of course Tiana knew who he was. Everyone did. And *everyone* was relieved he was dead.

Did that make what Carson did all right? She didn't know.

Tiana obviously knew there was a reason she'd asked, but she let it go. "Relationships aren't easy," she said instead. "Everyone does stupid shit. You just have to decide what you can forgive and what you can't. Your man is one of the good ones," Tiana said with no hesitation. "Before you throw him away, I suggest you really search your heart to see if you can live without him."

Skylar nodded. She felt like she'd been thinking about nothing but what Carson had told her, and she was nowhere near a decision.

"Now, are we good?" Tiana asked.

"Why wouldn't we be?"

"Because now you know a bit more about me. I was in a gang. For all intents and purposes, I still am. I've done some bad shit. You gonna be okay with that?"

Was she? Skylar thought about it for a second, then nodded. "You've been nothing but good to me. I'd like to think we're friends."

"And Susan? You think less of her because she's got sticky fingers?"

Skylar shook her head. "No. It's wrong, and I have a feeling she knows it, but that doesn't change the fact that she's selfless and always looking out for me."

"Right," Tiana said. "You judge people by how they treat you, not by what they look like, the color of their skin, or their past. It's one of the things everyone around here really likes about you. So I have to wonder . . . why are you that way with your friends, but not your man?"

Skylar blinked in surprise.

Tiana was right.

But . . . killing people . . . that was different than stealing and doing drugs, wasn't it?

As if she could read her mind, Tiana said, "At the risk of ruining our friendship, I'll repeat, I've *killed* people. Does that change the way you think about me?"

Skylar couldn't even imagine the older woman next to her killing anyone. She shook her head slowly.

"Right. If you can overlook me doing *that*, and I'm just your neighbor, I'm guessing you can probably forgive your man for just about anything."

Skylar licked her lips. She was tipsy from the two shots she'd done but was thinking more clearly than she had since Carson had told her what he and his team did for a living. "Thanks, Tiana."

"Anytime," she told her.

Skylar stood, and Tiana followed suit. She walked Skylar to the door and put a hand on her arm before she could step outside.

"I never found a man who looks at me like yours looks at you," Tiana said softly. "If I had, I would've never let him go. Maybe my life would've gone differently. Cut him some slack, Skylar."

After nodding, she walked back to her apartment and went inside. She locked the door, remembering how the last thing Carson had said to her was to lock the bolt behind him. Even after she'd shut him out and asked him to leave, he'd still been concerned about her. Been thinking about her safety.

The blank look on his face once more flashed in her brain. Skylar had hurt him. She'd been the one always begging him not to hurt *her*, but when push came to shove, she'd hurt him just as badly.

She had some more thinking to do, but she already knew she'd reacted very badly. Maybe the timing wasn't right, maybe he shouldn't have left the way he had without trying harder to make her see his side of things. Though, she hadn't really let him explain. She'd cut him off and thrown up a wall between them. She knew she wanted—no, *needed* to talk to him. She just hoped he'd make it home so she could do so.

Gramps was right. If Carson was in the Army doing what he was doing, she wouldn't think twice about it. She'd be proud of him. Proud to know he was protecting his country. Why was it different now that he was out? Now that the military had kicked him and his team to the curb for doing exactly what they'd trained them to do? It didn't seem fair.

With her mind still reeling, Skylar sat on her couch. She wanted to turn her brain off, to stop thinking about everything, but she couldn't.

Tiana had been a gang member. Susan was a kleptomaniac. The friendly couple down the way sold drugs. Her world had been spun on its axis, and yet . . . life went on. She was still Ms. Reid, kindergarten teacher.

She thought about Shawn and how happy he was to have his new job at Silverstone Towing. She thought about the fifty-dollar tip Carson had left at Rosie's Diner that first date they'd been on.

"We need to talk," Skylar whispered to her empty apartment. "Come home soon."

There was no answer, but just speaking the words out loud made her feel better. She wasn't sure what the future held for her and Carson . . . but she was ready to give their relationship another chance.

Maybe it was the wrong decision. Maybe she'd go to hell for it. But she wasn't ready to give Carson up. She loved him. All of him. She just needed him to get home so she could tell him.

Chapter Sixteen

"I can't believe you called her," Bull bitched to Gramps on the plane on the way back to Indiana.

They'd found Mostafa right where their intel had said he'd be. In the middle of a fucking Al-Shabaab training camp. They'd done surveillance, witnessing the American teaching the teenagers and young men about American culture and, later in the day, how to use grenades to cause the most damage.

The four men had snuck into his tent as planned and killed him with one of his own knives.

They were now flying back to Indianapolis. Willis had already been informed of the death of Jehad Serwan Mostafa and was elated. Their partnership with the man had worked out well over the years, and Bull knew he should feel some satisfaction that they'd gotten another terrorist off the streets, so to speak. But he couldn't make himself feel much of anything.

Other than annoyance over Gramps's interference in his relationship with Skylar.

"You were a fucking mess," Gramps reasoned with no remorse in his tone. "And I was pissed. I just wanted her to know that she'd fucked up. Besides, I know what it's like to have regrets. About not saying something you should've to a woman, about not doing more to make things work."

"It still wasn't your place," Bull said.

"Maybe, maybe not. But as your friend, I'm always going to have your back," Gramps said, not upset in the least. "If that means telling your girlfriend that she's being a douche, that's what it means."

"Don't call her that," Bull said ferociously.

"Not cool," Eagle agreed.

"*I* would've called her if I'd thought about it," Smoke added.

"Fuck," Bull said, running a hand through his hair. "We promised we'd never let a woman get between us. And I refuse to let my relationship fuck us up. If Skylar can't deal with what we do . . ." His voice trailed off, and he shrugged.

"So that's it?" Eagle asked. "You two are done?"

Sighing, Bull shook his head. "No. Not yet. We've both had time to think, and I know I didn't handle things nearly as well as I could've. I shouldn't have left her without at least trying to explain things better. I'm going to see if I can convince her to talk to me when I get home. I'll go over to her place tomorrow and see if she'll answer the door. I love her. I'm not ready to throw in the towel on what we have. She's it for me. I feel it in my bones. But she has to come to terms with what I do. Somehow."

"You think she can?" Smoke asked.

"I don't know."

"She called you an assassin," Gramps reminded him.

"Aren't you supposed to be trying to keep us together?" Bull asked a little grumpily.

"Yeah, but when someone hurts my friend, all bets are off," Gramps returned.

Bull looked at the three men sitting around him on the plane. He was lucky as fuck to have found them. When he'd joined the Army, he'd had no one. These men were now his family, and they'd proven over and over that they had his back—on the battlefield, in the boardroom, and now when it came to his relationship with Skylar. "She means everything to me," he said quietly. "I don't know how that'll change things between us as a team, but I'd do just about anything for her," he said.

"Including quitting Silverstone?" Eagle asked. There was no censure in his tone, just curiosity.

"I don't know," Bull said honestly. "I don't want to. I believe in what we're doing. Remember when we were in Lima in del Rio's compound, and behind door after door, we found abused and terrified women and children?" Bull asked.

When everyone nodded, he went on. "What if we *hadn't* done what we did? What if Rex hadn't called to tell us he'd found his wife and the person who'd kidnapped her a decade ago? The man would still be ruining lives today. He'd be kidnapping other women, selling children to depraved people to do horrible things to. But now he's dead, and those prisoners in his compound are all free. Yes, there will be others who try to take his place, and there will always be those who want to make a buck on someone else's suffering, but I feel as if we made a difference. At least in some people's lives. Every evil asshole we take out means we've saved someone from suffering. Somehow. Someway.

"I don't want to stop. Not yet at least. But if Skylar tells me she can't be with me if I'm a part of Silverstone, *I'll* be the one suffering. She's everything to me. Even after such a short time, I know my life will be a hollow shell of what it could be if she leaves me. I'm not sure I'm strong enough to let her go."

"Even if that means you're miserable?" Smoke asked.

"*Will* I be miserable?" Bull countered. "She makes me happy. I never laugh so much as when I'm around her. She's so clueless sometimes I can't help but shake my head in exasperation. But she wants so badly to do good in the world. I feel honored to be around her. And if I let her go, what will happen to her? What if someone takes advantage of her goodness? I wouldn't be able to forgive myself if she got hurt and I wasn't there to keep her safe."

"Basically, you're screwed," Eagle said with a chuckle.

"Not if I talk to her and get her to understand," Bull said. "Maybe there's a way I can have both her *and* Silverstone."

"You really think it's a possibility?" Gramps asked.

"I'm counting on it," Bull told him. "I'm not sure I can survive with only one or the other."

"You know we'll do whatever we can to help," Eagle told him.

"Just let us know what you need, and we're there," Smoke added.

"And I'm happy to call her again and try to talk some more sense into her," Gramps threw in.

"Thanks, guys. I appreciate that more than you know. I want you to like her, to accept her."

"We do," Gramps said. "If she's yours, she's ours. Simple as that."

Bull felt his heart swell. He loved these men. He'd never told them and probably never would, but the feeling was there just the same. "Thanks. When we get home, I'll go to my place, get some sleep, then head over to her apartment in the morning. If she won't open the door, I'll think about what to do next. But I'm counting on Sky at least being relieved that I'm back safe, enough to get me in the door. I'll figure out what to say depending on how things go."

"It's not much of a plan," Eagle said with a chuckle.

"Just wait until you find *your* woman," Bull told him. "You'll see how easy it is to figure out the right thing to do when she's pissed at you."

"Touché," Eagle said. "Well, you know we're here if you need backup."

Bull nodded, and the foursome fell silent. The truth was he had no plan in mind. None. Just getting her to open the door seemed a huge hurdle right now. But he hadn't lied—he hoped she cared about him enough to have been worried for his safety. He'd be winging what he said after he got inside her apartment.

~

Jay watched from the edge of the woods. The parking lot was nearly empty. This was his chance. He had the stash house all ready. His plan was to bring her there and wait out any search parties. He'd even join in if he thought things were secure in his hiding place. No one would suspect him. Yes, he had a record, but he didn't have an official address, so no one knew he'd been living near the school.

He'd snatch her and wait long enough for the search to slow down, then he'd take her away. Make her love him. And they'd live happily ever after. Just thinking about it made Jay's heart beat faster. He'd planned this day for so long, and it was here. All his fantasies were about to come true.

Staring at his target, he quickly made his way across the parking lot. He'd practiced this in the early hours of the morning. He knew exactly how long it took to walk across the lot and through the broken gate. He also knew exactly how long it took to run back the way he came, through the woods, down the block, to the abandoned row house he'd already prepared.

He was doing this. *Finally.*

~

It was finally Friday, and Skylar was more than ready for the weekend. Even having taken the one day off, she felt the week had dragged. She couldn't keep Carson out of her mind. She kept thinking about what Tiana had told her, and she knew today was the day Carson and the others were supposed to get back from their mission. She had no idea where they'd gone or who their target had been, but she couldn't help worrying.

Would Carson even let her know he was back?

If she called Silverstone Towing, would whoever was on dispatch tell her if the guys had returned?

What if they'd been injured—or killed? Would she ever find out what had happened to them?

She had more questions than answers, and her head was pounding. Her students had been unusually rambunctious all day, and she was ready to go home.

Today was also Sandra's last day coming to her room when the after-school program ended. Shawn was going to pick her up around six, and then next week he'd start working from eight to four at Silverstone Towing.

It meant Skylar could go home at five. She always stayed until the after-school program was over, just in case. She usually got her planning for the next day done and then could relax when she got back to her apartment.

Skylar was leaning against the building, lost in her thoughts, when movement caught her attention. She turned to glance toward where Sandra was playing on the monkey bars—and couldn't believe what she was seeing.

A man was running across the playground with the little girl in his arms. He had his hand over her mouth and was almost to the broken gate leading to the parking lot.

Running faster than she'd ever run before, Skylar took off after them. She almost screamed for help but knew no one was around. She was better off saving her breath.

Thankful she was wearing flats, Skylar slammed through the gate, her feet hurting as they pounded against the asphalt of the parking lot.

She didn't even hesitate to follow the man and Sandra into the trees. A branch slapped her across the face, and she brushed it aside impatiently—and barely stopped in time to keep from running right into the man.

He was still holding Sandra in an iron grip. The little girl was squirming and wiggling in his grasp, but it didn't seem to faze the man. He was tall, at least half a foot taller than Skylar. And he was *big*. He had a beer belly that protruded in a grotesque way from beneath the T-shirt he was wearing. He had longish greasy brown hair that hung in his eyes, his jeans were dirty, and his pasty skin gleamed with sweat.

The fingers that were across Sandra's mouth were also dirty, and Skylar saw scars on them. Just seeing his hands on the little girl was enough to make her sick.

"Let her go," she growled as menacingly as possible.

But the man just laughed. "I don't think so."

Skylar was doing everything possible to keep her fright hidden. She took a step closer—and the arm around Sandra's waist dropped, making her feet land on the grassy ground beneath them. But the man didn't give her a chance to get away. He pulled out a wicked-looking knife from somewhere behind him. Skylar could only assume he had some sort of sheath strapped to his belt.

One hand was still pressed over her mouth as he brought the knife to Sandra's throat. "Here's the deal—if you make a sound, I'll gut her from here"—he pointed the knife to her throat—"to here." He slowly drew the knife down her body to point at her belly. "Understand?"

Skylar really wanted to call his bluff. He wouldn't have gone out of his way to kidnap Sandra if he was just going to hurt her . . . would he?

She wasn't going to gamble with the girl's life.

Without taking his gaze from Skylar, he squeezed little Sandra's face in his hand. "And if *you* make a sound, I'll gut your pretty teacher in the same way. You keep quiet and do what I say, and she lives. Your teacher keeps quiet, and *you* live. Got it?"

Sandra nodded frantically.

The man slowly removed his hand from Sandra's face. "Good girl. I knew you were smart. You and me are gonna get along just great."

Then he started backing away, through the trees, the knife pressed to Sandra's throat.

Skylar followed, feeling helpless. She wanted to bum-rush him and snatch Sandra out of his grasp, but that knife kept her from doing anything stupid. The blade was rusty but serrated, so even if it was dull, he could do more damage to the little girl than she'd be able to survive.

She considered running in the opposite direction to get help, but she didn't see anyone in the immediate area, and the thought of the man disappearing with Sandra wasn't something she was willing to risk. Threatening the little girl was just as effective as if he was holding a gun to Skylar's own head. She couldn't overpower the man, but she wasn't willing to run away either.

She knew this wasn't going to end well for her, but she literally didn't feel as if she had any other choice. She was damned if she did, but Sandra was damned if she didn't.

"Get up here, and walk in front of me," the man ordered.

Skylar didn't want to turn her back to the guy, but she hoped that by doing what he wanted, she could bide her time and figure out a plan.

"What's your name?" the man asked Sandra.

When Sandra stayed silent, Skylar looked back and saw a frustrated look cross the guy's face. He pressed the tip of the knife to the little girl's neck, and a bead of blood welled. "I asked you a question," he said in a low growly tone. "You answer me when I talk to you," he ordered.

"S-Sandra."

"Sandra," he breathed. "A beautiful name for a beautiful girl." Then he ran a hand over her hair, his gaze sliding down her body.

Skylar felt sick to her stomach, and her adrenaline spiked. She wasn't going to let this monster hurt the little girl. Not on her watch.

"What's *your* name?" she asked quietly.

He looked up, and Skylar shivered. The look in his eyes was pure evil. She could see the intent to hurt in his gaze. "Me? I'm Jay. Jay Ricketts," he said, looking down at Sandra. "Hear that, honey? My name is Jay, and you belong to me now. You're mine to take care of. To nurture. To make feel good. Just as your job is to do what I say and make *me* feel good."

Skylar swallowed the bile that had risen up her throat. She memorized the man's name. If it was the last thing she did, she was going to let someone know who'd kidnapped them.

They walked until they came out on the other side of the copse of trees, and Skylar's hopes of seeing someone, of bringing some sort of attention to them, were dashed. The street was deserted. Shouldn't there be more people out and about on a Friday afternoon?

They walked between a row of run-down houses, and Skylar could hear people talking and laughing from the open windows they passed, but she didn't dare make a noise. Jay had picked up Sandra and was carrying her on his hip. He had the knife in his free hand, and while it wasn't pressed against Sandra's throat anymore, Skylar knew he could still mortally wound the little girl before she could wrestle her out of his hold.

She was frustrated and terrified, but desperately tried to hold herself together.

They walked for another ten minutes or so until Jay stopped them at the back door of a half-standing row house. There was a foul smell coming from inside the building, and it took everything Skylar had not to gag.

"In," Jay said, jabbing Skylar with the knife.

She gasped in pain and grabbed her back where he'd poked her. She looked down at her hand and saw her palm was smeared with blood. Despite knowing if she took one step inside the condemned building, it was highly likely she'd never come out, she did as Jay ordered. She literally had no choice.

Grabbing hold of the doorjamb, she ducked under the board blocking the door, Jay right on her heels. He poked her again with the knife, and she let out a small screech.

"Quiet!" Jay hissed. Skylar turned to see he'd put the knife back to Sandra's throat. Tears fell from the little girl's eyes—and rage rose within Skylar.

"I'll be quiet if you stop hurting me!" Skylar hissed back at the man. She knew she shouldn't push him, but she couldn't help it.

Instead of getting mad, the guy smiled. His rotting teeth reminded her of the Grinch. It was an odd, fleeting thought. "She's got some spunk," Jay said more to himself than to Skylar. "This might be fun, after all. Go downstairs," he ordered.

Skylar took a deep breath through her mouth, trying not to inhale any more of the noxious stench in the room than she had to.

She carefully picked her way down the stairs, which were falling apart. One of the boards broke under her foot, and she just kept herself from screaming out in fright as she almost fell down the stairs headfirst. The man behind her didn't say a word. He still had Sandra in his arms, and Skylar prayed he wouldn't fall down the stairs, taking her out in the process and injuring them all.

She made it to the bottom and into the basement. If anything, the smell down here was worse than it was upstairs. Not wanting to know what had died down here, Skylar looked back at Jay. He pointed to a door to their right. Making her way around old tires and piles of trash and trying not to step in the puddles of unknown liquid that were all around her, Skylar docilely went to the door he'd indicated.

She pushed on it, but the door didn't move.

"Put some effort into it, bitch," Jay sneered. "It's not that heavy."

Skylar swallowed the retort that was on the tip of her tongue. She regretted just following Jay meekly. She should've screamed her head off and gotten someone's attention. Maybe she should've run off to get help . . . but either action would've led to her losing sight of Sandra. There were too many cases of children being abducted and disappearing forever. No matter what happened, she was better off sticking with Sandra and doing everything in her power to help the little girl.

When she finally got the door open, Skylar's stomach lurched. This had obviously been thought out. This was no spur-of-the-moment decision on Jay's part.

The room they were in had probably been some sort of storage area at one time. There was a tiny window high up on one wall, and Skylar could see nothing but weeds in front of the glass.

There was also a mattress on the floor and some filthy bedding on top of it. Other than that, unlike the rest of the basement, this room was completely empty. Jay had obviously removed anything that might be used as a weapon or to help Sandra escape.

"Go sit on the mattress," Jay ordered Skylar.

Not wanting to be that far away from Sandra, she said, "You don't have to do this. It's not too late to walk away."

Jay laughed again. A low chuckle that grated on Skylar's nerves. "But I don't want to walk away," he told her. "I've waited a very long time to find the perfect girl. And when I saw little Sandra playing, I knew she was mine. Now . . . *go. Sit. Down.*"

His voice turned mean, and Skylar wanted to cry. She slowly walked over to the mattress and sat.

"Put that on," Jay said, motioning to something to her left with his head.

Looking to where he'd indicated, Skylar saw something peeking out from the gray blanket next to her. After lifting it, she jerked in surprise as two cockroaches scampered away when their sanctuary was disturbed.

Under the blanket she saw an old rusty chain. And on the end of it was a shackle.

She looked up at Jay in horror.

"You heard me," he said, bringing the knife up and using it to caress the side of Sandra's face. The girl flinched away from him, but she didn't make a sound.

Knowing if she put that chain on, she was as good as dead—and Jay could disappear with Sandra, and she wouldn't be able to follow—Skylar hesitated.

"It's not time for me to leave yet," Jay said, as if he could read her mind. "You be good and put that on, and everything will be fine."

Skylar knew it wouldn't be fine, but frankly, she had no choice. The chain clanged when she picked it up, and the sound made her wince. She studied the end and realized that Jay had gotten a handcuff from somewhere and attached it to the chain.

"Put it around your ankle," he ordered.

"It's going to be too small," Skylar protested.

"Not my problem," Jay said unsympathetically. "It wasn't made for an adult."

And *that* made her blood run cold. Thinking about poor Sandra with this thing around *her* ankle made her sick.

Moving slowly, Skylar wrapped the handcuff around her ankle. Maybe she could just pretend to fasten it. Then when Jay left her alone, she could open it and get the hell out of there.

She looked down at her ankle—and the second she took her eyes off Jay, he moved.

He rushed toward her with Sandra still in his arms and grabbed the metal around her ankle, squeezing hard. The metal clicked as it latched and dug into her flesh.

Skylar once again yelped in pain as the metal squeezed her ankle.

"I know what you were thinking," Jay scolded. "I'm smarter than you, and I've planned a long time for this. Nothing and *no one* is gonna mess it up." He then dropped Sandra suddenly, and she landed on her butt on the mattress next to Skylar.

Ignoring the pain in her ankle, Skylar immediately reached for the little girl. Sandra burrowed into her arms and tucked her head against her shoulder. She was shaking like a leaf, and it made Skylar mad all over again.

"What exactly is your plan?" she asked a little belligerently, feeling braver now that Sandra wasn't being held at knifepoint.

"Well, I suppose there's no harm in telling you, as you certainly aren't going anywhere," Jay said with an evil laugh. He paced in front of her, playing with the knife, spinning it around and around as he outlined his "plan."

"I expect there'll be a search. There often is. My Sandra was supposed to be picked up around six. When she isn't there, people will panic. The cops will be called. Within an hour, the entire school grounds will be crawling with people. They'll be walking all over my tracks, so search dogs will be useless. They'll put out flyers, offer rewards . . . all to no avail. I might even go and join in the searches. But in a few days, when there's been no sign of the poor missing girl, people will start to go back to their regular lives."

Skylar was horrified. Not because of what he'd said, but because he was probably right. She'd watched enough crime shows to know that tracking dogs worked with their noses to the ground. They followed a trail of human scent, but if too much time had passed or if the area had been contaminated by too many police, searchers, and other well-meaning bystanders, the dogs wouldn't be able to do their jobs.

"Then what?" she asked, needing to know where he planned to take Sandra. Because it was obvious he couldn't keep her here forever. No, she was certain he had a location in mind.

"You know, you being here is your own fault," Jay said conversationally, not answering her question. "If you'd have gone for help instead, you wouldn't be in this situation. Anything that happens to *you* is no fault of mine. Although I have to say, having you here is actually a good thing. I expected more trouble out of my girl. But she's being quiet as a mouse."

Then he lunged and grabbed Skylar's free hand. He held the knife to the base of her pinkie finger and looked into Sandra's eyes. "If you scream, if you make any noise whatsoever, I'll cut off your teacher's finger. I'll do it right in front of you, and it'll be *your* fault. Even if I'm not in the room, I'll know. I have cameras outside, and they'll pick it up if you're in here trying to get someone to notice you. Not to mention, no one around here will think twice about a little screaming. They're more likely to go in the opposite direction. I've done my homework, and this neighborhood is shit. No one cares about anyone, and they won't lift a finger to help you. In fact, they might decide to hurt you. *I'm* not going to hurt you, Sandra, not if you don't give me a reason. I love you."

Skylar wanted to puke. She had no idea if the little girl even understood all of what Jay was saying, but *she* did. And it was horrifying. But she held as still as possible; the blade felt extremely threatening against her skin.

Without moving the knife, Jay switched his focus to her. "And if *you* do anything that I don't like, I won't use the knife on her . . . no, I don't want to mar that beautiful face." He stroked Sandra's cheek with the back of his fingers, and Skylar shivered in revulsion. "I'll take what I want from her right in front of you—and you won't be able to do a damn thing about it," he threatened.

Skylar knew that had been his plan for Sandra all along, but it still made her recoil in horror.

"I won't try to be gentle, won't try to make it good for her . . . if you know what I mean. So you be good, and your precious student won't be hurt."

He was sick. Demented. Sandra was only *five*! What he was saying was incomprehensible and terrifying.

"I won't try anything," she said quietly, just wanting Jay to back away. To stop touching her and especially to stop touching Sandra.

Jay smiled and stood back up. "Remember, even when I'm not here, I know what's going on. So don't do anything stupid. Take care of my Sandra for me, and everything will be all right. I'll be back later with some dinner."

With those parting words, Jay walked back across the room. He ducked through the door, shutting it behind him. Skylar could hear some sort of lock being placed on the door, and her heart dropped.

"Be good!" Jay called out before she heard his footsteps retreating up the stairs.

Sandra shuddered in her arms once more, and Skylar tightened her hold on the little girl.

They were in big trouble—and she had no idea what to do.

~

An hour after the plane had touched down, Bull was at Skylar's apartment. He'd tried to tell himself to wait, to go over in the morning, but he couldn't. He needed to make things right between them. He had no idea if he even could, but he had to try.

Exhaustion pulled at him. He'd never been able to sleep that well on planes, especially not after a mission. So far, he hadn't regretted anything he'd done for Silverstone, but he couldn't help going over every step he and his team had made after the fact. A mental after-action review to see where they could improve so the next mission would go even smoother.

Knocking, Bull frowned when he could hear no movement from inside the apartment. Looking at his watch, he saw it was eight o'clock. Skylar should be home from work by now. The nasty thought that maybe she was on a date rose within him. But Bull quashed that idea. She wouldn't do that to him. Even if she thought they were over, he didn't think she'd turn around and find another man in less than a week.

"You lookin' for Sky?" a voice said to his left.

Bull jerked and mentally swore. He had to be tired if he'd allowed someone to sneak up on him like that. Turning, he saw Tiana standing in her doorway. Her brows were furrowed, and she looked concerned.

"Yeah. You know where she is?" he asked.

Tiana shook her head. "Haven't heard anything since she left for work this morning, but it ain't like her to not be home this late."

"Could she be running errands?" Bull asked.

Tiana shrugged, but he could tell she didn't think that was likely. "Look, she's been upset this week," Skylar's neighbor said. "I know the two of you had a fight. She didn't tell me what it was about, but she wasn't happy. We talked, and I did my best to make her feel better, but I might've scared her."

Bull straightened. "You scared her?" He didn't mean to sound so harsh, but he hated to think about Skylar being frightened of anything, especially someone she thought was her friend.

"Relax, Hulk," Tiana said without seeming upset in the least. "She was talkin' about how she found something out about you and wasn't too happy with it. I tried to help by tellin' her that everyone's got secrets, including me. Told her I used to run with the Vice Lords."

Bull's expression didn't change on the outside, but inside, he was already mentally moving Skylar out of this apartment.

"I'm out," Tiana said, but her voice lowered. "Mostly. But I still have some connections. If something's happened to Sky, you let me know, and I'll take care of whoever hurt her."

Now Bull was surprised. "You think something's happened to her?"

"Sky's never late. She's got a predictable routine. Something's up."

Bull agreed. He nodded. "I'm heading to Eastlake. See if maybe she's still there."

Tiana reached under her shirt and pulled out a piece of paper. "My number. You need any help, call me. I know the Vice Lords ain't exactly the kind of help most people want, but I give you my word that they'll do whatever it takes to either find our Sky . . . or dole out street justice to anyone who messed with her."

Bull took the number. He'd learned to never turn down help, no matter if it came from an ex–gang member, a relative of a terrorist who was sick of the killing, or a random civilian on the street. "Thank you," he told her.

"Don't thank me, just bring Sky home," Tiana said in a hard tone before turning around and slamming her door.

With a sick feeling in his gut, Bull ran down the stairs two at a time and got back into his vehicle. He drove way too fast toward Skylar's school—and he knew something was very wrong when he got within a few blocks. He hit the Bluetooth in his car and called Eagle.

"Yo, what's up?" Eagle said as he answered.

"I can't find Sky, and I'm nearing Eastlake, and something's going on."

"Hang on," Eagle said in a tone that Bull recognized as his "work voice."

He'd called Eagle because he knew the man had a police scanner. If something was happening, he could listen in and figure it out. He heard tinny voices coming from the scanner as he pulled into an empty lot across the street from the elementary school. There were cars parked everywhere. He'd never seen so many people at the school before, even during the day.

Then he saw groups of people wandering around with flashlights—and his adrenaline spiked.

Bull saw who he thought was Shawn Archer standing by the front doors of the school, and he grabbed his phone and turned off the engine.

"Shit," Eagle said through the phone. "There's a missing kid. Cops got a call around six fifteen from the school. A dad arrived to pick up his daughter, and she wasn't there."

"It's Sandra," Bull said, immediately feeling sick. "Archer's here." Then he thought of something, and as he climbed out of his car, he looked toward the teachers' parking lot. "And Sky's car is still here."

"So she's probably there helping with the search," Eagle said calmly.

"Yeah," Bull agreed, but his stomach was in knots.

"I'll call the others, and we'll meet you there," Eagle said.

"Thanks," Bull told him. He knew his friends were just as tired as he was, but they wouldn't hesitate to come out to help in the search for a missing child. Even if it wasn't Sandra, time was of the essence when it came to any abduction.

After clicking off the phone, he made a beeline for Archer.

The second the other man saw him, he broke off his conversation with whoever it was he was talking to and started running toward Bull.

"Is it Sandra?" Bull asked without beating around the bush.

"Yes," Archer said, his voice breaking on the single word. "When I arrived, she wasn't here. The secretary went down to her classroom, and no one was there."

"What did Skylar say?"

Archer looked confused. "Nothing. She's not here either."

And there it was—confirmation that the unease he was feeling wasn't misplaced.

Bull knew without a doubt that whoever had taken Sandra had most likely taken Skylar too. His Sky wouldn't allow one of her students to just be snatched, not without putting up a hell of a fight or voluntarily getting herself kidnapped in the process.

After spinning on his heel, he started to walk back to his car. He had some things he needed to get from his vehicle before he began the hunt for both Sandra and his woman. Namely, his weapon.

"Bull!" Archer called out.

Bull turned to face the man.

"She's all I've got," he said in a miserable, desperate voice.

"We're gonna find her," Bull said confidently. He didn't know how, but he wasn't going to give up until both the little girl and her teacher were home safely.

Refusing to let his worry overwhelm him, Bull headed to his car. His Silverstone team would be here soon, and then they'd be on the hunt. *No one* took what belonged to him.

No fucking one.

~

It was past midnight, and Skylar was exhausted, but she couldn't sleep. Sandra had dozed here and there, but she was too scared to sleep for more than ten minutes at a time. Every little noise had them both jumping.

"Do you think anyone will find us?" Sandra whispered.

Jay had returned once, and he'd forced Sandra to sit on his lap on the other side of the room. He'd told her all about their new life and how great it was going to be. He'd run his hand over her hair and rubbed her back.

Skylar had never been so relieved as when he'd left them alone again. He'd said the search had begun, and he needed to keep watch.

"Yes," Skylar said with as much confidence as she could muster.

She wondered if Carson had gotten back from his mission. He'd said that he should be home tonight, but she suspected if things didn't go as planned, it could still be days before he got back. She tried not to think about that.

"You heard Jay. Everyone's already looking for you. They'll find us."

"I don't like when he touches me," Sandra whined. "Daddy always says if anyone touches me and I don't like it, I should scream and run away. But I can't do that, because he'll hurt you!"

Skylar felt heartsick. Jay wasn't as dumb as she'd hoped. By using his threats of harm, he'd basically paralyzed them both. She wasn't willing to call his bluff and risk him doing unspeakable things to Sandra, and the little girl wasn't willing to do anything to make him mad, because she didn't want her teacher to be hurt.

"I know," she told her. "Why don't you close your eyes and try to sleep again, sweetie," Skylar soothed, wanting the girl to escape from the horror they'd found themselves in, at least for a while.

"Ms. Reid?"

"Yeah, Sandra?"

"I'm glad you're here with me."

"Me too, Sandra. Me too." And she was. The thought of how scared the little girl would've been if she were alone with Jay was too dreadful to imagine.

Skylar shifted on the bed and winced as the handcuff dug into her ankle. Every time she moved, the damn thing seemed to get tighter. Jay hadn't double-locked it, so it was likely it *was* getting tighter. Her foot had tingled as if it had been asleep earlier, but now Skylar could barely feel it. She'd tried to break the chain, which had been useless. It was fastened tightly to a pipe in the wall across the room. She was well and truly stuck.

But Sandra wasn't.

If Skylar could get rid of the one thing Jay wanted most, he couldn't use Sandra against her. After looking around the room, she focused on the small window in the wall. It was too small for her to get out of, even if she could find a way to get out of the handcuff or break the chain, but Sandra was tiny. *She* could get out.

But was sending the five-year-old out to wander around a strange and dangerous neighborhood the right thing to do? She'd never forgive herself if someone else snatched up Sandra for his or her own nefarious reasons. But then again, with the search going on, the little girl might run into someone who was looking for her. The more people looking meant the better the chances someone would find Sandra.

Though, Skylar had seen for herself how far they were from the school. Yeah, it wasn't miles and miles, but to a five-year-old, it might as well be on the other side of the city. And there was no guarantee that the search would even go in this direction. Besides that, Jay hadn't lied. Where they were, it wasn't safe. Even though they'd only been there for a few hours, Skylar had heard several gunshots.

Shivering, she decided that at the moment, they were better off where they were. Jay had said himself that he was going to wait a few days to let the search calm down. He was also checking on them way too often. If Skylar was going to get Sandra out the window, she had to have enough of a head start to be able to escape. If Jay caught them in the act, or too soon after Sandra left, it was possible he'd find her again. Which would be bad.

So Skylar had to wait for exactly the right time to make a move.

And if the perfect time never came . . . it was possible she'd lose Sandra forever.

Holding the little girl tighter, Skylar closed her eyes and prayed that someone would find them before Jay could put his plan to take Sandra away in motion.

Chapter Seventeen

"Fuck!" Bull swore viciously as he stood in the middle of yet another block of houses around Eastlake Elementary School.

Eagle, Smoke, and Gramps were next to him, and he saw the frustration he was feeling reflected on their own faces.

It was Sunday evening. They'd been hunting nonstop for forty-eight hours.

And so far, they had nothing. It was as if Sandra and Skylar had disappeared into thin air.

The tracking dogs that had been brought in hadn't been able to pick up their scents because too many people had tromped through the area, contaminating the scene and rendering the dogs' skills useless.

For the first time, he got an inkling of what his friend Rex must've felt like a decade ago when his wife had been kidnapped. One second she'd been there, and the next she'd simply been gone.

Bull knew the first forty-eight hours were the most important in any abduction, but they'd found nothing to give them any clues as to where the pair might've gone.

The only clue they'd found was some tamped-down vegetation in the trees on the other side of the teachers' parking area. Whoever had taken Skylar and Sandra had obviously watched them from there. It was the perfect vantage point. When Bull had lain down in the exact spot, he'd been able to see the playground, the doors to the building, and anyone who was coming and going.

It made him killing mad to think the man might've been lying in wait when he and the others from Silverstone Towing had been there, showing the kids their trucks.

Smoke had remembered the gate to the playground had been broken, and they all figured that had made it even easier for the kidnapper to get to Sandra.

After his team had talked it over, they'd concluded Sandra had most likely been snatched from the playground, and Skylar had gone after her, getting herself taken in the process.

Bull could think of no other reason for them both to have disappeared at the same time. Skylar would've fought like hell if it had just been her, but if Sandra's life was at stake, he knew she wouldn't have done anything to further threaten the little girl.

So where did that leave them?

Nowhere.

"We need to regroup," Gramps said quietly. "Bring in more resources. We aren't doing anyone any good wandering around aimlessly."

"Sky's still here somewhere," Bull said firmly. "I don't think she's been taken out of the area."

"There have been search parties all over this area," Eagle said. "They've knocked on every door in a half-mile radius. It's highly unlikely they're still here."

"They are," Bull insisted. He looked at his friends. "I know you think I'm crazy, but she's here. She's waiting for me to find her, but her time's running out. I can feel it."

"What do you suggest?" Gramps asked.

"I don't know!" Bull growled in frustration.

"How about this," Smoke suggested. "We go back to Silverstone and get the drones. We'll put 'em up and see if we notice anything wonky." Then he lowered his voice. "You also said Skylar's neighbor volunteered to bring the Vice Lords into this . . . I think it's time for that."

Bull nodded. He hadn't wanted to be indebted to the street gang, but if they could find any speck of information about where Skylar was, or what had happened to her, he'd take it. He'd do whatever he had to do in order to bring Sky home.

Time had run out.

Skylar had hoped someone would find them before now. But Jay had come in earlier and gloated that no one knew where they were, and the search was being scaled down, just as he'd predicted. It was time to move to the next part in his plan . . . taking Sandra somewhere far away.

And Skylar wasn't going to let that happen. No way.

She was hungry. Hungrier than she'd ever been in her life. She hadn't eaten more than a few bites of hamburger since she'd been kidnapped on Friday night. As far as she could tell, it was now sometime in the very early hours of Monday.

Jay had brought a McDonald's Happy Meal to Sandra on Saturday morning, and the little girl had offered to share it. "When I was hungry, you shared your food with me," she'd said.

Skylar had wondered if the food had been drugged, but she'd been too hungry to care. She'd only taken a few bites of the hamburger. Even cold, it had been one of the best things she'd ever eaten.

But it was time to get Sandra out of this nightmare. Everything had been quiet for hours, and Skylar knew it was now or never.

She shook the little girl gently. "Wake up, Sandra." It was pitch dark in the room, which Skylar thought actually made this a bit easier. The little girl couldn't see how scared her teacher really was. "Are you awake?"

"Yeah."

"It's time to see if you can fit out that window."

They'd talked about this and agreed that it was the only way. Skylar was so proud of the little girl. She was obviously scared, but was willing to do what she could to get help. "You remember what to do?"

"Run," Sandra said softly. "Stay in the dark. See if I can find an open business. Or a police officer. Or anyone who looks friendly."

"Right," Skylar praised. "And I know it's hard, but I need you to try to remember where this place is. Before you run away, look back at the house. Memorize any numbers of houses you see. It's really, *really* important."

Sandra nodded. "Because they need to come back and get you too." Her voice dropped even more. "I wish you could come!" she whimpered.

"Me too, but I believe in you. You're smart, Sandra, and I know you can do this. Whatever happens, though, do *not* come back. Understand? No matter what you hear." The last thing Skylar wanted was Jay seeing her and threatening to kill her teacher to make the little girl come back. "Once you're out, keep going."

"I will," Sandra promised.

"And I'm sure whoever you find to help you will call your daddy, and he'll come right away. Come on, let's do this."

Skylar wanted to warn the girl some more, but she also didn't want to freak her out. Jay had been touching her more and more in the last two days, and she knew it was just a matter of time before he did something to really scar Sandra for life.

She also knew if Jay came downstairs and found Sandra gone, he'd kill *her*. Not that he hadn't already planned to. He wasn't going to drag her along when he left. She knew it deep in her bones. Her life was already forfeit.

As long as Sandra got free, that was all that mattered.

She stood up and ignored the pain in her ankle. She couldn't feel her foot anymore, and last she'd looked at it, when it had still been light outside, her toes had been blue. It wasn't a good sign, but her foot was the least of her worries at the moment.

They walked toward the window. The chain wasn't long enough to go all the way to the wall, but she could get close enough that Sandra could stand on her shoulders and lean over to get to the window. Skylar crouched to let Sandra climb up. She swayed and put a hand against the wall to get her balance. She didn't want to fall and hurt Sandra in the process.

They'd practiced earlier, and it was a good thing, because in the darkness, Skylar couldn't see anything. "Ready?" she asked softly.

"Ready," Sandra said.

"It's just like climbing on the monkey bars," Skylar reassured her. "Just slide the window open, and I'll hold your feet and help you through."

The sound of the window squeaking as it slid open seemed extremely loud in the quiet night air.

"Before you go, look outside. Do you see anyone?" Skylar whispered. She figured it was highly unlikely Jay actually had cameras outside, as he'd claimed. He'd worn the same clothes the entire time he'd been holding them captive, and he smelled as if he hadn't showered in at least a few weeks. If the man had money to buy cameras, then he'd probably have stashed her and Sandra somewhere more secure . . . and farther away from the school. At least, that was Skylar's hope.

"I don't see any people," Sandra whispered back.

"Okay. Remember, find a house number, then run as fast as you can, Sandra," Skylar whispered.

"I'm ready," she said, and began her climb toward the window.

Skylar leaned forward as far as she could while still remaining upright, and she held her breath as Sandra hoisted herself to the ledge of the window. She could only see her shadow, but one second the girl was on her shoulders, and the next she was gone.

Sandra forgot to close the window after she'd gone out, but Skylar knew it didn't matter. Jay would find out soon enough that the girl was nowhere in the room, and there was really only one way out since he kept the door locked.

Skylar hobbled back to the mattress and did her best to bunch up the blanket and make it look like Sandra was curled under it. She sat on the mattress and put her hand on top of the blanket, as if she were comforting the little girl. She had no idea when Jay would be back, but she was going to be ready for him.

Either he came back first and realized Sandra was gone, or her rescuers would arrive. She could only hope it was the latter.

~

Sandra was scared to death. It was really dark outside, and she had no idea where she was. She'd done what Ms. Reid had said, though; she'd looked back and memorized the only number she could see.

Four, one, five, she said mentally. *Four, one, five. Four, one, five. Four, one, five.*

She didn't want to forget it.

She knew she was little, but her daddy always told her she was the smartest little girl in the world. The man who'd taken her and her teacher was *bad*. She knew that too. He'd threatened to hurt Ms. Reid, and that scared—

Suddenly, she went flying through the air.

She'd tripped over something in the dark. She landed on her hands and knees and cried out in pain.

She wanted to go home. Wanted her daddy!

How long she lay on the ground crying, Sandra had no idea, but when no one came to help her, no one came to pick her up and kiss her boo-boos, she took a deep breath.

Four, one, five. Four, one, five.

She started moving, but not quite as fast as she'd been running before. She didn't want to fall again. And she was so tired. And scared. The shadows all looked like monsters reaching to grab her. When Ms. Reid had talked to her about running away, it hadn't seemed too scary. But now that she was alone, in the dark, she was terrified.

Then Sandra started to wonder if that Jay guy knew she was gone. Maybe he was chasing after her! He'd make her go back, and then he'd make her sit on his lap again. She didn't like that. She liked it when she sat on Daddy's lap, but Jay touched her legs in a way that made her scared. He also rubbed her back and told her she was pretty. She liked being pretty, but she hated how he looked at her.

Four, one, five. Four, one, five.

Sandra was walking slower now, trying to figure out where to go. Suddenly she heard a loud bang. Then another. And they sounded close.

Shaking in fear, she looked around and saw a small house to her right. Without thinking, she ran toward it and got on her hands and knees. It hurt her scrapes, but all Sandra could think about was getting to safety.

She crawled under the porch and scooted all the way to the back corner. No one would see her from the road. If Jay came after her, he'd walk right on by.

As she held on to her knees with her hands, Sandra began to cry quietly. She was lost and scared, and she just wanted to go home!

~

At six o'clock in the morning, a man walked his dog down the sidewalk. He'd seen on the internet that the girl and teacher who'd gone missing from the school nearby still hadn't been found. It was a shame. He wasn't exactly a saint himself—he'd done his share of bad shit—but he'd never hurt a kid. He had scruples.

He wasn't normally up this early, but one of his regular clients wanted a hit. Usually he didn't give a shit about his clients' needs, but the guy had offered to pay him triple, he was that desperate. So he'd agreed to meet him a few blocks over.

The hood was quiet at this hour. Not that he was too concerned. The teardrop tattoos on his face were enough to keep most people from crossing him. The pit bull on the end of the leash also helped to enhance his scary image. Of course, no one knew the dog would most likely lick someone to death before he'd actually bite. His bark was simply an invitation for people to come closer so they could pet him.

When he turned the corner, a squirrel ran in front of the sidewalk, and his dog decided that was an offer to play. The pit bull jerked the leash out of his hand and went tearing after the small rodent.

Swearing, the man ran after his dog, yelling at him to come back, but of course the dog ignored him. He ran straight toward a small house and started digging at the edge of the porch, trying to get underneath.

"Damn dog," the man muttered. He grabbed hold of the dog's collar and pulled—but the muscular animal jerked back so hard the man tripped and fell over onto his ass. He scowled and crawled toward his dog, ready to smack his ass to get him away from the porch.

But something moving under the deck caught his attention.

At first the man thought it was just the squirrel his dog had been chasing . . . until whatever it was blinked.

"Shit," the man said, pressing his face closer to the latticework. "Hello?"

"Four, one, five," a child's tiny voice said.

"Holy fuck!" the man exclaimed.

"Four, one, five," the little girl said again. "Can you help Ms. Reid? Four, one, five . . ."

Because he'd just watched a news clip on the missing little girl and her teacher, the man knew immediately he was looking at the missing Sandra Archer—and that her teacher's name was Skylar Reid.

All thoughts of the drug deal he'd been heading toward flew from his head. He realized his dog had been trying to widen a small hole the girl had probably used to get under the porch in the first place. He held out his hand. "Come on, baby. I'm not gonna hurt you. I bet you're scared, huh? I'll help you."

"Four, one, five," Sandra said again.

The man tilted his head. "I don't understand."

"That's near where Ms. Reid is. Four, one, five."

His heart beating out of his chest, the man nodded. "Okay. Four, one, five. Got it. Come on, let's get you home."

Then, to his relief, the child slowly began to crawl toward him. When she got closer, he could see that she was covered in dirt. Her hair, once so nicely braided, was falling out and sticking up in all directions. Her cheeks had tear tracks on them as well as a liberal amount of dirt.

But he'd never seen anything so beautiful in all his life.

She was alive and, while moving slowly, seemed unhurt. He might be a drug dealer, but he abhorred people who hurt kids. *No one* should hurt a kid.

The man's dog now sat silently, his tongue sticking out of the side of his mouth.

"Is your doggy nice?" little Sandra asked.

She'd reached him then and allowed him to put his hands under her arms and pick her up. "He sure is," the man told her. Then he picked up his pit bull's leash and began to walk as fast as he could toward the convenience store around the block. At no time did his distaste for the cops enter his mind. He actually wished there was one in front of him right that second. He had to get this precious girl home to her dad. Now.

~

Bull hadn't slept more than a few hours in the last three days. He hadn't been able to. Every time he'd closed his eyes, he'd had nightmares of finding Skylar's dead and mutilated body.

They'd called in every marker they could, including getting Willis from the FBI involved. The man had actually flown in from DC, where he lived and worked, and so far, even with his help, along with the help of other agents from the Indianapolis field office, they hadn't found shit.

Bull was beginning to think the worst. That his beautiful Skylar was gone forever.

He and his friends were going door to door, *again*, to the town houses around the school, asking if the residents had seen anything. Their search had been frustrating and disheartening, but Bull wasn't going to give up. He wouldn't *ever* give up.

His cell phone rang.

"Bull here."

"It's Willis. Sandra's been found."

Those three words had Bull headed for his car. Gramps was at his side, and he gestured to Eagle and Smoke, who were at the residence next door. They fell into step behind him.

"Where?"

"She's at a convenience store about half a mile from Eastlake."

"I *knew* they were still in the area," Bull said with satisfaction. "Where's Skylar?"

"She's not here. I'm sorry, Bull," Willis told him.

"Fuck!"

After they got into his car, he took the time to tell Gramps where to go and put the phone on speaker, then ground his teeth as the FBI agent continued talking.

"Apparently some drug dealer found Sandra hiding under the porch of a house this morning. He claims he was simply out walking his dog, but I don't know anyone who does that in *this* neighborhood."

"I don't give a shit if he was going to sell dope to the fucking president. All I care about is finding Skylar. What did Sandra say?"

"We're giving her a chance to be reunited with her dad before we try to talk to her."

Bull wanted to protest. Wanted to demand Willis get Sandra to tell him everything, but he took a deep breath. "We'll be there in ten minutes or so."

"I'll be looking for you." Then Willis ended the connection.

"Hold it together," Eagle ordered.

"I am," Bull said, lying through his teeth.

No one said a word as Gramps drove like a bat out of hell through the mostly empty morning streets to get to where Sandra had been found.

Not even waiting for the car to stop when they arrived, Bull was out and on his way inside the convenience store. He saw Sandra sitting in a back office on Archer's lap. The large man was openly crying, but he was also smiling. He was obviously relieved his little girl was safe but hadn't yet recovered emotionally.

A man holding the leash of an extremely mean-looking pit bull was standing off to the side. He was giving all the cops in the store foul looks, and the officers were definitely keeping their eyes on him as well.

Not caring who the man was or what he might've been doing on the streets at six in the morning, Bull walked right up to him and held out his hand. "Thank you," he said without preamble.

The man eyed him, but eventually shook his hand.

"Skylar Reid is my woman, and while I'm pleased as fuck that you found Sandra, I can't relax until I find Sky."

The man's demeanor immediately changed to one of empathy. "Sorry, man, I looked around, but all I saw was the kid."

"Where?"

The man gave the address of the house Sandra had been hiding underneath, and Bull nodded, making a mental note. That was his next destination, as soon as he'd talked to Sandra.

He started to go to the office, when the man stopped him. "When I found her, she kept saying 'Four, one, five.' Over and over. I didn't know what she was talking about—then she said that's where her teacher is."

Bull looked up in surprise. "You're sure?"

"Sure that's what she said? Yeah, I'm not fuckin' deaf," the man said a little belligerently. "Look, I'm not happy to be questioned by the cops, but I'm sticking around anyway. I told them everything I know. A bunch of them are out canvassing the area already. Except these assholes left here to watch *me*." He rolled his eyes. "Anyway, anyone who hurts kids is an asshole."

"Agreed," Bull said. "Thanks for doing the right thing."

"Didn't do it for you," the man retorted.

"All the same. Thank you." Then Bull was done with the man. Eagle, Smoke, and Gramps were waiting for him next to the office.

He strode toward the door, and the second Sandra saw him, she wiggled to get down from her dad's lap. Archer held her tight for a second before reluctantly letting her go. She ran straight for Bull, and he went down on one knee and caught her.

"Mr. Carson!" she shouted.

"Hey, little one," Bull said as gently as he could. He wasn't feeling very gentle at the moment, but he wouldn't do anything to scare Sandra more than she already had been. "You okay?"

"I was really thirsty and hungry, but I got some snacks!" she said.

"That's good. Now I need you to think really hard and tell me everything you remember about who took you and where you've been for the last few days," Bull said softly.

"Four, one, five," Sandra said immediately.

"What is that?" Bull asked, hoping like hell it really *was* where Skylar was being held.

"The numbers I saw before I ran away. Ms. Reid almost fell through the stairs in the house when she went down. It's falling apart and smells *really* bad! But after I crawled out the window, Ms. Reid told me I had to look back and see if I could find any numbers. They were the only ones I could see."

Everything in Bull wanted to run out of the store and get in his car and find Skylar, but he forced himself to stay right where he was. "What else? Who took you? What happened? Can you remember?"

She looked up at him, as if he'd just asked the dumbest question ever. "I remember. I was playing on the monkey bars. The man came out of nowhere. He was big—his belly stuck out to here." She pantomimed someone with a very fat belly. "He grabbed me before I could scream and started running. He had his hand over my mouth, and when he stopped, he was breathing really hard, but Ms. Reid was there. He told her he'd hurt me if she yelled, and then told me he'd hurt Ms. Reid if I screamed.

"We walked and walked and walked until we got to the house. He made us go in, and we went down the stairs to a little room that smelled bad. He put a chain on Ms. Reid and made us stay there. He brought me a Happy Meal once, but we were soooo hungry! And I had to pee in the corner. It was gross! Then he held me on his lap and told me stories about how we were gonna move away and be really happy, and when I told him I wanted to go home, he was angry.

"Ms. Reid said I had to get away. So she helped me up to the window. It was too small for her to fit, and she had the chain on, so I had to do it. I ran and ran and ran, but then I heard loud bangs and got scared, and I hid, and then the man with the nice doggy found me and brought me here.

"Four, one, five," she said again earnestly. "Are you gonna go get Ms. Reid away from the bad man?"

"Yes," Bull said. Her story made sense for the most part. He'd let the cops get more details. But he had two more questions before he could search for Skylar. "What was the bad man's name? Did he tell you?"

"Jay," Sandra said without hesitation.

"Do you know his last name?"

"Crickets?" Sandra said, scrunching her nose, as if she wasn't sure what she'd said was right.

Deciding it didn't matter at the moment, Bull asked what he *really* wanted to know. "Was Ms. Reid hurt when you left?"

Sandra stared at him, as if she were much older than her five years. She nodded. "The bad man poked her a few times with his knife. It hurt, and I saw blood. But she didn't cry. And the chain around her ankle is really, really tight! It was bleeding. She kept it under the blanket most of the time and didn't let me see. But I knew anyway because she moaned in her sleep when she moved her leg."

It took everything in Bull to keep calm.

"I'm scared," Sandra whimpered. "The man said he was gonna take me away today. That's why I had to go out the window. I'm afraid he's gonna hurt Ms. Reid when he finds out I'm gone. She wasn't s'posed to be taken with me!"

Bull palmed Sandra's cheeks, his hands completely covering both sides of her little head. He looked her in the eyes and said, "I'm gonna go get Ms. Reid. Do you believe me?"

Sandra nodded.

"Good. Now you go back to your dad. He was really worried when he couldn't find you. He needs more kisses and hugs."

Sandra turned to look at her dad and nodded. Bull kissed her on the top of the head and stood as she scampered back to her dad.

Bull walked out of the office, past the man who'd found Sandra, past the half dozen police officers, and headed for his car once more, with Eagle, Smoke, and Gramps at his heels.

Smoke's eyes were focused on his phone, and the second they were inside the car, he said, "I've got six addresses within a half-mile radius with the numbers *four*, *one*, *five* in them."

"Which ones are *just* four, one, five?" Bull asked.

"You know those might be the only numbers she saw. That might not be the exact address," Eagle said cautiously.

"It is," Bull said firmly. "I know she's only five, but Sandra's smart. If she said she saw four, one, five, that's the address."

"There's only one with that address," Smoke answered.

"Let's go," Bull bit out.

Without hesitation, Gramps started the car, and they were off. Bull knew he should probably wait for the police, but he wasn't going to let Skylar spend one more second at the mercy of the man who'd kidnapped her. He had Silverstone at his back. As long as this Jay guy hadn't fled already, he was as good as captured.

Bull just hoped Skylar was still alive to be rescued. He knew desperate men did desperate things, and he prayed that Jay hadn't killed Skylar in a fit of rage when he'd realized the object of his obsession had escaped.

Chapter Eighteen

Skylar held her breath when she heard footsteps on the stairs. This was it. Jay was going to find out Sandra was gone, and he was going to be pissed. Since the little girl's escape, Skylar had prayed that she'd hear the sounds of the cavalry coming to her rescue, but other than the occasional gunshot, all had been quiet.

She was scared out of her mind for Sandra. What had happened to her? Had she made it to safety, or was she still wandering around, lost and frightened? Skylar wanted to cry. If something happened to the little girl, she'd feel guilty for life. But she hadn't had a choice. Helping her out the window had been her only chance.

There wasn't anything in the room that Skylar could use as a weapon against Jay, but she wasn't helpless. Her dad had made her take a self-defense class when she'd been in high school, and she'd gone to a few refresher courses since then. She'd be hampered by the chain around her ankle, but she wasn't going down without a fight.

Hearing the sounds of Jay unlocking the door to the room, Skylar took a deep breath.

All of a sudden, she felt extremely calm.

If she died in the next few minutes, so be it. But she would injure Jay as much as possible and be sure to get his DNA under her fingernails as well. He wouldn't get away with this. Skylar knew he'd find another girl to obsess over, and that one might not have the luck to be kidnapped with an adult.

The door opened—and Skylar could've laughed at the comical way Jay's eyes went wide at the sight of her standing next to the mattress. The lump of blankets was still under the thin sheet, but as much as she'd hoped he'd think it was Sandra, it was clear he didn't.

"Noooooo!" Jay screamed.

Flinching, Skylar held her ground.

"You fucking *bitch*!" Jay said, his hands curling into fists. "Where is she?"

"Probably back with her dad by now," Skylar taunted. Maybe she could freak him out enough to have him running scared. "She's been gone for hours. I'm sure she's with the cops right this second, telling them exactly where she was being held. If I were you, I'd get the hell out of here before they come find you and throw you behind bars."

But instead of her words scaring him into leaving, they inflamed him even more.

"I'm gonna kill you! Then I'm gonna find my baby girl. You can't keep her from me!" he seethed.

This was it.

Taking a deep breath, she tightened every muscle in her body, ready to do whatever she could to keep him from killing her. Because it was obvious by the rage on his face, that was his plan.

Jay was across the room in seconds, reaching for her. She put her arm up to deflect him, but he grabbed it, hitting her in the face.

It hurt. A lot. But Skylar didn't go down.

Instead, she lowered her head and lunged forward, headbutting him as hard as she could, the strike making her head spin, then swiftly reached up to try to gouge his eyes.

The unfortunate thing was in every class she'd taken, the common advice had been to hurt her assailant, make as much noise as possible, then run like hell. In her case, she could do the first two, but not the last. She was well and truly stuck because of the chain around her ankle.

Grunting, she did her best to fend off Jay's blows. But he had the upper hand in almost every way. He outweighed her, was taller, and was extremely pissed at her for helping Sandra escape.

But Skylar didn't give up. She hit, punched, kicked, scratched, and did whatever she could to bring the man down.

Glancing up, she saw that the window was still open, which gave her a sliver of hope. She had no idea if there was anyone close by, but if there was, she wanted them to hear her. Hell, she wanted the people who lived down the *block* to hear her.

She opened her mouth to scream, but Jay acted before she could get a sound out.

"Oh no you don't," Jay muttered as he grabbed her around the neck, spinning her around until her back was against his front.

Knowing she was extremely vulnerable in this position, Skylar did everything she could to get away from him, but it was no use.

Suddenly, she saw the same knife he'd hurt her with that first day.

She had no idea where he'd stashed it while they'd been fighting, but now he held it to her throat and chuckled when she whimpered.

"What're you gonna do now, Ms. Reid?" he asked.

There was only one thing she *could* do.

Ignoring the fact that he might slash her throat as soon as she made a sound, Skylar opened her mouth and let out the loudest bloodcurdling scream she could manage.

~

Within minutes of leaving the convenience store, Silverstone pulled up to 415 East Forty-Sixth Street. It was a cloudy day, and the early-morning sun hadn't penetrated the thick clouds yet. The entire neighborhood looked foreboding, but Bull didn't hesitate. He jumped out of the car and headed for the row of dilapidated houses.

Sandra had said the numbers were the only ones she had been able to see, so she and Skylar had to have been held there or nearby. He started at house 415. Gramps was close behind him as he crept around to the back of the structure. There were no fences, which he was thankful for, as it made his job much easier.

He examined the intact doorway and windows to the old house. He didn't see anything that led him to believe the structure had been disturbed.

Glancing over at Eagle and Smoke, who'd gone to the house next door, Bull saw Eagle motioning for him. Within seconds, Bull and Gramps were there. He immediately saw what his teammate had found.

A dark-red, smeared handprint on the doorjamb.

Putting his hand beside it but not touching it, Bull knew it was Skylar's. His own hand dwarfed hers, but the print wasn't so small as to have been Sandra's.

After nodding at his teammates, he took point and quickly ducked under the wide board that was nailed across the door. He made not a sound as he entered the building. He wanted to surprise this Jay guy and take him down before he could use Skylar as a shield.

Remembering that Sandra had said they'd gone down some stairs, he made a beeline for the basement. Their target could be anywhere, but Bull had a driving need to find Skylar before he hunted down the kidnapper.

He'd taken one step on the rotting stairs when he heard the most frightening thing he'd ever heard in his thirty-six years. A scream that made the hair on his arms stand straight up.

Skylar. And she was in big trouble.

Gripping his pistol tighter, Bull gave up all pretense of being quiet. Skylar needed him, and he'd be damned if he took even a second longer to get to her.

His foot went through one of the boards on the stairs, but it didn't trip him up. He rushed down the stairs in seconds and quickly made his way across the basement toward the door at the back. There was a padlock hanging from a board next to the door, and without hesitation, Bull kicked open the door and burst into the room.

Inside, there was a man with his arm around Skylar's chest. He had a knife in his other hand, which he held to her neck. Bull's eyes met hers, and he could see that she was petrified. Seeing her that way infuriated him even more.

Seeing that desperate look in her eyes . . . it was wrong. He hated seeing her scared. Hated knowing some of Skylar's innocence and naivety had been stripped from her in such a brutal manner.

Eagle, Smoke, and Gramps fanned out around him, preventing Jay's escape. But Bull didn't care about the man getting past him. All he cared about was getting that knife away from his woman's neck.

"Put the knife down!" Smoke ordered.

"It's over," Eagle added.

"Come on, man, you don't want to do that," Gramps said.

Bull's focus narrowed on his target. This was familiar. He and his team had done this before. The others distracting the target by talking to him while he focused on eliminating the threat.

Unfortunately, the man wasn't a complete idiot. He hunched down behind Skylar, making himself less of a target.

"Get away from the door!" Jay yelled. "I'm taking her with me. Get out of my way!"

"How are you gonna take her with you when she's chained up?" Gramps asked reasonably. "Just put down the knife, and let's figure this out."

"There's nothing to figure out!" Jay yelled. "She ruined everything. *Everything!* If she'd just minded her own damn business, me and my Sandra would be long gone by now! She wasn't supposed to stick her nose in where it didn't belong!"

Bull wasn't even listening to what the man was saying. He was concentrating too hard on figuring out the best way to end the threat to Skylar.

His gaze flicked to hers for a split second—and he was entirely surprised at what he saw.

Instead of the terror he'd found in her gaze seconds ago, she looked almost calm. She was standing still in Jay's arms now, as if simply waiting for Bull to get her out of the predicament she'd found herself in.

But the man *did* have a knife to her throat, and Bull needed to end this.

Skylar mouthed his name and stared back with all the confidence in the world. It scared the hell out of Bull because he had no idea what she was planning. And he had no doubt she was planning *something*.

Eagle had just said something to the man, but Bull hadn't heard him.

He saw her arm flex a fraction of a second before it moved.

Then Skylar's hand flew down between Jay's legs.

Because his knees were bent as he tried to hide behind her, she easily reached her target. She grabbed hold of her captor's dick and squeezed as hard as she could.

Jay let out a high-pitched scream, and his hips jerked as he tried to get his junk out of Skylar's hand. But as he moved, so did the knife. A short bright-red line of blood formed on her skin, and her eyes widened in shock.

But his little wildcat didn't let go. If anything, she tightened her grip, her knuckles turning white. Jay's screams hadn't stopped, but now they increased in pitch.

He shoved Skylar away from him as hard as he could. She went flying sideways, hitting her head on the wall of the storage room before crumpling to the floor in a heap.

Her actions had provided what Bull needed—a clear view of his target.

Two gunshots exploded in the small room, making Bull's ears ring, but he didn't even wait to see if Jay was down. He knew his team would take care of the man.

Bull always hit what he aimed for—and by taking the knife and Jay's hand out of the equation, he wouldn't be a threat anymore.

Holstering his pistol was second nature, and by the time he'd reached Skylar's side, his weapon was secure once more.

Gently rolling Skylar onto her back, he prayed harder than he'd ever prayed before. The bastard might've broken her neck when he'd thrown her into the wall. Bull's entire life flashed before him in the split second it took to meet her gaze.

Green eyes filled with pain stared up at him. "Bull's-eye," she whispered.

"Fuck," Bull gasped. *"Fuck."* He couldn't seem to get anything else out. He was too relieved she was alive to speak.

Blood was oozing out of a small cut on her neck. It obviously wasn't too deep, but Bull couldn't stand the sight of blood on her.

"Here," Eagle said, reaching around him and holding out a wad of gauze. Bull pressed it against her neck, but she didn't even flinch.

"I've called the police and paramedics," Gramps informed him.

Bull nodded, not taking his gaze from Skylar's.

"Sandra?" she asked softly.

"She's fine," Bull told her. "She got scared and hid under a porch most of the night—that's why it took us so long to get to you."

"But you came," she told him. Then she reached up and grabbed hold of his arm with a surprisingly strong grip. "I was wrong," she whispered before her eyes closed, and she went limp.

"Fuck!" Bull swore.

"We need to get this off her ankle so we can get out of here," Gramps said in a tight voice.

Bull looked down Skylar's body and saw his teammate kneeling by her legs. He pulled up the leg of her pants, and Bull growled. Her ankle was in bad shape. The handcuff had dug into her skin, and it was bleeding and looked infected. Her toes were blue, and it was obvious the blood flow had been restricted for some time.

Without missing a beat, Smoke reached into one of his pockets and came out with a handcuff key.

Skylar moaned when the cuff was unlocked, and Bull's muscles tightened. He knew that had to have hurt if she was moaning while unconscious. A hand on his shoulder kept him from leaping across the room and killing the man wearing zip ties and moaning about his dick being broken.

Bull was done. He wanted Skylar out of this putrid hellhole. Out of this house. He stood, then leaned over and ever so gently picked up Skylar. Smoke walked by his side, keeping the pressure on the bandage on her throat. Her head wasn't bleeding where she'd hit it against the wall, but that didn't mean she didn't have a brain injury. He stepped around the man writhing on the floor and headed for the stairs.

The second they were out of the house, Bull took a deep breath. Freedom. He knew from experience how clean and fresh the air seemed after you'd been freed from captivity. He hated that Skylar now knew this feeling as well.

The sound of sirens coming toward them was loud, and doing his best not to panic, Bull strode quickly around the dilapidated row of houses. He could see pockets of people standing around, gawking, and he bitterly wondered where they'd been when his woman had been suffering and screaming for her life.

The second the ambulance came to a stop, Bull walked up to it and opened the back door, scaring the shit out of the paramedic who was about to exit.

He stepped up and inside the vehicle and lowered Skylar to the gurney. He moved to her head but didn't leave. No one was taking him from her. No way in hell.

Bull saw Jay being put into an ambulance, escorted by two police officers, and regretted for a second that he hadn't aimed for his head. He hadn't shot to kill, only to disarm and take him out of the equation. He'd put a bullet through the hand that had been holding the knife to Skylar's throat, then he'd shot him in the thigh as well, making sure the man couldn't run. But as he looked down at the paramedic who'd just removed the gauze so he could examine Skylar's injuries, Bull wished he'd shot the asshole in the dick and ended his life once and for all.

Within seconds, the ambulance was moving. Heading for the hospital.

Leaning down and ignoring the man who was doing his best to assess Skylar's condition, he kissed her temple and whispered, "I love you, Sky. Don't leave me."

She didn't even twitch in response.

~

Skylar glanced toward the door of her hospital room, her eyes heavy with exhaustion. It was late, and the sun had long since set. She'd woken up in the emergency room while being examined by a doctor and nurse. She had a concussion and a couple small puncture wounds on her back, but her ankle had been the worst of her injuries. Even though the slice on her neck had looked bad, compared to the infection and loss of circulation in her foot, it was nothing.

She hadn't lost any of her toes, although the doctor said it had been a very close call. If it had been even just a few hours later, she might've lost her entire foot.

She'd been told she'd be in the hospital for a few days so the doctors could monitor her, but she knew she'd been lucky. Very lucky. Jay had planned to kill her. The fact that she was still here amazed her.

Looking over at Carson talking to the night nurse made her sigh in compassion for the poor man. He'd been at her side ever since the doctor had allowed him back into the emergency room. They hadn't had a moment to themselves, as Smoke, Eagle, Gramps, the cops, the doctors, nurses, employees of Silverstone, her fellow teachers, and even a few reporters had all been in and out all day.

Her parents had shown up almost immediately after she'd been admitted. They'd been frantic the entire time she'd been missing, and they had been staying in a hotel nearby so they could help search for her. Her mom had cried when she'd seen her, and even her dad had tears in his eyes. Carson had been a huge help, reassuring them that she was all right. They were currently at their hotel, but were going to come back the next day and probably every day until she was discharged. Skylar didn't mind. She hated that they were so worried, and visiting reassured them that she was going to be all right.

Seeing Sandra looking safe and happy, however, had been the highlight of her day. Their relationship had changed from mere teacher and student. Shawn had cried and told her she was now a permanent part of his family.

Telling the police detective everything that had happened hadn't been difficult, although Skylar knew Carson hadn't been happy to hear she'd willingly put herself in danger. She'd tried to explain that there was no way she would've let Jay Ricketts take Sandra away by herself, and even though she suspected the police detective had understood, she wasn't sure Carson did.

The click of the door closing caught Skylar's attention, and she looked over at Carson. Moving her head was uncomfortable because of the knife wound and her concussion, and she couldn't help but wince.

In seconds, Carson was in front of her. "Are you all right? Do you need another pain pill?"

"I'm okay," Skylar told him. "I just forgot for a second."

Her overprotective, attentive boyfriend growled.

Skylar held out a hand to him.

He stared at it for a second, but instead of taking it, he leaned down and began to unlace his combat boots. He walked over to the wall, turned off the overhead light, detoured to the bathroom to turn on that light instead. Then he removed his shirt before gently repositioning her in the bed, just enough to give him room to lie down next to her.

The second his arms closed around her, Skylar sighed in contentment. She'd been poked and prodded all day. She'd been given a sponge bath by a very talkative nurse. Had reassured her countless visitors that she was fine, that it was Sandra who she was worried about.

Now, in the dim light coming from the bathroom, Skylar fully relaxed for the first time since she'd regained consciousness.

Her head rested on Carson's chest, and her arm was flung across his belly. Her neck was sore, but she ignored it, needing to feel Carson against her more than she cared about a little pain in her neck. Her ankle was bandaged, and she carefully rearranged her leg so it was still elevated on the pillows at the foot of the bed. She wiggled a bit, then sighed once more.

"Comfortable?" Carson asked.

"Yeah."

"You still hungry?"

"No." After hearing she hadn't eaten anything since Friday night other than a few bites of cold hamburger, Carson had made sure she had milkshakes and bland snacks throughout the day.

Skylar had been thinking for hours about what she wanted to say to Carson, and now that she had him to herself, she didn't hesitate. "I was wrong."

"You said that back at the house," Carson said. "I didn't know what you meant."

"I did?" Skylar asked.

"Yeah."

"I don't remember saying it, but I'd been thinking about it a lot, even before the kidnapping, so I'm not surprised." She rolled her head back a bit so she could look him in the eyes, being careful with her stitches. "I was wrong to judge you so harshly," she clarified. "I said some things I regret. You were right. If you were in the military, I wouldn't even think twice about what you do. I would still worry about you, but I'd probably tell you how proud I was of you."

Carson shook his head. "You weren't wrong. What we're doing isn't legal. Maybe not even right."

"Bullshit," Skylar said firmly. "I'm not going to lie here and pretend it doesn't freak me out, because honestly, it does. But . . . I get it now. People like Jay Ricketts don't deserve to walk around doing the things they do. He wanted to do terrible things to Sandra. It made me sick. I'm glad you and your team were there to do what you do."

Carson had a look on his face she couldn't interpret, and Skylar frowned. "What?" she asked.

"Sweetheart, on a scale of one to ten on the evil spectrum, Ricketts is about a three."

"Seriously?"

"Yeah. He's sick in the head and a menace to society, but Silverstone doesn't go after threes. We target nines and tens."

Skylar gasped. "If Jay was a three, I don't even want to imagine what a nine or ten would be like."

"You don't," Carson agreed calmly. "My point is, we aren't running around killing people indiscriminately. We work with the FBI and Homeland Security and only go after the worst of the worst."

"People like Fazlur Barzan Khatun," Skylar said, finally understanding.

"Exactly." Then, after a beat of silence, Carson admitted, "But I *wanted* to kill Ricketts. He hurt you. Held you hostage. Tortured you and Sandra. I wanted to kill him so badly."

"But you didn't," Skylar said, bringing a hand up and laying it on the side of his face. "Because you're a good man."

"I'm not," Carson insisted. "You have no idea the blood that's on my hands."

Skylar shook her head gently. "You and your friends are good men who do bad things to bad people." She could tell her words were sinking in. "And I love you," she finished softly.

Skylar saw the emotion that had been missing from his face that awful day last week shining from his eyes. Then he gave her the best gift she could've ever asked for. He smiled.

A big smile that went from ear to ear.

It was beautiful. *He* was beautiful.

"I love you too," he said without hesitation. "You'll never know how much."

"I can live with what you do," she told him. "It scares me—I'll worry about you—but knowing you're out there making the world safer . . . I can be okay with that."

He closed his eyes and pressed his lips to her forehead. When he opened them again, she couldn't look away. "I promise it won't touch you, sweetheart. Ever."

"I believe you."

"Good."

As much as she tried to hold it back, Skylar opened her mouth and yawned.

Carson chuckled, and the sound sent goose bumps down to her toes. "Sleep, baby."

"You won't leave?" she asked.

"I'm not going anywhere," Carson told her.

"I want to go home," she whined. "*Your* home," she quickly clarified.

"You will. As soon as the docs say you're ready," Carson told her. "I'd like for you to stay there permanently," he added.

"Okay," Skylar agreed, already half-asleep.

"Okay?" Carson asked. "You'll move in with me?"

"Yeah."

"I'm gonna hold you to that," Carson warned.

But Skylar barely heard him. She was warm, comfortable, safe, and her belly was full. She was in the arms of the man she loved, who loved her back. She was asleep in seconds.

~

An hour later, the door to Skylar's hospital room opened silently. Expecting to see the night nurse, Bull was startled when Tiana let herself in.

It was way too late for visitors, but Bull figured Skylar's neighbor didn't really care about following rules when it came to her friends. She pulled a chair up to the side of the bed and stared at Skylar for a moment before meeting Bull's eyes.

"I'm sorry my connections weren't able to find her before she was hurt," she said so softly there was no chance Skylar would wake up.

Bull knew she'd called in favors with the Vice Lords. It seemed she wasn't as far removed from the gang life as she might've told Skylar she was. While Bull wasn't thrilled about the woman's affiliation, she was good to Skylar, and that was really all he cared about.

Besides, he was an assassin. Who was he to throw judgment around?

"It's okay," he told her.

"I'll come back tomorrow to see Sky, but I wanted to let you know that the VLs aren't going to let this go. Skylar isn't one of us, but she accepted me without any strings. The first day she moved in, she knocked on my door and informed me that women need to stick together, and if we were going to be safe, we had to watch out for each other. She didn't even know me. Didn't know my background. To her, I was just the older black lady who lived next door. What can you tell me about Ricketts?"

"He's a registered sex offender from South Dakota. He did a few years in jail for molesting a twelve-year-old. He left Sioux Falls without updating his address, and apparently he'd been staking out Eastlake for the perfect victim. He was going to take Sandra to Chicago and eventually move to Alaska and live off the grid. He planned to brainwash her into loving him and being his wife."

Tiana scowled and leaned forward. "He's not going to be a problem for you or Skylar or any little girls any longer."

"Tiana," Bull warned.

She held up a hand. "You know as well as I do that child molesters don't do well in prison. There's a code. No touching kids. He broke that. It wouldn't surprise me if he didn't last very long behind bars."

Bull wanted to protest. He didn't want to owe a favor to the Vice Lords, but he pressed his lips together.

"And this is *me* doing a favor for someone I care about," Tiana said. "I'm keeping other children safe. Understand?"

Bull did. "Thank you."

"I told you that Sky came over to talk to me," Tiana said conversationally. "She was upset that she'd learned something about you that she wasn't comfortable with. I don't know what it is, and I don't want to know. I told her that you were the kind of man who would do anything necessary to keep her safe."

"I am," Bull interrupted.

"She's a lucky woman," Tiana said. "Special."

"She's moving in with me," Bull blurted.

Instead of being pissed, Tiana smiled. "Good."

"You and Maria are welcome to visit her . . . us . . . anytime," Bull told her.

For a second, Tiana looked surprised, then she straightened in her chair. "Even knowing what you know about me, you'd invite me into your home?"

"Damn straight," Bull said. "*You.* Not your . . . er . . . associates."

"Understood."

"Thank you for watching out for her," Bull told her.

Tiana nodded. "Fuck with her, you fuck with the Vice Lords," she said without heat. "I just wanted you to know that Ricketts isn't your problem anymore."

Bull nodded, feeling more relieved than he probably should've.

Tiana then stood and headed for the door. She left without another word.

Bull tightened his hold on Skylar and kissed her head once more.

Skylar stirred. "Carson?"

Bull smiled. He'd never get tired of hearing her say his name before asking him a question. For a while, he'd thought he'd lost something special, precious, when she'd been having trouble accepting what he did. Then he'd thought he'd lost it when Ricketts had had a knife to her throat. "Yeah, sweetheart?"

"Remind me to do my lesson plans tomorrow. I don't want my absence to mess with my kids' education."

Bull chuckled. His Sky was always thinking about others before herself. "I will."

"Love you," she murmured.

And he'd never get tired of hearing that either. "Love you too."

Epilogue

Taylor Cardin let out a small screech of fright as a car in the parking lot spun its wheels and pulled right in front of her to get into a vacant spot. Putting her hand to her chest, she took a moment to catch her breath. She'd been about three steps away from being run over.

Before she could regain her equilibrium, a man leapt out of another car and began to yell at the guy who'd pulled into the parking spot.

The next thing she knew, the two men were going at it. Throwing punches and screaming at each other.

Backing away, Taylor looked around and saw there were several other shoppers watching what was happening.

Breathing a sigh of relief that she wasn't the only witness, Taylor backed up farther.

When one of the men quickly drew a knife, her eyes widened in shock.

Was this really happening?

Apparently, yes, it was.

One of the other bystanders yelled out that he'd called the police, but it didn't stop the fight.

"Holy crap!" a woman standing nearby yelled. "This is crazy!"

Taylor had to agree.

She knew she could cross into another lane and continue into the grocery store, but Taylor stayed put. She was the worst witness in the history of witnesses, and staying would bring her nothing but grief, but she couldn't make herself leave. It felt wrong to leave the scene before the police arrived.

Twenty minutes later, policemen had gotten the men separated and had dealt with their superficial wounds and were questioning everyone standing around as to what they'd witnessed.

"I'm Officer Nelson, can you tell me what you saw?" he asked her.

Taylor took a deep breath and gave him as many details as she could.

"Great. I need to get your information so you can testify if it comes to that."

Taylor glanced around and saw that several other witnesses were waiting impatiently for their turn to tell the policeman what they'd seen . . . but she had to fess up to her condition.

"I'm happy to give you my information, but I'm not going to be able to testify."

Officer Nelson looked up sharply at that. "Why not?"

"I have prosopagnosia. It's a condition where I have no facial recognition. I won't be able to identify which man was which when we're in a courtroom. I won't even recognize *you*."

She waited—and sure enough, she got the reaction she'd expected.

"So, what . . . you're like that woman in that *Fifty First Dates* movie? The one who had no idea she was going on a date with a guy day after day?"

Taylor did her best to tamp down her irritation. Even though she was used to people being insensitive and making incorrect judgments about her condition, it was still frustrating. "No. It's not like that. I don't have a memory problem. I can tell a judge and jury what happened. I'll remember the color of the cars and even what the men were wearing, but I won't be able to point out who pulled the knife and who didn't."

"Shit. That *is* a problem," the officer said. "Okay, just hang out here while I talk to the other witnesses. Then I need to talk to my supervisor and decide if we can even use your statement. Don't go anywhere, all right?"

Taylor pressed her lips together and nodded. She should've gone inside the store instead of doing the right thing by sticking around. She absently watched as the officer took notes while talking to the other witnesses. There were two women and three men. Not that it mattered. She wouldn't recognize *them* after they left either. She'd come to terms with her condition over the years, but it didn't make it easier to deal with people's curiosity about it.

She wasn't sure how long she'd waited, but it was long enough for the policeman to finish taking the other witnesses' statements and have a lengthy conversation with the other officers on the scene.

She was still standing off to the side with her arms around her belly, feeling as if she'd been forgotten, when she saw a man walking confidently across the parking lot toward Officer Nelson.

Because of her condition, she'd never really been able to tell if someone was "handsome" or not. For her, facial features tended to blur together. Unless someone had something very distinguishable about their face, something she'd be able to recognize later, it was literally as if everyone's face looked the same. She could still appreciate a well-defined physique, though—and this man was definitely in shape. And something about the way he walked—with no fear of anyone or anything around him—made her feel a pang of wistfulness.

Taylor *never* felt that way. She was generally scared of people. She always felt as if she was at the mercy of her environment. No one ever understood what her life was like with her condition, and she hated confrontation of any sort.

The man stopped to talk to Officer Nelson, and she saw him glance over his shoulder at her. He wore a T-shirt with Silverstone Towing written in large letters on the back.

Taylor stiffened. Did she know him? Did he recognize her? She had no idea. The guy didn't look upset, just curious.

For a moment, she wished she had a man like him. A man who looked in charge. Someone who could take control of any situation and protect her from the curious glances of people who felt sorry for her or were too nosy for their own good.

But boyfriends weren't in the cards for her. She'd learned that the hard way.

When the man turned and headed toward her, Taylor wanted to bolt, but she'd told the police officer she'd stay until he figured out what to do with her.

Holding her stomach even tighter, she took a deep breath and prepared herself for whatever the man had to say.

Please don't be a jerk, she thought, looking into his eyes as he approached.

About the Author

Photo © 2015 A&C Photography

Susan Stoker is a *New York Times*, *USA Today*, and *Wall Street Journal* bestselling author whose series include Badge of Honor: Texas Heroes, SEAL of Protection, and Delta Force Heroes. Married to a retired army noncommissioned officer, Stoker has lived all over the country—from Missouri and California to Colorado and Texas—and currently lives under the big skies of Tennessee. A true believer in happily ever after, Stoker enjoys writing novels in which romance turns to love. To learn more about the author and her work, visit her website, www.stokeraces.com, or find her on Facebook at www.facebook.com/authorsusanstoker.

Connect with Susan Online

Susan's Facebook Profile and Page

www.facebook.com/authorsstoker

www.facebook.com/authorsusanstoker

Follow Susan on Twitter

www.twitter.com/Susan_Stoker

Find Susan's Books on Goodreads

www.goodreads.com/SusanStoker

Email

Susan@StokerAces.com

Website

www.StokerAces.com